You Can Call Me Cooper

Cali Kitsu

Winnipeg, Canada

Published May 2024 by Deep Hearts YA, an imprint of Story Perfect Books.

Deep Hearts YA
PO Box 51053 Tyndall Park
Winnipeg, Manitoba R2X 3B0
Canada

Visit deepheartsya.com for more great reads.

Thank you for reading *You Can Call Me Cooper*.

In its original form, *You Can Call Me Cooper* was an adult novel before being rewritten as young adult with the characters aged down for this version. Please note that I have released an "Author's Cut" version of *You Can Call Me Cooper*, which is the adult version of *Cooper*. The story is very close the YA version, with the exception that the characters are twenty-one and older, and includes a prologue, deleted and extended scenes, deeper emotional intimacy, and on-page sex.

The sequel, *Only My Husband Calls Me Cooper*, follows the Author's Cut edition where the characters are aged up.

Thanks for your support!
Cali

Table of Contents

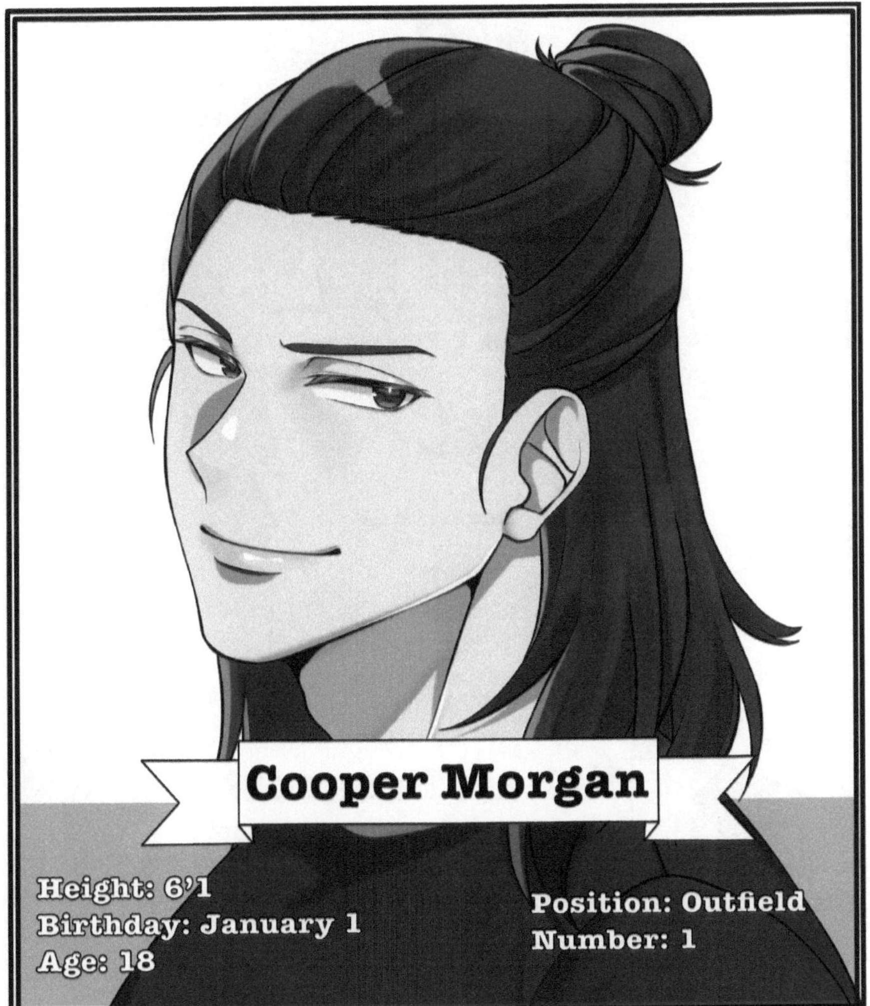

Cooper Morgan

Height: 6'1
Birthday: January 1
Age: 18

Position: Outfield
Number: 1

Ethan Prescott
Height: 6'0
Birthday: June 3
Age: 18
Position: Catcher
Number: 2

Luke Everton

Height: 5'11
Birthday: January 1
Age: 18

Position: Intern at Parson
& Associates Law Firm

Kory Collins
Height: 6'0
Birthday: July 10
Age: 18
Position: Lead Intern at Parson & Associates Law Firm

Chapter 1
Luke's Secret

"Damn it!" Coop screamed, as he missed yet another fastball during practice. He slammed his bat into home plate.

"Mac, maybe lay off the fastballs a bit, eh?" Kai yelled at the pitcher.

Coop's baseball game had begun to suffer lately; his mind was in a constant state of turmoil. He wasn't happy with school, he wasn't happy with baseball, and he certainly wasn't happy with his boyfriend, Luke. Today was an especially noisy day inside his mind, as it was the eighth anniversary of his mother's death. He slammed the bat down a few more times in frustration. He kept hearing his mother's voice inside his head: *Coop, you need to take care of Luke, no matter what. As long as you two have each other, everything will be fine.*

At eighteen years old, he felt like he'd finally reached a breaking point in his relationship with Luke. But every time he heard his mother's words, he changed his course of action and listened to her voice.

The harsh afternoon sunlight beat down on him, worsening his awful mood. He threw his helmet down and tied his thick black hair in a topknot. Kai started jogging over to him, but changed course, veering away to the dugout immediately, upon seeing his hair.

Coop stood seething at home plate and noticed Kai pulling his phone out. They'd been friends since they were little kids, so he had a pretty good idea of what Kai was doing. *Yep, go ahead, take a pic, send it to Luke. He's not at practice again, but here I am feeling like shit, while he's off skipping for whatever reason. I'm so sick of this.*

Earlier that day

Kory Collins sat at his desk inside the law office of Parson & Associates waiting for Madeline Parson to arrive. He reached in the drawer to his right and flipped through the tabs, pulling out a thick manila file, labeled *Luke Everton.* He reviewed its contents carefully once more, just as Madeline entered.

"Yes, I'm five minutes late, but you work for me," she said quickly, while sitting down. "Tell me what you need, you have ten minutes." Her curly red hair bounced as she spoke.

Not wasting any time, Kory slid the file across the desk. "Luke Everton. He's interviewing for an intern position this afternoon."

She slid her thin black glasses down from her head and looked down at the file, then back up to Kory. "My intern called me in here to talk about hiring an intern. You're joking, right?"

"Oh, come on, you know I'm more than just your intern. Flip to my notes, it concerns Tom Morgan."

"*The* Tom Morgan?" she asked, her face now focused solely on the contents of the file.

Met with Luke Everton today, stopped me following a seminar at the local library. He is looking to start a career as a lawyer. He is currently dating, in secret, Coop Morgan, son of Tom Morgan, real estate magnate. He is considering filing a lawsuit against a scout who harassed Coop, with knowledge of their relationship. Apparently, the scout, whose name Luke does not know, threatened that Coop would never get a professional baseball deal offered, if it were to be discovered that he was gay. Luke seems nervous and sure of himself at the same time. Very well-spoken and extremely intelligent.

Madeline took her glasses off and placed them on Kory's desk, leaning her head back quickly then snapping it back to Kory. "What the hell is this? Are you kidding me? I don't want to touch this thing with a ten-foot pole. I'm not hiring him."

Kory leaned back in his chair and tilted his head at her. "You're going to hire him, and you're going to be using a much shorter pole," he chuckled.

She shook her head as Kory nodded.

"Madeline, I have been helping out here since I was sixteen years old, hear me out. You owe me this much."

"Kory, you're eighteen and expendable, be serious. Don't get cute with me," she said.

"All that I'm asking is for you to make a phone call to the school," Kory said. "It's simple. Just tell them that you've received reliable information suggesting that one of the scouts in the program harassed Tom Morgan's son. That's it. Trust me, the school will do the rest. This won't even make it to court. The school will hear your name and do anything they can to weed this guy out."

She folded her arms and leaned back in her chair. "Well, before I decide, let me ask you, how are you certain that"—she glanced down at the file—"Luke is telling the truth, and how are you already convinced that he is worth a hire? You're the smartest eighteen-year-old I've ever met; what convinced you to ask me to intervene like this, before you've even interviewed him?"

"Because he's worth it. He's smart, motivated, honest, passionate, sincere, easy to talk to, he's put up with a lot, and can handle processing a lot of emotions. I've been meeting with him for six months. He's the real deal, trust me. He's not lying. I'd stake my life on that."

She pulled her head back in response. "So, you want to sleep with this guy?"

"Oooh, confidential information, Madeline," he answered, winking.

Her mouth dropped open, and her nostrils flared. "Are you serious? I have plenty of people that I—"

Kory interrupted her, "Stop. No. It's not like that. Do this for me, please?"

Madeline stood up and looked at him, as she headed for the door. "One call. I will make one call. Nothing else. I'll call this afternoon… and, Kory, this conversation never happened," she said, as she left the office, closing the door behind her.

Kory exhaled. *Wow, I imagined that would be harder. She's usually not so easily convinced. I need to fix this for him, so he can let it go. It's been weighing on him for too long.*

Luke stepped into the elevator of Parson & Associates law firm, wearing a navy-blue suit, which complimented his baby blue eyes and sandy blonde hair. He received the picture of Coop and text from Kai: *Ya boy is in bad shape over here. Where u at?*

He rolled his eyes and placed his phone on do not disturb, sliding it into his pocket. The text about Coop frustrated him, but he quickly regained his composure, as he entered the office of Kory Collins.

The secretary greeted him, "Good afternoon, you must be Mr. Everton. Mr. Collins will be with you in a few minutes. It says here your interview starts at 4:00 PM, so you're a bit early. You can take a seat wherever you like." Through the office window behind her, Kory Collins, a tall man, with sandy blond hair and a striking smile could be seen standing, talking on the phone. Luke watched as Kory sat down and put his feet up on his desk. He was quite impressed that Kory had his own office and that he was the one that would be conducting his interview. After meeting with him for months, he still didn't quite understand how Kory had so many privileges as a mere intern, but he knew that he must be good at his job since the head of the firm, Madeline Parson was allowing him to hire his own intern.

Luke sat in the office chair, head held high, while his mind silently tormented him. He was stuck in a cycle of awful memories, as he recalled a fight he had with Coop after graduation.

"Luke, you may as well just move into the estate with me now, there's no reason to stay at your dad's," Coop said.

"I actually already found a place. I've been waiting for the right time to tell you."

Coop seemed blindsided. "What? What do you mean you found a place?"

"Coop, you and your dad have done everything for me my entire life. I need to prove that I can do some things by myself."

"By yourself? Without me? What the hell does that mean?" Coop pulled a hair tie out of his pants and held it with his teeth, as he quickly flipped his head upside down and wrapped his hair in a topknot.

Luke grabbed his arm. "Woah, let's take it down a notch, okay? That's not what I meant. I just meant that I depend on you both for everything."

Coop put his hands on his hips. "Right, so? What's wrong with that? It's always been that way, now you have a problem with it?"

Luke held his hands and said softly, "Coop, listen to me. This means nothing. This changes nothing. It will be the same as it is now. We'll still be together."

The inner office door opened, and Kory Collins emerged smiling. "Luke, hey, buddy, good to see you. Come on in, have a seat," he said.

The two entered the office and sat across from one another at the large mahogany desk. "Can I get you something to drink?" Kory asked.

"No, thank you, I'm fine," Luke replied.

Kory pulled a file out of his drawer and laid it open on his desk. He looked at the papers inside slowly, while thumbing through them. Luke suddenly felt very nervous. This was his first interview, and he hadn't even told Coop about it.

"You alright? You look like you just saw a ghost," Kory joked, not looking up from the file.

"Oh, no, I'm fine," Luke said.

"Luke, relax, this is an interview, but it's not so formal that you should be nervous."

Luke smiled. "Thank you. I'm really so flattered that you asked me to come in. Crazy that you have this big office and a secretary...I really wasn't expecting this."

"I told you that I was more than just an intern, though," Kory said, with a smile. "Madeline doesn't treat me like the others." Kory pulled a highlighter out of his drawer and began marking up the papers in the file. "Alright, so, we've known each other for about, what, six months now, right?"

Luke nodded. "Yes, just about six months, that sounds right."

Kory clicked his tongue and shook his head in annoyance while going over the papers. "If I remember correctly, you originally switched your career objective because your boyfriend was being harassed a while back, and that incident is what you considered to be your turning point."

Luke felt a rush of nervousness. "Sorry, I'm not used to being in an office like this, and you saying these things just sounds so official." He started over. "Ahem, yes, the turning point was basically when he didn't tell me that the scout harassed him, we were seventeen at the time. I mean it's pretty typical for him, though. He'll never ask for help, even if he needs it. He's always been good at everything, minus communication, and feelings. I mean we haven't even..."

Kory cut in, "I'm sorry, not that I'm uninterested, or unwilling to listen, but for right now, I'm just looking for the turning point in your career objective, not your relationship. Originally, you planned to study sports medicine, but you changed your goal after the harassment, which occurred early last year, right?"

Luke's face felt flushed with embarrassment, he covered his mouth with both hands. "I misunderstood. Yes, yes, that's correct, that is when I decided."

Kory smiled at him and closed the file that lay in front of him.

"I failed, right? I...I'll see myself out," Luke said, as he stood up.

Kory chuckled and reached behind his desk into the small mini-fridge. He pulled out a cold bottle of water and passed it to Luke. "Sit. You didn't fail anything. People are always on edge when they come in. I'm used to it. Normally, people are nervous because I talk to them before they meet with Madeline, so it's understandable. That was, however, the first time a person has ever misunderstood an interview question and related it to their relationship problems."

Luke sat down and took a long drink from the water bottle, then placed it on the floor next to him. "I don't know what to say. I skipped practice today, which I've been doing a lot since I've been meeting you at the library. I haven't even talked to Coop about this, he doesn't even know I'm here. I think I just feel guilty, so everything is just coming out."

Kory pressed the speaker button on his desk phone. "Ms. Martin, please reschedule my last two meetings of the day. You can go home early after you've finished."

"Yes sir, I'll call them now," she cheerfully replied. The secretary was obviously thrilled at being told she could leave early.

"Alright, now, you have my full attention," Kory said. "We've talked about Coop plenty of times before, but what's got you especially upset today? I noticed earlier when you were in the lobby that you seemed deep in thought."

Luke's feelings began spilling out, word after word, for what felt like hours, and Kory listened. "It's just that we've been growing apart for so long. I feel guilty for not telling him about this, but at the same time, I'm mad."

Kory leaned back in his chair, putting both hands behind his head. "What are you mad about?"

"Tch, I'm mad that he's always been the same, and I never realized it. He hasn't once asked me where I've been going when I miss practice. He never asks about my classes and he's just so uninterested. It feels like we've been friends for a long time now, and nothing more. As I say that, I want to cry because he's always been my whole world."

Kory looked at him softly. "Sounds like you two just need to talk."

Luke glanced around the room, thinking about what he should say next. "Yeah, but like I said, he doesn't really like to talk about feelings. I want to be honest with him, but I don't want to hurt him."

Kory sat up straight, tapping a pen on his desk, staring into Luke's eyes. "I don't want to overstep. I want to be professional because you came here for an interview and Madeline will kill me if I come off as unprofessional. I think you'd make a great intern. The experience will help you decide if this is the right path for you, but I need to be honest here." He rubbed his temples and looked at Luke, then began tapping his pen again. "Listen, we've met up three times a week for the past six months, you haven't told him that you decided to change your career path, that you've been meeting with me, or that you're here on an interview. It doesn't sound to me like he is the only one who is bad at communication."

Luke nodded slowly. "I can't disagree with that."

Kory placed the pen down, looking straight into Luke's eyes. "That being said, I need to say something I've been thinking about for a while. The truth is that I find it hard to be objective with you because I'm interested in you personally. I hate seeing your face all sad like this. I've been respectful of your relationship, and I will continue to be because that's just my personality, but the second that you two break up, *I'm coming for you.* Now, if that makes you uncomfortable, I can find another associate that will take you on as their intern, no hard feelings. But judging from our interactions in the past half a year, I don't think you are uninterested." He tilted his head and waited for Luke's reply.

Luke could hardly believe what Kory just said. He was certainly not expecting his interview to end with a confession. A massive swirl of emotions overcame him. He wanted to stand and tell Kory how he felt, and briefly imagined walking over and kissing him passionately, instead of using words. What he was feeling for Kory was something hot, fierce, and urgent. He stood to reply, but quickly sat back down, as flashes of Coop played in his mind, bringing with them momentary feelings of betrayal, which he quickly shook off. His eyes met Kory's from across the desk, and he was suddenly filled with a confidence that he hadn't felt until now, accompanied by a new feeling of hope. "I'm interested," he said.

"I thought so. I'm happy to finally hear that," he said, unable to contain his pearly white smile.

"I, uh, don't want to wait, though…I want to just jump in, but I have to end things with Coop, first." Luke rubbed his thumbs together on his lap, avoiding further eye contact. He didn't trust himself right now, and he wanted to stay true to what he just said.

Kory nodded and swiveled slowly side to side in his chair. "Yeah, I know waiting is hard, but it's important to me that you are fully removed from any relationship before we get involved intimately. But, professionally, you got the job, and since you'll be working under me, I just need to know when you want to start."

Luke felt like his body was pulling him back and forth, as his lower half ordered him to let it loose, his brain told him to break up with Coop first. "Well, I need to talk to Coach and let him know that I'm leaving the team and then I'll end things with Coop. I'm going to tell Coach that I need to leave effective immediately. I'm not sure how that will go."

Kory flipped a pen between his fingers. "And what about Coop? What does that timeline look like?"

Luke sighed. "The same applies to Coop."

Kory folded his hands and rested his chin on his thumbs on his desk. "Alright, let's do this, I'm not rushing you with the relationship stuff. I've waited this long, a few more days won't be too difficult. The firm just got a huge case that I could definitely use your help with. There are probably a million copies and files that need to be made. It's a really complicated case. Madeline has two other interns, but I don't think one is going to last much longer because she doesn't follow directions well. That's why Madeline gave me the okay to hire you if I felt like you'd be a good fit. So, take your time with it, but not too much time, and I'll plan to just see you here on Monday. If you end up reaching out before then, well, great, but if not, then we'll at least have a firm date for you to start work."

Luke stood and approached Kory, slowly walking around the large desk. "Thank you, Kory. I'm really looking forward to working with you."

Luke hugged him tightly, and Kory stood to fully embrace him for the first time. "Luke, I want to hold you like this, but I really can't for much longer. Your face is too close…your body…is too close."

Luke felt a light throbbing below, he brought his face in front of Kory's. As much as he wanted to do the right thing, after being in a relationship with no intimacy for so long, he couldn't help himself. Kory quickly covered Luke's mouth with his hand, then softly kissed the back of the hand that separated them. "Let me walk you out," he said, while looking at Luke's flushed face.

Luke got into his car at 7:15 PM. He looked at his phone to see missed texts and calls from Coop, Kai, and Coach. He pressed the call button on the last one. "Hey, Coach, I'm sorry for missing again. Can we talk?"

"Of course, do you want to swing by? I'll be in my office for a little while longer."

Luke paused as he looked at the time, he didn't want to run into anyone from the team right now. "Is everyone already gone?" he asked.

"Yep, it's just me," Coach replied.

Luke drove to the school and sat in his car for a few minutes before going in. He was shaking and wasn't sure why. He looked down at his phone trying to decide if he should tell Coop everything before going in. As he looked at Coop's picture and texts, he couldn't help but feel a little guilty. Coop really hadn't done anything wrong, in contrast to Luke, who was ready to do much more than kiss Kory a few minutes ago. In fact, if Kory hadn't covered his mouth, there's no telling how far Luke would've gone.

No, I have to do this. It's not fair to him either, he told himself as he walked into Coach's office.

"Hey, Luke, have a seat and tell me what's got you in the mood to talk. I'm guessing it has to do with the reason you've been missing so much practice," Coach said.

Luke sat down and leaned back in his chair, staring at the ceiling. "Coach, there's not really a good way for me to say it. I'm not too sure of what I'm doing right now, honestly. I'm actually kind of scared."

"Well, if you can't look me in the eyes, then you haven't made up your mind on whatever it is that you're trying to decide."

Luke sat up straight and looked at Coach. "I want to quit. I got a job interning at a law firm. I'm really excited about it, it's a great opportunity, but I just feel bad coming here and doing this part."

Coach looked at him, studying his face. "Well, as someone whose been with you for a long time, I'm very happy for you and I'm proud of you."

Luke was definitely not expecting such a positive reaction, but he was happy, nonetheless. "Thanks, Coach."

Coach shook his head at him. "Don't thank me, because as your Coach, I'm pissed off. How long have you been chewing on this decision? Screwing around, missing practice, all while knowing you were going to leave. That's a crap thing to do, Luke. I can't believe you two kept this from me—"

Luke interrupted him, "What two? Do you know Kory?"

Coach was beside himself in frustration. "What? Who's Kory? No,

I don't know Kory. I'm talking about Coop. I can't believe you two would keep this from me. Damn it. We don't even have a decent backup catcher right now."

Luke struggled with whether he should tell Coach that even Coop was unaware of his plans. After listening to Coach yell for several minutes, he spoke up. "Coach, Coop doesn't know I'm quitting. He doesn't know any of this. He has no idea that I changed my major, or about the job, none of it."

Coach stood up, rubbing his hand down his face. "Luke, do the right thing. You've always been a team. Don't make a decision like this without talking to him."

Luke stood up. "No. No, I won't. He is not my whole world. I have my own life and my own decisions to make. I'm tired of worrying about everyone else. I'm done."

Coach sat down and looked at him, he raised both of his hands off his desk. "Seems to me, you've forgotten all about practicing HX4, since it sounds like neither your head, hands, heart, or your home have been with Coop or baseball for a while." Luke sat silent. Coach could tell he wouldn't change his mind. "Alright, well, how much time can you give me before you have to leave the team?"

Coop swam alone in the family pool, hoping to escape the torment of his mother's voice. The stars in the sky were beautiful, and the warm water was comforting, but his mother's words pierced through the silence in his mind, frustrating him, just the same.

Coop, take care of Luke. Coop, remember Luke isn't as fortunate as you, he doesn't have a mom. Coop, let Luke have that, we'll buy you another one. Luke is your best friend, he needs you…

He stood in the water and smacked his hand into it, making a big splash.

"Ooooh, loser Morgan, what are you smacking the water for? Who made the great Coop Morgan upset this time?" his sister, Ariel, teased him while walking into the pool area. She was now seventeen, and had grown to look much like their mother, Sam. Her long brown mermaid hair, soft button nose, tan skin, and green eyes were captivating, her attitude toward her brother, however, was not. She plopped herself on a pool chair and sat cross-legged looking at Coop.

He turned quickly to see her. "What do you want, Arie?" he asked, wiping the water from his face.

"I just wanted to check on you. I know normally this day hits you pretty hard. Not that I expect you to open up to me. God forbid you share your feelings." She rolled her eyes and looked at him.

Coop stood in the shallow end of the pool and threw his arms up at her. "If you already know that, then why are you here?"

"Yikes, gosh, you really are a jerk. I don't know how Luke has put up with you for all these years," she said.

Coop ignored her and climbed onto a long, black reclining pool float.

Not getting the reaction she wanted, she started again, "I'm here because I don't remember as much about mom as you do. So, I'm sad because it's the day she passed, but it's different for you. You have memories that I don't have. If I come here and try to talk to you, I may learn something about her that I never knew before. That would make me feel better. I'd feel like she was still here somehow."

Coop sighed. Although Arie was generally a brat, he did feel bad that she was stuck being raised without a mom. He turned his head to face her, grabbing the side of the pool, stopping his float from being pushed around by the pool jets. "Arie, listen, today sucks, yeah. I've been thinking about mom a lot more lately, but I don't really want to talk about it. I wish I could tell you something you didn't know about her, but all I really have are memories of her telling me to take care of Luke and seeming to truly care about him more than me."

"You can't really believe that? I mean you don't really think she cared about Luke more than you, do you?"

Coop looked up at the brightly shining moon. "Arie, I don't want to talk about this. I know she loved me, but it was just weird that she stepped in the way she did to take care of Luke. I mean his dad and our dad don't even talk to each other. What the hell happened between them? They were best friends for years. Now that I'm older, I find myself questioning everything. Sometimes, I think whatever it was that drove them apart had to do with mom."

She pulled her head back. "So, you think maybe Luke's dad and our dad, like, fought over her?"

"Isn't that the only thing that makes sense, Arie? Why else did she insert herself into Luke's life? Why would Luke's mom leave his dad when he was only a few days old? It makes sense to me that there was some kind of a fight over her."

Arie wasn't convinced. "Maybe? I mean, maybe she was just being nice. Everyone describes her as basically a walking angel... Dad says they never fought, and she was always smiling in pictures. I don't know, though. I've always wondered why Luke's dad doesn't bother with us after all that Dad has done for Luke. He practically considers him a son, while Luke's dad seems like he hates you. Of course, you are a jerk, though, so I don't blame him," she said.

"He doesn't hate me, he's just indifferent toward me. He's never once been mean to me."

Coop's phone beeped, signaling a text. Arie picked it up and looked at it, she put his passcode in and unlocked it.

"Hey, put my phone down, you don't even know my code. You'll get me locked out!" he yelled.

"*Oh my God*"—she cocked her head to the side—"0102, it's the same code you use for everything. Oooh, it's a text from Luke. He says he's going home because he has work to do, he sounds pissy. Do you want me to reply for you?"

Coop hopped off his float and stood in the water. "How do you know my passcode?"

She rolled her eyes and replied, "Your generation is all the same, you use the same code for everything."

"My generation? Arie, I'm eighteen and you're seventeen, are you serious right now? Dumbest thing you've ever said."

"Shut up. What should I text him back? Yikes, what are all these?" she asked, while scrolling through his texts with Luke.

"Arie, just text him and tell him it's okay. I understand. He's been busy with stuff lately. It's fine."

Chapter 2
I Can Fix Him

Kory stood in his office overlooking a desk cluttered with files and papers, while two other lawyers from the practice stood close by. They argued about the sloppy notes made by a former intern.

As Kory looked up, he saw Luke enter the lobby. He smiled and waved him in. "Hey, this is a nice surprise, I wasn't expecting you to start until Monday," he said. "Guys give us a few minutes. I'll have Ms. Martin notify you when it's time to reconvene."

Both men shuffled past Luke. They nodded in acknowledgement of him, but Kory sent them away so fast that they didn't have time for introductions.

"You didn't have to do that; I didn't mean to intrude. You're obviously very busy," Luke said. He eyed the massive piles of papers strewn on the desk.

Kory sized Luke up from across the room. "You told your Coach, but not Coop, am I correct?"

Luke's eyes went wide. "How could you even know that?"

"Luke, I'm training to be a lawyer, I read people's body language all day. Madeline has filled my head with so much knowledge on it, that I should be considered an expert at this point. Yours is screaming for help right now, which can only mean that you are not here for…well…sex, which is something that I am greatly looking forward to."

Luke bit his bottom lip and reached into his pocket, pulling out his phone. *Hello, Luke, I hope you are doing alright. I have a solution that I think will work out for catcher. I have to try and get a bunch of things approved very quickly in order for this to work, though. I want you to plan to meet me at Tagaloa's tomorrow night at 8:00pm. I'll let you know if anything changes.*

"You're not gonna say anything?" Kory asked.

"Sorry, that was a text from my coach. He wants me to meet him at Tagaloa's tomorrow night. I'll end things with Coop afterward. Today just won't work out for us to meet up."

"Okay, that's fine," Kory said. "No hugs, though. You stay over there. If you're going to be here, I have to put you to actual work." He gestured to the piles of papers on his desk.

"Right, just work," Luke replied, placing his keys on Kory's credenza.

For the rest of the day Kory watched in awe, as Luke diligently attended every task he was given, making copies, re-printing documents, finding files quickly, and even going on a coffee run for the group. *Just one more day,* Kory thought.

Coop sat at the bar of Tagaloa's Restaurant on Friday night, with a glass of beer in hand listening to Kai ramble on. "He's been missing practice like crazy these days. What's going on with him?" Kai asked, while wiping down the bar.

Coop took a sip of beer and shrugged his shoulders at him in response. "Kai, I have no idea, he texted me the same exact thing that he texted you. He said he was meeting Coach here tonight, and he'd try to meet up after. That's it." Coop took another large sip from his frosty mug.

The door of the restaurant opened, and a well-dressed man entered. Kai's mother did not welcome this customer, as she typically did for all others. Coop noticed Mrs. Tagaloa elbowing Kai in the side, he heard her whisper, "The Scout," while lifting her chin toward the door. Coop shook his head and sighed loudly, upon noticing Collin Pyle approaching him from the left.

"Could I have just a minute, Mr. Morgan?" he asked, standing behind Coop.

"Are you selling the same shit you tried to sell me last year? Not interested." Coop took a sip of his beer.

"I have something that I think you'll definitely be interested in," he replied, while flashing a large manila envelope.

"Tch, I doubt it," Coop said.

"Yo, you here for trouble, or what?" Kai asked, from behind the bar.

"Kai Tagaloa"—Mr. Pyle looked Kai up and down—"batting average of 185, GPA…even worse. I'm not here for trouble, and I'm certainly not here for you."

Kai's jaw fell open. "No, he did not just say that to me," he said under his breath.

"Come, have a drink with me, Mr. Morgan."

Coop reluctantly got up from his seat at the bar and walked over to an open table near the corner of the restaurant. His posture was terrible, as he slid down in his chair and leaned back, beer in hand. He'd already had a few beers, and really wasn't in the mood to play nice. Truth be told, he only came over to avoid making a scene. People were already starting to whisper, while staring over. Coop was always the center of attention and people were constantly interested in whatever he was doing. Customers in the restaurant immediately began discussing their opinions on Coop being there without Luke.

"Do you think he switched Luke out for this guy?" he heard

someone say. Coop shot an icy gaze toward the woman that made that comment. She widened her eyes upon noticing and looked down at the table.

Coop turned his attention back to Mr. Pyle. "Alright, out with it, what's in the envelope?"

"It's nice to see you, too," Mr. Pyle said with a smirk. "We'll get to the envelope in a moment. I'm a bit hungry, would you mind if I ordered something?"

"Ugh…unbelievable." Coop hung his head backward. "Whatever, man, last time I checked this was a free country, this is a restaurant, so if you're hungry, who am I to get in the way of what makes you happy?"

"Ha ha ha…there we go! Why do I feel like you aren't talking about food right now?" Mr. Pyle asked.

Coop crossed his arms. "So, you do have a brain in there, I'm glad you understood. Cut the shit, man. I'm not here to eat with you. I have stuff to do and I'm tired of looking at your face."

"Aww, see now, that's going too far. Many women find me handsome, should I take that last remark as a sign that you don't agree with them?"

"Do I look like a woman to you?" Coop asked.

"Hmm…no, Mr. Morgan, I can't say that you do. Although you've definitely grown since we last saw each other and your hair is slightly longer." Mr. Pyle reached across the table to touch the strands of hair that were hanging over Coop's shoulders.

Coop's head was facing down, looking at the table as he held his own face in his hands. His hair, which was half in a topknot and half down, framed his face. Since he was a few drinks in, his reaction was slow. He lifted his head as he saw the man's fingers touching the bottom pieces of hair that were resting on the table. "What the hell, man?" Coop quickly pulled the hair tie out of his hair and flipped his head upside down.

"Uh oh, the samurai knot is coming out," Kai said, still behind the bar.

Coop aggressively bundled his hair on the top of his head, knotted it, and stood up. "Thank you for wasting my time, once again."

The scout tapped the folder and gestured for him to sit back down. "Alright, alright, so you hate my face, and you don't resemble a woman. Let's move on, shall we?" Mr. Pyle asked.

Coop sighed and righted his posture, sitting back down. He didn't want to deal with this guy, but really wanted to know what was in the envelope.

"I'm here because I truly want to help you," Mr. Pyle said.

Coop scoffed. "Oh, really, and why is that?"

"Hmm, well, I rather like you, Mr. Morgan, and so do the people I work with. Everyone was so disappointed that we couldn't come to an agreement last time."

"Ah, so, it is the same shit as last time. What's in the envelope then?" Coop asked.

"Here. See for yourself."

Coop noticed Kai straining to see what was going on. He removed a stack of five pictures from the envelope. Some were of him holding hands with Luke, some were of the two of them kissing, and one showed them wrapped in each other's arms, with Luke's hand in a very compromising position. "First, these are hot, I think I'll keep them. Second, they're a bit dated," Coop said, stuffing the pictures back in the envelope.

"I agree, they are very hot. Which brings me to my reason for coming here."

Coop felt a change in the man's voice and interrupted him, "Wait, what did you just say? Are you here to threaten me, help me, or fucking hit on me? Because I'm honestly confused at this point."

"Hmmm, I suppose it's a bit of all three," Mr. Pyle replied.

"Ha," Coop said. "So let me get this straight. You try to get me to dump my boyfriend when I'm seventeen, by telling me no one will sign me if I'm outed, then you come back here a year later, after stalking me, to proposition me for sex?"

"Not quite, but close," Mr. Pyle replied. "See, it's like this, I know no one else has made you an offer, and we both know why. Now, I did have someone take these pictures, but background checks are part of my job. I certainly haven't been stalking you. I did notice that you weren't with Luke after practice today, so I thought if you two had broken up, or if you wanted to maybe...try someone new, I could help you out. Because if you give me what I want,"—he reached over and put his hand on top of Coop's—"I'll make sure you get an offer by the end of the week."

The large group from Parson & Associates Law Firm gathered for drinks at a beachside bar after ending their day early at 6:00 PM.

Kory and Luke were sitting across from one another, as Shay, another intern, approached. "Hey, Luke, you play baseball with the Morgan guy, right? Tom Morgan's son, what's his name? The guy with the sexy long hair and hot body?" she asked, while holding a blue martini in her hand.

Kory blew air from his mouth and looked at Luke, who was struggling with a reply.

"Um, I, uh, yeah, I know him. His name is Coop. He's, um, yeah," Luke stammered.

"Wow," Kory said, eyes wide, looking at Luke. *This is cute, he feels uncomfortable saying he's actually dating him. Now, is that because I'm here, or is it because he considers the relationship over? Or maybe he doesn't want other people knowing that he's gay?*

Shay put her martini down and sat close next to Kory. "That's great but how well do you know him, Luke? Could you, like, get me an intro?

I can follow you on your socials, then maybe we could plan like a group thing? Like karaoke or something. Damn, he would look good singing. Ugh, he looks good with his hair when it's all tied up, too, like a sexy little man bun." She pulled her long hair up in imitation and made a kissy face in the air. Her blonde hair dropped, and she looked at Kory, who was staring intently at a very uncomfortable Luke. She noticed Luke's expression and asked, "Oh, is he like dating your sister or something, Luke?"

"No, I don't have a sister," Luke said. "He is in a relationship, but something tells me he's going to be single soon. Although, I'm very sure you're not his type if I'm being honest."

Shay made a confused face and straightened her hair; she stood up while finishing her martini and walked away. Luke looked down at his phone. "Oh, shoot, I'm supposed to meet Coach at eight, and my car is at the office."

"That's fine, I'll drop you off, just let me know when you're done with your meeting, and I'll pick you up and bring you to get your car from the office," Kory said.

Luke whined, "But I really wanted to deal with Coop after—"

Kory stood and interrupted him, "It's okay, Luke, one thing at a time. Meet with your Coach tonight, deal with the rest tomorrow… I can wait."

That's it! Kai thought, after hearing Collin Pyle's proposition to Coop. He grabbed a pitcher of beer and walked over, he planned to pretend he was only there to refresh Coop's beer. Only, he didn't walk, per se, as he actually slipped on a piece of ice and slid right into their table. *Whoosh!* Beer everywhere!

Coop, with beer dripping off his face, looked down at Kai, who was now on the floor. "Smooth," Coop said.

"Damn," Mr. Pyle said, wiping his pants. "This is a $1,200 suit."

Kai's mother came from the back with a towel in hand. She stepped over Kai, who was lying flat on the floor, and began wiping Coop's face. She looked at Collin Pyle. "I think it's time for you to go," she said, shifting her gaze to the exit.

Mr. Pyle stood up from the table, still wiping his suit. "Fine, I gave you two chances, Mr. Morgan. Don't forget that." The entire crowd booed him as he left.

No one heard what they were discussing previously but the vibe was easy to read. Once the scout left, Kai stood up and took a bow to the sound of applause.

As Mr. Pyle stormed outside, he saw Luke heading in. He shouted in Luke's direction, "You've ruined him! I hope you know that!"

Luke saw the beer-drenched man and the white Mercedes he was getting into, but had no idea who he was, or what he was shouting about, so he walked inside without acknowledging him. He entered the restaurant and was greeted by the sight of Kai, soaked in beer, bowing to applause, and Coop, whose hair was being towel dried by Kai's mother. "Do I even want to know what happened here?" Luke asked.

Coop thanked Kai's mother and shook his hair out of her grip.

Luke walked over, grabbing a towel from the bar on the way. "What happened?" he asked Coop.

"Not much. Kai found his calling as a traveling clown," Coop replied.

Luke ran his fingers through Coop's hair and found it sticky with beer. "Let's hit the bathroom and try to rinse it. I'll see if Arie can come pick you up. You've obviously been drinking, so you're not driving."

"You can just drive me home, can't you?"

"I told you earlier; I'm meeting with Coach tonight. I don't think you should let him see you like this," Luke said.

"Alright," Coop replied, as they headed toward the bathroom together.

Typical—he didn't even remember that I was meeting Coach, Luke thought.

Opening the bathroom door, Luke noticed that Coop had stopped following him. He appeared to be moving some menus around on a table. "What are you doing? Is there something interesting over there? Come on, Coop, Coach is gonna be here soon." He gestured toward the open door and cocked his head to the side. "You just decided to straighten the menus for no reason?"

"No… Luke, what are you even asking me right now?"

The two walked into the bathroom, one behind the other. The bathrooms were nicer, cleaner, and more spacious than most restaurant bathrooms, with several stalls, lighted mirrors, and large sinks.

"What happened? They just changed the drinking age to eighteen last month, and you're already wasted. You've had, probably what, like three beers or so? Your hair is drenched and you're all sticky. What did Kai do?" Luke asked while running his fingers through Coop's hair.

"Let's just talk about it later, I can't think straight right now. I just want to go home."

Luke, who was already on edge, rubbed Coop's shoulders. "Okay, well, if we aren't going to rinse your hair, let's get the sides out of your face. Where is your hair tie?"

Coop appeared to be confused or distracted, due to the alcohol, which only frustrated Luke more. He really wanted to get Coop out of there before Coach saw him in his drunken state.

There was normally a spare hair tie inside the waistband of Coop's uniform pants. Luke slid his hand around the outside of his waist feeling for one.

Kai's voice was heard outside the door, "They didn't leave, I'm telling you, they just went in the bathroom to rinse Coop's hair."

"Hair tie," Luke whispered, and held his hand out to Coop.

"Why are you whispering?" Coop asked him.

The bathroom door swung open; it was Kai. "See, here they are, I told you!" he yelled to his mother from the bathroom. "Uh, what the hell were you two doing? Your hair is a fucking mess, dude. Where's your hair tie?" Kai asked, in one breath.

"That's what I've been asking him," Luke replied.

"Asking him, huh? I've known you two long enough, and I didn't hear any talking in here before I came in," Kai said.

Luke rolled his eyes.

"Oh, wait, I pulled my hair tie out, when your mom came to help dry my hair, it's probably on the table," Coop said. Suddenly, his eyes widened, and he darted out of the bathroom.

The envelope is inside the menus; I gotta stash it somewhere else. Maybe I'll just ask Kai to hang on to it for me. I'm pretty sure he heard everything that happened anyway. Coop hurried over to the table, and grabbed the hair tie, stuffing it inside his waistband. He reached inside the menu's and was shocked to find the envelope was gone. Frantically, he searched around the table, then shook all the menus out one at a time.

Tap, tap, tap, Coop looked out the window toward the tapping sound. Wendy stood outside, holding the envelope, smiling. She motioned with her hand for him to come outside.

Coop panicked and ran out of the restaurant. He held his hand out toward her. "Give me the envelope, Wendy. I'm not in the mood for games."

Wendy Miller was no friend of Coop's, she was a conceited, snobbish girl who only wanted the things she couldn't have. "People usually greet one another first; you really are rude, Coop."

Coop sighed, he was drunk and not thinking clearly, he was also afraid that Luke would come out at any moment and see the pictures. "What do you want, Wendy? Give me the envelope that you stole."

Wendy rolled her eyes at him. "I didn't steal anything, it was sitting right on the table, carefully tucked in a menu. I saw you place it there. It looked like something you didn't want Luke to see. Imagine my disappointment when I looked inside. Why would he be upset by these? Wait, don't answer that. More importantly, why would you feel the need to hide them from him?"

"Wendy, seriously, give me the envelope. I'm not gonna stand out here and talk to you about Luke."

"Tsk, tsk, tsk, I think that it would be very bad for you if I posted these on social media. The guy in the expensive suit seemed to think they were worth something, too. So, let's make a deal."

"*Wendy*, just tell me what you want, damn it!"

She paused for a moment. "I want you to let me take a shot at you, let me see if I can excite you," she said flirtatiously while slowly waving the envelope at Coop.

"What? Why would you? I… You can't, it won't work. I'm not interested in you. Do you want money? I can give you money."

She shook her head and got closer to him. "I want to know if I can do it. I don't believe that you are only interested in Luke. I really don't. All you have to do is stand there."

"Listen, I can't think straight, and Luke is probably looking for me. What you're saying doesn't make sense. What would you get out of this? I'm telling you that I'm not interested. Just give me the envelope."

"Coop, shut up. Listen, you'll be famous one day, everyone knows that. It will be a great story that I can tell my friends for years to come. The story of how I made you want me, and then left you standing here, all alone."

"This is not going to go the way you think it is. Honestly, I don't like making girls cry, but I don't give a shit at this point. Go ahead and try, I'm not touching you, at all. Also, I'm telling Luke the second this ends, so don't even think you're going to try and blackmail me twice."

Ethan Prescott pulled up to Tagaloa's restaurant at 8:00 PM. He looked at his phone, there was a text from his dad: *Running late, be there soon.*

"Great, I'll just sit here then." He turned his car lights off and opened the windows of his lifted white Jeep.

"Damn it, stay still," he heard a woman's voice saying.

Ethan was suddenly staring at the most bizarre sight. He saw a tall, muscular, handsome man, standing with his back against a wall. *Wait, that's Coop Morgan, I thought he was...* His thoughts were quickly interrupted as he saw the screaming woman moving very close to Coop. She was wearing a very tight pink dress and had short blonde hair that shook as she pleaded with him. *What is she begging him for?* Ethan was deeply engrossed in the scene. He leaned his head near his open window to try and hear, but choked as a light breeze blew through his car. *Oh, man, she smells terrible. Her perfume is awful.* He looked on, as he saw Coop quickly put his hair in a topknot. *That looks good, he's got nice hair. Oof, he looks really pissed, though. What the hell is happening?*

The woman brought her hand to his cheek, as Coop twisted and put his hands straight up in the air. *Okay, he looks like he's surrendering to the police, or something. Maybe I should step in?* Ethan placed a hand on his door handle.

"Stay still, Coop, you said I could try!" Wendy screamed.

Coop squirmed. "Ugh, it's gross, I can't. Just hurry up!"

Wendy went in for a kiss, placing her mouth on his for a fraction of a second, as Coop squeezed his mouth shut, facial muscles strained— "I can't, get off me, I'm gonna puke." Coop leaned over, dry heaving. "Effing disgusting," he said, while spitting on the ground.

Wendy threw the envelope down and stormed off.

Coop quickly grabbed the envelope off the ground and stood up straight. He was still wiping his mouth and spitting as Arie pulled up in her black Mustang GT. She revved the engine at him and yelled out the window, "Hey, loser Morgan, hurry up and get in. You better not puke in my car."

Ethan watched as Coop left in Arie's car. *What the hell just happened?* He removed his hand from his door and leaned back in his seat.

Luke stood in the bathroom, listening to Kai explain what happened with Mr. Pyle. "No, no. This is *not* happening again!" Luke screamed. "What do you mean, Kai? Did you just stand there like an idiot and watch it happen?"

"Woahhhh, calm down," Kai said, backing up. "I didn't just stand there, but what the hell was I supposed to do? Do you think Coop would have been happy with me getting involved? He would have flipped out. I went over trying to break it up nonchalantly, and, well, although it didn't go the way I wanted it to; the guy left and I'm pretty sure I ruined his suit." He smiled cautiously at Luke, hoping for a smile in return.

Luke held a hand on his own forehead. "I'm sorry, Kai. It's not your fault. I have a lot going on right now. I shouldn't have yelled at you."

Kai patted him on the shoulder. "What time are you meeting Coach?"

Luke pulled his phone out of his pocket to check the time. There was a missed text from Arie: *Hey, I got him. Can you bring his car home for him? I assume you're coming over after, anyway.* He quickly texted her back: *Sure.* He noticed the time and answered Kai, "Coach is probably here already. Let's go."

Luke and Kai glanced around the restaurant; Coach hadn't arrived yet. "Kai, I'm gonna sit over here and wait for him," Luke said.

Kai nodded and walked around the bar to help with a few customers. Luke was beyond frustrated as he sat down at a corner table. His mind was once again in turmoil. *He left and didn't even say goodbye to me. I can't believe the scout came back again…I'm making the right choice.*

Luke's thoughts were interrupted as Kai's mother yelled, "Talofa, Coach!"

Coach walked in and behind him was a gorgeous man, with shaggy, light brown hair, tan sun-kissed skin, and big brown eyes. His build was muscular, but not overly so. Luke had no idea who he was, and he wasn't expecting anyone else to join them. The man approached with Coach, and Luke stood to shake his hand.

Coach started, "Hey, Luke, this is my son."

The man reached his hand out to Luke. "Hey, I'm Ethan Prescott, nice to meet you."

"Nice to meet you, too." Luke said, as the three sat down.

Coach looked at Luke, who sat politely but seemed a bit off. "Hey, sorry, I forgot to tell you that Ethan was going to join us. I wasn't sure he was coming until this morning."

"No problem. I'm happy to finally meet him," Luke said, smiling at Ethan.

Ethan didn't seem to hear the compliment or notice Luke smiling at him. Coach knocked lightly on the table, bringing Ethan out of his trance. "Whaaat? What are you knocking at me for?" Ethan asked.

Coach smiled at Ethan, then spoke to Luke. "Ethan is going to be our new catcher. His transfer will take place immediately. I need you to be at the field tomorrow morning, so I can introduce him to the team. It's important that you're there. I've moved a bunch of things around quickly to make this happen. Don't even think of telling me that you can't make it. I'll text everyone after this and let them know we have a mandatory team meeting tomorrow."

"Wow, um. Okay, wow. I don't know what I'm feeling right now," Luke said.

Ethan seemed confused by Luke's response. "What's wrong? Didn't you want to leave the team?" he asked.

"I do. I have someone else, I mean something…else, that I want more. My heart hasn't been in it for a while. I'm dragging everyone down at this point." He looked up at Ethan, whose eyes were still wide at the *I have someone else* slip-up. Luke shook it off and continued, "They're a great bunch of guys. You'll have no problem fitting in."

"I can think of one person he may have some trouble with," Coach said.

Luke looked down at the table, then back up to Coach. "Coop… yeah…maybe…"

Ethan spoke up, for some reason their shared sentiment that Coop wouldn't work well with him, seemed to really get under his skin. "Why would I have trouble with him? I watched a few of his recent games, he's not dropping his hips enough, and he seems unfocused. I think he needs to make a few adjustments to his back leg, his right elbow, and then deal with whatever it is that's got him so distracted."

Luke was stunned. "Wow, that was crazy accurate. You picked up on all that from watching footage of him?"

Ethan shrugged his shoulders. "Well, yeah, I mean he's the star, right? I can fix him."

Luke shook his head. "Maybe you can if you can get him to listen to you. He doesn't like people critiquing him. He's stubborn like that, he never asks for help."

Coach agreed, "Yep, that's Coop."

Ethan looked straight into Luke's wavering eyes. "I can fix him."

Chapter 3
I'm Done With Us

Luke sat inside Coop's car, hugging the steering wheel. He told Arie he would drop his car off, but he was suddenly feeling hesitant. He found himself unable to move from the parking spot, frozen in the reality that he would be ending their relationship tonight. *Why can't I move?* he wondered. His phone rang, interrupting the deadlock within. He saw the name that was calling; instantly he lifted his head, put his seatbelt on, and started to drive. He answered the call on speaker. "Hey, Kory, I just got done with the meeting. I'm so happy you called."

"Of course, I called," Kory said. "When I dropped you off, I told you I'd pick you up after you finished. I'll leave now and head that way."

"Oh, um, no. Sorry… I'm actually driving Coop's car right now. I need to drop it off for him."

Kory was silent.

"It's no big deal, he was drunk when I got there, a whole bunch of stuff happened, his sister had to pick him up… Yeah, so I'm just dropping his car off…" Luke sniffled, trying to hold back tears.

Kory remained silent, then finally asked, "Are you crying?"

Luke broke down in a fit of tears and frustration. "I just can't anymore. I can't do it. I have to end this, now."

Kory exhaled deeply into the phone. "Luke, listen to me. You don't sound good. I think you should have a clear head when you do this. I don't want you to regret anything. Sleeping on it may help you feel better."

"No, I'm doing it tonight. I should've done this a long time ago."

Coop stood in his room across from Luke, who was enraged after he explained what happened at the bar earlier. He didn't want to hide it this time, he told Luke everything that happened and passed him the pictures. He felt like he hadn't done anything wrong, so he wasn't too concerned with how Luke would react.

Luke thumbed through them in disbelief as he looked at Coop, whose hair was in a topknot. "Great, Coop. This is great. Help me understand your thought process here. I don't want to tell my boyfriend about these old-ass pictures of us, so I'm going to kiss this girl, get the pictures back and everything will be fine? I don't understand this!"

"Luke, she didn't kiss me. She tried to put her mouth on mine for not even a second. I did nothing. I didn't even touch her."

Luke looked at him like he was the stupidest person in the world. "Coop she had her mouth on your mouth, do you know what that is? It's called a fucking kiss! You let her kiss you, Coop! How could you do something like that? This is just like last time, damn it!" Luke held a hand on his own forehead.

"What's like last time? When did I ever let anyone else try to put their mouth on mine?"

Luke shot him a look of pure disgust at his phrasing. "I'm talking about the last time this scout came around and you decided not to tell me about it."

"What do you mean? I did tell you about it."

"Coop, are you serious right now? You said it was a bad deal, you conveniently left out the fact that you wouldn't be signed because of me, because of us!"

Coop sighed. "First of all, I wasn't going to sign anyway, and you should remember that. All I wanted at that time was to protect you. I didn't care about the deal. I just didn't want you to find out what he said and get hurt. Wait…who even told you about this?"

Luke held one hand on his head, while the other hand told Coop to stop. "Alright, enough… I'm done with this…us… I can't."

Coop pulled his head back. "Done with what? With us?"

Luke kept one hand on his forehead, nodding. "Yeah, Coop. I'm done with us."

Coop grabbed Luke's hands. "Luke, look at me, what are you saying right now, you can't be serious?"

Luke pulled his hands away. "I am serious."

Coop covered his mouth with his hand. "Luke, I'm sorry. I shouldn't have let her do that."

"Coop…we've been going down different roads for a long time." Coop shook his head in shock and sat on the side of his bed, while Luke walked over to face him. "Look at me. Why did I meet with Coach today?"

Coop stared at the floor. "I don't know, probably because you've been missing practice all the time lately."

Luke scoffed. "Why don't you know? Because you didn't ask, right?" Luke continued, "Okay, so, why have I been missing practice?"

Coop stared blankly. "I…I…I don't know." Luke tilted his head and half smiled at him. Coop folded his hands on his lap and looked at the floor. "So, why have you been missing practice? What did you meet with Coach about?" Coop asked.

"I got a job interning at a law firm."

"What? Since when were you even interested in becoming a lawyer?"

Luke softened his tone and smiled. "It's kind of a long story, but I originally met this guy when the law firm was holding a seminar at the library. I approached him to talk about what happened with the scout last year. For the past six months, I've been meeting with him, instead of going to practice. He's the one…that gave me the internship. It's an amazing opportunity."

Coop quickly pieced things together. *It definitely sounds like he's into this guy. I guess he's been thinking about breaking up for a long time, too…. I feel kind of happy right now for some reason. Why is that? Shouldn't I feel more upset? I actually feel relieved.* Coop leaned back on his bed and stared at the ceiling fan in silence, while Luke paced around the room slowly. The realization that he wouldn't have to put Luke first anymore hit him, and in that moment he could only feel grateful.

"Hey… I'm happy for you," Coop said, softly.

Luke stopped and sat on the bed beside him. "Yeah?"

Coop nodded.

"Thanks…but I did keep it from you, so part of me has felt really bad about that," Luke said.

Coop shook his head, still lying down. "No, don't feel bad. I didn't ask…. If I cared, I would have asked. It's like you said, I had already moved on from the romantic part of our relationship a long time ago. Lately, I'd been feeling like I wanted to end things, too."

They continued talking for several hours. Luke looked at his phone, it was 2:00 AM. "Hey, I, um, don't have a car here with me, not sure if you already realized that."

"Well, you're not borrowing one of mine. Now that we aren't together, I can finally tell you; you are a terrible driver…worse than Arie."

Luke whacked him with a pillow. "Well, what should I do, then?"

Coop stood up, pulled out Luke's favorite red track pants, a white T-shirt, and tossed them over to him. "It's fine, just stay. You can use the guest room if you're uncomfortable."

Luke began undressing while standing beside the bed. "Uncomfortable? Around you? I could never be."

The two brushed their teeth and laid down in Coop's bed. They turned with their backs facing one another, on opposite sides of the bed.

"Oh, by the way, I met Ethan Prescott tonight," Luke said.

"Ethan Prescott? Coach's son?"

"Yeah, he's gonna be my replacement."

Both Coop and Luke fell asleep within minutes. A tremendous weight had been lifted from them.

Chapter 4
Luke Gets Loose

Kory fell asleep in bed around 1:00 AM, with no text or call from Luke shown on his phone. He placed the phone on his pillow next to his face, so he wouldn't miss his call. He opened his sleepy eyes again at three, still no notifications. He sighed and turned back over in bed, closing his eyes.

Just after seven, a notification rang loudly next to Kory's face. Kory's eyes remained closed as he sat up in bed, feeling around for his obnoxiously loud phone. He held the phone close to his eyes; he'd barely slept and couldn't see that well yet.

Luke: *Hey, sorry I didn't get back with you last night. I did it.*

Kory wasn't thinking clearly, and he didn't exactly read that the way Luke intended it. *What? He did what? Sex? No, what?* Kory wiped his eyes awake and took a deep breath. He wrote out several texts in reply, but deleted each one, thinking they each sounded horrible in their own way. As he struggled, another text came in.

Luke: *Hey, sorry if I woke you. We broke up. So, I believe the words you used were something along the line of, coming for me, if I'm not mistaken. If you want me, pick me up at 9:15am at the baseball field.*

Luke: *Lol my first time sending a text like that. I hope it came off as playfully sexy. Or at least sexy.*

Kory: *Make sure you're showered. I'm coming for you...*

Luke: *I've already worked out and showered. Funny you mentioned a shower, I pegged you for a dirty guy.*

Kory: *I am. See you at 9:15.*

The entire baseball team gathered in the meeting room. Coach and Luke stood in front of the group, while the rest of the team sat in chairs. "Good morning, guys. Sorry to pull you in early on a Saturday, but I've got an announcement to make that requires you all to be here," Coach said.

Coop suddenly felt like all eyes were on him, as Luke made eye contact with him from the front of the room. Coop shook his head and silently mouthed *not me* to the teammates looking at him.

Coach said, "Effective immediately, Luke will no longer be our catcher."

Kai stood up first. "What? What the hell?"

Other members joined him in shock, asking questions rapidly, some shouting, some standing. Coop sat silently in his seat. He couldn't wait to get out of there.

"Ethan, right on time," Coach said.

Coop looked up and saw the most perfect face he'd ever seen, atop a perfectly toned body. Ethan Prescott walked in, wearing a pair of slim fitting gray athletic pants, a long sleeved tight black shirt, and a pair of black sneakers, with white soles. Coop was having trouble taking the sight of him in. He was quite picky and honestly hadn't found himself attracted to anyone, which was another reason he stayed with Luke for so long. Even in a locker room full of well-built, usually naked, athletic guys, he was uninterested. This feeling that came over him was completely foreign and he could barely think straight. *Damn, he's really hot...more than hot... everything I'm seeing is perfect... What is this weird warm feeling in my chest? My heart is beating so fast,* Coop wondered, rubbing his chest with his palm.

Coach announced, "Team, this is my son, Ethan, he is Luke's replacement. He'll be wearing the number two."

The team stared at Ethan, and Luke tried to make light of the situation.

Luke rambled on about how his replacement is smarter and faster than he ever was anyway. He then tried to make a joke; it was something about the new number two being better looking too.

Ethan introduced himself, following the terrible pun from Luke. Coop was mesmerized as Ethan spoke, his teeth were bright white and perfectly aligned, and his big brown eyes were very expressive.

Coach put Coop on the spot. "Coop, you're the captain, do you have anything to add?"

Coop walked to the front of the room and approached Ethan. "Hey, I'm Coop, it's nice to meet you. If you need anything at all, you come directly to me." He smiled brightly, and the two shook hands. Their hands joined a little longer than what one would consider a normal handshake. *Why don't I want to let go of his hand? It's so warm...and it feels like I'm meant to hold onto it....*

Coop gently released his hand, and turned to face the team, in his best head of the team manner. "Alright, so, this was a shock to everyone, including me. Now, some people don't understand the word commitment..." He smirked and winked at Luke.

"Right...yes, that's me," Luke jested along.

Coop continued, "But the rest of us here, do. I'm proud as your captain to see the dedication and frustration that you're all feeling right now. And as a teammate of Luke's, I share that. However, as his friend, I'm happy for him. Thankfully, Ethan Prescott has stepped in to save our asses. We've all heard Coach talk about him before, of course, most of us assumed he was merely a figment of Coach's imagination, but we can all see"—he pointed to Ethan, and the two exchanged a smile—"he isn't. I know that with his help, we can win the Championship this year. Everyone, please give Ethan a warm welcome!"

As the meeting ended and Coop and Luke went their separate ways, Coop felt lighter than he could remember in a long time. He got in his car and saw Luke sprinting toward a bright-red, sporty Audi. *Someone else is going to take care of Luke now. I don't have to worry about him anymore. This is the best I've ever felt. I didn't realize that ending our relationship would make me feel this way. Why do I feel so happy?*

Outside his car, he heard someone shout, "Ethan!"

Ethan… Coop looked in the opposite direction and saw Ethan standing in the parking lot talking with a few of the guys. *I hope I didn't look stupid in there. What did I even say to him? He's making my brain all crazy. I want to talk to him, maybe I should go over there? No, I can't. I don't recognize myself right now. These feelings are so strange. I should just go home.*

Coop started his car and stole one more look at Ethan before pulling away.

Kory waited patiently in the parking lot for Luke to arrive. He'd waited six months to finally have Luke all to himself, and now the day was finally here. Hearing people talking near his car, he straightened his seat into a sitting position. Luke's smiling face appeared outside the passenger window. Kory unlocked the door, and Luke quickly sat inside.

"Good morning, I couldn't tell if you saw me or not," Luke said, as he buckled himself in.

"Good morning, do you want to stop and grab something to eat? Or I can make you something at my place? Whatever you want."

"Mmm, no thanks. I already ate," Luke said, with a smile.

I want kiss him. But it's better if I wait until we get to my place, Kory thought. He listened to Luke recap the events of the last twelve hours, as he finally pulled into the large employee parking garage. Once he reached the third level, he spotted Luke's red Range Rover. There weren't any other cars parked, since the office was closed for the weekend and this level was exclusively for Parson & Associates employees.

Kory parked beside Luke's car. "Alright, follow me to my place, it's only about a fifteen-minute drive," Kory said.

Luke gave him a disappointed look, and sat unmoving in the passenger seat.

"What are you looking at me like that for?" Kory asked.

"No, it's nothing… You lead, I'll follow." Luke turned and grabbed the door handle.

Kory leaned over, placed two fingers inside the neckline of the tight-fitting, brown T-shirt that Luke was wearing, lightly rubbing down from the bottom of his hairline. Then he hooked the collar with a tug inside his shirt. Luke turned to face him, and Kory wrapped his hand around the back of Luke's neck, bringing his face closer. Luke leaned in, and Kory aggressively pulled him into a forceful, commanding first kiss.

"Mmph…mmm…mmm…" Luke moaned through the sloppy kiss.

"I've been waiting so long to do that," Kory said, pulling back.

Luke licked his lips. "It's been so long since I've been kissed…and I've never been kissed like that." He dragged a finger over Kory's pants. "Can I try something else?" Luke asked teasingly. "I've been watching a ton of porn, so I could do this right."

Kory reclined his seat back. "I'm not sure porn is the best teacher, but I've been dying to feel every piece of you." Kory kissed him again, then their lips parted, and Luke moved further down. He ran his fingers through Luke's hair and whispered through the moans, "Yeah—mmmnn—like that, that's a good boy, Luke." After a few moments, Kory leaned his head back. "Finally…"

Luke sat up slightly, looking at Kory, then he neared Kory's ear, whispering, "No, I'm not good. I'm bad. I deserve to be punished for making you wait so long."

"Come here," Kory said, still tingling from how good Luke made him feel. He pulled Luke into a quick soft kiss, allowing just a light amount of tongue on the outside as he pulled back. "You did so good. Now, let me catch my breath and then it's your turn. But I would prefer if we did the next part at my place."

Luke's face felt flushed, and his normally neatly-styled hair was a mess. "Did I do okay, really? It was my first time doing that. I hope it was alright."

Kory looked at him, confused. "Yes, it was good. It was very good. The best." He smiled at Luke, who grabbed the water bottle from the cupholder and sipped from it.

Luke wiped his lips and looked at Kory. "Okay, I'll follow you to your place."

When they pulled into the driveway and got out of their cars, Luke was amazed at the giant beachside home. "How is this your house? We're the same age…I can barely afford my one-bedroom apartment and you have this.

Kory took Luke by the hand, quickly leading him inside through the front door. "My dad left it to me in his will. We can talk about that later, come on. I've waited long enough."

"It's so nice in here," Luke said. "Are you gonna give me a tour?"

Kory pulled him straight into his bedroom. He spoke quickly, "Sure, here's a tour. Look, it's a bed." He pointed to the walls. "That's a painting of some conch shells, there's a panorama of the ocean, and here are a bunch of fluffy pillows." He placed two hands on Luke's chest, urging him to lay on the bed.

Kory cupped Luke's face in his hands, kissed him softly, and crawled on top of him. The instant their lips touched again, Luke felt the fire between them.

Time passed as they explored each other and the depths of their quickly growing passion. Afterward, Luke looked at the clock, seeing it displayed 1:17 PM.

"Hey, I'm not complaining, but is that how long this normally takes? We started hours ago; how can we do this every day?" Luke asked.

Kory looked at him from across the room. "Already thinking about next time, huh?" He walked over to Luke, who lay in the sweat-covered, wrinkled sheets and smiled down at him. "That was worth the wait. I knew it would be," Kory said, while rubbing Luke's cheek.

Luke was truly spent at this point. He looked up at Kory through hazy, half-lidded eyes. "Thank you for waiting for me," he mumbled, with his eyes fully closed.

Kory smiled. "We should clean up before you fall asleep, the sheets are all messed up, too."

Luke didn't move, he was past the point of exhaustion. He was vaguely aware of Kory heading into the bathroom.

He heard the sound of the water running and tried to force himself to wake up, to stand. "Ouch! Son of a…. What the hell?!" he shouted.

Kory appeared quickly from the bathroom, placing clean, folded sheets on the nightstand. He stood over Luke, who was slumped over in defeat. "Hey, hey, you can't stand like that. You know that, right? It was your first time; didn't you know it would hurt afterward?"

Luke lifted his head and looked at him. "Riiight, well…I did not know that I wouldn't be able to walk, but I do now. Help me?" he asked, reaching his arms up.

Kory smiled and scooped him up from the side, carrying him into the bathroom and placing him gently into the warm tub. Luke winced as he became immersed in the water.

"You good? Or do you need me to stay in here?" Kory asked, noticing Luke's uncomfortable expression.

"I'm as good as I'm going to be, I guess. It's fine," Luke replied, shifting in the tub.

Kory quickly gave him privacy, and Luke sunk into the warmth of the bath. *That was amazing but, holy shit, I feel like I can't stand.* He stretched out, trying to get comfortable. The large tub was much nicer than the one he was used to in his apartment.

After several minutes, Kory stepped into the bathroom again. "You, okay? I ordered Nick's Pizza for us; you must be starving."

"Yes, pizza, feed me pizza. I was good and now I hurt. Ugh, and I didn't even bring extra clothes with me," Luke said, sticking his bottom lip out.

Kory smiled at him. "My brother uses the spare bedroom whenever he gets in trouble with his girlfriend, which is pretty often. I think you guys may be about the same size, you can borrow whatever clothes he has in there if you want."

Luke made a face in resignation. "Well, I don't have much of a choice. Are we really the same size?"

Kory chuckled. "I think so height-wise, but your ass is a bit... thicker maybe, I don't know—"

Luke put his hand up from the tub and tilted his head. "Did you actually just say I have a thick ass?" he asked, feeling a bit embarrassed.

"Well, what do you want me to say? It's perfect, it's just rounder than his or something. That's not a bad thing. It's a perfect thing." He winked.

"I have never been told such a thing before. I don't even know how to respond to that. Help me up," Luke said, reaching up with his arms.

Kory helped Luke into a standing position. "Did the bath help?"

"I feel a bit better, but I don't want to do anything for the rest of the day." They left the bathroom, and Luke sat uncomfortably on Kory's bed. He looked over at Kory, as he rubbed the smooth navy-colored sheet. "Hey, you changed the sheets, these are really soft."

Kory smiled, looking in his dresser. "Yeah, I planned ahead. Figured we'd use a lower thread count for the dirty stuff."

Luke frowned as he looked at his reddened knees and elbows. "Next time I want soft for both, my knees and elbows are feeling kind of irritated."

Kory tilted his head at him. "Look at you, already spoiled, making demands. It's not like we were on sandpaper, you just aren't used to that position." He smirked playfully, while continuing to look through his drawers. "Alright, if we aren't going to go anywhere, then how about sweats? Those should fit that juicy ass," he joked, winking at Luke.

Luke, still wrapped in only a towel, tried to warm himself, rubbing his arms. "Yes, yes, fine. Just give me something to wear, I'm cold…and don't call my ass juicy!"

Coop sat in front of his laptop on Saturday afternoon, completely bored. He wasn't sure what to do with himself. He'd already exercised, gone for a swim, and did some extra work for The Morgan Family Foundation, the charitable branch of his dad's company. His father officially put him in charge of the charity after graduation. Coop worked from home in his spare time and didn't stick to a normal work schedule. He had a team of employees that ran the day-to-day operations alongside employees from the other branches of Morgan Enterprises. Recently, his father had a brand-new multi-story office building constructed across town. Coop had only been there once; he wasn't interested in being stuck inside an office all day. His father didn't mind him working from home, although he had been pressuring him recently to try and find an assistant to help with things. Right now, he didn't feel like playing baseball, or doing any more work, but he did think of one thing that seemed to hold his interest…or, rather, one person; Ethan Prescott.

For the most part, Coop didn't like to use social media, he felt it was flooded with negativity. He also wasn't a fan of random messages from people he didn't even know, which seemed to be a regular occurrence anytime he logged onto a social site. But today, his curiosity for Ethan pulled him quickly into multiple sites. He wanted to know more about him. Meeting Ethan today was strange, he'd always known he existed, since Coach talked about him often, but finally meeting him felt somehow different than when he'd met other people. He found two profiles, both on the same sites that Coop was on, and like Coop's profiles, they weren't used often. There were only a few pictures, and they seemed to be older.

Coop pulled one picture up and studied it. The same warm feeling overcame him. He leaned back in his desk chair and put his hands behind his head. *What the hell is this feeling? He makes my chest feel warm…I don't get it. I feel like I need to be near him… What the hell is wrong with me? I don't even know him. But, damn…he's the first guy I've ever seen that I really want to…*

Coop shook his head and yelled down at his crotch which was suddenly stirring, "Hey! What the hell are you thinking? You're making me feel like a pervert. I can't be feeling like this about a guy I've barely talked to. Get down."

He quickly closed Ethan's profile, and an advertisement for online cooking classes appeared. He figured now was as good a time as any to distract himself with a new hobby. He grabbed his laptop and went into his kitchen to try and learn the recipe that was shown. It was a beginner recipe for a baked chicken and spinach casserole dish. Luckily, he had all of the ingredients on hand.

This is good, I'll learn to cook. I need a new hobby anyway… Maybe I can cook for Ethan one day. He shook his head at the thought.

He really had no idea what was going on, he'd never thought of anyone this much, not even Luke. It wasn't exactly a sexual feeling, or a feeling of lust, or curiosity, the thing that frightened him was this overwhelming want to just be near him.

He dove headfirst into the recipe and forty-five minutes later, the dish was complete. It came out pretty well for a first attempt at cooking. He took a few bites and then sealed the rest in an airtight container.

With the rest of the afternoon ahead of him, he went back upstairs and decided to work more on The Foundation's gala plans for the summer. Since his dad let him take over, he wanted to be sure he did just as good a job as he'd done last year with the inaugural gala. He went into his work email and began reading letters from organizations requesting help with funding.

Coop could never say no to someone in need. As he read each heartfelt request, he sorted them into folders and prepared a strategy that would allow him to help each one in at least some way. He was torn between which charity would receive the majority of gala donations, but he still had time to decide.

Chapter 5
The Traveler

Following a busy night in between the sheets, Luke found himself at a loss, as he lay beside Kory the next morning.

"What's wrong?" Kory asked.

"Nothing, I'm just thinking. I forgot that we have to work tomorrow. I'll need to stop by my place later and grab a suit and some other things. Also, it will be weird at the office, don't you think?" Luke asked, rolling over to face Kory.

Kory gave him a half smile, while brushing his hand lightly through Luke's hair. "Why would it be weird? I'm not like man-bun, I'm not going to hide that fact that we're together…unless that's what you want. Which, if that is the case, I'll need a pretty convincing argument for."

Luke couldn't believe his ears. "Man bun? Ohhhh, you're talking about what Shay said the other night. And here I thought I was dating someone mature," he said, rolling his eyes playfully at Kory.

"I don't know why you thought I was mature," Kory joked. "But I have been wanting to talk to you about that. I wasn't going to bring it up, but I guess I should. Are you uncomfortable with people knowing that you're gay? Is that why you guys hid the fact that you were dating?"

Luke pulled his mouth to the side in thought. "You know, we never talked about it. It just felt like something that we didn't want people to know. Maybe it was a little bit of both of us being afraid. Coop wasn't openly affectionate, so I think I just kind of followed him. He never seemed jealous, or needy, or lovey-dovey. I understand him a little better now, but at the time I just felt like something was wrong with me. I often wondered if he would be different with someone else, but I never brought it up. I think I felt like we were okay for so long, because he was always protecting me… I took that as him caring about me, but that was really the only type of affection he showed. Honestly, it felt like he protected me because he felt obligated to or something…like there was something wrong with me and I needed to be protected."

Kory rolled on his back and pretended to be asleep. He let out a loud exaggerated snore, then peeked one eye open, smiling at Luke. He pulled Luke in close to him. Luke laid his head on his chest, as Kory rubbed his fingers through his hair and lightly ran his fingertips over his shoulders.

"Luke, there was never anything wrong with you. You two just weren't meant to be. It's easy to confuse feelings of comfort and familiarity with love. But speaking of work, I feel like I should tell you, Madeline already knows that I'm into you. She'll take one look at you tomorrow and know we're sleeping together. No question about it."

Luke sat up. "Madeline Parson? *The boss*? How can she know? This is terrible. I'm going to get fired before I even start," Luke said with a hand on his forehead.

Kory sat up and pulled Luke next to him, sitting against the headboard, which squeaked with their weight. "You unofficially started the other day, remember?" Kory joked, shooting Luke a playfully witty smile. "Stop freaking out, Luke. Madeline is the top defense attorney in the state, she reads people all day long. They don't call her the boss without reason. She is a shark, through and through, and your sweet ass will be like chum in the water for her, if she thinks you're hiding something."

"Riiiight, but what do I do then? I'm not embarrassed about being with you or being gay. I just don't know how to act around other people when I'm with you. Look at the other night, we weren't even dating yet, and I almost fell out of my chair. I don't know what's okay, and what's not."

Kory said softly, "Just be you. Do what feels right. Don't worry about other people and what they think. I'll talk to Madeline tonight."

He kissed Luke gently, leaning across his body, as Luke looked at him. Kory's eyes signaled he was ready for another round. Luke slid beneath him and wrapped his legs tightly around.

Ethan Prescott was still unpacking things inside his dad's home Sunday afternoon. He was happy about the break away from his overbearing mother, whom he loved, but he still didn't feel comfortable at his dad's. Ethan flipped to a blank sheet on his large easel, which he used for drawing. He stared at the paper and only one thing—well, one person—came to mind. Cooper Morgan.

He recalled two nights ago when he watched Coop struggling to keep a screaming woman off him in the parking lot, he remembered how uneasy Luke's hesitancy made him feel, but most of all he remembered the handshake that he shared with him. Ethan looked at his own hand in remembrance of the warmth that he felt when their hands touched. He was certain that he must have been grinning from ear to ear when it happened, that or he may have looked like he was a crazy person. He couldn't quite recall what he did outwardly. He could only remember the feelings that were pulsing through his body as their hands joined, and their eyes met.

He decided now wouldn't be a good time to draw, or he may draw something that he wouldn't want others to see. He couldn't believe the thoughts he was having. When it came to finding boyfriend material, Ethan was unappeasable. The fact that he'd seen someone he felt was utterly flawless and would be playing on the same team as him, was almost too much for Ethan to bear.

He didn't struggle in locker rooms as a gay teenager, because he found most guys his age pretty gross. They were always talking about girls in disgusting ways, and since Ethan was a bit of a mama's boy, he wouldn't ever be able to date someone who talked negatively about women, even if the people doing the talking felt like they were complimenting them. Ethan also liked things very clean, which was the opposite of men in locker rooms, literally and figuratively. Mostly he felt that things would just be too difficult, in general, if he was in a relationship…but when he thought about that handshake, he began to once again think of something that he wouldn't find too difficult…and that was one thing he really shouldn't draw.

"Ethan?" his father called outside the door.

"Yeah, come in."

His father walked in and studied the room. "Looks like you're almost settled in. Do you need anything? We can run to the store if you do. I'm free for the next few hours."

Ethan knew his dad was just trying to spend more time with him, but he figured they'd be spending more than enough time together since he was the team's coach. Still, he felt like he should meet him halfway, even if he didn't actually forget anything. "You know what, Dad; I think I should run to the store for a few things. If you want to ride with me, that would be great."

"Yes!" His dad gave him a thumbs up. "Let's take your Jeep, though. I haven't driven with you in such a long time, I want to see how those new tires feel."

"I was gonna drive anyway, Dad. I'm not letting you drive; you can barely see. I don't even know how they let you coach baseball. You should be wearing glasses. The other day at the meeting I'm pretty sure you were pointing at the wrong people a couple of times."

His dad put his hands on his hips, what Ethan said about him needing glasses was something that Ethan's mother had pointed out on many occasions. He joked, "Oh, I didn't realize you'd turned into your mother, you little potato." He shook his head. "Making fun of me within forty-eight hours of moving in; your mother has definitely rubbed off on you."

Ethan's mother's side of the family was Italian; among the many names that his grandparents gave him as a small child, potato was just one of them. Of course, when his Nonna or Pop Pop called him that, it didn't bother him, he was used to it. Besides, his mother called him a million different things, she was constantly gushing over her precious son. But his father had the most boring sense of humor ever, and his jokes often fell flat. Still, Ethan couldn't help but think it was kind of sweet that his dad threw his potato nickname into the mild banter he tossed at him.

"Well, Dad, I'm not sure about—" Ethan's phone rang interrupting their conversation. "Ooh, its Mom, you're in trouble. I'm gonna tell her what you said," Ethan teased.

"Don't answer it, Ethan. Please. She knows everything… Probably had some weird feeling about me talking about her. She'll drive here and kill me if you tell her I was making fun of her. Just send it to voicemail… Do the right thing." His dad winced as Ethan's finger hovered over the accept button on his phone.

Ethan hadn't gotten to tease his dad in a long time and felt like now was as good a time as any to start.

"Hi, Mom," he answered the phone, and smiled at his father.

His dad grabbed Ethan's keys off his dresser and dashed out of the house, with Ethan running behind him. He climbed inside Ethan's Jeep, sitting in the driver's seat.

Ethan stared up at him. "Dad, do not turn my car on, it doesn't want you to drive it. Get out."

"What is happening?" his mother asked.

His father pointed to the phone, telling him to hang up, while his finger came dangerously close to the start button inside the car.

"Mom, I'll call you later, everything is fine." Ethan ended the call without waiting for a reply.

His father knew what was coming. "You shouldn't have answered it, now she's gonna…"

Ethan's phone rang. It was his mother calling back. He sent it quickly to voicemail.

"That's not gonna work and you know it," his father said, leaning against the steering wheel.

Ethan smirked. "Well, since I have turned into my mother, like you said, I can bet you that she calls me two more times, then starts calling you. What do you think?" Ethan's phone rang again, he held up two fingers and raised his eyebrows.

"Fine, I'll take that bet. I'll wash your Jeep if you're right," his dad said.

Ethan made a disagreeable face. "Does my Jeep look like it's dirty? No. Try again, this call is almost at voicemail already."

"Fine, I'll give you the inside information about anyone on the baseball team, and I'll take you out to dinner. Before you say that you already know everything from watching film, I'm not talking about that. I'm talking about personal details because something tells me—"

"Deal," Ethan said.

Ethan's phone rang again as his father still sat inside the driver's seat, with Ethan standing outside. Ethan pumped his eyebrows. "She's gonna call you now, guaranteed."

Sure enough, his dad's phone began to ring. He dropped his head and climbed out of the driver's seat. If he didn't answer it, Ethan's mother really would drive there, or call the police—either would not be out of the realm of possibilities for her. His father walked toward the front door and locked it. "Hi, Gina, nothing is wrong, we're just having a father-son talk." From where Ethan was standing, he could hear his mother yelling loudly at his father.

"Okay, yes, yes, I'll protect the little bean. Goodbye." He got into the passenger seat beside Ethan, who started the car with an amused smile on his face. "Don't smirk at me like that! You know better than to answer the phone and hang up on her. Now there's a fifty percent chance that she really does drive here."

"Nah," Ethan replied. "She would've called me again if she thought something was wrong. Now, about that information."

Ethan looked at his father whose knees bounced a bit nervously in the passenger seat. "What are you fidgeting like that for? Did Mom make you that nervous? She's not gonna come here, at least not right now, she hates driving at night."

His father shook his head in reply. "No, I'm not worried about that. It's just, listen, if you're gonna ask me about the guys on the team that's fine, I agreed to that. I really can't uh…answer any questions about their parts, though."

Ethan tapped the brakes and his father's head swayed and hit the seat. "Brake check… What the hell did you just say to me? Do you think I'm interested in that?" Ethan asked, while holding in the urge to laugh.

His dad was visibly relieved. "Nope, I think you're gonna ask me about Coop."

Ethan continued to drive without a reply. *How the hell did he know I was interested in him? Was it that obvious? I thought I played it off pretty well. Anyway, I'm not interested in second-hand information about him. I'd rather learn that for myself, but I'm still confused about what happened the other night…*

"I want to know about Luke," Ethan said.

His dad was clearly not expecting that. "Luke? He's not even on the team anymore. What do you care about him for?"

"A deal is a deal. I'm trying to figure something out and just based on what I saw the other night, I want to know if I'm right."

"You really have turned into your mother," his father joked.

While Luke had gone home to grab some clothes for work, Kory called Madeline in preparation for Luke's first day tomorrow.

"Madeline, I know what I'm doing, I'm just letting you know so you won't torment him tomorrow," Kory said into the phone.

"So, he's one hundred percent not involved with Tom Morgan's son—what's his face—anymore?" Madeline asked pointedly.

"No, that's over. You told me not to ask but did you—"

Madeline interrupted him. "*Stop*. If I told you not to ask, don't ask. At this point, I have no idea what you're referring to, but I won't even entertain it if you start that way. I'll see you tomorrow morning." She ended the call without another word.

Kory placed his phone on the coffee table next to the couch and exhaled, sinking back into the comfortable gray leather. Now that he officially told Madeline about dating Luke, he felt relieved. It would have been impossible for him to hide his relationship with Luke from her, anyway.

Kory's doorbell rang, the camera showed Luke standing at the door with an overnight suitcase propped against his leg. Kory opened the door. "Can I help you, sir? Are you lost? I see you have a suitcase there, are you looking for your lover's house?"

Luke raised his eyebrows. "Role play, or are you just being funny?" he asked.

Kory grinned wide, looking down at his watch. "It's too late for a sexy man like you to be outside looking for your lover's home. You can stay the night with me." He pulled Luke through the door, as Luke wheeled his suitcase inside.

Luke was intrigued, as Kory led him into the kitchen. He still wasn't sure how far Kory was going to take this, but he was enjoying it all the same.

Kory handed him a glass of ice water. "You must be thirsty, here drink this. You look like you've had a long day. Let me show you…my bedroom."

"Thank you," Luke said, accepting the glass and taking a sip. His blue eyes teared up as he held in his laughter, looking at Kory, who was taking his pretend role very seriously.

"I've never thought about role play, that was fun," Luke said. "Short, but fun. Wait, I almost forgot, can I hang my suit in your closet? It shouldn't be wrinkled yet, but I need to get it out quick."

Kory suddenly pressed Luke onto his bed and climbed on top of him. He got right back into character. "There's no rush. I have a steamer if you need it in the morning, little traveler."

A few hours later, he carried Luke into the shower with him. They brushed their teeth, and fell fast asleep, looking forward to Luke's first official day at the office.

Kory and Luke arrived together at the office at 9:00 AM Monday. Kory held his hand as they entered the elevator. The two had a quick round on the couch before their morning shower, and Luke still felt a little flushed. He fanned his face with his hand and looked at Kory. "It's a bit hot, don't you think?"

"You look like a guilty person right now. It's okay, I told you, I spoke to Madeline last night. It's fine. Just breathe." He stood in front of Luke and straightened his tie, giving him a quick kiss before the doors opened.

Ms. Martin looked up smiling from her desk. "Good morning, Mr. Collins, Mr. Everton. Madeline brought in bagels from that New York-style bagel place you like, Mr. Collins; they're in the break room. I'm supposed to tell her the moment you walk in."

Luke really hadn't been called Mr. Everton professionally before. He thought it was kind of strange that the secretary who was certainly older than both he and Kory, referred to them that way, but since it was an office, he understood.

Kory sighed. "Give me ten minutes before you do that," he said, closing his office door behind himself and Luke. She turned her chair around and looked at them through the inner office glass windowpane. Kory held up both hands signaling ten minutes, before he closed the window blinds blocking her view.

He held Luke's shoulders. "Okay, right now, I need you to pretend you aren't nervous. Madeline's going to think I dragged you in here against your will if you walk in there with that look on your face. She is very nice, really. She even brought bagels in for your first day. It's going to be fine." Kory quickly kissed him, and Luke nodded silently. He inhaled and opened the door, then they headed to the top floor of the building.

Madeline greeted them quickly, as they got off the elevator. She wore a gray pencil skirt and a sleeveless, black, high-neck top that was tucked in. Her black high heels added another inch or two to her small frame. "Everyone, Luke is here, come greet the new intern," she called down the hall.

Five lawyers emerged, and they all headed into the break room, following closely behind Madeline. The vibe was very casual, as the partners introduced themselves.

Two of the partners, Marcus and Andrew, shared immediately that they were married to each other and had recently adopted a child.

Marcus complained that he would have rather had a dog, while Andrew shoved him playfully. Luke was comforted by the warm welcome. He fit in well with the crowd, despite being thrust in front of the majority of the company on his first day. The meet and greet ended, and they headed back down to the office.

Kory opened a side door inside the lobby of his office, showing Luke his own office space. "This is yours, but you really won't use it that much. I'll need you near me at all times, unless I'm dealing with something confidential. It's your space, though, you can do whatever you want with it. Ms. Martin ordered your door plate last week, so it should be here soon."

Luke smiled as he looked around the small office. The window inside overlooked the town, and he could see the ocean in the distance. "Thank you, for this opportunity, Kory. I really don't know what I did to deserve all of this."

Kory pulled him into a warm embrace. "You really have no idea, huh?" He kissed Luke on the forehead and led him into his office, where a group of lawyers were waiting.

Chapter 6
Hair Training

Monday afternoon, Coop loaded his gear into his trunk for practice. Arie approached him from the side. "Loser Morgan, you wanna talk?"

Coop sighed and closed the trunk. "No, I don't and I'm sure you know that. What would I want to talk about? We talked the other day… I think that was enough for the year."

She looked at her freshly painted baby pink nails. "Yeah, but you got dumped, so I figured I should try and see if you were experiencing what we normal people call feelings… I'm not sure if you've heard of them."

Coop didn't like that. He didn't feel like he got dumped. In his eyes, he'd wanted to leave Luke a long time ago, so it was more of a joint decision than a dumping. His pride wouldn't allow her remark to stand. "I did not get dumped. What are you even saying? You really are dumb. You're in honors classes, right? Don't you have to be smart to be in those? I know that when I took advanced placement classes, I was the smartest one there. I had to take special tests to get in. Has the school changed their standards? I haven't been on campus in a while, is that what happened?"

She raised her middle finger at him. "You're saying you didn't get dumped? That's not the way I understood it. I heard it was a big fat dumping, along with Luke leaving you for a really hot guy who graduated like a year early or something…some super fine guy from a law firm. That's gotta hurt." She crossed her arms and awaited his reply.

Coop swung his door open and sat inside his car. "Arie, I do not care. I am not upset. I could not care less about any of what you just said. What have I done that would make you think I feel anything other than relief? This is why talking to people is stupid. The other day you forced me to talk to you, and I told you how I felt then and there. That didn't change just because we broke up. I have nothing else to say about this. I'm gonna be late for practice now."

Coop indeed arrived extremely late to the team's first practice since Luke's departure, with his hair in a topknot. He didn't feel like being there, following the discussion he had with Arie. He was sick and tired of everyone bringing up Luke. *Why can't people understand that we separated because it's what we both wanted? Why do people expect me to cry about it? Shit, here comes Kai. I'm not in the mood for him either. Everyone is pissing me off today.*

"Kai, don't start with me, just toss the ball," Coop said, holding out his glove.

Kai tossed the ball with a nod. "Topknot and you're late. You're still pissed about this morning?"

Coop caught the ball then hung his head backward, sighing loudly. He tossed the ball back. "Kai, what part of don't start with me sounded like 'do you think you could piss me off some more?' Damn it. I got Arie bothering me, Mac's over there with a stupid look on his face, you texting me about Luke this morning…so damn aggravating."

Kai caught the ball and shook his head. "Fine, I won't say anything. Just toss the ball in silence, bro. You're gonna have to swap partners soon, though. I don't know who's brave enough to come over here when you got your samurai knot going on. Coach will make us swap, though, so some poor sucker is gonna get stuck with you."

Coop scoffed. *Maybe I should just go home. I don't feel like practicing.*

Coach's whistle blared loudly, signaling it was time to swap partners. Other teammates quickly paired up, while Coop continued to wrestle with whether he should leave or not. He saw Ethan approaching…and he suddenly felt happy looking at him. That warm feeling crept into his chest again, and the want to be near him pulled deep from within. Instinctively, he took a few steps toward him. *What the hell is happening? I feel like I'm being pulled in by some invisible force; but it's not invisible, it's him, all of him. I want to be near him, but why? I feel like…*

From behind him, Mac the pitcher, said to another teammate, "Hey, look at Luke 2.0. Is he really gonna try to talk to Coop?"

Coop knew Ethan heard the comment when he stopped his approach, pretending instead to want to partner up with Kai who had already left Coop's side.

Coop's posture dropped, along with his briefly happy mood. He turned quickly toward Mac, but when Mac noticed Coop's fuming face coming toward him, he quickly darted next to Coach in the dugout. Coop walked over and gave Mac a look of warning.

Mac avoided eye contact and engaged Coach in conversation, hoping Coop wouldn't hit him since he was next to Coach.

Coop stared him down for a minute or two, then decided it wasn't worth it to fight with him. While standing in the dugout, he found himself in a mental debate over Ethan. *I would have just punched Mac, if he hadn't hidden next to Coach. Such a jerk. But why did him saying that make me so upset? I felt incredibly happy when I saw Ethan coming toward me, what a weird thing. Is it really so strange, though? He is definitely the best-looking guy I've ever seen. But, still, that handshake the other day, it was like he didn't want to let go either…right? What is making me feel this way? Thinking about him makes me feel hopeful or something…*

A text from Arie interrupted his thoughts.

Arie: *Hey, let me know if you need help getting all of Luke's stuff out. I still have some stuff over here of his. Text me when you're done with practice.*

Coach snapped his fingers in front of Coop. "Hey, you showed up late, now you got your phone out at practice, looks like you're in a mood," he said, pointing to Coop's hair. "Why don't you and Mac go practice together. You've been struggling with fastballs. Go swing the bat a little, and take that murderous look off your face, while you're at it."

Coop nodded, grabbed his bat from the bench and walked out to the field, with Mac following behind him. Standing in the batter's box, he pulled his top knot out, and put his helmet on. The rest of the team finished their initial warmups and moved to the dugout. Coop's game continued to suffer, as he missed the first three pitches from Mac. He leaned his head back in frustration and dropped his helmet on the ground. "Mac, you're really starting to piss me off," he said. He pulled his hair tie out of his waistband and tied his hair in a topknot again.

Ethan noticed Coop's frustration from the dugout and really wanted to help him. He had yet to find a way to give Coop the tips that he had for him. Ethan casually approached him. "Hey, do you have plans after practice?"

Coop was removing his batting gloves, staring down Mac. He was trying to decide if he wanted to punch Mac in the face. He answered Ethan quickly, not understanding that his question was an invitation, "Yeah, I do."

Ethan, feeling rejected, returned to the dugout alongside Kai. "Let me tell you what you did wrong there," Kai said, putting his arm around his shoulder.

Ethan looked at him in confusion. "What did I do wrong? What do you mean?"

Kai stood in front of him. "See, Coop's hair indicates his mood. So, when it's in a topknot, like it is now—we call that his Samurai knot. That means Coop's in a bad mood. Someone pissed him off, something is going wrong, or he's just freaking out. We avoid Coop at those times. Next, we have the half pony—Coop's feeling good, took time on his appearance, he also leaves it like that when he's playing baseball. Doesn't like when the side pieces get in his face."

Ethan didn't know what to say. "Uhh, thank you, I guess, for telling me—"

Kai interrupted him, "Bup, bup, bup. Not done. Now, if Coop's hair is down; he's feeling wild. He's usually drinking, or partying, or he's getting ready to mess around. This is his playful hairstyle. This is when you ask him to join you for a drink, or whatever it was that you were just trying to ask him. So, let's review. Samurai knot equals danger. Don't engage, don't ask him for something you really need, or critique him…just, I don't know, run? Maybe? Half up, half down, eh…it's 50/50. Now, what is the sweet spot?"

Ethan replied enthusiastically, "Down, when it's all down!"

Kai patted him on the back. "Good job, buddy."

"I have a question," Ethan said.

"Sure, what is it?"

"What does it mean if he ties it down? Like low in the back, down here?" Ethan held an imaginary ponytail at the base of his head.

Kai made a face in disgust. "Coop would never do that to his hair. That's a terrible hairstyle. Who would do that?"

"I don't know. I've seen people with their hair like that before. I didn't think it was so strange."

"You thought wrong. It is strange and it would look terrible," Kai replied.

Ethan stood shaking his head. "How can the style of someone's hair mean so many things?"

"Who knows, but you're welcome," Kai said, with a smile.

After practice, Coop walked into the storage room inside the main estate, carrying a box of Luke's stuff. Arie was supposed to meet him there, but she hadn't shown up yet.

The room contained many of his mom's old things. He opened one of the boxes to find a small pink book. *Sam's Diary* was written on the inside cover. As he opened it, an old high school picture of his mother, father, and Luke's dad, fell out. His dad stood in the middle of his mom and Levi. His mom looked beautiful in her cheerleading uniform, while his father and Luke's dad were in their baseball uniforms. His dad and Luke's dad had their arms draped around each other's necks, their heads pushed together, and were smiling brightly, while his mom stood to the left of his dad, making a peace sign with her hand. Coop stared at the picture and studied it for a while.

Man, what happened to these guys? Coop wondered. He decided to flip through and see if he could figure out what the conflict between his dad and Luke's dad was.

Angela came by today. It was awful. I'm so upset. I don't even know what to do.

She's divorcing Levi. She told me that she hated him. When I asked her why, she demanded to talk to Tom. Obviously, I wasn't going to let that happen. She told me that she hated Luke, and never wanted to see him or Levi again. How could anyone hate their baby? She was always such a weird girl.

She told me that their wedding night was the only night that they'd ever had sex. Gosh, I can barely write this. I'm shaking. She said that while they had sex, Levi kept closing his eyes and looking away from her. Then she said that Levi actually called out, "Tommy." It took everything in me not to react when she told me, now that I'm writing this, I feel even worse.

She said that she went to her mom's house for a few weeks after, and figured Levi knew why, but he just didn't say anything. She was prepared to get the marriage annulled but found out she was pregnant. So, she waited until Luke was born. What am I supposed to do? Coop is sleeping in his crib right now. He's so precious. How can she leave Luke? It's not his fault. I feel gross.

The first time we slept together was the night of Levi and Angela's wedding, too. Of course, Tom didn't want to go to the wedding. I mean, I suppose I've always kind of suspected why. I keep reliving that night over and over in my mind, but it's just too icky. I felt that Tom was disinterested, but I thought it was because it was our first time, and we still weren't even officially dating yet. He'd honestly never really seemed interested in me that way.

I think I finally understand.

But Tom is MY husband. Tom loves me, right? I know he does. But does he love Levi? Who am I kidding? He probably always has. Is it just a different kind of love? Can you love two people? Or am I just a substitute? Am I just…just here? I feel guilty. I feel like it's my fault that they aren't together. It's not my fault, though. They haven't spoken in over a year. Did they talk about their feelings? Does Tom already know?

What do I do? I feel responsible. I have to help. I can help Levi raise Luke…surely Tom will agree to that. If he loves Levi, then maybe he would—God, what am I saying? Does Tom actually love him? Would this hurt Tom? Would it hurt Levi? No, I can't worry about that. I'm going to talk to Levi tomorrow. I have to. I need to let him know that I know everything. How do I do that, though?

Do I tell Tom? What if Tom wants to leave me? Would I be okay with that? No…no…I can't lose Tom. I love him so much, and I always have. This is my fault. I knew that Tom never felt the same for me. He's never looked at me the same. Still, I know he loves me…maybe it's just a different type of love. Whatever it is…I can't lose it. I'm sure he'll agree to us stepping in to help with Luke. I don't want to hurt him, but I don't think I trust him enough to tell him what happened. I can't risk it. No.

This is the only thing I can do. I can help Levi—damn it, Levi. Why did he do this to begin with? I already know the answer. This was because of Tom's family. Tom's father would never have allowed it. He still wouldn't...I guess that's the reason. Maybe? Well, it is the only thing that makes sense. I deserve to be loved; I deserve to have Tom.

What do I do? I have to help Levi. Luke won't have a mom to care for him. That's not fair. Should I leave, so Tom and Levi can be together? What do I do? I don't think I can tell anyone about this. I feel so alone.

Coop sat there alone, in complete shock. His hand trembled lightly as he stared at the pages. He closed the diary and gripped the small book tightly. His knuckles were white with frustration.

What the hell, What the actual hell? I can't believe this... This is why Luke was forced on me? Because my mom felt guilty? It wasn't her fault. It's my dad's fault or Levi's fault...I don't know whose fault it is, but it's not my mom's fault. Maybe it is her fault... What a stupid idea.

I can't even understand what the hell I just read. So, were our dads a couple? Did they have a secret relationship? Or was it one-sided? I'm so confused. Is my dad gay? Is that why he never cared about me and Luke being together?

My mom said that she suspected how he felt, but what does that mean? I wish she were here. I just want to talk to her. My dad married my mom...why did he fucking marry her? My whole life...my whole life Luke was forced on me. Is this why I've never felt anything real for him? I think this is the first time I've felt anything about him...but what is it? What do I even feel? This is bullshit.

Just...wait, did my dad know how Levi felt? I need to understand this, and I can't, it makes no sense to me. Luke's mom left because she found out her husband was in love with my dad. What the hell did that have to do with Luke? He was just a baby. It's not his fault that his dad was in love with my dad. In all this time she still hasn't reached out to him either. So many fucking secrets.

I need to talk to my dad…no, I need to tell Luke. He deserves to know everything, too. I don't even know what I'm feeling…

He sat in the room for a while longer and read through a few other pages. It seemed like he shared more than a few traits with his mom. He called Arie, who didn't answer, which was typical for her. He then called Luke, which he hadn't done since the breakup.

Luke was standing in Kory's office, looking over files.

Kory said, "Right, so here are pictures of our client and—" Kory looked down to see a picture of a young Coop in a baseball uniform on Luke's phone. *Coop Calling*, the screen read.

Luke felt conflicted, they were in the middle of his first big assignment, but he knew he needed to answer the call. "I'm sorry. He wouldn't be calling if it weren't important."

"Go ahead and answer it, I'll wait in the lobby," Kory said, kissing Luke's forehead quickly as he left.

Luke answered the phone on speaker, "Hey Coop, What's up?"

"Hey, you need to come over. I found something in the storage room."

"I'm at work right now. I can't just leave…"

Coop scoffed. "Luke. Would you just…. You need to see this."

Luke heard the tension in his voice. "What did you find? What are you talking about?"

"I found out why our dads don't talk, and the reason your mom left. You need to come here and see it for yourself."

My mom? Our dads? Luke felt like he was going to vomit. He was having trouble breathing and found himself unable to respond. Covering his mouth with his hand, he looked at Kory through the glass.

Kory opened the door and leaned into the room, concern on his face. "What's wrong? Look at me, Luke, why do you look like you are about to cry? What do you need?" He came closer and held Luke's face in his hands.

Luke placed his hands on top of Kory's. "Okay, Coop, I'm leaving, and I'll be there in a few," Luke finally responded.

"Here, sit down for a minute," Kory said guiding Luke to his office chair. "What's going on? Why do you need to leave?"

Luke was fighting the urge to cry. He'd given up trying to find out why his mom left a long time ago. The repressed feelings of anger and the awful remembrance that she'd abandoned him all rose to the surface. "I'm sorry. I just—I'm not completely sure. Coop said that he found something, I can't really explain it. I'm just freaking out. Can I leave early and make up the hours?"

Kory kissed his forehead. "How about this? You can leave work early; I'll drive you and wait outside. Afterward, I'll make you dinner, and we can talk about whatever this is. Deal?" Kory grabbed his keys and suit jacket.

Luke agreed, and Kory drove him to Coop's family estate. The security guard, Tony, stopped Kory's car at the gate, but quickly let them pass, seeing Luke in the passenger seat.

As they entered the Morgan estate, Luke guided Kory to the correct parking area. Kory whistled. "This is tycoon level…wow," he said as he parked in front of the main estate home. Luke took a deep breath, kissed him quickly and headed inside.

Luke came barreling through the door to the storage room. He was out of breath from running up the stairs and through the long hallways of the main estate. He flopped his body on the floor next to Coop in between several boxes.

Coop passed a small book to him. "Why are you giving me your mom's diary?" Luke asked.

"Just flip to a few days after we were born," Coop said, leaning his head against the wall.

Luke read the pages in disbelief, while holding his hand over his mouth. He started to cry. "This is…this is…too much."

Coop nodded at him slowly. "Indeed, it is," he said.

Luke was still piecing things together. "So, were they a thing? Were they actually together? I don't know which part I'm expected to process first. So, my mom left *me* because my dad was in love with your dad. Your mom felt guilty and decided to help raise me…and my father knew all of this and kept it from me. I mean that's the truth, right? Out of everyone here, there's one person who obviously knew everything— that's my father.

"This actually doesn't tell us if your dad knew, because it sounds like your mom didn't tell him…but maybe your dad did know? I mean, are both our dads gay? I kind of suspected mine was, but I'd never really thought about yours before."

Luke covered his mouth with his hands. "Holy shit. Your mom and your dad have only felt bad for me my whole life—I've been a charity case to this whole family…even to you. You had no choice here either. My whole life has been one giant lie."

Coop stood up and said, "Well, I'm going to talk to my dad. I need to hear his side of this. I have to find out what really happened. Definitely not what I was expecting, though. I always thought it was my mom they fought over, not that they were secretly…I don't know. It does explain a lot, though. I've never seen my dad go on a single date. I just assumed it was because my mom passed away. Now, I'm kind of wondering if all this time he's just been waiting…"

"Waiting for what?" Luke asked, looking up.

"I don't know, maybe for your dad? How should I know? I'm just as confused as you are." Coop picked the box of Luke's things up and stood in the doorway. "Packed up your stuff for you. Come on," he said walking toward the door.

Luke stood up, unsure of what to do. He felt like his whole life he'd only been a burden to everyone. Looking around the room that he'd been in so many times, he somehow felt like he didn't belong. It felt unfamiliar and cold. He struggled to keep his own emotions in check, feeling like he owed Coop for all the years he was forced to be his friend. "I don't know what to say. Do you want me to go with you when you talk to your dad? I know you don't like to talk about feelings. I can be there when you talk to him." He passed the diary back to Coop.

"No, thanks. I'm good."

Luke held his hands out. "I can hold the box, you've done enough for me," he said.

Coop smiled at him. "Don't be so dramatic. I can hold the box. Let's go."

Luke followed behind him, feeling extremely conflicted. They walked down the stairs in silence. Luke held back tears, wanting nothing more than to cry in Kory's arms.

Coop placed the diary on the kitchen counter on the way to the front door.

Kory waited anxiously for what seemed like forever. His phone rang, it was Madeline. She started, as normal, without a greeting. "I forgot to tell you; I did the thing last Wednesday that you asked me to. Shut up, don't ask questions. Think, if you can't remember what I'm talking about. I like Luke, by the way. He's very nice to look at, better than the stale men that normally flood the halls. Very well spoken, although if I had to guess, you two probably had sex right before you got to work. He seemed mildly nervous but pulled it off. Treat him right or I'll take him for myself." She hung up before Kory got a single word in.

Kory leaned back in his seat, wondering if what was happening was the result of him asking Madeline to intervene. *Damn it, is that what's happening right now? The scout thing? I wasn't sure if Madeline did it, so I didn't mention it. I need to tell him about that. I would have already, but it slipped my mind. He was so upset, and I hate that I don't know why. I want to take him away from all of this.*

He looked down at his watch, then checked his phone. *No messages, no call…what's taking so long. He's been in there a while; how long should I wait until I text him? Look at this place, it's huge. That alone tells you enough about Luke's character, he was completely uninterested in Morgan money.*

With his eyes fixed on the front door, he saw Coop emerge briefly. He watched as Coop passed a large box to Luke, then walked back inside. Kory quickly got out and walked over. He took the heavy box from Luke and opened the passenger door for him, then placed the box in the trunk and got inside the car.

Luke sobbed hysterically with his head in his hands. Through tears, he asked, "Can I stay the night with you again? I don't want to go to my place and be alone."

Kory cradled Luke's head and kissed his face, wiping his tears away. "Of course, you can. You don't think I'd let my little traveler out into the night when he's so distraught?"

Luke nodded, with the slightest hint of a smile. "Okay. Can we talk about this when we get there? I just want to cry for now, is that okay?"

"Luke, you don't need permission to cry and I'm certainly not going to force you to talk. I'm here if you need me to listen, but don't force yourself."

This can't be about the scout, he's way too upset. He's crumbling to pieces right now, what the hell happened?

Mr. Morgan walked into the kitchen to grab a quick snack. He saw an out-of-place pink book on the counter. It disrupted the all-white aesthetic in the room, so he noticed it immediately. As he picked it up, the book opened to the same page held by the photo of himself, Levi, and Sam. He held the book open with one hand and studied the picture with the other. He quickly read the page that described the incident with Luke's mother as he sank onto a stool at the counter.

His hands were shaking, holding the picture. He wondered how the diary ended up on the kitchen counter. His heart ached thinking of Levi. *Why didn't he tell me? Does he still feel the same? How could Sam keep this from me? She knew all along. All this time...has Levi been thinking about me? He must have been so embarrassed when that happened... I can't believe this. I need to talk to Levi. I can't do that. What would I even say?*

Damn it, if Levi had just trusted me, trusted how much I loved him, this never would have happened. But where would I be? I wouldn't have Coop or Arie. Luke wouldn't be here...my father would have disowned me. Is it wrong that part of me hopes Levi still feels the same? Should I hope he's been as miserable as I've been? This hurts...my heart hurts. I can't hold these feelings in any longer.

Tears fell from his eyes as Coop entered the kitchen.

He wiped his eyes and took a deep breath. *I need to talk to Coop. I have to be honest with my son.*

Mr. Morgan pulled the stool out next to him with his foot. "Sit," he said to Coop. He tapped the diary and looked at him. "Let's talk about this."

Coop sat down. "Yeah. I think we should. I don't understand anything right now."

Seeing Coop willing to listen gave him the confidence to move forward with complete honesty. He hadn't been strong enough to be honest with Sam, and he'd always regretted that. He'd kept his feelings for Levi buried for so long, the raw emotions that rose to the surface refused to be contained.

He explained that he and Levi were in love, but it wasn't really accepted when they were in high school. He went on to say that although he didn't care about what people thought, Levi decided, alone, that it would be best if they broke up and went their separate ways. Levi was only concerned with what would happen to Tom. He felt strongly that Tom's life would be ruined if people found out, and since he loved Tom, he thought them separating would be the best thing for him. He held back the urge to scream thinking of it. He remembered the fight he'd had with Levi, when they broke up and how angry and hurt, he was. He tried to hide his frustration and continued calmly explaining things to Coop.

He noticed that Coop's right knee was bouncing under the counter, along with his facial expression which said that he'd heard enough. "I'm sure you have some questions, but there isn't much more to say. I don't know what else was in the diary but—"

"Wait, Dad. Just wait. So, what about mom? How did Mom get tied up in this…mess?" he asked.

"Sam was our childhood friend. She was very special to both of us. She wanted to go out with me for a long time, but I wasn't really into her like that when we were younger. It wasn't until the night that Levi got married—"

Coop slammed his hand on the table, interrupting his father. "Enough! I've heard enough! I can't listen anymore!" Coop stood up, infuriated.

Mr. Morgan wasn't sure exactly what Coop was angry about, since he didn't really react to any specific point in the conversation. The only times he'd ever seen Coop get upset were either over baseball or if someone was bothering Luke. Since baseball wasn't a factor here, he thought he may be reacting this way because of Luke.

Ignoring his outburst, he said calmly, "I heard Luke leaving a little bit ago, I'm sure you shared this with him. How did he take it?"

"What the fuck? How the hell should I know what Luke is thinking?"

Mr. Morgan remained calm, even though Coop was screaming and cursing at him, for the first time in his life. "Coop, calm down."

Coop shook his head at him. "No, I'm done being calm! Who cares about Luke? God, you guys forced him on me my whole life, do you even realize that? Both you and Mom, because of your own guilt! Can you even understand what I'm feeling? My whole life people have ridiculed me for not wanting to talk about my feelings. How could I talk about my feelings, when the only feelings I had were the ones that both you and Mom forced me to have? Birthday parties, baseball games, in every situation I had to put Luke first. Anything I had was shared with him, even the love I received from my parents. I still don't understand how inserting yourselves into Luke's life made any sense. Holy shit…I can't believe this. What about Mom, you didn't even fucking care about her!"

Mr. Morgan stood up quickly from his chair. "*Enough!* Watch your mouth, son. I loved your mother and treated her well." He stared Coop down, as Coop stood defiant against him.

"No, I won't watch my mouth! I'm not a kid! This is such bullshit! You didn't even want me. It's no wonder you've always treated Luke so well; he's the son of the man you loved. He's the son that you wanted." Coop turned and walked out of the kitchen toward the front door.

Coop's words hit him hard, and his heart that had been silent for so long, felt like it was being ripped apart with every step he heard Coop take toward the door. He yelled, "Coop, get back here! Coop, listen to me! I'm sorry!" His screams quickly turned to sobs as he slid down on the floor, leaning against the wall, crying. "I'm sorry, Sam…I'm sorry, Coop…I'm sorry, Luke. I didn't want to hurt anyone…"

Coop sat in his bedroom, desperately trying to reach Arie. He wanted to be the one to explain to her what happened, before their father did. Arie finally answered after a few texts. She came in through the door to see her brother in a complete state of shock. He explained what happened, and she took it much better than he did.

"How are you okay with this?" Coop asked her.

"Well, hello, I'm Arie. It's nice to finally meet you, you are my brother's feelings, if I'm not mistaken. I've been wanting to meet you for a long time," she joked. "Coop, it's like this, Mom is gone, that sucks. Did she feel like she wasted her life? I don't think so. I haven't read the diary, but I don't believe she did. To me, it sounded like she really loved Dad. Yeah, she felt guilty, but at some point or another, we all feel guilty about something. Did she need to insert herself into Luke's life and basically force him into our family? That's difficult. From your point of view, he was basically your partner from the time you were kids, whether you liked it or not, so, yeah, he was forced on you. But you guys are still friends, despite breaking up, so who cares? Did her being involved help Levi? Sheesh, I don't know about that. It must have been really hard for him for a multitude of reasons. I can't even imagine how Dad felt when he read that, and how he's felt all these years…. If I were him, I'd run to Levi right now. I mean, he just found out some pretty heavy stuff, and he's been alone for so long. For Luke, eh…I'd probably just be mad at my dad at this point, or society. True story."

Coop was stunned looking at Arie. He wondered how she was able to process all of that so quickly. There was truth in what she said, and as much as he understood that; he still didn't feel any better. "I can't just accept all of that, Arie. It's not right. I don't want to talk any more. I just want to be alone."

Kory pulled into his driveway and walked Luke inside, carrying the box for him. Luke couldn't shake the feeling that he didn't belong anywhere, his whole life he felt like everyone had been lying to him. After crying for the majority of the ride home, he felt an immediate sense of peace and comfort, as soon as he entered Kory's home.

Luke headed straight for Kory's bedroom. He removed his tie and took his jacket off, lying flat on his back on the comfortable bed. He smiled, thinking of all the two had done in the last few days and rubbed his hand on the comforter.

Kory came in, carrying a clear-handled glass teacup. He passed it to Luke. "Here, this is hot, so don't burn yourself. It's chamomile and lavender tea, it should help you relax a bit."

Luke sat up and took the cup, admiring the swirled glass etching on the sides. "Thank you, that was very sweet of you to make this for me," Luke said, smiling.

"Are you hungry?" Kory asked.

"No, but thank you."

Kory sat beside him. Luke explained what happened with the diary, and his mother and father. Kory sat in shock, his eyes widened, disrupting the confidence of his normally composed face. "Well, that is…a lot. I'm stunned, honestly, and it's pretty hard to surprise me. You should talk to your dad, though."

Luke shook his head resolutely. "No. I don't want to. All these years, he's known why my mother left. It was his fault. He never took the time to explain what happened. He should have told me. Not only that, but he knew this whole time why the Morgan's were always going out of their way for me. Why did he allow Coop's family to do that? Seems really shitty to me to let the man that he was in love with, and his wife, help raise me just because he screwed things up with my mom. That's not even it, though, he didn't screw things up with my mom, he never should have even married her or dated her for that matter. You have no idea how nice Coop's mom was, she must have been hurting so bad, and my dad just let it happen. Besides that, he has never once thanked Coop's dad for anything. He's always acted so entitled, at least that's how it always seemed. It seemed more like he felt like the Morgans owed him for something. None of this is okay…I'm too angry to talk to him. I have no respect for him right now."

Kory blew air from his mouth. "Of course, it's your choice when you want to talk to him. Your relationship with your father is good, though, and he did stay and raise you. Kept a big secret, or two, from you, but he still took care of you. I'm sure he loves you very much. Let's just see how you feel tomorrow."

Chapter 7
I Know Everything

Kory awoke at 6:05 AM Tuesday to Luke sitting on top of him. "Well, good morning…I guess you're feeling better," Kory said.

Luke slid his hands underneath Kory's shirt and rubbed up his chest. He nodded at Kory.

"This position is gonna get you in trouble. Pretty brave waking me up like this." Kory quickly flipped Luke onto his back.

Noticing the time, Kory knew they'd already spent way too much time in bed this morning. He rubbed Luke's face, completely enamored with the sight of him. Luke lay tucked against his chest. The feeling of Luke in his arms, in his bed, was the best feeling he'd ever known.

The two stared at one another, neither wanting to leave the comfort of the others embrace. "I wish we didn't have to work today, but we do," Kory said.

Luke patted Kory's chest lightly. "I know, I just want to stay here with you."

Kory kissed him on the forehead and stood beside the bed. "Me too, but we should shower now, or we'll be late."

Luke stretched his arms toward the ceiling.

Kory looked at him softly. "You want me to carry you into the shower?"

Luke maintained his position and stuck his bottom lip out. "Yes, spoil me. I want to be carried after that. It just feels right since you did it the first time."

Kory scooped him up and kissed him quickly on the mouth. "I'll always carry you, then," he said.

The two quickly showered and readied themselves for work. Luke borrowed a suit from Kory's brother's closet, it was a little tight in the bottom area, but Kory didn't think he should point that out.

His ass looks really good in that suit. I don't really want him to wear it to the office. Everyone is gonna be checking him out. What the hell am I thinking? It's fine. He'll be with me all day anyway, he thought.

"Ready to go?" he asked Luke.

"Yep. As ready as I'll ever be. I feel a little uncomfortable wearing your brother's suit, though."

Kory smiled. "Don't worry about it. Suit looks good on you." He grabbed his briefcase, and they left for the office.

Kory stopped at a traffic light and looked at Luke. "The most important thing to remember in our business is maintaining eye contact. You must control your eyes at all times when dealing with clients or coworkers. It's the first giveaway to a person's true intentions. Even if you're lying, or wavering, you maintain eye contact. Never break it first and definitely don't look at the ground."

Luke nodded. "Okay, yeah, I remember you telling me something similar before. I can do that."

Kory placed a hand on Luke's leg. "There's something else. You signed a bunch of waivers and NDA's yesterday. Those apply to all employees at the firm. Meaning there are some things that, legally, I can't share with you. It's dicey, at best, because we're interns, so technically some things are acceptable for you to have overheard... but you're also my boyfriend, so that may make things a bit more complicated. We'll need to devise a way to share information in a way that doesn't implicate either of us in some situations."

"Riiight…like a secret code," Luke said.

Kory adored Luke's innocence. "You're cute. Yes, kind of like that. For instance…wait…first, don't ask questions that will implicate either of us when I tell you this, okay?"

Luke tilted his head. "Is this practice or a real thing you're telling me?"

Kory sighed. "Fail. See, now if you hadn't asked that, and later on what I'm about to tell you came out, I could've said you misunderstood and that this was just a training scenario. But if you ask me like that, I don't want to lie to you, so I'll end up implicating myself."

Luke bit his lip. "Sorry, start again."

Kory smiled softly at him. "There was a problem that you originally came to me about. It's been taken care of. You know nothing, I said nothing, and no other lawyers were mentioned. But this problem that weighed on you for a long time, has been dealt with."

Luke sat deep in thought as they pulled into the parking garage, then said, "I think I understand. So, I'll just kiss you and say nothing else." He quickly planted a kiss on Kory's lips.

Kory took him by the hand, and they walked into the elevator. "Good job," Kory said.

Madeline stood near Ms. Martin's desk, waiting for Kory and Luke, as they stepped off the elevator. Kory looked at her and rolled his eyes, still holding Luke's hand. "Madeline it's too early, give us a few minutes to settle in," he said, walking past her.

Luke smiled and greeted her while being pulled along.

"Stop," Madeline said. "I'm taking him with me." She pointed to Luke. "I need his help; the other intern quit yesterday."

Kory tightened his hold on Luke's hand. "Which one quit? Shay?"

Madeline walked to the elevator and motioned for Luke to come over.

Kory felt Luke pull toward Madeline. Luke seemed conflicted looking back and forth between the two. "Just wait," Kory whispered and gave his hand a gentle squeeze.

"Yes, whatever her name was, with the long blonde hair. Total flake, always distracted instead of doing what she was told. She thought she was cute and acted a little too flirty with Andrew yesterday, and you can imagine how Marcus responded to that. Looked at me like I would save her. Anyway, she sent me an email with her resignation early this morning."

Kory scoffed. "You, save someone? From Marcus, no less… that's funny." He kept his grip on Luke's hand.

"Tell me about it. He's even more jealous than you, and that's saying something," she said.

Kory pulled his head back. "What are you talking about? When have you ever seen me jealous?"

She pulled her glasses down to her nose, and waved her hand, gesturing in Luke's direction. "With this one, just yesterday and today, it looks like you're deliberately trying to keep him from me. What, are you afraid because that suit is a little too tight on his cake?"

Luke seemed embarrassed by her comment. He tugged uncomfortably at his suit jacket with his free hand.

Kory wasn't all that surprised she'd noticed Luke's ass; she was always very observant. "You really don't miss a thing. Fine, I'll send him up in a few minutes."

Madeline pressed the elevator button and looked back at them. "Luke, I want you in my office at 9:20, not a minute later."

Kory quickly shut the door to his office, with Luke inside. He closed the blinds, then held Luke's face in between his hands. "Listen, it will be fine, she already knows we're together and she likes you. You already have two things in your favor. I'm her favorite, so she won't mess with you too bad. With that being said, she is going to try and figure you out. Quickly. She does a lot of rapid questioning, which she's known for. It's how she catches people in lies. Answer honestly and maintain eye contact. If you don't think you should answer something, then don't; ask her the same question back, but change it around a bit. She likes to be challenged, despite the way she talks to people. I'll call her in a few and make her send you back. She probably doesn't even need anything. She would just ask me if she did. She's just lying and using Shay as an excuse. Just don't bend over in front of her, and you'll be fine."

Kory could tell that Luke was nervous, but he had a strong urge to reenact their steamy morning. He pulled Luke into his arms and kissed him deeply. Luke melted quickly into Kory's embrace and responded with an even deeper kiss than Kory could allow in the moment.

Kory pulled back. "I just told you not to bend over in that suit. If you keep kissing me like that, what will she see besides your juicy ass?" Kory lightly spanked him on his bottom.

Luke cleared his throat, as he straightened his pants and tie, then headed to Madeline's office.

I'm not afraid, I'm not afraid…this is fine…. Luke repeated to himself in the elevator.

Madeline's office was huge. Certificates of accomplishments and various degrees covered the walls. She sat behind her desk, leaning back in her chair, her legs propped on her desk and crossed at the ankles, staring at her phone, her glasses pulled down her nose.

Her door was open. "Knock, knock," Luke said as he approached.

She looked at her phone, then back up to Luke and said, "Nine seventeen, good job. Take a seat."

Luke tried to maintain eye contact, but he was intimidated quickly by the many psychology accolades around the room. *I have nothing to hide, why am I so nervous?*

Madeline straightened her posture and looked at Luke. "Help me understand something," she said. She slid two phones across the desk to him. They were both opened to a social media site. "Why can't I get a date…with either of those, with a normal man?"

Luke calmly scrolled through the profiles, mildly confused. The first reflected her actual name, with a picture of her sitting at her desk, surrounded by papers, smiling. *This one is terrible…zero interest shown from the entire internet.* The next profile had the letters XXX mixed in with her name, an expletive and the word "Bo$$." Luke covered his mouth with his hand, seeing the picture of her smiling, showing a lot of cleavage, and the posts that followed. *Where do I start with this? Why would she… Be confident,* he reminded himself. "I don't use social media, I really don't. Honestly, though, these are both terrible." He slid the phones back across her desk.

She put her glasses back on top of her hair. "Well, why are they terrible? Explain."

Luke maintained eye contact. "Well, the first one is terrible because you look like a workaholic with a messy desk. You're using your real name, which I'm sure some people find intimidating. Your posts are boring, and no one will ever see them. The second one, I don't even know where to start. The username is disgusting and suggests way more than you looking for just a date with a normal man. The picture is also…not good."

Madeline interrupted him, "Who doesn't like a nice pair of boobs? Also, I could date a woman, too. Don't assume things."

He pulled his head back and raised his hand. "I don't like a nice pair of boobs, and I didn't assume anything. You asked me why you couldn't get a date with a normal man. Those were your words."

She leaned back in her chair nodding slowly. "I like you. You're good. Not afraid of pissing the boss off, huh? It's a shame Kory scooped you up."

Luke raised his hand again. "I'm not into women. At all."

"Well, listen, the boob profile, that last intern made for me. I told her that no one was paying any attention to me, and I was having trouble meeting people. She made that, and I just figured it was normal. There's a lot of messages on there, but it's not anything I'd be interested in on a first date," she said, winking at him.

"Well, I met her only briefly, but I wouldn't have trusted her with this. That was a bad call," Luke said confidently.

Another man entered, immediately sitting down next to him. He appeared to be around the same age but had a very cocky disposition.

Madeline was obviously mad, she flicked a pen forcefully across her desk at him and his intrusion.

"Hello, who asked you to come in here? Who do you think you are, Liam? I'm having a private conversation. You can leave."

He glanced casually at Luke. "Is she sleeping with you yet?" he asked. He pulled a lollipop out of his pocket, unwrapped it and stuck it in his mouth.

Luke's mouth dropped open, and Madeline smacked her hand on the table. "Don't make me call Kory in here, get out. Go get the signatures on the Simons case before I take it away from you. You little puke."

He raised his palms outward, while remaining seated. "No, no don't call your dog in here. But you may need to let him off his leash for the Simons case. It's getting a little too deep for me."

Luke sat straight-faced, while thinking, *Her dog? His leash? Don't make me call Kory? What the hell was all that?*

"What happened?" she asked. "That was a done deal. You only needed to get her to sign in two spots. How could that be too deep for you?"

Liam sighed as he sized Luke up. "Nice suit, guy," he said while looking Luke over. He turned back toward Madeline. "The client wants Kory. She said she likes dealing with him better. Well, she asked for you, then she asked for Kory, when I told her you didn't have time."

She shook her head in annoyance. "Liam, those are two very

different things. Get up and fix it. The deal is sitting in the chamber already. What the hell is wrong with you?"

He rolled his eyes. "Sorry," he said.

"No, there is no sorry. Fix it now. If this deal isn't done by 1:00 PM, I'll fire you. Get out." She pointed toward the door.

Liam got up and left the office without saying another word.

"Now, you," she looked at Luke, "what are you so distracted for? He asked if we were sleeping together, and you didn't even reply. Then, you sat there frozen as he called Kory my dog and looked you over. Is that what's bothering you?"

Luke shook his head. "No, that's not it. I've dealt with people like him before…I just have a lot on my mind."

"Spill it. We're friends now. I need a new friend anyway."

Luke remembered that Kory warned him to be careful around Madeline, but he also didn't want to lie. "It's just family stuff. I found out some alarming news last night and I'm still a bit shaken. I probably shouldn't tell you that, though."

She smirked at him. "There is nothing that you could say that would surprise me. I'm quite familiar with your history." She reached into the small refrigerator beside her desk and pulled out two pink glass bottles of sparkling water. She slid one across the desk to Luke, and held the other in her hand.

"Thank you," Luke said, taking the bottle. Luke raised his eyebrows and leaned back in his chair. "If I may, I'd like to challenge that," he said.

She let out an exaggerated breath, then spoke quickly without pause, "Luke Everton, eighteen, born January 1, to Levi and Angela Everton, abandoned by Angela Everton and raised by your father, after she discovered your father was in love with your ex-boyfriend's father in the dirtiest of ways. Your very rich ex-boyfriend, harassed by a scout for being gay, was too afraid to seek out his own feelings and you both stayed trapped in an emotionless relationship, until you met the one and only wonderkid, Kory Collins, with a head of gorgeous blond hair and an ass that doesn't quit. You two immediately started dating after said break up, which occurred just a few days ago and have been knocking boots ever since." She sipped from her bottle. "How did I do?"

Luke's mouth dropped open, and she smiled brightly at him.

"I know everything, I told you."

Chapter 8
My Worthless Father

Coop was still distraught and frustrated on Tuesday morning. He decided to call Coach, to try and lose himself in some practice. Coach answered on the first ring. "Hey, Coach, sorry to, uh…bother you on an off day, but I'm having a bit of—never mind. Can I…can I please come use the cages for a bit. I'll lock up after I'm done. I don't want to be at home right now."

"You okay, Coop? You sound upset, and not the kind of upset I'm used to hearing from you."

"I'm…I'm…" He sighed, trying to keep his emotions in check. "I just need some air."

"Of course, but I want you to stop in my office first. I'll be here for a little bit longer this morning."

Coop arrived with his hair in a topknot, and his mind a complete mess. He walked into Coach's office, across the hall from the locker room. He closed the door and sat across from him.

Coach folded his hands on his desk. "What's going on, Coop? Something tells me you aren't here just because you felt like getting in some extra practice."

Coop sat silently with his head in his hands on Coach's desk.

"Coop, listen. At some point you gotta start trusting that there are people who want to help you. It's okay to ask for help." Coach's voice was growing more concerned by the minute. "Alright, you don't want to talk, that's fine, too." He looked at his watch. "I have plans in another thirty minutes, but until then, why don't you just sit, and I'll be here to watch over you. You're okay here."

Coop sat silently with his head in his hands for a long time. Then he started to cry. Coach stood up from his desk and patted him on his back, while Coop cried with his face in his hands, for what felt like the first time in his life.

Ethan had plans to meet his father in the parking lot. As he pulled in, he texted to tell him that he'd arrived. He waited a few minutes and after not receiving a reply, he walked inside toward his father's office.

Through the office window, he saw Coop crying with his head in his hands and his father comforting him. He felt a strong urge to go in and try to help with whatever was going on. But as he reached for the door handle, he realized that he had no right to try and interfere with whatever was happening.

He went into the locker room and lay on his back on the bench in front of Coop's locker. He couldn't understand why seeing Coop cry made him feel this way. He felt powerless. Being Italian, he was used to big feelings from his mother, so he was rarely affected by other people's emotions. This was different, though. Seeing Coop cry, hurt him on a level that he couldn't comprehend.

I need to help him, he thought. *I feel like I can make whatever is wrong, better. What right would I have to go in there, though? I've barely spoken to him. Everything in me is pulling me toward him. My heart…it's almost like it's reaching for him.*

He lay there for a long time until he heard his phone ring. His dad called to cancel their plans for the day. Ethan didn't ask any questions. He got up and headed back to his father's house.

Coach listened to Coop explain what happened, and the two talked for a long time. As Coop left, he gave him a big hug and told him he'd always be there for him. A few minutes later, Coach texted both Luke and Coop's fathers, telling them that they were urgently needed at the school. He received quick replies from both, that they were each on their way.

Coach headed out to the parking lot. He had to be careful here; he knew that if one pulled in and saw the other, there was a hundred percent chance that both would leave, if he weren't there to stop them. Coop's dad, Tom, pulled in first, he got out of his car and walked over to Coach. "Am I in trouble, Paul? What's going on?" he asked.

Coach was annoyed with him. "Yeah, you are. I talked to Coop this morning."

Before Tom could respond, Levi pulled into the parking lot. Tom looked at Coach after seeing him pulling in. "Shit, are you serious, Paul? You called him here, too? I'm leaving." Tom started walking back toward his car.

Coach pointed at him. "Tom, don't you move from that spot. I kicked your ass once in high school and I'll do it again."

Tom held his hands up in resignation, standing in front of his car. He was a well-built man, but was no match for Coach when he was in fighting mood.

Levi sat in his car staring at Coach, who motioned for him to get out. Levi rolled his eyes, got out and leaned against the front of his car. The three stood in a triangle, with Coach in the middle, and Levi and Tom both standing near the front of their cars. They were parked just one space away from each other.

Levi was agitated and confused. He held one hand on his hip. "Why am I here, Paul? Did something happen with the boys?"

Coach was extremely frustrated, as he pointed at both men. "You two. I've had enough of this shit! It's been like eighteen years since you've spoken. Damn it! We came up with HX4. What the hell? Did you just forget it? Avoiding each other like idiots. Well, guess what? I'm not fixing this shit for you!" he shouted.

Levi still seemed confused, but he apparently didn't feel the need to be polite. He yelled with his head cocked to the side, "Who asked you to fix anything, Paul? Why don't you fix your own problems first?"

Tom added, "Yeah what about Gina? Why haven't you patched things up with her?"

Coach had both hands on his hips and shook his head at them. "Man, you two are still the same. Levi, I told him earlier and I'll tell you, too. I kicked both of your asses in high school, and I'll do it again."

Levi pulled an eyebrow down in disagreement. "You kicked his ass, not mine."

"Bullshit," Tom said.

Levi looked at Tom in disbelief. The first word he'd spoken to him in eighteen years was that? He couldn't believe his ears. He sassed Tom, with a hand on his hip, "What did you just say?"

Tom finally made eye contact with Levi. "I said, bullshit. He definitely did kick your ass."

Levi's mouth dropped open. He narrowed his eyes and sassed Tom again, "Oh are you talking to me? Don't you need to have your secretary speak for you?"

Tom's mouth and eyes both widened at Levi's remark. "*What?!*" he screamed.

Coach stood in the middle of the two. "I don't have time for this, guys. You both just need to talk."

"Why?" Levi asked, throwing his hands up in frustration.

Coach gestured to Tom, who let out a long sigh before replying, "The boys found Sam's diary."

"And?" Levi asked with a shrug.

Tom looked at the ground and didn't respond. Coach shook his keys in the air, as he got into his car. "I'm leaving. I had to cancel plans with my son over this. Use your heads, guys."

Levi narrowed his eyes looking at Coach. "I hate you, Paul."

"Same," Tom said, looking at Coach.

Coach yelled out the window, "Yeah, well I love you both!" He left the two standing in the parking lot alone.

Tom leaned against his car. Levi couldn't help but notice how good he looked. Tom had clearly come from his office, he was dressed in a tight-fitting, black designer suit. It complimented his deep green eyes and perfectly styled black hair.

Levi stood against his own car. Tom's burning gaze raked over Levi's form. He was wearing gray slim fit designer pants, a tucked in white button-down shirt, complimented by a navy vest and gray blazer.

They both stared at each other for a few minutes in silence. This was the closest they'd been in eighteen years, and the first time they'd truly been able to take in the sight of each other, alone.

Levi spoke up first, "What did the diary say?"

Tom didn't reply, instead he opened the door of his car and handed him the small, pink book. The two were now only three feet from one another following the handoff of the diary. The book opened on its own to the page that described Angela coming over, thanks to the photo that served as a bookmark. Levi pulled the picture out and admired it. He was filled with even more regret after seeing it. He tried to smile, but his face wouldn't allow him to. There was too much pain and sadness. He tucked the picture into the back of the diary and read the page. He put his hand on his mouth as he read further on. He closed the diary and sighed, with tears in his eyes. "Oh, Sam…" he said.

Tom stared at him silently. He was dealing with his own mixed bag of emotions.

Levi looked up at Tom. "I…I don't really know what to say. How is Coop?"

Tom snickered at him. "That's funny."

Levi cocked his head to the side, placing his hand back on his hip. "What's funny?"

"You asked about Coop. When have you ever given a shit about him?"

"What the hell was I supposed to do, Tommy? I'm not you. I couldn't stand it," he said while crying.

Tom shook his head repeatedly upon seeing him cry. "No, no, no. You do not get to play the victim here."

Levi looked at him, as he wiped his tears. "And who do you think the victim is?"

"Everyone involved except you."

Levi wiped a few tears with the back of his hand. "Oh, I'm not a victim? You think I wanted to marry Angela? You think I wanted to say your name, while I was forcing myself to have sex on my wedding night? Do you think I liked looking at a carbon copy of you, making out with my son? Do you think I liked being alone? Do you think I liked watching my son cry his eyes out over what happened with that sleaze bag scout. Fuck, Tommy. It was a nightmare. I literally had a front-row seat to the thing that I tried to protect you from."

"You lost me at the end there. What sleazy scout?"

Levi quickly explained what happened with the scout. As he finished, he found himself confused. "Wait, how did you not know this?"

Tom held one hand on his own forehead. "He said he just got a bad offer, and he didn't want me to interfere. He wasn't too interested in signing right after high school anyway."

Levi pulled an eyebrow down. "Riiight, but the scout just came back, though. I guess you didn't know that, either."

Tom shook his head and sighed in frustration. "Why didn't he tell me? This kid…he just can't bring himself to ask for help."

Levi smiled softly. "Who does that remind you of?"

They both looked at each other. "Sam," they said at the same time.

Tom folded his arms on the hood of his SUV and laid his head on them, face down. He truly didn't know what to do. He closed his eyes for a few minutes, silently considering everything he'd just learned this morning. Suddenly he felt a warm hand on his back. Levi's gentle touch rubbed away the pain that he'd carried for so long.

"Tommy, I'm sorry."

Tom lifted his head, turned, and pulled Levi close, wrapping him in a strong embrace. No words were spoken between them. Levi looked up at him, and the two stared in silence at one another. Tom held Levi's face in his hands and pulled him into a deep, passionate kiss. The last time they'd kissed they were clumsy teenagers, but now they were men, full grown men, with needs that had not been met in a long time. Their kiss was hot, loud, and wet. Levi lightly moaned as he tried to keep pace with Tom, who felt like he may swallow his face whole at any moment.

Tom suddenly grabbed Levi's shoulders and stepped back slightly, bringing an abrupt end to their lascivious kissing. Levi looked at him confused, and stood silently watching, as Tom pulled his phone out and dialed a number. He held a finger up to Levi as he spoke on the phone, "Tony, listen, Levi is going to come through the gate in a few minutes, let him in." Levi's eyes went wide, as Tom maintained eye contact, with a very serious expression on his face. "Yes, Levi Everton. No, I won't be with him, I'll be there shortly after. Thanks."

Levi crossed his arms and tilted his head to the side. Tom slid his phone in his pocket and sighed, looking at Levi. "I am very angry with

you. You should know that, but after that kiss, I know you aren't going to leave me again," Tom said.

Levi looked at him softly. "No. I won't." He reached for his hand, but Tom pulled back, avoiding contact.

"I'm not done. I am mad, Levi. I know you suffered, but it was not easy for me either. I'm not interested in talking because there is nothing else left to say. You apologized, like you should have a long time ago, and that's fine…but that's not what I need right now. Right now, I want you to listen to me very carefully. *You* are to go to my home and call me when you get to the main estate. I will direct you further when you get there. I'm going to stop off and grab a few things that we'll need. Do not call me until you are at the entrance to the main estate. Do you understand me?"

Levi was confused, but pretty aroused by the way Tom spoke to him. "Um, okay, I can do that. Yeah, I'll call and tell the office that I'm not coming back today," Levi said.

Tom shook his head and pointed his keys at him. "No. You will *not*. I did not tell you to do that, did I? Can you follow instructions, yes or no?"

Levi nodded. "Yes. I can but…"

Tom tilted his head and raised his eyebrows inquisitively.

Levi started again, "Yes, I can. I can do that. I'll head over now, and I'll call you when I get to the main estate entrance."

Tom opened his car door and sat inside. "Straight there, Levi," he said as he closed the door.

Levi walked quickly to his car and sat inside. He spoke aloud to himself, "What the hell just happened? What am I doing? Is this real?"

He tapped the sides of his face and looked in between his legs, sure enough it was real. He had just made out with his Tommy, after all these years. His heart pounded incredibly fast, as he relived the sensation of their mouths tangling together, and the taste of Tommy's minty tongue. He looked to the left and saw that Tom's SUV was stopped.

"Shit, he must be waiting to make sure I leave." Levi started his car and headed toward the estate.

Tom resumed driving as Levi pulled out of the parking lot.

Levi arrived at the gate and lowered his window. Tony, the security guard, approached. "Whoa! I don't even need your ID. You're definitely Levi. Luke looks just like you. No doubt about it."

Levi smiled. "Thank you. You must be Tony, it's nice to meet you. Which way to the main estate?"

Tony quickly explained to Levi how to reach the main estate.

When he parked and got out of the car, he called Tom.

"Tommy, I'm here. This place is bigger than I imagined. What do you want me to do now?"

"Open up the glass door, that's facing you and head to the right," Tom instructed him.

Levi approached the door. "With what key? I don't have a key," he said.

Tom sighed. "The door isn't locked, why would it be? Was it easy for you to get in there? I never lock it. Go inside like I told you."

Levi pouted. "You know you're being kind of fresh with me, Tommy." He walked through the doors and made a right inside.

Tom didn't reply to Levi.

"Okay, now what? Where do I go now?" Levi asked.

Tom replied, "Go up the stairs. Try not to fall, you always were very clumsy…"

Levi knew that was true, given all of the times he'd fallen, tripped, or spilled something in front of Tom. "Well, I can't argue with that," he said.

"*You*…won't argue with anything."

Levi's eyes widened. He was really getting hot from the tone in Tom's voice. He reached the top of the stairs, the long hallway had two closed doors on the right and one on the left in the middle, which was open. "Go in the door that's open," Tom said.

Levi asked, "How did you know I was upstairs? Weren't you afraid

I would fall, since I'm so clumsy?" He listened closely, waiting to hear if Tom would laugh.

Tom sighed. "Levi, listen to me. I'm not going to play games with you right now. I'm not laughing, I don't think anything is cute, so just do as I say."

Levi furrowed his brow and walked into the large bedroom. "You really like the grays and whites, huh?" He looked around the room. "Wow…Tommy, it smells like seagrass and Bergamot, is that a candle I'm smelling?"

At thirty-seven years old, Tom finally felt secure for the first time in his life, knowing that his Levi was in his room. He could barely contain his excitement, but, truthfully, he knew he wouldn't be able to take it easy on Levi, after all these years of pent-up frustration. He wanted Levi to know what he was in for.

"Levi, get in my bed. I'm almost there." He hung up the phone, without waiting for a response from Levi.

Tom sped quickly through the gate and headed inside. He nearly fell, as he rushed upstairs to be with Levi. He flung the door open and looked at Levi, in the middle of his king-size bed. He eyed his slender, toned upper body that peeked out from beneath the sheets, and slammed his bedroom door shut. "I am so mad at you. You know that, right?" Tom asked.

Levi nodded. "Yes, I do."

Tom unbuttoned his black vest, and pulled his tie off, while gazing at Levi. He opened a few buttons on the top of his shirt and untucked it. "Do you agree that this is your fault?" he asked.

Levi nodded. "Yes, I do. I'm sorry."

Tom unbuckled his belt and walked toward Levi. "Do you agree that you should be disciplined?"

Levi's eyes widened in excitement. "Mmmm…yes, I do."

Tom licked his lips and stood on the left of the bed, then reached over and squeezed Levi's cheeks together with his right hand. He whispered, "Show me how sorry you are."

Levi crawled from the middle of the bed to the edge where Tom stood. He looked up at him with lustful eyes, propped himself on his elbows, and unbuttoned Tom's pants, carefully unzipping and tugging them down. Tom quickly kicked them off and stood towering above Levi in his tight black briefs.

"Bend over in the middle of the bed, Levi."

Levi did as he was told, bending over quickly. Tom removed his shirt and got on his knees behind him. He spanked Levi's firm ass. "Lift your ass higher, don't be lazy."

"Tommy, please. I really want it," Levi, whined.

Tom spanked him again. "You'll get it when I'm ready. You've been craving this all these years; what was your plan, Levi? Were you gonna just keep living without me?" Tom cracked him on the ass again.

"I'm sorry… I was wrong… I just wanted what was best for you."

"Don't move," Tom commanded.

Levi remained on elbows and knees, while Tom got off the bed and grabbed his phone. He knelt behind Levi and rubbed his back softly. "I know…I know…It was mostly because of my parents."

Levi nodded face down, as Tom continued rubbing his back softly with one hand. Tom reached over and pressed call on his phone, leaving it on speaker, causing Levi to lift his head at the sound of a phone ringing.

"What do you want?" a cranky old voice answered over the speaker.

Tom took a deep breath—and spanked Levi again. "You like that, Levi? Tell my worthless father how much you like it. Tell him it's his fault that we've been miserable."

Levi responded without hesitation. "I like it, Tommy, yes, I did leave you because of your father."

Tom wrapped his arms around Levi's waist and softly pulled him into a sitting position. There was only silence on the other end of the phone.

"Listen, old man, I have never needed you. I'm going to take him now, like I should have been doing for the past eighteen years," Tom said, then ended the call.

Levi sobbed as Tom held him gently from behind on his lap. Levi turned to face him, and Tom kissed him on the cheek. He tugged the comforter up and wrapped it around Levi, then squeezed him tight again, pressing their faces together.

"I have never needed anyone but you, Levi."

Tears streamed down Levi's face, while Tom held him close. "Shhhh…it's okay now," Tom said while he rubbed Levi's back.

"I can't believe you just did that," Levi said, wiping his own tears.

"Well, I haven't talked to him in probably eighteen years. When my mom passed, he tried to get me to thank him for my success. I told him that I hated him then and there. He brought you up and then I just lost it. He told me that I was lucky to have found someone who cared more about our family's reputation than love. I thought that was pretty sick and I let him know it…and now he can sit around alone, surrounded by only his money, knowing that true love will always find a way."

Levi kissed Tom's cheek. "I don't want you to be mad at me anymore," Levi said, as he laid his head on Tom's shoulder.

"Okay…I won't be."

Levi suddenly remembered something and pulled back from Tom's embrace. He slid off the bed, and wrapped himself tightly in a gray throw blanket, then walked across the room. He picked the brown paper bag up from the dresser and asked Tom, "What did you need to get before you came here?"

Tom smiled and sat against the headboard of his bed. He covered his bottom half with his comforter and looked at Levi. "Go ahead, look inside."

Levi excitedly brought the bag over to the bed and dumped its contents out. He smiled big, as he saw what was on the bed: lube, condoms, and a bag of their favorite candy from high school. Levi popped open the bag and unwrapped one of the watermelon flavored hard candies, popping it into his mouth.

"Mmm…it still tastes the same. Do you remember what we used to do with these, Tommy?"

Tom nodded, beckoning him with one finger.

Levi eagerly crawled up the bed and pressed his mouth against Tom's. "Mmm…you're right, it does taste the same," Tom said after sucking the candy into his own mouth.

The two swapped the candy back and forth a few times through kisses, until Tom pulled it out and placed it on the empty wrapper. "Okay, enough games. How do you want it?"

Levi's face brightened in excitement. "Well, I know I said I didn't want you to be mad, but I would be lying if I said I didn't like the rough talk earlier."

Two hours later, both were finally satisfied. Levi fell asleep shortly after the last bout.

Tom lay next to him looking at his phone, moving a few things around with his schedule. He emailed his secretary and told her to notify Levi's office that he would be out for a few days. Levi was the boss anyway, so it was unnecessary for Tom to even have done that, but he wanted to make things as easy as possible for him from now on.

Tom texted Coop and Arie in a group text:

Tom: *Hey, I need you both to come to the main estate later. I want to clear the air. Levi will be here, and probably Luke, too.*

Arie: *Nah, I'm good. ILY. Don't need a convo.*

Coop: *I don't need a conversation either.*

Tom: *Coop, it's important to Levi & I that you're here.*

Arie: *So, I'm not important?*

Coop: *Yeah, why doesn't Arie have to go?*

Tom: *She said she was good. You did not.*
Coop: *I'm good*
Arie: *lollll*
Tom: *Please try to make it Coop.*
Coop: *Fine*

Levi stretched and looked up at Tom smiling. "Mmmm, I was almost afraid to open my eyes."

Tom leaned down and kissed him. "Why would you be afraid of that?"

Levi snuggled in close, sitting up. "I've had many dreams of this happening and each time I awoke you weren't there, Tommy."

Tom could relate to what Levi was feeling. He'd dreamt of this many times, too. "But did your back hurt when you woke up those times? Because honestly, mine is pretty sore."

"How can your back be sore?" Levi asked. "Look at you. How often are you working out to stay in shape like this? I'm gonna tell you right now, I'm not doing whatever crazy exercise routine you're doing. So don't think that because we're back together, I'm gonna start lifting weights and I don't know trucks…or whatever the hell has got you so buff."

Tom gave him a quick kiss on the mouth. "I don't want you to. Your tush is perfect, soft like a marshmallow."

Levi playfully smacked him in response.

"I texted Coop and Arie. Coop says he'll try and come. Arie's not interested. You should call Luke."

Levi sighed. "I don't know, Tommy. He just started this new job with this guy he likes and I—"

Tom tilted his head. "He started a job with a guy he likes? Since when?"

"I think his first official day was yesterday. Was yesterday Monday? Anyway, yeah, it's at a law firm. I didn't get the name of the firm, but the guy's name is Kory. I know he'd been meeting Luke a few times a week for a long time. I think they met originally because of the whole scout business."

Tom's jaw dropped open. "So, he was cheating on Coop?"

"How should I know? I just can tell he really likes this guy. He's talked about him for months. He just accepted the position the other day. I don't think he cheated on Coop, though."

"If you meet with a guy and don't tell me about it, even once, that's dishonest. You're saying he did this for months?"

Levi shrugged. "I guess so…"

Tom walked across the room over to his dresser. He picked up a seafoam-colored candle and sniffed it. He brought it near Levi's nose. "Is this what you smelled when you came in?"

Levi inhaled. "Yes! That is amazing, what is it?"

Tom spun the candle, showing him the label: *Seagrass and Bergamot.*

"See how good I am?" Levi bragged.

"Well, of course you're good with smells, running that winery, you must work with so many scents for all those new wines, my little enologist." He pinched Levi's cheek.

Chapter 9
Twins

Back at Parson & Associates, Luke was still being held captive by Madeline. Her desk phone rang loudly at 1:00 PM. She answered it on speaker, without waiting for the other party to say anything. "No, you can't have him back. I'm keeping him. Let's split custody. You have him at night, and I'll have him during the day." She grinned at Luke.

The other party hung up without any words spoken.

"Uh-oh. I've done it now," she said as she looked toward her door.

"What was that about?" Luke asked.

"Oh, Collie, be with me, he'll be here any second," she said biting her lip, still looking toward the door.

"Who, or what, is Collie?" Luke asked.

"My dead fiancé…" she replied.

Ding. The elevator sounded as it reached the floor. Madeline quickly pulled a file out and put it on her desk pretending to look at it.

"Let's go, that's enough," Kory said, pulling Luke up from his chair by the hand.

Madeline looked up from the file. "Wait, wait, wait…ah, forget it, go ahead. I've had my fun. Thanks for your help, Luke."

As they got in the elevator, Kory pressed the door close button rapidly, then pulled the stop button as the doors closed. He pushed

Luke against the side of the elevator and kissed him aggressively. He pulled back and started kissing his neck and face, then loosened his tie so that he could kiss Luke's collarbone. "Lunch break," Kory said.

Luke held onto him for dear life, as Kory kissed and rubbed his body, then stepped back and pressed the button for their office floor.

Their office was empty, as Ms. Martin had already gone to lunch. Kory continued kissing Luke passionately, leading him backward into his office and locking the door behind them. The room was only dimly lit by the sunlight peeking through the back window, which was blocked by a large portable dry erase board.

Kory picked Luke up and sat him on his desk. His strong hands rapidly stripped Luke from the waist down. Luke slid lightly on the shiny mahogany wood. Luke leaned back on the desk and Kory leaned over him, his body close. This was hot—hotter than being in the bedroom.

The intercom sounded, just as the two finished getting dressed. Luke's face was red, and he panted heavily while sitting in the office chair. Kory stood over him and tried to help fix his hair for him.

Ms. Martin spoke on the intercom, "Liam is here, do you want to see him?" she asked.

"No. Tell him to send whatever it is in an email. I'm busy."

"Got it," she said, ending the call.

A moment later they could hear Liam's voice through the walls. "What the hell does he mean he's too busy? His lights are off, for crying out loud."

Kory flipped the light on.

"Hey, asshole, I know you can hear me, open up," Liam yelled as he pounded on the door.

Kory didn't like that. He quickly opened the door and grabbed Liam by the collar of his shirt, pulling him inside. He enunciated each word slowly, as he shoved Liam backward. "What. Do. You. Need?"

Liam noticed Luke sitting in the chair and pointed at him. "You again? Who are you? I've seen you twice today."

Kory held his hand up to Luke, signaling him not to answer.

"Liam, if you have seen someone twice, then shouldn't you introduce yourself?" he asked.

"Why should I? He was sitting in Madeline's—"

Kory pushed Liam against the wall and lifted his chin at him.

He looked at Luke. "I'm Liam Collins, nice to meet you."

Luke looked at their faces carefully and pointed. "Liam Collins?"

Kory nodded. "Yes, this is my twin brother. I told you that we looked nothing alike. Fraternal twins and complete opposites."

Luke hadn't seen a picture of Kory's brother and didn't remember his name. He did remember that Kory said he really didn't like his brother, though, and the behavior that Luke witnessed from Liam earlier, lined up perfectly with everything that Kory had told him about his twin.

"Wow, I'm learning all kinds of things today," Luke said while standing. He walked over and extended his hand to Liam, "I'm Luke Everton, Kory's—"

"Boyfriend," Kory interrupted, looking at Liam.

Liam shook his hand and smiled, then looked at Kory. "Boyfriend? You called him your boyfriend? Since when do you date anyone?"

"What do you want?" Kory asked. "Why are you here? Aren't you supposed to be getting the signatures on the Simons case?"

Luke looked at him, remembering what Madeline said earlier. He raised his eyebrows awaiting Liam's response.

"I need help. The client doesn't want to deal with me. She likes you better."

Luke's cell phone rang, and he quickly walked outside of Kory's office.

"Wait, is that my suit he's wearing?" Liam asked.

Luke stepped into his own office; the one he'd only seen momentarily until now. He answered the phone on speaker, while laying it on his desk. "Hi, Dad, what's up?" he asked dryly.

His dad sighed. "I want to talk to you about what happened."

Luke rolled his eyes, as he played with the pens on his desk. "Dad, I already know enough. My new boss already knew everything too, so I guess it was somehow public knowledge. I can just ask her if I have any questions."

Levi scoffed at Luke's response, but then seemed taken aback by what he said. "Her? I thought you were going to work with the guy you liked, Kory? Isn't he your boss? You've never referred to Kory as her."

Luke tapped a pen on his desk in annoyance. "My boss, Madeline Parson, the managing partner of our firm. She knew everything, without me even uttering a word. Kory is my supervisor, but she is the boss."

"Maddie? Maddie is your boss? Oh, come on…her father was your mother's divorce attorney and Maddie went to the same school as us. I'm not surprised that she knew everything, she was always very smart."

Luke clapped his hands sarcastically. "Great, great, really. Everyone knew except for me."

His father sighed. "Meet me at Tommy's tonight, okay? Give me a chance to explain some things, please?"

Kory knocked on the door, entering before Luke could respond. "Luke, I need you with me. We're starting back up, and I need to fill you in on what you missed," he said.

Luke nodded at him. "Dad, I'll try. You're talking about the main estate, right? Or do you mean the meeting wing?" he asked.

Luke heard Mr. Morgan respond softly in the background, "Main estate."

Levi repeated, "Main estate."

Luke hung up in annoyance.

"You okay?" Kory asked, as Luke fell into his chest.

"Did you sleep with Madeline?" Luke asked, with his head tucked. Kory pulled back and looked at him.

Luke stammered through tears, "I can't take anymore…I…I'm so mad that everyone knew about everything when I didn't… I know it's none of my business if you did…because it was before me…but…please, please be honest with me."

Kory shook his head and wiped away his tears. "I will always be honest with you, Luke. Even if it hurts. This, however, will not. Madeline was engaged to my dad for about two years, he passed away before they got married."

Luke took in his words, then smiled. "Phew. I couldn't have taken any more today."

Kory continued wiping Luke's tears, then said, "Let's go, we're taking the rest of the day off. Grab your phone." Luke nodded as Kory led him by the hand.

"Ms. Martin, tell Madeline that something came up and we'll both be out for the rest of the day," Kory said.

She saluted in reply. "Yes, sir."

He smiled at her playful response. "Don't leave before five, I'm not kidding."

"Have a good afternoon, Ms. Martin," Luke said, as Kory walked him in the elevator, trying to shield his tear-streaked face.

They went to Luke's place, so he could grab a few things for the rest of the week. He opened the door to his small, neat, one-bedroom apartment. "Can I get you something to drink?" Luke asked.

"No, thanks, I'm fine. This is nice," Kory replied, as he looked around.

"Thanks, it's not much but I got it by myself. I'm happy with it for now. My lease runs out in another month, I think. I've lost track of the days at this point."

Luke pulled a large suitcase out of his closet and placed it on his bed. Kory wrapped his arms around him from behind. "Awww, my little traveler has an even bigger suitcase. So cute."

Luke giggled. "I left the little guy at your place, so I have to use this one. How many days should I plan for? Are we working this weekend? Oh crap, I forgot about Kai's birthday party on Friday night.

I also have two classes, one tomorrow night and one Thursday night." Luke held a conversation with himself, without any input from Kory, who stood chuckling while embracing him.

"Just pack it all up," Kory said.

Luke looked over his shoulder. "What? Pack what all up?" he asked.

Kory embraced him tighter from behind. "All of it. Just stay with me until you feel like coming back…or just stay with me forever."

Luke turned around and looked at him. "You don't mean that. You just feel bad because you see how tiny this place is compared to that beachside mansion you live in."

Kory shook his head. "No. I do mean it. Luke, I've been waiting for you for six months, it's felt like an eternity. I've worked around people older than us for the past two years; what we have is something people spend their whole lives looking for. I don't ever want you to leave. I'm serious."

Luke looked into Kory's love-struck eyes. He felt truly wanted, for the first time in his life. He wrapped his arms around Kory's waist as Kory embraced him. "I will always want to be with you," Luke said. He tried to hold back tears, as Kory rubbed his back.

Kory walked over to the small closet and squished a bunch of suits and shirts together, lifting them off the rod in one motion. He raised his eyebrows at Luke. "Okay?" he asked.

Luke nodded. "Okay."

Kory took the large stack of suits and carried it to his car. Luke packed up most of his dresser and a few extra things, while Kory grabbed a box from the closet and filled it with shoes and hats. Luke emanated happiness, as he sat in the car next to Kory.

"What are you thinking about?" Kory asked.

"I've just never felt like anyone ever wanted me. I feel so happy, even with everything that's going on."

Kory smiled at him. "I've always wanted you."

Luke knew that was true, he'd wanted Kory for a long time, too. After just the few days they'd spent together, the two had already tangled more times than he could count. He twisted lightly in the passenger seat, rubbing his back, and said, "Well, that much is obvious, my back can attest to that."

The two carried all of Luke's things inside Kory's home. Kory led Luke into his home office. "I don't want to put anything in the guest room, you're not a guest here. I don't like the way that feels. It makes it seem temporary. Put whatever you want in this closet, just until I make room. I'll put everything else in the bedroom."

Luke liked the sound of that. He smiled widely as he opened his suitcase and placed a few things in the closet. His phone rang and he hung his head backward as he answered it. "Yeah?"

"Are you on your way?" his father asked. "Coop is already here. We're just waiting for you."

Luke was confused. "Wait, why is Coop there? Why are we doing this together?"

Kory walked over, placing a hand on Luke's shoulder, and lifted his chin at him curiously. Luke covered his hand with his own. "Ugh. Fine. I don't really want to, though. I honestly couldn't care less at this point, Dad. I'm happy. Isn't that all that matters?"

Luke heard Coop's voice in the background of the call. "Well, that sums my life up."

"Luke, listen, you're on speaker phone. I wasn't expecting such a selfish remark from you. Just get over here." His father ended the call.

"Uggghhhh, I don't want to," Luke whined, looking at Kory.

"What's up? Where is Coop and what is happening?" Kory asked.

Luke sighed. "I guess my dad meant that he and Mr. Morgan would talk to us together at the same time. That wasn't explained to me earlier."

"Why do you need to be together for that?" Kory asked.

Luke unbuttoned his shirt and looked at Kory. "Exactly, that's what I want to know. He actually called me selfish; can you believe that?" He took his shirt off, grabbing a new one from a hanger.

"Hmmm, well, I only care about your happiness," Kory said. "So, I don't think it was selfish, but I'm thinking that if I were your dad in his current situation, the last thing I'd want to hear from my son is that he only cares about his own happiness. But I'm biased, so I think you said nothing wrong."

Luke stood with a white polo shirt on, and a pair of brown athletic pants unbuttoned, looking at Kory. "Let's just cuddle in bed. I don't want to go."

Kory refused, even though it was hard for him. "No, not until you're done, so button up." He grabbed his keys and wallet, and opened the door leading to the garage. "Come on, let's get this over with."

Luke reluctantly buttoned his pants and put his shoes on. He kissed Kory softly as he walked past him into the garage. The struggle on Kory's face was clear to Luke; he, too, wanted to stay and cuddle. But the responsible part of him won out, and they got in the car.

Kory reversed out of the garage and headed toward the Morgan Estate. He kept a hand on the inside of Luke's inner thigh, close to the warmth of his crotch. A silent promise that once he was finished dealing with things, Kory would give him what they both wanted.

Coop sat in the family room on a gray leather recliner in front of Levi and his dad. He'd spent most of the day trying to sort out his own feelings, which proved to be quite difficult for him. After meeting with Coach, he came home for a swim, then dove into Foundation emails for the rest of the day. As he read the desperate emails from others, he truly felt that he had no right to pity himself in his current situation. He also felt a tinge of happiness any time Ethan's face crept into his mind, but his intermittent frustration wouldn't allow him to focus on whatever it was that was going on there.

His father and Levi wanted to wait until Luke arrived, so they wouldn't have to explain everything twice. Coop stared at the two of them, already mildly annoyed. Levi seemed like a completely different person. His personality was much brighter and happier than Coop had ever seen. Not to mention his own father who seemed to be intent on smothering Levi to death with attention or kisses—both seemed possible at this point. Either way, Coop felt like it wasn't fair for the two of them to be sitting there like this, not when so many people were hurt. As much as he didn't want to be there, he was looking forward to venting more of his frustrations, particularly toward Levi.

Luke came in from the front door and sat on a recliner beside Coop.

There was only silence for a minute or so, before Coop decided he would lead things off. He looked at his dad and Levi in frustration. "I don't understand what I'm looking at right now. I've been sitting here for fifteen minutes and you two haven't been able to keep your hands to yourselves. Is this real? I don't understand. You guys were so crazy in love that you just decided to stay apart, and now, less than eight hours of getting back together, you two look like you were never apart. What the hell?"

Levi tilted his head in response to Coop. "What's your question? You're saying what the hell, what do you mean, what the hell?"

Luke jumped in, "What he means is—"

Coop put his hand up toward Luke. "Don't speak for me. Thank you."

Coop spoke to Levi, "Well, Mr. Everton, you see, I just found out that my father didn't even want to be married to my mother, which means that my father also did not want to have me or my sister." He could tell that both his dad and Levi were ready to interrupt him. "Please don't interrupt me. It's the truth. So, my mother was married to someone who didn't even love her the way that she loved him, while my sister and I were raised by someone who has only been thinking about you for the past eighteen years. He only wanted one person as his son, and he's sitting right there." He pointed to Luke. "My entire life I was brainwashed into thinking that Luke was everything, that nothing else mattered. For years and years everything I did revolved around making Luke happy. That, of course, wasn't Luke's fault. It was yours, Mr. Everton. If you had just been a little braver, then maybe you two wouldn't have wasted so much time and hurt so many people. I can't understand looking at the two of you how you were ever separated. Honestly, if you told me right now that you'd secretly been together all this time, I would believe it. This is just very weird seeing you guys like this. Then you got Luke over here, openly saying that as long as he's happy, who cares about anything else; his statement perfectly sums up the last eighteen years of my life. It's all just a big slap in the face."

Luke cut in, "Yeah, Dad, that's what he means by what the hell. What the hell were you thinking? Who would marry someone they didn't care about? Who would do something like that? How could you have left Mr. Morgan if you loved him so much? Do you even realize what our relationship did to the two of us? Coop literally felt obligated at every step to only care about me. It's no wonder he never talked about his feelings. What could he have felt? He wasn't allowed to feel anything!"

Tom rubbed Levi's back trying to comfort him as tears fell. Levi sniffled looking at Tom. "They're right, Tommy. It is my fault."

Coop's dad wasn't going to let this continue, when Levi was already crying. "Listen, both of you, I understand that you're both frustrated, but you can both shut up now. You have no idea what it was like to be gay at that time. Right now, you two can go off and hold hands, walk around, skip in the park, and have a great time, but back then things weren't so easy. Actually, it's still not easy for many people. Either way, while I didn't agree with Levi's decision and I still think it was the wrong one, I understand why he did it. You two have no idea what a different time it was. We live in a very open community, so you two haven't been really exposed to much ridicule, plus you kept your relationship a secret—"

Luke interrupted him, "I'm dating a man right now, I'm not afraid of what anyone thinks."

Coop found Luke interrupting his dad funny. He'd never seen Luke challenge him; it actually made him respect him a bit more.

Levi saw Coop's slight smile and asked Luke, "Speaking of your new boyfriend, Tommy and I were wondering if you cheated on Coop?"

Coop put his hand up to Luke and spoke to Levi, "Why do you either of you care if he did? I don't care if he did. We weren't sleeping together; we were basically brothers that held hands. Who cares if he cheated on me?"

"I didn't," Luke interjected.

Levi and Tom were mumbling about the fact that the two hadn't slept together. They were both pretty shocked at that revelation.

Levi looked at Coop, then at Luke. "Are you sure that you're gay? What do you mean you two never slept together? How could two guys your age be together for as long as you two were and not have done that?" He looked at Tom. "Tommy if we were together at their age, we definitely would have been sleeping together. Am I wrong?"

Tom turned his body toward Levi. "I don't even know what to say to that. I can't believe that you just said any of that. That was a lot."

Luke raised his hand. "I am sleeping with Kory. Yes, I am sure I'm gay. Thank you, Dad. Rather a weird thing to ask. Actually, that was all weird. Are you just weird?"

Coop could hardly contain his smile. He thought everything that just happened was funnier than he'd thought anything was in a long time.

Levi patted Tom's lap. "I'm sorry. I really am, I'm sorry for everything that I caused. It's all my fault. You're both right. I should have been braver, but I loved him so much and I couldn't stand a vision of a life where he would suffer because of me. Also, we are both very happy to have you as our children, so regardless of how we felt or didn't feel about your mothers, we love you both very much. If you want to keep yelling at me, that's fine. You won't say anything I haven't thought of myself."

Tom rubbed Levi's arms and kissed him on his tear-covered cheek.

For some reason listening to everything made Coop feel better. Just a few minutes ago, he was beyond annoyed with his dad and Levi, and now as he looked at the two, he felt softer and could see the love that they had for one another.

A few more words were said between them, and they all went their separate ways for the night.

Luke sprinted to Kory's car and quickly sat inside. "Phew, glad that's over. I feel better. Wow. Much better." He kissed Kory all over his face, then buckled himself in. Luke summarized their meeting while Kory drove and listened intently.

"Right, then I told my dad that this was all his fault and Coop agreed. It was kind of nice tag-teaming him. I feel a little bad, but they're going to just go for it now, so what's the use in being upset? The past is the past. You are my present and my future. If they're happy then it's not really right for me to be upset. Especially when I have you." Luke leaned in and kissed his cheek. "Oh, Friday night is Kai's birthday party. He texted asking if I was coming. I haven't answered him yet. Do you want to go?"

Kory looked at him as he pulled into his garage, leaving the garage door open. "It would be nice to meet your friends. I, personally, would rather come straight home and just be with you after work. But we can go if you want. Up to you."

"I'll think about it," Luke said, stepping out of the car. He looked in the distance. "It's so nice here, you can hear the waves crashing at night, and the breeze is so much stronger right next to the ocean like this."

Kory smiled opening the inside door to the house for Luke. "After your class tomorrow night, we can go for a walk on the beach if you feel like it."

Luke slipped his shoes off by the door and walked into the home office. His suitcase lay open on the small navy couch inside. Piles of his clothes were scattered on the computer desk and small coffee table.

He pulled his suitcase off the couch and sat on the floor with it. He changed his voice, using a meek and lightly suggestive tone, and said, "Kind sir, I've come from an awful place. My lover threw me out and it's so late. I don't have anywhere else to go. Is there anything I can do to repay your kindness for letting me stay here?"

Kory looked down at him. "Oh, you poor little traveler, why don't I show you where the shower is and then we can talk about remuneration." Kory bent down and scooped him off the ground, carrying him toward the bathroom.

Luke widened his eyes exaggeratedly. "Oh, wow, you're so strong. I've always wanted to be carried like this. It's so comforting."

Kory smiled at him. "After you make your payment later, I'll carry you like this again, little traveler."

Luke giggled, and the two got in the shower together.

Following the verbal beatdown from their sons, Levi and Tom went back upstairs to Tom's bedroom. Levi grabbed his keys off Tom's dresser. "Alright, well, I'm gonna go home, I guess."

Tom stood in front of the door and blocked it. "Nope."

Levi was thrilled that Tom wasn't going to let him leave, but felt more aroused by Tom's show of dominance in blocking the door. "What? Do you want to hit it one more time?" Levi asked, as he put his keys on the dresser and gestured to the bed.

Tom grinned widely, and approached Levi from behind, whispering in his right ear, "Levi, I've waited eighteen years to have you beside me, I'm not spending another night away from you. Never again," he said, wrapping his strong arms around him.

Levi melted into his arms. "How could I ever have doubted you?"

Tom chuckled. "I don't know. I think it's like the kid said earlier, maybe you're just weird."

Levi gave him a playful shove backward.

Tom pulled him back into his arms. "You're my little weirdo."

Chapter 10
Tattletale

The next morning, the traveler was very sore. He leaned over a still-sleeping Kory and kissed his cheek. "Hey, we gotta wake up. We'll be late for work."

Kory squinted his eyes and pulled Luke close. "Nope, don't wanna," he said, closing his eyes again.

Kory's alarm sounded, making his eyes quickly pop open.

Luke smiled. "I told you it was time to get up."

"Whoo…my little traveler did some work last night," Kory said, giving Luke one more squeeze.

Luke smiled and rolled out of bed. "Ouch, ugh, my back, no, my neck, ugh, ouch everywhere."

Kory smiled at him, walking toward the bathroom.

Luke slowly walked into the closet and flipped through several suits. He called out, "Hey do we have to wear suits every day? I noticed yesterday some other guys weren't wearing them."

Kory returned carrying a few ibuprofen pills, and a glass of ice water, he handed both to Luke. "Here take these, then you need to come eat. You shouldn't take them on an empty stomach."

Luke smiled brightly. "Thank you." He swallowed the small pills and drank some water.

"Always dress to impress," Kory said. "Suits are mandatory on court days, or for any client meetings, there are also a few other instances, but those are the main two. I wear a suit most days, but that's because I never know what Madeline is going to have me do. You should always wear a tie, that's a good rule of thumb. Thankfully, the jacket isn't always necessary, with the sweltering heat. We have to stop in and see Judge Murphy this morning, so today we both need suits."

After stopping in the office briefly, Luke and Kory, dressed in designer suits, entered Judge Murphy's private chambers. Kory tried to calm Luke, who stood nervously beside him. "Don't worry. Just remember what I said. Try not to smile, she'll see how soft you are if you do."

Judge Murphy, a large woman with short black hair, entered, followed by the prosecutor.

Kory addressed the Judge, "Good morning, your honor." He gestured to Luke. "I'd like to introduce, Luke Everton, he's our newest intern."

Luke approached confidently and greeted her, shaking her very strong hand.

Kory looked over at the other attorney, he was a small weasel-looking man, in a brown suit. "Luke, this is 'name redacted for privacy purposes', the prosecutor in this case."

The weasel-man spoke, "Starting in already, Kory? You could at least introduce me properly. You're like a miniature version of your boss. So rude."

Kory ignored him.

Luke was confused at the immediate hostility, but held a straight face.

Judge Murphy sat behind her large brown desk, and the three men sat across from her. She looked at Luke and gestured toward Kory and the other attorney. "These two are always going at it. Nature of the business." She smiled lightly at him, then picked up a file from her desk and held it toward Kory. "What happened?" she asked him.

After several rounds of arguments, the consensus was that Liam screwed it up. Kory smoothed things over, and the client agreed to come to the courthouse and sign the papers within the hour.

When they arrived at Kory's car in the parking lot, Luke hunched over, breathing rapidly. "I thought I was gonna die. She was so intimidating."

Kory patted him on the back. "Nah, she actually likes me. Wait until you meet some of the other judges. They'll really scare you. She at least tried to comfort you."

On the drive back to the office, Kory asked Luke to call Madeline and update her on the status of the case.

Madeline spoke loudly through the speaker, "Luke, talk fast, what is it?"

Luke raised his eyebrows and looked at Kory, who shook his head at her greeting.

"Hi, Madeline, how are you?" Luke asked.

She sighed into the speaker. "No. Stop. Get to the why you're calling part. Don't waste time."

Luke started over, speaking quickly. "The Simons case is closed out. Kory fixed it." He ended the call.

Kory's mouth dropped open in shock.

Luke looked at him innocently. "What? She wanted me to hurry. Should I not have hung up on her?" He covered his mouth with his hands.

Kory blew air from his mouth. "I guess we'll see what she thinks about it, when we get back to the office."

Pulling into the parking garage, Kory felt pretty nervous. He worried that Madeline was really going to yell at Luke. He wouldn't be able to protect him from her wrath, as much as he'd like to. Although Madeline let him have free rein over a lot of things, if she felt like Luke disrespected her, who knows what she might do.

"Do you think she's gonna be mad?" Luke asked, closing his door and stepping out of the car.

Kory shrugged. "We're about to find out. Just stay close to me."

Kory held Luke's hand as they stepped off the elevator onto their floor. Ms. Martin gave Luke a troublesome look, then shifted her gaze to Kory.

"Why are you looking at him like that?" Kory asked, then paused, seeing his brother through the office window. "Why the hell is Liam in my office?"

Ms. Martin pulled her mouth to the side. "Madeline came down here mad as hell, who knows about what. She told Liam to sit there until you got back. He's been there for about fifteen minutes, hasn't moved from that chair. You know I don't trust him, I watched him through the reflection on my monitor. I'm supposed to let her know as soon as you get back. Are you back? Or do you need a few minutes?"

"Give me a head start, call her in ten minutes. Thank you," Kory said. Luke smiled behind him and waved at her, as he was pulled into the office.

Kory closed the door behind them. "Are you here because of the Simons case? Or something else, Liam?"

"Oh geez, I don't know…" Liam replied sarcastically, not looking up from his phone. He pulled a lollipop out of his mouth and threw it in the trash.

Kory snatched his phone away from him.

Liam screamed as he tried unsuccessfully to pull the phone from Kory's hand. "Hey, that was a ranked match! Give it back!" The twins weren't similar in size, so it was pretty obvious that Liam wouldn't be able to overpower Kory. Liam's disposition was cocky, but he definitely wasn't as strong.

"What are you thinking playing games in the office? You're here to work, not screw off," Kory said, while holding onto Liam's phone.

Liam challenged Kory, "Oh, oh, I shouldn't be screwing off at work...then is regular screwing, okay? Your light was off when I came in after lunch yesterday, and your door was locked. Then you slammed me against the wall, and I almost choked on the smell of sex in the air."

Luke's face turned red, and he looked down at the floor, standing behind Kory.

Ms. Martin, sitting right outside, facing the opposite direction, definitely heard that. She clapped her hands at the remark and nodded her head. Kory picked up a bouncy stress ball from his desk and lightly tossed it against the glass. Her body jolted at the sound. She continued looking at her monitor and gave him a thumbs up over her head.

Ding! The elevator opened, and Madeline came out swinging. She screamed as she walked quickly into the office, "*Luke!*"

Liam backed up against the wall wincing. Kory stepped in front of Luke, blocking her path.

"Get outta my way." She shooed Kory, flicking her wrist at him. "*You!*" she screamed at Luke. "I can't believe you hung up on me!"

Luke replied calmly, "Now wait a minute, you told me not to waste your time and to get to the point. I only did what you asked."

She cocked her head to the side, then turned to face Liam with a snarl.

Liam, still wincing against the wall, pointed to Kory. "Kory and Luke had sex in the office!"

Ms. Martin gave a loud "Mmhmm" from her chair around the corner.

Madeline slammed the door shut, almost falling as her high heel turned in a bit. Liam chuckled and covered his mouth.

She stood with her arms crossed, glaring at Kory and Luke. Luke challenged her, remembering their conversation yesterday. "Didn't you say you were going to fire Liam if he didn't get the signatures? He didn't, Kory did."

Kory backed up Luke. "You did say that. I'm not gonna protect him. It was not an easy fix this morning, either."

Madeline pointed to Kory and Luke. "Sit," she said.

Liam chuckled, likely glad the heat was off him.

She turned to face Liam. "You." She let out a large sigh and started again, "What am I supposed to do with you? Your father's gone and now what? I'm supposed to just keep taking care of you?"

She looked at Luke and Kory. "Now, you two think it's okay to have sex in an office, when there are people around?"

Luke raised his hand. Kory took Luke's raised hand and brought it down, holding it in his own.

Madeline pointed at the two. "Well? Which one of you is going to speak?"

Kory looked at her, he squeezed Luke's hand under the table. "There wasn't anyone in the office. It was lunch time. By the time Liam and Ms. Martin came in, we were already done," Kory said.

Madeline pulled her glasses off the top of her head and sat down across from the two.

Liam still stood against the wall to the left, he grabbed his phone off the top of the filing cabinet where Kory placed it earlier. He held it, looking down at the screen.

Madeline, remembering something, pulled her phones out, and started to place them on the long table, then paused, holding them both in her hand. She pointed at the table and looked at Kory. "You cleaned this, right?"

Kory put his face in his hands. "Of course, I did. Also, that was yesterday. Not today. He was just trying to distract you from his colossal failure."

She side-eyed Liam, who was too busy looking at his phone to notice, and slid both her phones over to Luke.

Kory watched, perplexed as Luke grabbed them without hesitation.

Luke quickly glanced at the phones, then back to Madeline. "Wait, before I look, which one is the boob one?"

Liam's head shot up, while Kory's eyes almost fell out of his head. Kory turned to Luke. "What did you just ask her?"

Luke shook his head and patted his shoulder in response.

Madeline said, "The one on your right is the spicy one. I changed the pictures, though. The boobs are gone."

Luke looked down at the phone on the left first. The profile picture was changed to a picture of Madeline in a tight white dress standing near her bright red corvette. She had several new posts, all of which received no likes. He shifted his attention to the spicy profile, cringing as he looked down. The picture was changed, replaced with a picture of Madeline from when she was much younger. Madeline was in her early thirties, but this picture showed her in her twenties, she was holding a pink popsicle, smiling, and wearing a red bikini.

Luke dropped his head, then raised it, looking at her silently.

"What? What's wrong with these?" she asked. "You didn't give me much to go off, yesterday." She placed her glasses back on her face.

"Give me a minute," Luke said, clearly trying to gather his thoughts, while Liam hovered over the back of him looking down.

Liam was now fully invested in what was on the phones. He reached in between Luke and Kory and scrolled on one of the screens. "Thought you said this was spicy? I guess you don't know spicy, Madeline," Liam said.

Luke shook his head, looking at Kory. "How are you two actually brothers?"

Kory spoke over his shoulder to Liam, "She said the spicy one was on his right, not her right, genius."

Liam looked down at the phone beside it and scrolled. "Psssh, this name is too much for me. I wouldn't even look at this. Why is there a picture of you from like twenty years ago or something? This looks like a fake account," he said.

Madeline grabbed the red stress ball that Kory threw earlier and hurled it at Liam. "*I didn't ask you!*" she yelled.

Kory pleaded with Madeline, "Can you please leave? I have the Rhodes case that you asked me to deal with, and I already wasted half my morning because of that moron." He looked at Liam, who resumed his previous position leaning against the wall.

Liam, who now had another lollipop in his mouth, looked at Madeline's profile on his own phone. "This is embarrassing, how could you post this? Anyone else would be fired," he said.

Madeline leaned back in her chair and looked at the three men in the room. She motioned for Kory to slide her phones back. Grabbing her phones, she looked down. "So, either I post too much or not enough? I don't understand. One of you explain it."

Luke spoke, "Well, the thing is that you are trying to get noticed in essentially a large crowd. So, it's not just how much you post but what you're posting and who you're saying it to. Right now, you aren't doing either of those things well."

"Exactly," Liam agreed.

Madeline folded her arms. "So, if I'm understanding correctly, I'm basically in a huge area of people in constant motion. I am essentially sitting off to the side, trying to get people to look at me and right now they are just walking by without even hearing me yell at them. Is that right?"

Luke thought that was a pretty good way to explain it. "Excellent analogy, with a few corrections. Right now, you're not even whispering, no one sees you and you're being trampled under their feet."

Liam reached down for Madeline's phone.

She looked at Liam. "Yeah, you fix it, then maybe I won't fire you. No, wait, let me see your account, first," she said.

Liam held tight onto his phone. "Hold on, you can't see this account. Let me log out of this one and into the one I use for streaming." He showed her the screen after pulling up his profile.

Her eyes lit up at the massive number of followers on Liam's profile. "What? How is this possible? How can anyone like you? Do they know you? How did you do this?"

Liam then pulled up Luke's profile, showing Madeline that Luke hadn't posted anything in over two years. "See, now all these people are paying attention to him, and he's not even doing anything. Kinda pisses you off, right?" he asked, while smirking at Luke.

She stood up and pointed at Kory and Luke. "I want you both to stay late working on the Rhodes case this week."

Kory shook his head in disagreement. "Luke has classes tonight and tomorrow, and we already have plans for Friday night."

She opened the office door and looked back at Luke. "Are you sure that you don't want to take an office upstairs next to mine, Luke? We could make you my second personal intern. Your stipend is pretty small right now, because you're under Kory."

Kory rolled his eyes.

Luke smiled. "I'm happy working under him, I'm learning a lot."

She threw her head back. "Hahaha, don't say such dirty things. We all know how much you're learning *under* him. The damn table leg is loose from your lesson yesterday. Call maintenance to fix it."

Madeline pointed at Liam. "You, come with me. You're gonna fix this. It's your punishment."

"Liam, wait, toss me your keys real quick!" Kory shouted. Liam, without thinking, tossed his keys to Kory, who caught them. He quickly pulled the spare key to his house off and tossed them back.

Liam looked at him strangely. "Did you just take your house key back? Are you that mad about the Simons case?"

Madeline interjected from the elevator, "Who cares if he's mad? I'm mad. Move your ass and help me fix this."

Liam dragged his feet behind her, begging, "Can't you just fire me instead? Please? I still have money left. I don't even need this job."

Kory walked over to the right side of the table and jostled it. "Oops, I guess we did knock it loose," he said.

Luke's face was flushed with embarrassment, then he remembered something. "Wait, I'm confused. So, I know your dad passed away right before I met you, I remember you telling me that. I also remember you saying that he was the state attorney, so how did both you and Liam end up here?"

Kory blew air from his mouth. "That's kind of a long story. I looked up to my dad a lot when I was little, but after my mom passed, I saw him in a different light. I watched as he would, in my eyes, prosecute innocent people without remorse. He was very arrogant, like Liam. He knew he was the best and he wore that title proudly. For me, I watched and saw people that truly had no chance, despite their pleas. Sometimes, he locked people up that deserved it, but when it was someone innocent begging for leniency, he couldn't have cared less. There was no innocent until proven guilty. Everyone was just guilty. I hated that. Madeline's father was my dad's rival in my eyes. He would always push him, sometimes winning, but always managing to help the wrongly accused. He wouldn't take on cases where he didn't feel the person was worth defending. In other words, he didn't defend the bad guys."

"How virtuous of him," Luke said.

Kory continued, "Yes, and that's why I came here at sixteen and started an internship. He was, of course, shocked and my dad was livid, but all the same, he was happy to have me. Madeline on the other hand, will defend anyone, for anything. One day, after meeting privately with a judge, like we did this morning, my dad and Madeline decided to get coffee and really hit it off. There was a ten-year age difference between them. Anyway, they got engaged soon after, with plans to marry in two years, and my dad had a heart attack around a month before the wedding. Liam had always worked near my dad, so he clung to Madeline and joined us here. I guess he sees her as a mom, he's really protective of her, despite his actions. I think he feels like he's taking care of her for my dad in some way. She feels like she's doing the same. It's a weird dynamic."

Luke took it all in silently, the only mother he'd known was Sam, and she was never mean, or bossy, but he did sense a sort of motherly vibe between Madeline and Liam. "She does kind of come off as a mother to him, maybe a strict one," he said.

"Yeah, I think she feels obligated to. Alright, any more questions? If not, we really have to get back to work." He smiled and pulled Luke in for a hug.

Luke said, "Just one more question. Why did your dad give you the beach house? Did he leave Liam something else?"

"Yep. Money, lots of money. Don't know why or how he decided, but at some point, he had written in his will that I would have the beach house, Liam would get an obscene amount of his money and Madeline got everything else."

The rest of the day passed quickly as they pored over the files. Kory looked at the clock on the wall. "Alright, let's get out of here, so you aren't late."

Luke smiled. *He has to be the most considerate person I've ever met. I didn't even have to remind him about my class.*

Kory flipped the office light off, and they headed for the parking garage.

"I'm sorry to make you leave the office," Luke said, getting into the passenger seat of Kory's car. "I know we still have so much work to do. I should've thought ahead and drove myself in this morning."

Kory shook his head as they drove home to get Luke's car. "No, it's fine. This way you can change out of your suit before class, too."

Luke looked at the time, as he ran into the house. "I'm supposed to be there by six and it's already five fifteen. I'll never make it." He quickly ripped his suit off and dressed in a pair of jeans and a lightweight crew neck maroon sweater, and sneakers, with no socks. Luke grabbed his laptop and keys, then flipped the light off.

Kory stood near the door holding the key that he took from Liam. "Here you go," he said, as he handed the key to Luke.

"That's why you took the key from him. I should have known. Thank you." Luke gave him a quick kiss and slid the key onto his key ring.

They drove away in their own cars, as Luke headed to class and Kory headed back to the office.

Luke arrived in class at 5:59 PM, right before the professor started speaking. He sat in a seat near the back of the crowded classroom. He pulled his laptop out and put his thin, black-framed reading glasses on. He received a text from Kai:

Kai: *Yo, are u coming to my party? Or not? U didn't txt me back.*

Luke: *I think so. I want you guys to meet Kory. Just depends on if we finish up work in time. Been super busy. Awesome and I love it but busy.*

Kai: *Dope. See u guys Friday.*

As he closed the text stream, he scrolled to Kory's texts. His whole body felt instantly hot. He looked at the text he sent him from the day that they got together and remembered the events that followed. He unintentionally let out a very soft moan. The person next to him gave him a nasty look in response. Luke covered his mouth in embarrassment. He was unable to concentrate for the rest of the class.

As the class ended, the professor called Luke over to meet with him. Luke explained that he was now an intern at Parson & Associates, which the professor was quite proud of. "That's wonderful, Luke. They are a top-tier firm. They didn't call me for a recommendation, though, how strange," the professor said, stroking his small goatee.

Luke smiled. "Thank you. It pays very well, too."

The professor turned his head to the side and said, "Wow, in my day when you were an intern, you were just a grunt getting coffee. Now you get picked up by an elite firm and they're paying you? Times have changed. Well, listen, if you find yourself involved in something big, just let me know. You can always take this class online. It's only necessary for you to be here in-person on certain days. I do love having full seats, but you feel free to do what works best."

"Thank you, Professor," Luke said. He left the classroom and headed to Kory's place.

Luke pulled into the driveway and saw the inside lights on. The garage was closed, so he wasn't sure if Kory was home or not. He approached the front door and used his key for the first time. As he turned it, he exhaled deeply as it opened. He walked around the large home, calling for Kory, but didn't receive a reply. He went into the bedroom and heard the shower running. Quickly, he stripped himself and walked into the bathroom. Changing his voice into the meek, lost traveler, he looked at Kory through the glass door. "Oh my, sir, I've wandered into the wrong home during my travels. I'm so dirty, though, could I possibly shower with you?"

Kory slid the shower door open and pulled the lost traveler inside with him.

Chapter 11
Dirty Dancer

Thursday morning, Ethan Prescott awoke at seven, already looking forward to the evening. Tonight was his first game with the team, and he was more than excited. Although he wasn't able to talk to Coop yet, he was still hopeful that he may be able to pull him aside before the game.

Kai had texted the entire team about his party earlier in the week, and since Ethan was in the group text, naturally he received the invite too. He paid close attention over the past few days to see if Coop said that he was going or not. If he was going, then Ethan would definitely be there, if he wasn't, then Ethan had no interest in going.

He sat on the couch in the living room and watched more footage from the team's previous games. He wanted to be sure he had a good feel for all the pitches he would be receiving tonight, and he also wanted to get a few more looks at Coop's stance.

His dad walked in and patted him on the shoulder. "You ready for tonight?" he asked.

Ethan stared at the video which happened to be paused on a close up of Coop's bottom half. "Yeah, Dad, I'm good. I'm just looking at something."

His dad looked at the screen, then back to Ethan. "What, uh…

what are you looking at here? Coop's, uh…what the hell are you looking at?"

Ethan furrowed his brow and pointed the controller at him. "What do you think I'm looking at, Dad? Hmm? I'm here in the living room, with my stat book staring at a video of the last game."

His dad pointed to the TV. "Looks to me like you're looking at his ass, if you really want to know."

Ethan had a pretty good sense of humor and could tell that his dad was frazzled, so he thought he'd push him just a little further. "Well, you don't know me at all then. I'm not interested in the back side of him, Dad. What he's got in the front is what matters to me."

Ethan quickly jotted down notes on Coop's stance, which is what he was actually looking at.

"Alright, sorry. I'll leave you to it," his dad said, walking away.

Coop sat in his kitchen on a video call with a few employees from the Foundation. A couple of them were arguing about something that he felt was pretty stupid. Apparently the two women, were fighting over a man in another branch of Morgan Enterprises. Several times he had to verbally break them apart. One of the women gave Coop a serious attitude and threatened legal action if he didn't act according to her best interest. Coop was in a pretty good mood before this call, but now after hearing that, he was on edge. The last thing he needed was for his dad to think he couldn't handle things. He spent the next forty-five minutes trying to smooth the situation over. The meeting ended and he wasn't feeling too great about where things stood with the two women.

He received several texts from Kai who was trying on different suits for his birthday party. The text included pictures of Kai in an all-white suit, a cobalt blue suit, and a black suit with silver palm trees.

Kai: *Yo…Which one?*

Kai: *For my party*

Kai: *U like them all?*

Coop: *Whichever one you like.*

Kai: *I think the white one. Luke texted me btw and said he and Kory are coming.*

Kai: *Wait, I'm not sure if he told u about him. Forget I said that.*

Kai: *Did u already know? I feel bad now.*

Kai: *Coop for real…I wasn't trying to piss u off if I did.*

Coop: *I don't care Kai. Not sure why you would think I would.*

Arie texted Coop next:

Arie: *Hey I forgot to give you Luke's stuff the other night. Can u bring it 2 him?*

Arie: *Hellloooo don't just leave me on read. Can u do it or not?*

Arie: *Fine. Ignore me. I'll just give the stuff to Levi.*

Coop: *Good.*

Now Coop was in a really bad mood. He couldn't imagine a more annoying sequence of events. The only thing that could be worse would be if his dad and Levi showed up to his game together. He didn't feel like explaining what happened to his dad with the women from the Foundation, and since he didn't like to lie, he really hoped they wouldn't be there.

He went upstairs, loaded his gear into his bag, and left a few minutes after, headed for the baseball field.

Coop arrived at the field with his hair in a topknot. Ethan spotted him as soon as he walked in the locker room, and he remembered Kai's hair training. *Again with the topknot? How can he be pissed already? Maybe whatever happened yesterday is still bothering him. I really wanted to try and talk to him before the game. This sucks.*

Ethan watched as Kai walked over to Coop. "Yo," Kai said.

Coop looked at Kai. "Yo," he replied.

Kai smiled nervously, tension clearly in his body from where Ethan watched. "Let's kick some ass today, Coop."

Coop looked at Kai, put his earbuds in and walked away without another word.

Ethan let out an "Oof" from across the locker room.

After the game, the team headed to the locker room to celebrate their win. Ethan's dad pulled him aside, before he joined the rest of the group. Music blared from the open locker room door.

"Do me a favor, make sure that when you watch the tape, take note of those pitches that Coop struggled with. Don't just note the good stuff," his dad said.

"Of course, I always note everything. You don't need to tell me that."

Coach looked inside the locker room and patted Ethan on the shoulder. "Alright, get in there, go celebrate with the team. The dancing has already started. Kai's got his winning playlist on."

Kai shouted, "Whooo, that's how we do it!"

Ethan entered to find Kai dancing on top of a bench. Standing below Kai was Coop, his hair down, black uniform pants unlaced, shirtless and dancing. *Holy shit, holy shit, holy shit,* Ethan thought. Coop's movements were obscene. Ethan stood frozen staring at him. *I don't even know which part of him to look at....* He felt his lower region begin to stir. Coop's sweat covered, muscular body, coupled with his deep V, was too much for Ethan to bear. *I gotta get out of here!*

Coop looked up and saw Ethan standing frozen near the locker room entrance. "Good game!" he shouted to Ethan.

Ethan, who was having some difficulty controlling his thoughts, stood in disbelief as he heard Coop's voice call to him. Coop raised his eyebrows at him and began to approach. Ethan was in shock. *He's walking over here...no, no, no. MOVE, FEET!*

Coop put his hand on Ethan's shoulder and squeezed it. "You good? Did you need something?"

Ethan, very aware of his growing situation below, shook his right shoulder out of Coop's grip and replied, "Yeah, good game." He quickly headed toward the back side of the locker room. *What the hell was I thinking? Where the hell was I looking?* Ethan smacked himself on the forehead.

He glanced back and saw Coop still standing there, confused, staring at the hand that Ethan had shook off his shoulder.

Kai walked over to where Coop was standing and nudged his arm. "See, that was nice, he's cool, right? And, I mean, you know I don't swing that way, but that boy is *meow*," he said, as he raised his hands like cat claws.

Coop furrowed his brow in reply, pulled his hair tie out of the side of his waistband, and tied his hair in a topknot.

Kai raised his hands in confusion as Coop walked away. "Hey, what did I do? Why did you topknot me? You can't be mean to me; tomorrow is my birthday!"

Coop ignored him as he walked toward the cool down area of the locker room.

Ethan stood unmoving in the ice-cold locker room shower, lost in his thoughts. *Okay, he's hot, but I already knew that. How are his abs so defined? His whole body. I can't take it. I've never had these thoughts in a locker room before. His hair was down, and he seemed happy. I need to finish my shower and ask him out for drinks. Wait…how did that interaction with him just end?* Ethan's eyes widened and he put his hands on the side of his face. *Oh no, I shook him off. I felt my body responding to him, so I pulled away…*

"Shit," he said aloud, as he turned the shower off. He quickly dried off and wrapped a towel around his now-calmed lower half.

He walked around the other side of the lockers to where Coop was before his shower but didn't see him there. *Oh, don't tell me he already left.* He moved quickly through the rows of lockers and found himself in the doorway of the cool down room. Ethan coughed harshly at the sight before him.

Coop, who was sitting in the ice bath with his eyes closed and head back, jerked his head forward and opened his eyes. "You, okay?" he asked Ethan.

Ethan hunched over, covered his mouth, and held his right hand up. "I'm fine, just choked on air or something."

"Choked on air, that's a new one." Coop leaned back and closed his eyes again.

Ethan regained his composure and steeled his nerves to ask him out. "H…h—" was all that came out, as he stopped himself from speaking. *Oh, no. His hair's in a topknot. Forget it.*

Coop jolted his head up and made eye contact with him. "You want me…or something?" he asked in what sounded like a deliberately teasing tone, as he stood up slowly from the ice bath.

The sound of a knockout bell rang loudly in Ethan's head, as he was faced with a naked Coop, dripping wet, only a few feet away. Coop pulled his topknot out, shook his hair, then slowly wrapped a small white towel around his bottom half. Ethan was frozen in place, as he futilely tried to avoid staring at Coop's lower region.

"What's with you, today?" Coop questioned as he approached him.

"Sorry, I just wanted to apologize for earlier," Ethan quickly replied.

Coop was now only a foot or so away. "Apologize for what, exactly?" Coop asked, as his eyes searched Ethan's naked tanned chest.

Ethan suddenly realized that he, too, was only wrapped in the same small white towel. *Oh no, it's happening again,* he thought as his body

began to react. "Sorry about walking away earlier when you were talking to me," Ethan answered him.

"Ohhhh that. No big deal. I was more shocked by you pulling away, like I was gross or something." Coop closed the last bit of distance between the two of them and locked eyes with Ethan. Coop's face and body were now extremely close. He spoke softly and deliberately near Ethan's ear, "I mean, I guess we technically aren't friends, so I shouldn't have done that."

Too close, too close, too close… Ethan desperately tried to imagine himself anywhere else.

"Ethan, you in here?" his dad's voice called.

Coop's face and wet body remained close. He looked into Ethan's eyes and answered for him, "He's right here, Coach." He flashed Ethan a mischievous smile and walked away.

Coop got dressed, grabbed his gear, and headed to his car. He sat in the driver's seat, thinking about the last few minutes. *Well…that was…something.* He suddenly felt a throbbing below, as he remembered the sight of Ethan's thick, solid chest and the smell of his clean body, fresh from the shower. He looked down at his crotch and scolded it, "You shut up down there. We can't think these things about him. It's not right. We don't even know how he feels."

Coop awoke the next morning at five and hopped on the treadmill. He flipped the screen on to watch footage of last night's game. Normally, he watched his own performance and critiqued it, but this morning he skipped the film to a certain catcher wearing the number two. "Damn, he's fast," he said, as Ethan stole second base. He watched intently as Ethan, who currently had a good lead in between second and third, leaned his body, readying to steal another base. The inning ended and he watched as the camera showed a frustrated Ethan walking back to the dugout. "What's he so pissed about?" Coop wondered aloud. Coop reversed the footage and watched Ethan slide on his chest into second base. "Did he get hurt?" He continued the cycle of pausing and reversing. "He doesn't look hurt, what the hell is it?" Coop left the footage paused on a close-up of Ethan's face and studied it; his chest instantly warmed again.

Later that afternoon, the team won another game. Coop went 1–4, striking out three times, with one homerun. He was not pleased at all with his performance. The rest of the team discussed Kai's party, which was being held later that night at his family's restaurant. Coop stood in his tight black underwear, getting dressed in front of his locker. His hair was in a topknot and his gold chain with the number one on it was pressed against his tan skin.

Kai bounced over, fresh from the shower, wrapped in a towel. "Hey, man, you gotta snap out of it. It's my birthday! Plus, we won, who cares about the strikeouts?" Kai spritzed himself with his cologne, as Coop jerked his own body away from the overspray.

Kai jumped into a pair of sweatpants, just as Ethan entered, still in uniform. Kai shouted, "Hey, number two! You coming to my party tonight?"

Ethan's eyes looked past Kai to Coop, who was standing in his underwear. He slowly shifted his gaze from Coop's bulge and seemed to be trying to read Coop's expression before he answered.

Coop smiled brightly and said, "You should come…it would great if we both do…I mean, we should come, go…we should… coming would be good…"

Kai pulled his face back. "What the hell are you saying to him, Coop?"

Coop noticed Ethan blush at his fumbled invitation. *Okay, well I did say it would be great if we both…he seemed to pick up on that. Maybe he's into me.*

Kai walked over to Ethan and put his arm around him.

Ethan pulled his head to the side, and asked Kai, "Hey, what kind of cologne is that?"

Kai smiled. "Why, do you like it?"

Ethan made a disgusted face. "No, not at all. Sorry, but I think it smells awful."

"Ha!" Kai said. "What is the deal with you guys? This cologne smells great."

Coop shouted, "What's your girlfriend's name, Kai?"

Kai looked confused. "I don't have a girlfriend. You know that."

"Yeah…but what was the last one's name?" Coop asked.

Kai furrowed his brow in thought. "There was no last one…you bastard." Kai walked over to Coop and pushed him. "Oh, my cologne is terrible, so that's why I can't get a girlfriend?"

Coop was already dressed and smiling, his hair was down.

Ethan headed to the showers on the other side of locker room. As Ethan walked away, Kai playfully teased Coop. "Hey Coop, he hates my cologne too. That reminds me of you and Luke."

That instantly frustrated Coop. "Wow. You're an idiot."

Kai pulled his head back in response. "That sounded different than when you normally call me an idiot, are you mad?"

Coop slammed his locker shut. "Everyone really needs to stop the comparing him to Luke shit. You're so loud right now. He's not Luke, you guys need to just lay off him." He tied his hair in a topknot and walked away.

Coach entered the locker room and saw Kai on the bench, looking rather miserable. He sat down next to him. The teammates around them were whispering about something.

Coach asked, "What happened, Kai?"

Kai sighed. "It's my fault, I guess. Coop just…he won't listen. He gets angry so easily all the time now. I've never seen him like this."

Coach shook his head slowly, and patted Kai's back. "He's going through a lot right now. There's a lot at play here. I don't think it's your fault… I think Coop's heart has been lost for some time. He's gotta figure it out on his own."

"Yeah, but why won't he just let me help him? He doesn't ever tell me anything. It's like he's stuck in one place right now. He's the best player on this team, and he's just standing still as his game gets worse, while doing nothing but getting pissed about it."

Coach clicked his tongue. "It's not so simple, Kai. He needs someone, or something, to help him move forward. I'm not sure who, or what, but you can't force him. You've been friends for a long time. If he hasn't asked you for help yet, he's not going to. That's just the way it is. But speaking of moving forward, have you talked to Luke?"

Kai smiled. "Yeah, he's doing good. Really loves his job. He's supposed to be coming to the party tonight," Kai paused and lightly scoffed at his own thoughts, "I just don't understand. The two of them always shared everything. How can one be fine and the other not?"

Coach stood up from the bench. "Well, like I said, I think there are a lot of things at play here, that you don't know about. I will say that in my opinion, this is more about Coop just growing as a person. He just has to decide to move forward."

"Thanks, Coach," Kai said, while Coach patted him on the shoulder.

Coach smiled as he walked away. "Anytime, Kai. Do me a favor and make sure Ethan goes to your party tonight. I think it will be good for him."

Ethan stood up, following the end of the conversation from the other side of the lockers. He slowly walked into the shower, lost in a memory. *"Coop, Coop, Coop!" He could still hear the crowd cheering as he stood and watched from the other field, when he was ten years old. "Did you see the Morgan kid? Wow, he's something!" Ethan could still feel his mother pulling him, as he stood with one hand on the fence, looking over.*

As the warm water washed over his body, his gold chain with the number two clung to his neck. *I really wish I didn't hear all that... I'm going to that party tonight.*

Chapter 12
Say My Name

Brightly colored balloons and streamers were strung around the walls of Tagaloa's restaurant. Music blared loudly, and the room was packed full of guests for Kai's birthday party.

Coop sat at a table on the far side of the room, facing the door. He'd never put so much time and effort into his appearance before, but he really wanted to look good for Ethan. He was dressed in slim-fitting gray designer pants, a form-fitting, long-sleeved, black, button-down shirt, and black shiny loafers. His shirt was tucked, and he left the top two buttons open. His tan skin and pecs were extremely eye catching. He wore a gold watch, which complimented his gold number one chain. His hair was down, and he had an extremely thin, black elastic headband on.

As people continued to pile in, Ethan entered. Coop noticed him immediately and stared in awe, his heart raced, at the sight of Ethan's gorgeous face. He looked perfect in his tight, white, button-down shirt, navy pants, and matching leather loafers. His white shirt only had the top button open, and it was perfectly tucked in.

Upon entering, Ethan saw his reason for coming, staring straight at him. He took two steps toward Coop from the door and froze as his gaze reached Coop's headband.

Kai, wearing a neon pink boa, oversized sunglasses, a white suit, and a silver birthday boy crown, noticed Ethan and swarmed him. He wrapped his arm around him and guided him to the bar, quickly handing Ethan a shot glass full of something from a tray on the counter.

Coop was frustrated. *Shit, you idiot, Kai. He was definitely coming over here. I'll give him a minute and walk over there. I'm tired of waiting.*

Luke entered only a few moments later, dressed in a slim-fit, burgundy suit with a white collared shirt, tucked in and buttoned to the top. He wore clean white sneakers and no socks, his ankles showing. Luke headed over to Coop, who sat waiting for Kai to walk away from Ethan. Coop barely noticed him until Luke leaned in close to his ear, and whispered, "Nice headband."

Coop's eyes remained locked on Ethan at the bar. He noticed Ethan glance over his shoulder as he drank, what Coop counted to be his second shot.

Luke sat down in the seat beside Coop, smiling from ear to ear. "You look good, Coop. You feeling better about the dad stuff?"

Partygoers started to gossip, seeing the two sitting next to each other. Coop reluctantly pulled his gaze from Ethan, to converse with Luke. "Yeah, I mean if they're happy, why shouldn't I be happy? You're happy, they're happy. That's what matters."

Luke cocked his head to the side and raised his chin at Coop.

"Ah. Don't look at me like that, Luke. You know me too well. I thought that was enough to get you to leave me alone."

"No. It's not. I'm quite familiar with that tone. What happened in the game? Spill it."

Coop leaned back in his chair. "I hit a homerun in the eighth that sealed it," he said, in a voice lacking any emotion.

Luke leaned in closer. "Riiight…what about the rest of the game?"

Coop watched as Ethan took another shot at the bar and glanced over his way again. *He's thrown back at least three shots already, and every time he looks over here, he looks like he's waiting for Luke to leave, or maybe he's waiting for me to go over there?*

Coop sat up straight. "Luke, you're so annoying. Can you leave?" he joked.

Luke tapped his fingers on the table. "I'm waiting…"

Coop rolled his eyes. "Okay, I went 1–4, struck out three times."

Luke's mouth dropped open. "What? Why? I thought Ethan was supposed to be like a genius or something… Is he here?"

Luke followed Coop's eyeline and saw Ethan sitting at the bar. He saw something in Coop's eyes that he'd never seen before as Coop stared at Ethan. His face lit up looking in-between the two.

Coop noticed the shift in Luke's expression. He knew Luke was gonna tease him a bit.

"He's really good-looking, maybe even better-looking than you. You gonna ask him out?"

Coop rolled his eyes at Luke's remark and smiled.

Kai, who hadn't noticed Luke come in until now, danced his way over to the table and started talking to him. Coop got up and walked to the bathroom.

Luke laughed loudly, drawing Ethan's attention from the bar. Ethan was confused and lost in thought, *What? Where is Cooper? Why is Kai sitting in his seat? I gotta go find him.* As soon as Ethan made up his mind to find him, he realized he couldn't exactly stand straight after drinking so many shots and sat back down.

Ethan was quickly surrounded by several women. "Wow, you're so cute, and you smell good, too," one woman said, placing a hand on his shoulder.

Ethan looked at her. "Please don't…" He found himself unable to get a complete sentence out. He'd taken four shots since he'd sat down and was really feeling frustrated.

Ethan saw Coop emerge from the bathroom as one of the women in the group cackled loudly beside him at the bar. She placed a hand on Ethan's shoulder and moved in closer.

"Oof, stop," Ethan said. "Please don't touch me." He looked at Coop through glassy eyes, silently pleading for his help.

Coop darted over to Ethan, without thinking, pushing through the group of women that surrounded him. He stood beside him, as one woman said, "Hey, Coop, you want to join us, we're trying to get Ethan to play, but it would be better if you joined us, too."

Ethan decided to down yet another shot, but spit it out of his mouth at hearing her suggestion. He shook his head. "Pfft…. You wish," he said while looking at women.

"What did he just say?" one woman asked.

"Who cares? He's so hot," another replied.

The smell of the women nauseated Ethan. He'd always been very averse to strong smells, especially women's perfume. "Oof, you all smell terrible," he said.

Coop leaned in close to Ethan's face. He whispered, "Hey let's get out of here, let me take you home."

Ethan liked the change in smell, but he remembered what Coop said to him yesterday and still wasn't exactly sure what Coop meant by it. He was also very drunk. "Oh, are we friends now?" he asked Coop.

Coop knew that Ethan was just repeating what he'd said back to him. He didn't respond, and instead he began helping him up.

As Coop wrapped his arm around him, Ethan's face leaned into Coop's exposed chest. Coop was only an inch or so taller than him, but Ethan's current state wouldn't allow him to stand properly. Ethan breathed in Coop's scent, and his body relaxed even more, making it even harder for Coop to move him.

The girls reluctantly cleared out of the way. Coop headed for the exit, Ethan tucked tight, with his right arm wrapped around him.

"First its Luke, now its Ethan," Wendy shouted from behind.

Coop kept his eyes forward, maintained his grip on Ethan with one hand, while lifting his other hand and raising his middle finger at her.

As the two left the party, Ethan tried to right his posture, while Coop held onto him with his very strong right arm draped over his shoulders. Ethan nearly tripped, his face again was pressed squarely in the center of Coop's exposed chest. Ethan stopped walking and inhaled deeply, once again. This time however, he didn't move following the breath. He closed his eyes and kept his face there, as he spoke through a muffled voice, "Mmmm you smell so…damn good."

Coop tried hard not to hug him, finding himself extremely giddy at the moment. After several seconds, Coop, looking down said, "Uhhh, Ethan?"

Ethan looked up, his eyes half closed. "Yes, your highness?"

Coop thought that was hilarious, he held onto both of Ethan's shoulders. "What? Did you just call me your highness?" he asked, grinning from ear to ear.

Ethan, with his face still in Coop's chest said quietly, "You're so mean to me. Everyone is so mean to me."

Coop felt hurt by that even though he knew Ethan was drunk. "I could never be mean to you, Ethan." He turned Ethan's body and said, "Come on let's get you home."

From the other side of the parking lot, someone called out, "Hey Coop, nice home run today!" Coop nodded and smiled. He noticed Luke, who appeared to be waiting for someone by the restaurant door.

Ethan looked forward, as the two started walking again, with Coop still guiding him. "I hate that name," Ethan said.

Coop was confused. "What name?" he asked.

Ethan scoffed. "What else could I be talking about? Coop, Coop, Coop, oof, blech."

Coop nearly fell over laughing but held onto Ethan.

Ethan continued, eyes half closed, "I mean it, all the time it's Cooper Morgan this and Cooper Morgan that, Cooper, Cooper, Cooper. So exhausting."

Coop was stuck in a giggle fit, as he opened his car door, while guiding Ethan inside. He couldn't understand what was happening inside himself. It was as if all the feelings that he'd never felt before came pouring out. Hearing Ethan call him Cooper changed something in him. He knew he wanted Ethan, but just the sound of his name from Ethan's mouth filled him with extreme emotions. The want that he felt turned immediately into a need, a need for Ethan to say his name again…a need to hold him close and never let go.

Ethan frowned in the passenger seat. "Are you laughing at me right now?"

"No. I mean, no one calls me Cooper, you just said it so naturally… I've never let anyone call me that."

He looked up at Coop. "Ohhh my God…. Well, what am I supposed to call you? It's your name, isn't it?"

Coop felt the happiest he'd ever felt, looking at him. "You can call me Cooper," he said, as he reached to buckle Ethan in.

With Coop's arm reaching around him, Ethan widened his eyes to see Coop's gold number one chain, dangling in front of his face. Ethan pinched the charm in between his fingers, "Hey, is that mine?"

"What?" Coop asked, as he looked down at Ethan, finding it extremely difficult not to kiss him.

Ethan, still with Coop's charm pinched in between his fingers, pulled his own chain out with the number two on it, he tried looking down to examine both.

Coop hadn't noticed that they both wore the same chain and style charm number. He smiled at the realization and pointed to Ethan's charm. "No, see, yours is right there."

Ethan didn't respond. As Coop finished buckling him in, Ethan closed his eyes and fell asleep. Coop stood next to him, with his car door still open, gazing in adoration at a sleeping Ethan. *What have you done to me? How can you make me feel this way?*

Coop heard Luke's laugh from across the parking lot, he looked up quickly, then looked back down to Ethan's sleeping face. He rubbed the back of his hand softly on Ethan's cheek.

Ethan, still asleep, nuzzled Coop's hand, then brought it to his mouth, and lightly kissed the inside. He mumbled, "Mmm…you smell good," and released Coop's hand.

With that light kiss, Coop's lower half joined the rest of his body in excitement and began to react. He quickly closed Ethan's door and got into the driver's seat. He stared for a few moments at the inside of the hand that Ethan kissed. Reversing out of the parking lot, he headed for Coach's house. As he stopped at a red light, he looked down and inwardly scolded his body. *No. Down, down, get down. He's drunk. I know you're excited, but you gotta get down.*

When they arrived at Coach's home, Ethan remained asleep. Coop tried to rouse him gently, to no avail.

Ethan was now talking in his sleep and giggling. "Cooper, push me on the swing, just a few more times, please…no, I want vanilla cupcakes."

Coop laughed loudly at that, which still didn't wake him. He called Coach on the phone several times, with no answer. He noticed that there was an unfamiliar car along with Coach's in the driveway. He quickly went and knocked on the front door. After a minute or so, he gave up, returned to his car, and started driving. *I'll just bring him home with me. It's not like I can take his keys out of his pants, and just walk into Coach's house.*

Chapter 13
Your Cologne

While he waited outside Kai's party, Luke talked with a few friends. Some people didn't even know that he left the team yet.

His phone rang with a call from Kory. "Hey, are you here? I don't see your car," he said, looking around.

Kory whispered into the phone, "Oh, you can't see me, but I see a very sexy traveler, in a nice burgundy suit right now. I can only dream that he runs over here and lets me do dirty things to him."

Luke looked in the distance, and saw Kory smiling brightly across the parking lot, he happily ran into his arms. The two kissed rather intensely in the parking lot, each trying to press their tongue further into the other's mouth. Luke pulled back and said, "Come on, let me introduce you to everyone real fast, then let's leave."

Kory smiled. "Sounds good."

The two held hands and walked toward the restaurant. "Well, you won't get to meet Coop tonight. His car isn't here anymore… I hope he talked to Ethan," Luke said.

Kory furrowed his brow. "Ethan, the guy who took your spot on the team?"

"Mmhmm, same guy. You should've seen the way Coop looked at him. Gave me chills. Like you looking at me with my suitcase."

The two entered Tagaloa's holding hands. Kai spotted them and split through the crowd to greet Kory. "Hey, I'm Kai. It's nice to meet you," he said, shaking Kory's hand.

"Happy birthday. It's nice to meet you. I've heard a lot about you," Kory replied.

From behind them, Wendy said loudly to another woman, "Holy…look at him, he's wearing an effing emerald-green suit with a black turtleneck…standing next to Luke in his burgundy suit, they look like Christmas. Damn, let me open my present, please?"

The other woman replied, "Tasty. Now that Coop's gone, maybe we can slide in with Luke."

Luke watched Wendy and her friends checking them out, he'd heard their loud remarks and tucked in closer to Kory, giving his hand a squeeze.

Wendy looked Kory up and down. "You do what you want with Luke, but that other guy is giving off some serious daddy vibes. I need to know who—" She stopped upon noticing Luke holding Kory's hand and Kory kissing Luke's cheek. She rolled her head in circles, "Ugh…damn it."

The women sitting at the bar continued staring at Kai, Kory and Luke who sat at a table nearby. Luke called over, "Hey, Wendy, do me a favor and keep your mouth away from this one. If you can control yourself, that is."

Wendy spun around on her barstool. "Oh, you got some balls now? Are you mad that I kissed Coop? It was gross anyway, he screamed like a little b. I'm not interested in that one next to you. He's making it very obvious that he's here with you. You and Coop tried to hide that shit, and it pissed me off. I'm not trying to mess with a guy like him," she pointed at Kory.

Luke cocked his head to the side, as Kory pulled him close, wrapping his arm around him.

Luke wasn't finished. "Riiight, but Coop told you he didn't want to, and he made it clear that he wasn't into you, and you still forced it. We call that sexual assault in our business."

Kory nodded, while rubbing his shoulder.

"Oh Lord…calm down, I barely touched him. Anyway, he just left with Ethan, so I wouldn't worry too much about him." Wendy smirked.

Luke smiled wide as he looked at Kory. "Oh good, he left with Ethan!"

Kai walked over to Wendy "Don't try to start trouble," he warned her loudly. "I haven't seen my friend in a while, and I'd like to enjoy myself at my party."

Kai returned to Kory and Luke, who were tonsils-deep in each other's mouths. Kai knocked on the table, "Hello, there are people here…maybe you should do that somewhere else."

Luke wiped his mouth. "Sorry, Kai, he just tastes so good."

"I'll take your word for it," Kai said, winking as he sat down.

Kai talked about baseball, and Kory shared some stories from his time on the soccer team. The two hit it off immediately, with Luke barely getting a word in. Several old teammates came over to talk to Luke, praising Ethan's efforts as catcher, which made Luke really happy.

Kai's mother rolled a big three-tiered chocolate cake out on a serving cart, and everyone sang *Happy Birthday* to him, as he danced along to the song.

Kai sat down and dug into his cake. "I love chocolate cake. So good. Almost makes up for not having a girlfriend," he joked.

Kory pulled his mouth to the side. "Hmmm, you're a good-looking guy, you're on the baseball team, your parents are successful. What's the deal? Your cologne is on the strong side, but that can't be it, can it?" He looked at Luke, as Kai's mouth dropped open. Luke nearly choked on his cake. "What's wrong, did you think that was rude?"

Luke shook his head no, repressing the urge to laugh.

Kai said, "Yes, yes, I did. You guys, Coop, Ethan, Luke, now you;

everyone is always talking smack about my cologne." He took another bite of cake.

"I apologize, I didn't mean to offend you," Kory said.

Luke looked at Kory softly. "Don't apologize, he needs new cologne. Listen to how many people have already told him. He refuses to try another one. This has been going on for years."

Kory and Luke talked with Kai for a little while longer, then headed home in their own cars.

They barely made it through the door before they stripped each other of their suits.

Luke pushed Kory forcefully onto the bed and planted a small bite on his neck. "I've been waiting to taste you all night," Luke said, as he licked the bite mark.

Kory grunted at the feeling of Luke atop him, he couldn't wait any longer. "I need you, now."

Chapter 14
You're Such A Tease

Coop took a deep breath as he pulled into his side of the estate at 11:00 PM. He walked around and opened the passenger door. He spoke softly to Ethan, "Hey, you gotta get up, okay? Or else I'm gonna have to carry you."

Ethan sat unmoving, eyes closed. Coop decided the best way to get him up the stairs would be piggyback style, so he grabbed ahold of Ethan, who was deadweight at this point, and put him on his back. Ethan wrapped his arms tightly, hanging them around Coop's neck. Coop finally had a good grip on him, he kicked his car door shut quickly.

Tony, the security guard, was doing his nightly rounds and shouted from a distance, "Hey Coop, what's the matter, Luke have too much to drink?"

Ethan screamed suddenly, "I'm not Luke! I'm Ethan! I'm Ethan!"

Tony replied, "Oh, sorry, didn't mean to—"

Coop quickly carried Ethan inside, cutting off Tony's apology. Ethan's head lay back down, and he lightly kissed Coop's neck. "No. Ethan, we're walking upstairs. Definitely don't do that to my neck right now." Coop felt him fall asleep again. "Also, is there any way you could wake up? You were awake like five seconds ago. Can you do that again?"

he pleaded with Ethan, while cautiously carrying him up the stairs, into his bedroom.

Coop placed Ethan carefully on his bed and covered him with a spare blanket. He paced back and forth beside the bed, his mind racing with thoughts. *Okay, he kissed me three times, once on my hand, and at least twice on my neck. I definitely didn't imagine that. I loved it when he called me Cooper…his face is so cute… I wish he was awake. I really want to talk to him. This is okay that I brought him here, right? I tried to bring him to Coach. I'll sleep on the opposite side, it's fine. I don't think he's gonna wake up any time soon. Okay, let me just take a shower.*

Following a shower, and a scolding of his manhood, Coop got a few things ready for Ethan. He placed them in the bathroom and climbed gently into the other side of the bed. He fell asleep almost immediately, comforted by a completely new sense of peace with Ethan beside him.

Ethan stretched and turned his head to see an unfamiliar clock showing the time of 3:00 AM. He squinted his eyes and tried to focus inside the large, dark room. He looked to his left, to see a shirtless, sleeping Coop next to him. Suddenly, he remembered a few fragmented things from earlier in the night. He held his forehead, as he tried to piece everything together. He looked over again, in disbelief, that Coop Morgan, lay sleeping beside him, shirtless no less. He cupped his own face with his hands. *I'm actually in his bed. Wow, he is seriously gorgeous. Would it be okay if I touched his hair? I wonder if it's soft? I'm not mad that he's shirtless, wait, he's shirtless in bed with me!*

As he looked again to his right, he saw what appeared to be a large bathroom. He carefully slipped out of bed and went inside. Using only the moonlight that came in through the window, he tried to find a light switch. Ethan flipped what he believed to be the light switch, only to find the sauna to be turned on instead. He quickly flipped the switch back down and flipped the next switch and jumped. "Oof, wrong again," he said as the sound of music quickly turned on and off. He peered outside the door to see Coop jostling a bit in his sleep. Ethan winced as he tried the third switch. *Please, please, please just be a light and not like a rocket or something.* He sighed in relief as the bathroom was quickly illuminated by a nice, soft white light.

The bathroom attached to Coop's room was gigantic. There was a huge glass door shower, a sauna, double sinks, a large window overlooking the pool, and a private toilet area. On the counter, there was a towel, a washcloth, a pair of black track pants, a white compression shirt, a toothbrush in plastic, as well as a pair of underwear with tags attached. *This must be a dream, right?*

There was also a note that read: *Ethan, if you wake up before me, you can wear these, or you can wake me up and I'll bring you home. I tried taking you to your dad's, but he didn't answer the door. There are directions for the shower on the back of this note. Cooper :)*

Ethan's whole body was inexplicably warm. *What is this feeling?* After a quick shower and a thorough towel drying of his shaggy light-brown hair, he slipped into the clothes that Coop set out and gently climbed back into bed.

He looked at the clock which now displayed 3:30 AM. *I can't ask him to bring me to my dad's now, it's already so late. But how am I supposed to sleep with him next to me like this? I'll just lay here until morning. I can look at him, though, right? I mean there's no law against staring at a sleeping person, is there?* He gently turned to face Coop and lay there staring at Coop's perfect face, wondering if it would be okay if he held him. *No, no, that's not okay. You can't hold people without their consent.* Ethan then rolled onto his back and closed his eyes.

The silence lasted a few minutes before it was broken by Coop's sleepy voice. "Ethan?"

Ethan squeezed his eyes shut tighter and didn't respond.

"Ethan, are you awake?"

Ethan didn't respond again. *Why am I pretending to be asleep?* he asked himself, as he lay completely still, eyes closed.

The bed shifted as Coop rolled on his side to face him. He reached over and rubbed the back of his hand softly on Ethan's face. He then reached for the gold number two charm, that was lying flat on Ethan's tight white shirt and firm chest.

Coop spoke softly, "Hey, I really like you. I have for a while. I don't really know how to say it to you. It's all so surreal to me. I feel so many things right now that I've never felt before…not for anyone…and I've barely even spoken to you. How is that even possible? My entire life I've just been going through the motions, doing what was expected of me. I felt like everyone else was living, and I was just existing, without a purpose. When you called me Cooper today, everything just fell into place for me. It was like my whole body felt warm from the inside out…" he paused for a moment.

Ethan was finding it very hard to remain asleep but stayed true to the role he'd chosen.

"I want to be with you, Ethan. I want you to be mine. I want to protect you, hold you, and kiss you. I want to make you happy. I saw those girls near you tonight, and I almost lost it. I don't want anyone else to hit on you. I just wanted to pick you up and throw you over my shoulder. I just…how would I even explain this to you if you were awake? I've been pulling away from getting close to you, because it's all happening so fast in my mind. I really wanted to kiss you in the locker room yesterday. How can I feel so strongly for you already? I feel so many things every time I see you. I mean, I feel them until Kai shows up and says something stupid."

Ethan suddenly laughed, and Coop froze.

"You're awake?" Coop asked.

Ethan, whose eyes were watery with unshed tears, looked over at him and nodded his head.

Neither said anything as they lay locked in a desperate stare.

Coop broke the silence first and stammered, "I-I-I'm…that was too much… I wouldn't have said all that if I knew you were awake."

Ethan struggled with a reply as he stared in awe at Coop's perfect face. "I don't really know what to say… I—"

Coop interrupted him, "It's okay. You really don't have to say anything." He rolled onto his back.

Ethan lay silent, still trying to process what just happened. Coop sat up, and Ethan reached his hand over to his back and rubbed it. Coop's soft skin was hot to the touch, it felt like there was literally a fire within him.

"Wait…" Ethan said. "Cooper, I can tell that you meant what you said, but it's just, I mean, I do feel the same things when I look at you. But every time I tried to get close to you, I was pushed away."

Coop turned toward him. "When did I ever push you away?"

"I guess 'pushed away' isn't the right way to say it. More like I felt like I was in the way."

Coop paused, his gaze flicking back and forth as he desperately tried to think of what Ethan was talking about. He laid back down and turned to face him. "Why would you feel that way? What did I do to you, specifically?"

Ethan shook his head softly. "Nothing to me directly; you just seem like you're always pissed off or upset about something. I started to think maybe it was because of me."

Coop closed his eyes and sighed. He put his left hand on Ethan's face. "It was never because of you. I have a problem asking people for help. I just kept finding myself conflicted. I felt myself wanting to hold you, and at the same time, I had this childish feeling that you could save me."

"Save you from what?"

"I don't know, from life, I guess. I just…I'm not really sure how to explain it. It's like nothing I do matters. But when I look at you, I feel different, it's like something in me sparks up and my heart feels all warm. I can't explain it, it must sound stupid."

"When did you start feeling like nothing you do matters? Was it when…L-Luke left the team?"

"No, no, this has nothing to do with him," Coop answered resolutely.

Ethan sat up and covered his face with his hands. "I shouldn't have said that. I'm sorry."

"Why are you sorry? I want you to ask me things. I don't want to keep anything from you," Coop said.

Ethan sat up and flipped his legs over the side of the bed. "All right, let me try and get this all out. Cooper, I really like you too. I'm drawn to you in so many ways. I also feel things for you that I don't think make sense either. I want to know everything about you. But right now, I just need to be sure I'm not dreaming or hallucinating."

Coop walked around to Ethan, who looked up at him with hopeful eyes. Coop took both of his hands in his and asked, "You like me?"

"I really do but isn't that weird? I mean, how can I feel this way? It's so strong, this feeling. It's like I belong here, right now. I don't know if that makes sense."

Coop bent down and looked into his eyes. "It does, because I feel the same."

"Could you let me kiss you, maybe?" Ethan asked.

Coop shook his head and moved in. He gently opened Ethan's lips with his own, and the two softly kissed, as Coop slowly allowed his tongue to meet Ethan's. Coop held Ethan's face in his hands, slowly pulling back from the kiss.

"Mmmmmm, okay, I gotta stop," Coop said.

Ethan looked up at him. "Was that bad?"

Coop shook his head and leaned back in for another kiss. He went in with more force this time, and they kissed deeply, holding each other's faces. Coop finished with a soft kiss and pulled away again. "Mmmm, no, no. I have to stop," Coop said.

Ethan was now panting from the forceful, hot kiss. He wiped his wet lips with the back of his hand.

Coop's alarm sounded loudly. He looked at Ethan and shook his head while smiling. "I pulled back because I can't do the things I'm thinking of right now." He looked down at his black track pants and scolded the tent that was below. "Hey, listen, we gotta go for our morning run. Cut it out. He just said he liked me. You get back down. It's not your turn yet." He smiled and shrugged.

Ethan looked in between his own legs and said, "Yeah, same goes for you. Cut it out." Then he looked up at Coop and asked, "Do you really have to go for a run right now?"

"Well, I'm gonna need a minute or two thanks to someone," he said with a wink, "but yeah, I exercise at 5:00 AM every day."

Ethan nodded slowly while maintaining eye contact. "Mmm... that explains it."

"Explains what?" Coop asked.

Ethan pulled one eyebrow down and gestured at Coop's body. "Explains all these rocks that you're always flaunting."

"I'll take that as a compliment." He looked at Ethan, as though he could see through his shirt and licked his lips. "I can't start thinking about your body right now, Ethan. I'm still trying to get him to calm down," he said, as he pointed to his bottom half.

Coop walked over to his dresser and grabbed a pair of black gym shorts. "Do you want to run with me?" he asked Ethan, before he closed the drawer.

"I don't think I can run right now," Ethan said.

Coop smiled at him. "No worries, just give me a sec." He walked into the bathroom and closed the door. "In case you're wondering, I'm changing in here because I don't trust myself to take my pants off in front of you right now."

Ethan then heard Coop, playfully addressing his piece. "Hey, listen, you gotta calm down, buddy. I know you're excited, but we can't attack right now. You gotta chill. Stay down."

The bathroom door opened, and Coop smiled at a giggling Ethan who sat on the bed shaking his head. "Alright, I'm good, he's gonna listen. Let's go," Coop said.

Ethan was confused, he stood up and looked at him. "Wait I told you I couldn't run, though."

Coop walked over to him and grabbed his hand. "I know, come on."

"I don't even have my shoes on," Ethan said, as he was being led down the long, dimly lit hallway.

"You don't need shoes," Coop said. He smiled as the two walked hand in hand.

"I don't want to be barefoot outside," Ethan replied, making a sour face.

"Ew, me neither," Coop said. "We aren't going outside, though." He pulled Ethan's hand to the left and led him into a large room full of exercise equipment.

"Wh…where, what?" Ethan looked around astonished. His eyes couldn't process everything fast enough. The in-home gym featured a giant wall-size TV screen, two treadmills, an elliptical, weight benches, and a few other machines that Ethan didn't recognize, as well as two large recliners.

Coop looked at Ethan's shocked face. "You're adorable. You know that, right?" He passed him a large controller and gestured to the massage recliners. Ethan looked at him in awe, as he sat on the soft, smooth, black leather chair.

"I normally watch footage in the morning during my run, but you can watch something else if you want."

Ethan looked at Coop and then at the controller. "Wasn't my fiasco in the bathroom what woke you up earlier? I don't think I can be trusted with this," he said, as he passed the controller back to Coop.

"You want to watch last night's game?" Coop asked.

"Sure, that's good." Ethan beamed at him from the recliner. Coop started running as the giant display came alive with footage of their win yesterday. "I don't need to see myself strike out again. You can skip this part. Let's just get to you."

Coop sped the recording up to his turn at bat. They watched together as Coop struck out, with three strikes in a row. "Can you please tell me what I did wrong here? Be gentle though, remember I just poured my heart out to you a few minutes ago."

"Pffft…okay, okay, well, it depends on what sense you're asking that in. Like, do I see mentally what's happening, or physically?"

"Both," Coop replied.

"Yeah. I see it. It's plain as day."

Coop had never asked for help with his game before, not from anyone. The words came out, without even a thought, "Will you help me, please?"

Ethan nodded his head and approached the TV "The team our dads were on came up with HX4 right? Head, hands, heart, home. So, let's start with that. Head, no problem here, you're facing straight, that's good. Hands, you have your hands where they should be, nice firm grip."

Coop nodded along, as he listened and watched.

Ethan continued, "Now, here we have the problems. Next is heart. Can you pause this? Right there."

Coop paused the footage as directed, on a close-up of his own face. "My face is the problem?" he asked.

Ethan shook his head and chuckled. "Not exactly, but yes. Look at this extremely sexy man." He smiled over at Coop, who responded with a wink. "Now really look at his eyes. Where is this man's heart? Does he seem like he's really interested in this game?"

"No," Coop said, as he shook his head.

"Which leads to what?" Ethan raised his eyebrows.

"Not reaching home," Coop replied.

Ethan nodded. "And then last, but not least, physically." He pointed at Coop's hips on the screen. "The main thing is that your hips have gotten really stiff all of a sudden, compared to your previous seasons. You need to drop them a bit more."

Coop looked on in disbelief that Ethan was able to analyze him so quickly. "Ethan, that was amazing. How did you figure that out so fast?"

"Honestly, I noticed it a long time ago, but couldn't find an opening to tell you."

Coop shook his head, remembering Ethan's words from earlier. "I'm sorry, Ethan. I feel bad that my stubbornness made you feel like you were in the way. You definitely weren't."

Ethan tilted his head and smiled at him. "There's no need for an apology. As far as I'm concerned, this guy on the screen"—he pointed at the screen and then back to Coop—"you two, are different people. The Cooper that I'm looking at got a lot off his chest this morning, and hopefully I was able to make him feel a little better."

Coop shot him a megawatt smile. "Not just a little. You made me feel better than I can ever remember feeling. Really. Thank you."

Ethan blushed at his heartfelt reply.

"Alright, now, let's see your stance for reference," Coop said. He skipped ahead to Ethan's next plate appearance. Coop whistled as Ethan appeared on screen. "That guy looks like he knows how to drop his hips," Coop said, as he pumped his eyebrows at Ethan.

Ethan replied playfully, "Well, I'm a virgin, so I'm not so sure about that."

Coop looked back at the screen. "Me too."

Ethan scoffed. "Yeah right."

Coop looked over at Ethan, who had found his way back to the recliner. "It's true," he said.

Ethan's mouth dropped open. "How is that even possible?"

"The thing is that it just didn't happen. There were a couple times that I came kind of close, but that was a long time ago."

Ethan sat in disbelief at Coop's confession. "I'm not gonna pretend that I didn't know that you were with Luke, because I figured that out pretty quickly. So, what, did you guys just sit around and not kiss or touch each other?"

Coop nodded slowly. "Mmm pretty much. Yeah, just, like, kisses on the cheek and foreheads for the past year."

"Wow…I was not expecting that, I mean I saw you dancing in the locker room, and it definitely seemed like you, I don't know, had experience. Plus, I mean, I just assumed."

"Ha! I knew you were checking me out," Coop said. "Those last couple thrusts were meant for you."

Coop continued running on the treadmill and noticed Ethan covering his face. *He's so cute, he can't even look at me right now. I don't know if he's embarrassed, but I kind of am.* "Wait, you said you were a virgin too. Why are you making fun of me?" Coop asked.

"I'm not making fun of you. I'm just kind of trying to get the image of you thrusting and grinding…out of my head right now."

Coop looked at him and took a long sip from his water bottle.

Ethan took a deep breath in. "So, yeah, back to me, I am a virgin, yes. But the thing is, I wasn't really ever in a serious relationship with anyone."

Coop stopped running and entered his walking, cool-down phase. "Well, now it's my turn to be shocked. Ethan, please explain how someone who looks like you remained single and pure."

"I've always been taking care of my mom and playing baseball. Sex just seemed like it would be too difficult somehow."

Coop shook his head; he couldn't understand how Ethan could

think something like that. He'd been imagining it a lot recently and his only concern was that it would hurt Ethan. Coop was well aware that his size was much larger than any other guy that he knew. After being in locker rooms for years, he knew well enough that he was the king in that department.

"I don't think anyone would find sex with you difficult, Ethan."

Ethan's face became instantly flushed. Coop lifted his water bottle and squeezed a stream of water into his mouth, sticking his tongue out slightly and looking at Ethan.

"Wow…you're such a tease," Ethan said, staring at him.

Coop hopped off the treadmill and quickly approached. He stood in front of Ethan and placed his hands flat on the recliner, pinning him between his powerful, tanned arms. Beads of sweat ran from his neck, dripping down his chest. "Who's a tease?" he whispered, as he brought his mouth in front of Ethan's.

Ethan moved his mouth closer and locked eyes with him. "I think we both know who the tease is here, Cooper."

Coop broke the stalemate and pulled Ethan into a deep, enthusiastic kiss. Their tongues danced inside each other's mouths, as they turned their heads, each trying to get deeper inside the other.

"Mmmph—wait, wait," Ethan said as he pulled back. "Don't you live here with your dad? What if he comes in?"

Coop kept his face close. "This side of the estate is mine; he lives in the main house." He watched as Ethan bit his lip, seeming quite nervous.

"Okay, but still, I'd feel better if we were back in your room."

Coop scooped him up and threw him over his shoulder like a sack of presents. "Alright, let's go," he said. He patted Ethan's firm round ass.

Ethan was a well-built guy, his body was firm, top to bottom, he'd probably never been tossed over anyone's shoulder, and likely never imagined anyone could do it with such ease. Completely in shock, he yelled, "*Oh my God*, Cooper!"

They reached Coop's bedroom quickly. He shut the door with his foot, approached his bed and gently placed Ethan on it.

Ethan put a hand on his own chest and playfully hit Coop's abs. "I can't believe you just did that," he said while trying to catch his breath.

"Hmmm..." Coop tilted his head and straddled him. "You said I was a tease, right?"

Ethan locked eyes with Coop. "I did, and I stand by that. What are you going to do about it?"

Coop raised his eyebrows at him, "Alright, you asked for it." He began slowly kissing Ethan's neck and chest, then moved back to his mouth and the two kissed intensely.

"Can I see it?" Ethan asked, as he reached for the waistband of Coop's shorts. Coop shook his head, no, and kissed him again.

Ethan had called Coop a tease earlier, but in truth, Ethan was being the real tease here. "Mmm... You like it when I say your name, right? Cooper..."

Coop whimpered in need.

"Cooper...come on...let me see it." He reached for Coop's waistband again.

Instead, Coop ground his body hard against Ethan's, gently biting into the base of his neck as he did so. He was sure Ethan got a good feel, but he wanted to move past that, to push further, to drive Ethan wild.

He leaned down and pushed Ethan's shirt up, licking from his navel to his neck. "Damn...Ethan, your skin tastes so sweet." He helped Ethan pull his shirt the rest of the way off.

Coop looked down at him in awe and hunger. He tried to calm himself. *I have to slow down, besides, I don't have any condoms.* "I know we can't do this right now, but I really want you, and it's taking everything I have, to hold back."

Ethan nodded "I know, but please don't take your hands off of me, keep touching me…please? We can do other things."

Upon hearing his plea, Coop nipped at the base of Ethan's neck again. The heat from Ethan's body was incredible, overwhelming. He needed to be even closer to him. And then for the first time together, they both felt an indescribable pleasure, accompanied by goosebumps that covered their arms.

Chapter 15
What's In The Drawer?

The two laid next to each other panting. Coop grabbed Ethan's hand, brought it to his mouth, and kissed it. "I'll be right back," he said. He quickly walked into the bathroom, grabbed a washcloth, and wiped Ethan down. Ethan's face was flushed, as Coop leaned in and kissed him on the mouth softly.

"Let's shower," Coop said.

Ethan nodded and smiled at him.

Coop took in the sight of Ethan's naked body inside the shower. The need to be close to him was stronger than ever. After they both cleaned off, Coop pulled him close, letting the water wash over their bodies. He'd never felt so vulnerable with another person, but something in him sensed that Ethan was likely feeling the same. He kissed Ethan's forehead, and slid the shower door open.

Once they left the bathroom, only their bottom halves wrapped in black towels, Ethan realized he didn't have any clean clothes with him.

Coop was already prepared for this. He walked to the side of his room and motioned for Ethan to go inside the open door. The huge walk-in closet was lined with shirts, polos, button-downs, suits, uniforms, and shoes. It looked like a mini store.

"How is this real?" Ethan asked.

Coop shrugged his shoulders and smiled, as he reached into a drawer in the bottom of the closet. The drawer held several new packs of underwear and socks. He grabbed a pair of each and tossed them to Ethan, who stood in shock. "These should fit you," Coop said. "And you can wear whatever you want." He quickly grabbed a white polo shirt and black performance pants for himself. "I'm gonna get dressed and grab some water for us. I'll be right back."

Ethan's phone vibrated in his pocket. He answered it on speaker, so he could continue looking through the massive closet for something to wear. "Hey, Dad," he answered.

"Hay is for horses," his dad replied. "I was worried when you didn't come home last night. Everything okay?"

Coop shouted from behind him, "Let's go get breakfast," and tossed him a bottle of cold water.

Ethan nodded at him, moved the phone in between his chin and shoulder, and brought the bottle to his mouth.

"Is that Coop?" his dad asked. Ethan's eyes went wide as he drank from the bottle.

Coop winced. "Didn't realize you were talking to your dad. Sorry," he whispered.

"Yeah, Dad, he brought me home last night."

There was no reply from Ethan's dad.

"Dad, are you there?" he asked.

"Oh, okay, yeah, sorry… Wait, where is your car?"

"Cooper drove us here, I guess I left it at Kai's restaurant."

There was a long pause before his dad replied, "Okay. So, you won't be coming home for a bit?"

Coop, who now stood closer, heard the question, and shook his head, no, while smiling.

"Uh, no, I guess not. I think Cooper wants to go get breakfast."

Coop smiled big, as he enthusiastically nodded his head yes.

There was yet another long pause. "Alright, be safe," his dad finally said.

"Later, Dad."

"Bye, Coach," Coop added.

Coach looked at his phone as the call ended and smiled. Gina, Ethan's mother, stood across from him sipping from a mug. "Well, I think our son's gonna be alright," he said as he poured himself a cup of coffee.

Gina smiled at him. "Coop Morgan?" she asked, while looking up from her coffee.

He nodded at her and smiled.

"I knew it," she said.

"You knew what?"

"I did, in some way, ever since that day when he was little... Do you remember the junior championship?"

Coach sipped his coffee. "Of course, how could I forget it?"

Gina continued, "He was so upset, and after he finished throwing his little fit, the other field was chanting 'Coop, Coop, Coop' and it was like something in him broke. I just always knew somehow that Coop would be the only one that could fix it."

Ethan finally settled on an outfit to borrow. He looked at the pair of new underwear in his hand. "I'm sorry, but I have to ask. Why do you have brand-new packs of underwear and socks at the ready?"

Coop looked at him. "Eh, I'm kind of picky, I like to switch them out after a bit. If they lose that softness after a few washes, it just doesn't feel right."

Ethan slid into a pair of tan shorts with a long sleeve baby blue button-down shirt, which he cuffed so that his forearms were showing. He left the top button open and looked at Coop. "Look okay?" he asked.

Coop swallowed and looked him up and down. "You are literally perfect. I don't understand what I'm looking at right now. Is that even my shirt? When has a shirt I own looked like that on me?" He rubbed Ethan's shoulders and kissed him on the mouth.

Ethan gestured to Coop's body. "Please, look at you, I don't even know which part to look at. It's all so…oof."

Coop kissed Ethan's hand, held it, and led him out of the room. "Do the shoes fit you okay?"

Ethan wiggled his toes inside them. "They're good." As they walked down the hallway, Ethan was bright-eyed admiring the huge light fixtures and modern art that lined the hallways. "This place is huge. Do you ever get lost?" he asked.

Coop shook his head and chuckled. "Nah, besides, this is just my side; my dad's is much bigger."

"I don't even know what to say to that. Wait, what about your sister, she lives here too, right?"

"Yeah, but she lives on the opposite side. So, I'm on the left, Dad is in the main house in the center, and Arie is on the right."

"It must be nice to have so much space to yourself," Ethan said.

Ethan had lived his life being doted on by his mother. It wasn't a bad thing, his mother was very sweet and caring, but she definitely knew nothing of personal space. She wouldn't hear of Ethan moving out, she needed him with her, and Ethan felt obligated to stay. He had the opposite relationship with his dad. Whenever he came to visit, his dad was pretty busy with work, so Ethan felt a bit freer than normal. Even though the change in scenery was nice over the past week, Ethan still didn't feel at home at his father's house.

"Yeah, it's cool," Coop replied. "The three of us don't really see each other most days. Arie is usually off doing something, and my dad is normally working. It's pretty quiet."

Coop opened the glass door, and the two walked down the stone steps together slowly. They walked past Coop's black SUV and toward a large, detached garage. "We just walked past your car. I thought you said you didn't ever get lost," Ethan joked, while pointing his thumb over his shoulder.

Coop chuckled. "Very funny." He stuck his tongue out at Ethan and entered a code on the garage keypad. "Got something better than that." The door slowly opened revealing two cars, both black. One was a sporty BMW, and the other a Cadillac SUV.

Ethan gawked at both cars, then looked at Coop. "How am I even surprised at this point?"

Coop smiled at Ethan's surprised face. "Which one should we take?" he asked.

Ethan was still shaking his head in disbelief. "Let's take whichever one you like best."

Coop walked around the BMW and opened the passenger door for Ethan. "This one is my favorite," he said as Ethan sat inside. Before he closed the door, he looked down at Ethan. "Do you need help with your seatbelt?"

Ethan answered him in confusion, "Why wouldn't I be able to put my seatbelt on?" As soon as the words left his mouth, a memory of last night flashed in his mind. He remembered pulling Coop's chain and then rubbing his face against his hand.

Coop seemed to know exactly what Ethan was thinking. He smiled and pulled his chain out. "Kind of cool we both have the same chain with our numbers. The style is even identical. Sort of a crazy coincidence."

Ethan hung his head in embarrassment and buckled himself in. Coop closed the door, then jogged around to the driver's side.

"I don't know about you, but I'm starving," Coop said, quickly buckling in and pulling out of the garage.

"I'm hungry, too, but if I'm being honest, I'm suddenly feeling a bit embarrassed," Ethan replied, looking out the window.

"Embarrassed? About what?" Coop kept his eyes on the road, as he took Ethan's hand and quickly kissed it.

"I fear that list is very long, at this point," Ethan said.

Coop furrowed his brow. "How can I make it better for you?" he asked, as the two passed Tagaloa's restaurant and Ethan's Jeep.

Ethan pointed to the restaurant, while they drove by. "Wait, aren't we getting something to eat?"

Coop grinned and shook his head quickly side to side. "We're going somewhere new. I want to find a place where the two of us can eat and be alone."

Ethan looked over at him in awe. "Well, first, that was very sweet and I'm excited, so thank you. Second, how is this real right now?"

Coop shrugged his shoulders. "I don't know but I've never been happier than I am right now, with you sitting next to me."

Ethan dramatically leaned his head into the window, pretending to faint at the sweet comment. "Okay, alright, are you serious, or are you teasing me again?"

Coop raised one finger at him. "Don't you dare call me a tease while I'm driving, are you crazy?"

"Sorry, sorry, just kidding," Ethan said, with a smile.

Coop reached over and turned the driver's AC fan up on high. The shiny hair that hung just past his shoulders blew wildly. "Whew, okay, that's better," he said as he exhaled, and quickly turned it back off. "You can't get me all worked up when I'm driving."

They soon reached a cute beachside restaurant. "Oooh, Fregi's Beach Dive, this looks promising. You want to try this place?" Coop asked.

"Yeah, it looks good, I like the tiki vibe. Let's do it."

Coop pulled Ethan close as the two began walking to the dining area. Something about walking with his arm around Ethan felt so unbelievably freeing to him. Normally, when he entered a restaurant, all eyes were on him, and he carefully chose where to sit, based on the surrounding faces. He really didn't like it when strangers approached him, which they often did and he always felt uncomfortable when people touched him without his permission. But today, walking with Ethan, he saw no one else and didn't care who or what surrounded them. He had Ethan, and that was all he cared about.

Seat yourself, the sign read. Ten small tables, with thatch coverings, each adorned with artificial hibiscus flowers and orchids, were spread atop a large wooden deck overlooking the ocean. The restaurant was busy, with the only open table in the far back.

As they sat across from one another, Ethan, in contrast to Coop, looked a bit uncomfortable.

Coop tilted his head as he reached across the table and lifted Ethan's chin, staring into his honey brown eyes. He rubbed his thumb across Ethan's lower lip. "If I kissed you right now, would you be upset?" he asked.

"No, I wouldn't be upset, but there are so many people around, and they're all staring at you. One of them may throw something at me for blocking your face or something."

The way Coop felt with Ethan was something he'd only dreamed of. Now that he had this amazing feeling, he refused to care what anyone else thought. He leaned his muscular upper body across the table toward Ethan, his lips slightly parted.

A waitress loudly and abruptly interrupted, "Welcome to Fregi's! Do you guys want to hear the specials?"

Coop slowly backed away and looked at her, mildly annoyed with the interruption.

"I'll have a bottle of water, please," Ethan said.

Coop's eyes remained locked on Ethan, refusing to look up at the waitress. "Same for me, and I think we're good on hearing the specials, do you have a menu that we could look at ourselves?"

"Sure, suit yourselves," she said, seeming a little miffed as she walked away.

"*What* was that? Cooper Morgan, were you that mad that she interrupted you kissing me?" Ethan held back a laugh, fully amused by Coop's behavior.

Coop looked toward the area where a group of three waitresses gathered, then back to Ethan's face. "Maybe I was a little bothered. I didn't mean to be rude, though."

"Come here," Ethan said, as he leaned across the table toward Coop. Their lips met in a quick soft kiss.

A new waitress came over to the table. "Hi there, my name is Mandi, I'll be your server. Here are your waters and the menus. You guys take your time and I'll be back in a few minutes. Let me know if you have any questions."

"Thank you, Maaaaandi," Coop said. He took the menus and passed one across the table to Ethan, as Mandi walked away.

"Too much," Ethan joked. "Now that was too much. Is this your first time talking to people, or something?" Ethan couldn't contain his laughter, watching Coop's awkward interactions.

Coop was lost in Ethan's dazzling white smile, he stared at Ethan's perfect face. *What would it take to make him smile like this every day? I feel so warm and happy just being near him. I really do like him so much, so much more than I even realized.*

After a few minutes, Mandi bounced back over. "You ready, or did you need some more time?" She looked at Coop, who deferred to Ethan.

Ethan quickly scanned the long, pink, laminated menu. "I'll have the breakfast wrap, with a side of fruit, please."

She looked back to Coop, who was still undecided. "I'll have the pancakes with turkey sausage, please and thank you."

She collected their menus. "Sounds good, it will be up shortly," she said, as she walked back toward the kitchen.

"Ethan, remember when you said that you wanted to know everything about me?"

"I remember," Ethan replied.

"Well, I feel the same. I don't want there to be any secrets between us. So, go ahead and tell me everything." Coop placed his chin on both of his hands and smiled.

Ethan smirked. "You're too much. How can I possibly tell you everything, where do I even start?"

Coop thought momentarily and tapped the side of his head with his pointer finger. "I got it. We can play a game, like kids. I'll ask you a question, and you answer it."

Ethan tilted his head and dropped an eyebrow. "Now, that hardly sounds fair. I'll do it, but only if we take turns. You go first."

Coop: "What is your favorite color?"

Ethan: "Green, what's yours?"

Coop: "Black. What do you do on days that we don't have a game or practice?"

Ethan: "I go over game footage, record stats, or draw. Same question for you."

Coop: "Exercise, swim, and recently I started cooking and baking. What do you draw?"

Ethan: "Whatever I'm thinking about, usually."

A ringtone from Ethan's pocket sounded, and he pulled his phone out. "Sorry, it's my dad. Hey, Dad, what's up?"

"Hey, where is your stat book? I want to look at something, and I didn't see it on the counter where it normally is."

"Oh, sorry, I didn't think you'd need it since we were off," Ethan said.

A woman's voice spoke in the background, "Is that Ethan? Give me the phone. Hi, Mimmo."

Ethan looked at Coop's face in confusion, mouth agape. "Mom? What are you doing at Dad's? Did something happen?"

Ethan's mother sighed. "I'm hanging out with your dad. I'll probably stay for a few days."

Ethan was stunned, silent.

Coop looked at Ethan. "What? What's wrong?" he whispered.

His dad took the phone from his mother. "Here, just put him on speaker; it will be easier."

Ethan was still trying to process the fact that his parents were together, and that his mom was planning to stay at his dad's house for a few days. He stammered, "Uh, uh, okay, that's cool."

"Your old man is nothing if he isn't cool. Where is the stat book?" he asked.

"Oh, yeah, it's in my top drawer," Ethan said. Footsteps could be heard, as his dad walked across the home. The sound of a door opening, and a chilling realization hit Ethan. "Dad, stop! Stop, stop right now! Do not open my drawer!"

"Alright, alright. I didn't open it. What are you yelling about?" his father asked.

Coop's face brightened in curiosity. "What's in the drawer, why can't he open it?"

Ethan covered the phone. "Cooper, don't ask." Ethan held his own forehead. "Mom, take the phone and turn the speaker off."

Shuffling and beeps were heard, as she pressed wrong buttons before finding the right one. "Okay, I got it. What's up? What are you screaming about, sweetie?"

Coop leaned in to try and hear what was happening.

Ethan inhaled deeply. "Mom, listen to me, don't ask questions. Just do exactly as I say, please?"

There was no response from Ethan's mother.

"Mom, hello?"

"What?! I was waiting for you to tell me what to do. You said not to ask questions."

Ethan inhaled deeply again, visibly frustrated. "Go in my room and close the door. When you get inside, open my top drawer, and take out my stat book. Before you open it, I want you to please, please, for the love of all things…wait, do not let Dad follow you in."

Ethan heard the sound of a door opening and closing. He started again, "Okay, Mom, listen. I need you not to gawk, or stare, or comment. Just open the book to the clipped page, and quickly rip it out, tear it up, and put it in the garbage."

Ethan heard his drawer opening, and he winced while biting his lip.

The sound of the pages turning, and then, Ethan's mother shouted, "What the—Is this Coop Morgan's?"

Ethan slammed his head repeatedly on the table. "Mom, I said no questions, please don't stare, rip it up and give the book to Dad. Goodbye, forever." He hung up the phone and left his head on the table.

Coop tapped the table. "What was in the stat book?"

Ethan's face felt hot with embarrassment. "No, no, no, let's get back to the game."

Coop remembered where they left off, so he gave in quickly. "Okay, back to the game," he said. "It was my turn. What was in the stat book?"

"Okay, okay. I told you I draw…what I'm thinking about, and the last time I recorded stats was after seeing you in the ice bath."

"Wait…so you drew my….and your mom just…she saw it?!"

Ethan nodded slowly.

"How true to scale was it?"

After seeing and feeling Coop this morning, he could definitely say, it was nowhere near the size he drew, and the drawing didn't do justice to the real thing. But Ethan didn't say any of that. Instead, he reached across the table and playfully smacked him.

"What? I just wanted to know how good you draw," Coop said.

A new waitress interrupted their conversation, much to Ethan's delight. "Oh, thank you soooo much," Ethan said, as he smiled at her.

She placed their plates on the table, then turned and touched Coop's shoulder. "I know who you are. You're Coop Morgan, you're even hotter in person!"

Coop jerked his shoulder back from the contact and looked down at the table. Ethan could tell that Coop really hated when people touched him, he'd noticed it at practices and during games. Ethan knew he was the exception, of course. But as for strangers, Coop's reactions didn't hide the fact that he didn't like people touching him.

"Oof..." Ethan said, as he rolled his eyes. "Maybe you shouldn't touch people without permission," he mumbled.

Unfazed, the woman continued flirting with Coop. "Do you have a girlfriend? Can I give you my number?"

Coop looked up at Ethan, then over to her. "Sorry, I'm not interested," he said.

She looked at him in shock, but recovered quickly and turned to Ethan. "You're hot too, are you interested?"

Coop quickly placed his hand atop Ethan's. "Mine," he said, as looked up at her.

"Well, you can't blame me for trying. You guys enjoy your meals," she said, as she rushed back to the kitchen.

Ethan held Coop's hand, which lay on top of his, and looked at him. "Is that pretty common for you?"

"Is what pretty common?"

Ethan tilted his head and, using a high-pitched voice, imitated the waitress, "Oh wow, you're even hotter in person."

"I don't know…I guess, sometimes. Did that bother you? I think you're way more attractive than me if that makes you feel better."

"It's fine. I have to say, though, it was pretty hot when you grabbed my hand and said 'mine'." Ethan already felt that he belonged to Coop, hearing him say it made him feel warm, while the hint of possessiveness that he saw, caused a light throbbing below.

Coop pushed his plate across the table next to Ethan's. He walked around and sat on the small bench next to him. "I'd rather sit next to you. Can't have people thinking you're out here single."

Ethan leaned his head on his shoulder, and Coop responded with a nice, crisp smooch on Ethan's lips.

"I should have ordered pancakes. They smell amazing," Ethan said.

Coop cut into his pancakes and fed Ethan a few bites. "Let's trade," he said, seeing that Ethan was really enjoying the pancakes.

"No, no, I'll eat this," Ethan said, as he grabbed a strawberry with his fork and brought it to his mouth.

Coop intercepted the strawberry, using his teeth, and swapped plates with him. He grabbed the wrap and took a big bite. "It's fine, the wrap is great, but I'm keeping my sausage. You can have the pancakes." He poked the two sausages with his fork and put them on his plate.

A warm, salty breeze blew past the two as Coop gathered his hair in his right hand and fanned himself with the other. "Man, it's so hot, and I forgot to bring a hair tie."

"Are you upset?" Ethan asked.

Coop was confused, he had no idea why Ethan would ask him that. "Upset, what would I be upset about? I'm just hot." He rubbed his shoulder against Ethan's, and kissed him on the cheek.

"Alright, is it my turn to ask a question?" Ethan asked.

"Oooh, okay, yeah, hit me with it," Coop encouraged him.

"When did you first think you had feelings for me?"

"Well, I saw you the first day of the team meeting, and I just felt extremely interested, despite what was happening. I'm not usually drawn to other people, but I was immediately attracted to you. It was a really different feeling, though. At the same time, I was confused, probably just because of the timing. I thought you were the best-looking person I'd ever seen, and I really liked the sound of your voice. When I shook your hand, I didn't want to let go, there was like this force, keeping your hand in mine. That's definitely never happened before. After that, my heart just kind of warmed, as cheesy as that sounds, whenever I saw you. So, as soon as I saw you, is my final answer." He flashed him a wide smile.

Ethan blushed and kissed Coop quickly on the mouth.

Coop stared at him for a moment following the kiss. "Oh, I know. Why did you really come looking for me in the cool-down room? Were you gonna make a move?" He pumped his eyebrows at Ethan while grinning.

"Okay, well, you gave me a long answer, so let me do the same. I wanted to ask you out for drinks, like as soon as I met you."

"What? So, why didn't you?" Coop asked.

"Well, I kind of tried once, but you said you were busy. Then Kai gave me this whole speech and lessons on your hair and—"

"Kai did what?"

"He told me about your hairstyles and their different meanings. Like if your hair is in a topknot, you're mad, or if it's down, you're happy. If it's half up, there's a fifty-fifty chance of you being in a good mood."

Coop had never heard something so ridiculous. "So, when I mentioned not having a hair tie, that's why you asked if I was mad?"

Ethan winced. "Yes."

Coop sighed and held one finger up. "One second." He pulled his phone from his pocket and placed it on the table. He looked serious as he scrolled to a number, and pressed call on speaker mode.

"Hellllllllloooo, Coop," Kai answered.

"You're an idiot," Coop said, and hung up on him.

"Continue, please," he gestured to Ethan.

"Okay, so, he told me that if I asked you when your hair was in a top—"

A ringtone sounded as Kai called Coop's phone back.

"Hold that thought." Coop accepted the call on speaker without saying anything.

Kai's voice came loudly through the speaker. "Coop? Coop? What the hell, man? You call me an idiot and hang up on me? What did I do?"

"You are the king of all the idiots," Coop said to Kai, then hung up on him again.

"Do you really want me to continue? He's probably going to call back," Ethan said.

Coop nodded.

"Anyway, whenever I wanted to, your hair was in a topknot, so I didn't. The day of the ice bath, which was also the day that I saw you, well, air grinding—"

"Pretending it was you," he interrupted with a wink.

"Right," Ethan started again, "The day that you were, doing that, your hair was down, and I was going to ask you, but then you came over after—"

"Air grinding for you," Coop interjected.

Ethan spoke quickly, "Aaah, okay, okay, gosh, Cooper, you danced, you made me"—he gestured in between his legs—"you know…I got in the shower, and after I cooled off and found you, your damn hair was in a top knot again. Then you stood up naked, on purpose, asked me if I wanted you, and I don't even know, like, whispered in my ear. All while I had only a tiny white towel wrapped around myself. It happened again"—he gestured to his lower half—"and then you left. The End." Ethan quickly covered his mouth.

Coop had a habit of picking out one point in a conversation and coming back for it. It was normally the thing that whoever he was talking with cared the least about that he felt the need to clarify, but with Ethan he wanted to be sure to cover everything that bothered him.

"Ethan, in all seriousness, you shouldn't listen to Kai because, as I said, he's an idiot. I'm really sorry that you felt like you couldn't talk to me, though. That part makes me sad. I wouldn't have turned you away. That much I can tell you for certain. But, also, I mean, if you were turned on, you should've just acted on it. We were alone, I would've let you…. We could've felt the goosebumps sooner." He put his hand on Ethan's thigh and squeezed it.

Ethan covered his smile with his hand, looking to the side, seeming mildly embarrassed. Coop gave him a quick kiss on the cheek and whispered in his ear, "Let's get out of here."

Coop quickly paid for their breakfast, and they left holding hands.

Chapter 16
We're Together Now

Ethan's phone rang as they sat in the car. He turned the screen toward Coop. "It's Kai. He has literally never called me. Should I answer it?"

Coop shook his head no, and Ethan declined the call.

"Hey, I just realized I didn't ask you something important, Ethan."

"What is it?"

Coop looked at him softly. "Are you okay with people knowing that we're a couple?"

A couple, Ethan thought, his heart instantly warmed. "Well, of course, but are you okay with it? I feel like there's a lot of pressure on you. At least, that's how it seems. I don't want to add to it." He laid his head on Coop's shoulder.

Coop kissed the top of his head. "How would that add to it? If anything, the pressure of lying or hiding this would be too much. I only asked because I want to be considerate of your feelings. I'm about to do something that I can't take back. So, before I do, I just want to be sure that you want to be mine."

Ethan nodded, leaned in, and kissed him softly. "I already am yours."

Coop rubbed his finger across Ethan's soft lips and looked deep into his eyes. "How can we feel this way? How does this feel so right?" Coop asked.

"I guess it's no different than believing in love at first sight or being soul mates. I feel like, somehow, I belonged beside you a long time ago. Now that I'm here, I feel like I need to catch up on everything I missed and protect you from anything that comes our way."

Coop looked at him with lovestruck eyes and replied, "I'll protect you too." He leaned in and rubbed his hand through Ethan's soft shaggy hair, as Ethan peppered his face with soft little kisses.

Ethan's phone rang again, it was Kai calling for the second time.

Coop shook his head no, and Ethan declined the call again.

"I feel bad. Cooper, what if something's wrong? Like I said, he never calls me."

Coop pressed the speaker call button on his steering wheel, "Call The Idiot," he said.

Ethan's jaw dropped open. "Do you really have him in your contacts as The Idiot?"

"See for yourself." Coop motioned to the dashboard. The screen flashed *Calling The Idiot* along with Kai's phone number.

Kai answered, "Hey, Coop, what's up? Are you still mad at me for…I don't know, whatever I did?"

Coop raised his eyebrows at Ethan. "Ready?" he whispered and pointed to him.

Ethan, in tacit understanding, nodded. "Hi, Kai, It's Ethan."

Kai must have done a double take at his phone, as he stammered in reply, "E-E—hey, Ethan, what, uh, why are you calling from Coop's phone?"

Ethan held a finger up to Coop, telling him to be quiet. "Well, I saw that you called me, so I'm calling you back."

"Well, yeah, uh, your car is here," Kai said. "I wanted to see if everything was okay. Why are you with Coop?"

It was getting harder for Coop to remain quiet, so Ethan covered his mouth.

"Well, um, Cooper brought me home last night," Ethan said.

"Cooper? Who the hell is Cooper? You can't call him that! He'll flip out on you!" Kai warned Ethan.

Coop moved Ethan's hand off his mouth and spoke to Kai, "Hey, idiot, he can call me Cooper, you can't."

Kai remained silent for several moments, he was definitely in shock. He'd been Coop's friend for a long time, and he'd never heard anyone call him Cooper before. Now, Coop was even *giving* Ethan permission to say it. Kai had to be confused.

"Kai?" Ethan said.

"Uh yeah, gimme a sec, I'm just trying to work this out in my head."

"Don't hurt yourself, Kai," Coop joked.

Coop and Ethan were quite proud of themselves. The little jerks thought that Kai's reaction was hilarious. It was exactly what they wanted. The two realized at that moment that teasing their friends was something they both had in common.

After a moment, Kai started again, "So, last night, Wendy told me she saw you two leave together. I thought she was just starting trouble, like always, but I guess she wasn't."

"Who is Wendy?" Ethan asked.

Kai and Coop answered at the same time, "The worst."

Coop spoke loudly, "Listen, *we* are going back to my place, *we* just had breakfast, and you called him twice. *We* will come to get his car in a bit, after *we* go do a few other things."

"That's a lot of 'we's' I'm hearing, and since when do you go out for breakfast anywhere but here?" Kai asked. "You're gonna break my mom's heart, and mine too, from the sound of it," he joked.

"I'm glad you picked up on what I was saying. You're such a smart little idiot," Coop teased him.

"Why thank you," Kai said. He paused for a moment, then asked, "Ethan, did you really just call him Cooper screwing around, or did he really say you could?"

"He told me I can call him Cooper."

"Woooooow, just wow," Kai said. "I never thought I'd see the day. Well, congrats. Let me know when you guys are coming to get the car. I'll be here most of the day. The team left this place a mess last night and I'm still finding stuff in crazy places."

The call ended, and the two men looked at each other and smiled.

"People really don't call you Cooper, huh?"

Coop shook his head. "Never. You are the first."

Ethan leaned in front of Coops face. "I like that," he said, then parted Coop's lips with his own and softly swirled his tongue inside.

Coop pulled back momentarily. "Me too," he said, then gently finished the kiss.

"Where next?" Coop asked, as they finally pulled out of Fregi's parking lot.

"Do you think I need to get my car, or is it okay to leave it a bit longer?"

Coop shook his head. "It's fine, he was just being nice and checking in on you. We can grab it on the way back to my place, or we can get it later, whichever you want."

Ethan smiled. "I don't have a preference, driver's choice." *He's so much sweeter than any guy I've ever known. All morning he's been asking me what I want at every turn, just trying to make sure I'm comfortable. This feels so right…*

Coop squeezed Ethan's hand. "I need to grab some stuff from the store, if you're going to hang with me for the rest of the day. Is that okay?"

Ethan nodded, and Coop soon pulled into the department store parking lot. The two walked hand in hand into the large store, with

Coop grabbing a variety of things. He pulled Ethan around while holding a basket that was quickly filled to the top.

"What do you need scissors for?" Ethan asked.

"You'll see," Coop said, grinning.

"Chicken, spinach, sundried tomatoes." Coop called out ingredients as he grabbed them from the shelves.

After grabbing everything from the food section, they walked down the personal product aisle. Ethan, knowing full well what he wanted, and still a bit regretful that they couldn't do it this morning, reached forward, and grabbed a box of condoms and lube, then quickly placed them in Coop's handcart.

Ethan's bravery was commendable. As a virgin, he should've been far more afraid of what was to come than he was, especially given Coop's size. Those goosebumps he was looking forward to, would not be as easy to come by as the ones he felt this morning.

Coop was thrilled that Ethan took the initiative to grab the items. "Wow, that was the greatest thing ever. Here I thought I was going to have to explain that I wasn't being a pervert but prepping ahead. And you went and grabbed that stuff without any discussion whatsoever."

Ethan looked at him confused, as he dropped one eyebrow. "Cooper, after what we did this morning, what would make you think we needed to discuss anything further? It would only make sense to be prepped for whenever that happens. Also, just for the record, I think you are more of a tease than a pervert."

"You keep calling me a tease." Coop placed the overflowing basket on the floor and wrapped his arms around Ethan's waist. He spoke seductively, in a voice barely above a whisper into Ethan's ear, "You must have really liked what happened when you said that this morning." He lightly licked Ethan's earlobe.

"I think it was pretty obvious that I enjoyed it, *Cooper*." Ethan kissed his cheek and wiggled out of his grip. "Enough now, we're in a store."

After checking out, Coop tossed the two insulated bags he was carrying, as well as the one that Ethan had, into the trunk.

Chapter 17
Drunk People Can't Whisper

"Alright, let's head back to my place. The insulated bags will keep the cold stuff safe for at least a few hours, but better to be safe than sorry." Coop checked the rearview mirror, as he backed out of the parking lot. "You feel like maybe going for a swim? I don't know about you, but I'm still kinda hot."

Ethan nodded slowly. "That's why you bought another pair of swim shorts! Why didn't you tell me? I could've just grabbed mine from my—" This morning's incident with his mother flashed in Ethan's mind. *Never mind, I can't bring him over there right now. My mom will still have the picture fresh in her mind.* He cringed at the thought. "Actually, that's a good call. I don't want to go there right now."

"Yeah, honestly, I'd feel a bit embarrassed to meet your mom right now. I figured you'd insist on buying your own if I said they were for you, so I just grabbed them."

Ethan squished up his nose and pinched Coop's cheek. "Thank you."

As they approached the Morgan Estate entrance, a single car followed close behind, honking its horn loudly. "Oh no, anything but this," Coop said.

Ethan turned and looked behind them, as the gate slowly opened. "Is that your dad? Who is that with him?"

"Yes, yes, it is, unfortunately…my dad and Levi."

"Why is that unfortunate?" Ethan asked. He was a big fan of Mr. Morgan and Levi's early baseball days. He was getting pretty excited that he was going to meet them. He'd heard his father talk about both of them plenty of times, so he knew they were good people. He hadn't heard that they were together, but knew that they used to all be very good friends. His dad was a free talker, and he always said how he felt. If either were truly terrible, Ethan would've known it.

Coop slowly shook his head. "You'll see." The two luxury cars pulled into the main estate driveway, side by side. "Ethan let's run away. Let's just leave. Please…this is going to be hideous." Coop hung his head on Ethan's shoulder.

Mr. Morgan, who looked like a model, fresh from a photo shoot, tapped on the window. He was dressed in a pair of tight-fitting, plaid, designer pants and a black, short-sleeved, button-down shirt, which was tucked in. From behind him, Levi, wearing an equally stylish ensemble, approached, staring into the car.

"Go away," Coop said, as he pinned his face against the steering wheel, eyes closed.

"Well, it didn't work, your dad's still there." Ethan waved at him through the window and smiled.

Mr. Morgan stuck his face against Coop's window in an extreme moment of silliness. Coop looked up to see his father's face squished against the glass. "Dad! Get your face off the window!" Coop turned toward Ethan. "Okay, we have to get out now. I'm going to just ask for forgiveness for whatever happens. He's obviously in an extra crazy mood."

They both stepped out of the car.

"*My son,*" Mr. Morgan said dramatically, as he pulled Coop into a bear hug.

"Are you drunk?" Coop asked. "It's like noon. Get off me!" Coop pushed out of his father's grasp, as Ethan approached cautiously from the other side.

Levi stood beside Mr. Morgan and draped his arm around his neck. "Hi, Coop…and Ethan Prescott, if I'm not mistaken," he said, smiling brightly.

Coop introduced them in a flat voice, "Dad, Levi, this is Ethan. Ethan this is my dad and Levi." He took Ethan's hand and held it tightly, in a move that Mr. Morgan and Levi both smiled at.

Ethan reached his right hand out to shake their hands, and Coop pulled him back while wrapping his arms around him. "No, no, these are two drunk men, we don't go near them," he joked.

Mr. Morgan and Levi both chuckled and shook the hand that he successfully wiggled out of Coop's grip. "It's so nice to meet you both," Ethan said.

They both replied at the same time, "Likewise," and shot him bright smiles.

Ethan was starstruck. "I've watched a ton of footage of the both of you from high school. Your precision pickoffs are some of the best I've ever seen, Mr. Morgan." He turned to Levi, "And your direct throws from the outfield still give me chills, Mr. Everton."

"Oh, what a charmer this kid is!" Levi said.

"Nothing like his dad," Mr. Morgan added.

Coop pulled Ethan by the hand and brought him around to the trunk, while waving. "Okay, bye Dad and Levi, see ya later." He grabbed the bags out of the trunk and closed it.

Mr. Morgan's mouth dropped open, and Levi laughed while hunched over. "Tommy, he hates us, look he's pulling Ethan around like a puppy!"

Ethan tilted his head at Coop and whimpered, while making puppy noises.

Levi was in stitches. Mr. Morgan called to Coop, "Hey, we aren't done, come around back. Let's have a drink out by the bar."

Coop shook his head. "No. I don't want to do that. I want to go for a swim. You guys already had drinks. Come on, go away," he pleaded.

"Oooh, Tommy, he even pouts just like you. Look at his frown! Let's leave them to have their fun," Levi said. He put his chin on Mr. Morgan's shoulder.

"Not happening," Mr. Morgan replied, through a smile.

Ethan pinched Coop's chin playfully, as Coop hung his head in defeat. "Aww, come on, don't pout. It will be fine. How bad could it be?" Ethan asked.

Levi and Mr. Morgan led the way, while Coop and Ethan followed from a distance. Levi whispered to Mr. Morgan, "Coop held his hand, so are they dating? Why didn't you tell me this?" He nudged him while grinning.

"I didn't know. I had no idea. He's a good-looking guy, though, my boy has good taste."

"Coop is good-looking too; they look like a pair of celebrities."

Coop shook his head, while he walked hand in hand with Ethan. He shouted, "Hey! We can hear you. I know you think you're whispering, but you actually aren't."

Ethan felt a tad embarrassed, but also flattered that two people he admired thought that he and Coop looked like celebrities. Ethan never paid much attention to people's compliments. Much like Coop, he received them often, but hearing it from these two was almost validation that he was good looking enough to stand next to Coop, which was something he'd wondered about before.

"Oops, sorry," Levi said. He elbowed Mr. Morgan and tried to whisper again, "Why didn't you tell me I was being too loud?"

Coop yelled, "What is wrong with you two? Drunk people can't whisper, so please stop trying!" He shook his head in disbelief at the current situation.

The four approached opposite sides of the long, white granite-topped bar. Coop placed his bags on the couch, which faced the stone fireplace, then led Ethan back to the comfortable, padded, black bar stools. Ethan and Coop sat down first and watched as Mr. Morgan and Levi busied themselves.

"This is amazing," Ethan said, as he looked around the lavish outdoor area.

"Yeah, it would be more amazing if they would leave, though," Coop whispered.

"We're not leaving!" Mr. Morgan yelled.

"Does he think he's whispering?" Levi sassed.

Ethan laughed. "It's like I'm watching a TV show right now. You guys are so funny together," he said.

Mr. Morgan walked over to the attached outdoor kitchen and grabbed four beers from the fridge, as Levi took out snacks from the cabinet beside it. What started with the two casually walking back, turned into a speed-walking race to see who could reach the bar first. "Oh no you don't, Tommy!" Levi pushed in front of Mr. Morgan.

Mr. Morgan moved faster. Holding two glass bottles high in each hand, he sped past Levi.

"Ha! I win!" Mr. Morgan said, as he hopped onto his seat. He slid two bottles to Ethan and Coop.

Levi sat beside him, refusing to admit defeat. "You didn't win, you had glass, so I purposely let you get here first."

Coop opened Ethan's beer, then his own. The two clinked their bottles together and smiled, each taking a sip. Levi popped open a bag of chips and began to munch.

"So, what did you guys do today?" Mr. Morgan asked, as he sipped his beer.

Ethan noticed Coop's eyes widen. He decided to jump in since it seemed like Coop froze at his father's question.

"Cooper took me to a beachside café."

Mr. Morgan spit his beer to the right of the bar, and Levi choked on a chip.

Coop smiled and pinched Ethan's cheek, ignoring their reactions.

"Excuse me," Mr. Morgan said, as he patted Levi on the back, "did you just call him Cooper?"

"He said I could," Ethan replied, smiling at Coop.

"Well, now…you should know he didn't even let his mother, or I, ever call him Cooper. So, he must really like you."

Coop stared at Ethan. "I do really like him," he said, as he brought Ethan's hand to his mouth and kissed it.

Levi cleared his throat. "Ahem, well, I have never seen Coop blush in the eighteen years I've known him, and I've never heard him let anyone call him Cooper. Consider me equally in shock. I'm also somewhat confused, though, how long have you two been dating?"

Coop answered with stars in his eyes, "Since this morning."

Mr. Morgan looked lovingly at Levi. "Well…when you know, you know."

"Oh, Tommy, you're such a romantic," Levi said, as he nuzzled his shoulder.

Ethan felt warm and tingly all over as he watched the two.

Coop took another sip of his beer and stood up. "Alright guys, this was nice. We're gonna go. We want to try and get a swim in, and we still have to pick up his car from Tagaloa's at some point."

Ethan stood as Coop reached over and held his hand.

Mr. Morgan called out, "Wait, you're already leaving? What about dinner later tonight? We could fire up the grill or go out if you guys want."

Coop shook his head, as he grabbed the bags off the couch and headed toward his side of the estate. "No thanks, I have something else in mind."

"Oooh…mysterious," Levi said.

"It was really nice meeting you, thank you for the warm welcome!" Ethan shouted, as he was pulled away.

As they entered the foyer, Coop led them on a different path than the one they'd taken in the morning. "Where are we going?" Ethan asked, tugging on Coop's hand. "Is this the way to your room?"

Coop apologized and kissed Ethan's hand. "I'm sorry, I forgot you aren't familiar with the layout. We have to put this chicken and the other cold stuff in my kitchen. Thankfully, we had the insulated bags, I didn't think we'd ever get away from those two."

Ethan looked around as they entered a large open kitchen. It was beautifully designed and featured white cabinets, black granite countertops, and high-end black stainless-steel appliances.

Coop quickly placed the food items into the fridge and returned to Ethan's side.

"It was really nice meeting your dad and Levi. They're both so funny, and seem really happy together," Ethan said.

"Yeah, it's still kind of weird, but it's good. I mean it's new, but I guess also not new for them."

Ethan looked at him confused. "I don't know what happened with them. I heard my dad yelling about them being stubborn a bunch of times, but I never really asked about what happened."

"Well, it's a long story," Coop said. He pulled Ethan's hand, leading him toward the stairs. As the two walked up, he summarized everything that happened between his father and Levi, and Ethan cupped his hands over his mouth in disbelief.

After they walked inside his room, Coop placed the remaining bag from the store on his desk and sat on the edge of the bed. He patted his lap, signaling Ethan to sit on it. Ethan sat down and leaned back into

Coop's warm embrace, as Coop tilted his head and kissed both of his cheeks.

"That's really so tragic," Ethan said.

"Yeah, it is but see the thing for me is, like, a lot of people were hurt over Levi just being afraid. Luke's mom found out about the way Levi felt in a really bad way. She left, like, a few days after he was born. My mom stepped in and became a mom to Luke in her place. She felt responsible in some way. I don't know. Then she passed away from cancer when I was ten, and it was really tough. My dad and Levi just got back together after I found my mom's diary. They hadn't spoken in eighteen years. I mean Levi never came to any of our birthday parties, and if he came to games, he stayed far away from my dad. He was never mean to me, but he wasn't overly nice either. I honestly never knew why, I just figured he didn't like me."

"Who could not like you?" Ethan asked, as he turned and kissed Coop on the cheek. "You're perfect. You probably reminded him of your dad, if I had to guess. He said earlier that you looked just like him."

Coop smiled, eyes a little downcast. "Yeah, actually that's what he told me when he apologized. I feel like my mom also deserved an apology, though, and probably Luke's mom did, too."

Ethan studied his face. He really wanted to understand how he ended up staying with Luke for so long, or how they were even together to begin with. Their personalities were so different. "So, then you and Luke were basically raised together? You've always been in each other's lives?"

"We were, but whatever I felt for him in all that time doesn't compare to what I feel for you already." He squeezed Ethan tight as he kissed him on the cheek.

After a few moments of silence, Ethan said, "Wow. I think that makes perfect sense now. So, when you broke up it wasn't because one of you did something wrong to the other?"

Coop leaned his head back and sighed. "Well, honestly, I kept some things from him about this creepy scout who was harassing me and some other stuff, but, no, it wasn't truly because of that. We grew apart long before then. The spark was gone, or maybe it wasn't really ever there."

"Honestly, I asked my dad to try and help fill me in on you two earlier in the week, but he didn't know much. Did you break up right around the time that I got here?"

"Well, yeah, Luke met with you and your dad, and that same night we broke up. The night before I met you."

Ethan inhaled deeply as Coop rubbed his arms and shoulders from behind. "Wait, so, when that girl was trying to put her mouth on yours that night in the parking lot, what was that about? I remember getting there early and seeing it. It was definitely a bizarre sight. I almost jumped out of my car and pulled her off you. It made me really uncomfortable."

Coop shook his head. "Not my finest moment there. I can't believe you saw that."

Ethan shuddered. "I smelled it too, my window was down, and I could smell her perfume all the way in my car. It was awful."

"Well, the scout had all these old pictures of Luke and me. He tried to proposition me and I—"

"*What?* He tried to proposition you? For what? Sex?"

Coop nodded.

"Cooper, this is a crazy story you are telling me right now. How is this real?"

"I wish it weren't. Anyway, instead of just being honest, I tried to hide the pictures, and Wendy, who is the worst, found them. She told me she'd post them on social media if I didn't let her try to excite me. She was trying to kiss me, but I just couldn't let her. It was so gross."

"What the f—" Ethan held the sides of his head in disbelief. "Who would even...I, uh...okay, I get it now. Well, she failed miserably because I saw the whole thing. She forced her mouth on yours. That pisses me off."

Ethan turned around and licked Coop's mouth straight across his lips, as he pushed him on the bed and sat on top of him. Coop grabbed his ass and squeezed it tight.

"Cooper, I hate that those things happened to you, and I wasn't there. I know that sounds stupid, but I just feel upset thinking about it." Ethan pouted.

Coop looked up at him. "Don't feel bad. It's all okay. I have you now, and you're the only one I need."

Ethan leaned down and kissed him. As Coop pulled Ethan's ass down tight, Ethan's ringtone sounded. The two broke apart from the kiss. Coop held firm to Ethan's ass and refused to let go. Ethan sat up and pulled his phone out of his pocket, which was quite difficult given their position. "Hey, Kai, what's up?" Ethan asked.

Coop shook his head at him and reached for the phone, and Ethan passed it over. "Kai, what are you calling him for? You know we're together now, so what do you need?"

"*Together?* Like *dating?* Kidding, I'm kidding. Yes sir, I understood that from our conversation earlier. I was just calling to see if you guys were going to pick his Jeep up, or not. I'm only going to be here until around six. It's Saturday night, so we could all hang after if you want."

"Uhhhh, hold please," Coop said, as he put the phone on mute. "I have something I want you to do which will take a bit of time, then do you want to go get your car, so he leaves us alone? If we wait until later when he's about to leave work, he's gonna try to stay with us all night and I don't want that. I want goosebumps."

"Me too," Ethan said. "Goosebumps are a must tonight. So, I'd rather just be alone with you."

"Alright, then let's just go grab it now," Coop said.

Ethan climbed off Coop and walked over to the doorway.

"Kai, we'll be there in like an hour, hour and a half, or two hours to get his car… I don't know, soon. No, we're not hanging out after. Love you, bye." Coop ended the call before Kai could respond.

Kai Tagaloa stood in silence behind the bar of his parents' restaurant, staring at his phone. *Did he just say he loved me? When has he ever said that, even as a joke? He sounded really happy,* Kai thought, as he leaned over the bar.

"Ouch!" he screamed as his mother towel smacked him on his backside.

"What are you daydreaming about?" she asked. "Finish cleaning, you're not leaving until it's done." She picked at his thick, black curly hair that hung past his waist. "You need a trim; your ends are split."

Kai smiled and turned to look at her, as she released the curls. "Yeah, it's been a minute."

Kai's mother looked at her son's puzzled face and placed the towel she was holding on the counter. A few customers walked in, and she greeted them. "Talofa!" she said, smiling as the group seated themselves. "What's got your head in the clouds?" she asked, as she looked at Kai.

He shook his head and resumed cleaning. "It's nothing, Mom, Coop just told me he loved me."

She pulled her face back and looked at him. "When has Coop ever been so affectionate?"

He shook his head, as he pulled a piece of confetti off one of the walls. "Never," he replied.

Chapter 18
It Has To Be You

Ethan stood by the door ready to leave, as Coop stood up from the bed. "That was nice," he said smiling, looking over his shoulder at Coop.

"Eh, I was just joking with him. Sometimes I'm probably a little too mean to him." He shrugged his shoulders and gave Ethan a quick kiss. "Okay, now…" He turned Ethan's body toward the desk and stood in front of him. "Thank you for listening to everything I just told you before he called. That was probably uncomfortable for you, judging by the way you tried to jump me." Coop smiled as he walked backward, pulling Ethan toward the black desk.

Ethan looked down at the floor. "I was maybe a little jealous," he said.

Coop pulled him tight into an embrace. "Please trust me when I say this, you have nothing to be jealous of, Ethan." He held Ethan's face and looked into his big brown eyes, then leaned in and pressed their lips together gently while allowing his tongue to softly enter for a few momentary swirls.

He tried to pull back as Ethan deepened the kiss, bringing more heat than Coop could allow in the moment. He was torn between loving the taste and feel of Ethan's mouth and trying to behave himself. "Mmm, no, mmm, no," he moaned, and broke apart from the kiss.

As Coop pulled back, Ethan whined through half-lidded eyes, "Cooper, why not? Give me your mouth back…"

Coop squatted down and addressed Ethan's crotch. "Hey, listen, I need the guy up there to do something else for me right now. I'll give you attention later, but for now, I need you to shush." He popped back up to Ethan, who was holding his mouth in embarrassment. Coop adjusted his own pants.

He reached over and fished inside the bag from the store, quickly pulled out the scissors, and sat on his desk chair in front of Ethan. "Will you cut it for me?" he asked, holding the scissors up.

"Cut what…your hair?!"

"Yeah. My hair. Cut it."

"Cooper, what are you talking about? Why do you want me to cut it?"

Coop looked up at him with bright eyes. "I'm ready for something new, and besides, I don't want you to ever feel like you can't talk to me, or do anything, because you're trying to guess my mood based on my hair. You're too important to me. It's embarrassing that those things even happened. We could have been together sooner if it weren't for that."

Ethan leaned over and kissed him lightly on the lips, then stood back up. "It's okay, it's really not worth doing something so drastic."

Coop's eyes were resolute as he looked up at Ethan. "Do it, please. I really want you to," he urged him.

Ethan stood silent for a few moments as he studied Coop's face. He began pulling at sections of his hair, moving it in different ways. "Cooper, listen, I don't know if I can do it. Don't you have like a hairstylist or someone that normally cuts it for you?"

Coop shook his head. "Nope, I've always trimmed it myself."

Ethan was stunned, eyes wide. He held up three fingers to Coop. "Three things: First, I don't think I should be the first one ever to cut your hair, I'm definitely not qualified. Second, there is a big difference between a trim and a cut. And, lastly, what if I mess it up?"

"You won't mess it up, and if you do, it grows really fast. It would only take like four months for it to get this long again, seriously. There's a mirror right there, we can both watch as you do it, it will be like we're doing it together. I don't want anyone else to do this. It has to be you."

Ethan sighed in resignation and rubbed Coop's head. "Okay, okay, I'll try. But if I mess it up, it's not my fault." Ethan spun Coop's chair so that his body faced the oversized mirror that hung above his desk and stood behind him. "Where are the towels? I need to cover your shoulders with something."

Coop pointed to the bathroom. "There is a linen closet in there, just grab out whatever you need. I have a hair kit that I use for trims under the sink, too. I don't know if you'll need anything from that."

Ethan placed the scissors on Coop's desk and walked into the bathroom. *Is he crazy? Letting me cut his hair. God, what if I screw it up? He's so cute, it wouldn't matter looks-wise, but I don't want to make him mad if I don't do it right,* he thought, as he grabbed a towel and the hair kit.

Ethan appeared with the supplies in hand and covered Coop's shoulders with a towel. He opened the blue box and pulled a few clips out of the hair kit. He moved carefully and quickly while placing various clips in Coop's hair. "Alright, I'm ready, are you ready?" he asked Coop.

"Do it, but first..." Coop puckered his lips and tilted his head up.

Ethan leaned in for a quick kiss. He stood up straight and exhaled. "Alright, here I go."

The sound was sharp and quick from the scissors. Snip, Snip, snip. Huge locks of black wavy hair fell, piece after piece, for what felt like an hour, until the floor and Coop's shoulders were covered with it.

Coop smiled brightly in the mirror, as Ethan asked him, "Is it okay? Did I mess it up?"

His hairstyle was now similar to Ethan's, except Coop's hair was a bit thicker and black. He really liked his new, short shaggy mane. "Wow! Oh wow!" he said. He stood and leaned closer to the mirror, the towel on his shoulder fell, along with the hair on it. "It looks great! It feels so light," he leaned his head left and right, as he ran his fingers through it while staring at his own reflection.

Ethan asked him from his side in the mirror, "Do you really like it?"

"I love it. Thank you. You did so good."

Ethan breathed a huge sigh of relief as the two stared at one another in the mirror.

Coop pulled Ethan by the waist. "Hey, come put your face next to mine for a sec." Ethan leaned in and pressed his cheek next to Coop's while they both looked into the mirror. "Damn, we are good looking. I guess we do look like a couple of celebrities. You're still better looking, though."

They quickly cleaned up the piles of hair and straightened up the desk area. Coop continued glancing at himself in the mirror each time he walked by it. "Alright, let's go get your car," Coop said as he stood in the doorway, reaching out for Ethan's hand.

The two left the room and walked quickly down the stairs, toward the front door. "Why are you pulling me so fast?" Ethan asked, as the two were almost running.

"I don't want to run into them again and my car is on my dad's side of the estate, because of earlier. Come on, you're fast, let's go."

They ran the rest of the way to the car. As soon as they sat inside the car, Coop's dad and Levi could be seen rounding the corner, hand in hand. "Oh no, gotta go," Coop said, pressing the start button and quickly pulling out of the estate.

"Phew that was close, if we didn't run, they would've stopped us. My dad's probably not going to recognize me now," he joked.

"Your dad is probably gonna be pretty shocked. I can also imagine Levi fainting when he sees it, for some reason," Ethan said.

"He probably will." Coop chuckled, keeping his eyes on the road.

Chapter 19
Ethan The Wizard

There were a few cars in the parking lot of Tagaloa's, aside from Ethan's lifted white Jeep. Coop pulled into the spot beside it. "Those are big tires," Coop said, as they both got out and walked over to it.

"Yeah, they cost almost as much as the Jeep itself." Ethan did a quick scan of the outside checking for any damage, then opened the passenger door for Coop, who climbed in.

Coop sat in the passenger seat, while Ethan walked around the car, then joined him from the driver's seat. Coop noticed a very large book peeking out from beneath his seat. Before he could grab it, Ethan quickly placed a hand on it. "Oops, sorry. Let me move that," he said, picking the book up.

Coop was more than curious, he needed to know what was inside the book, given how quick Ethan was to move it.

"What is thiiiiiis?" Coop asked excitedly, playfully tugging at the book.

Ethan's face was flushed in embarrassment. "It's my art book, I left it in here after drawing the other day."

Coop smirked at him. "An art book? Oh…I get it, so you don't normally draw pictures of my naked body in your stat book?"

Ethan let go of the book, and Coop's head bounced back a smidge.

"I'm kidding, I'm kidding. Can I look inside, though?" Coop asked.

"Well, I've never let anyone else see it…but of course you can." Ethan bit his lip, nervously watching as Coop began thumbing through the pages.

Coop was silent, completely mesmerized while carefully examining each drawing. The thought and precision of someone with an innate artistic ability shined on every page. Coop continued turning the pages until he reached the drawings in the middle of the book, which showed Ethan's most recent work. "So, at this point, you were definitely thinking about me, and it looks like you were really frustrated, if I can read the meaning of these right here." He held the book open toward Ethan's gaze. A handsomely drawn Coop was shown frustrated, standing at home plate, while Ethan was drawn with a deep frown, looking at him in between second and third base.

Ethan nodded slowly. "Well, yeah, I told you I was. I wanted so badly to help you. I hated seeing how frustrated you were. I just kept feeling like I could fix it, but…"

Coop flipped to the next page and closed his eyes upon seeing the picture. "Ah, yes, the topknot makes an appearance." He sighed, looking at Ethan.

Ethan rubbed Coop's hair softly. "Okay, okay, let's go. You've looked at them all."

A piece of paper fell as Coop closed the book: *Hip placement, back leg, right elbow, unfocused, ask if he practices HX4, if so, he needs to work on heart, then home. He's perfectly built and extremely hot.* Coop made an exaggerated shocked face, as he finished reading it, while Ethan knocked his head against the driver's side window in embarrassment. "You thought I was hot?" Coop asked. He fluttered his lashes, while waving the small note.

Ethan lifted his head, while slowly dragging his right hand down his own face. "Will my humiliation never end today?" he asked aloud, looking at the sky.

"No, no humiliation," Coop said. "Thank you for letting me look at your work. It's amazing, you really are talented. Everything was so realistic. I've never felt anything looking at art before, but your drawings are just alive somehow."

Ethan turned his head and looked over at him. "Thank you. That may be the best compliment I've ever received about my art. My mom loves it too, she's always trying to grab whatever I'm working on."

Coop sat stone-faced at that comment.

"What? What's wrong?" Ethan asked while placing a hand on Coop's leg.

"Well…now that I've seen your art, I'm curious about how well you drew my…well, you know. On top of that, your phrasing made me really uncomfortable. You said your mom always tries to grab whatever you're working on." Coop shuddered, and Ethan playfully smacked him on his shoulder with the front and back of his hand. "Alright, alright, I'm sorry. I was just kidding. Let's just say hi to Kai really quick. Are you still up for a swim after?" Coop asked.

"Yeah, that sounds good," Ethan replied. They hopped out of the car and walked toward the door. "Kai is probably gonna flip when he sees your hair." Ethan ran his fingers through it.

"Well, let's give him something else to focus on then." He hoisted Ethan over his shoulder like a sack of potatoes and opened the door.

"Cooper, listen to me, put me down, come on," he begged through giggles. Coop playfully smacked Ethan's ass, as he walked toward the bar.

Mrs. Tagaloa grabbed a plate from the serving window. "Talo…" She froze in her usual greeting upon seeing a short-haired Coop, with a body slung over his shoulder.

Kai looked up while he filled a glass of beer for a customer. His mouth dropped at the sight, and the beer overflowed, as he held the switch open, completely stunned at what stood before him.

"Hi, Kai," Coop said, nonchalantly. Ethan laid upon his shoulder, waving behind it, to people who were whispering about Coop's hair, and the two of them.

Kai stood silent, mouth still open. Beer covered his arm, which he still had yet to move.

Coop, feigning confusion, tilted his head at him. "Oh, I know, you think it's rude that Ethan didn't say hi." He turned around so that Ethan faced the bar. "Ethan, say hi to Kai, he thinks you're being rude. That's why he's standing there like an idiot." He smiled at the crowd that now faced him.

Ethan looked up. "Hi, Kai. Cooper, please put me down now," he requested, while giggling.

Coop patted his ass firmly, twice. "Oh, I'm sorry, baby, you want to get down?" He gently placed Ethan on his feet. Ethan's face was red, and he stumbled just a bit while Coop held his shoulders upright. "Whoops, you're alright. I got you," he said, as he held him and helped him onto a stool. Coop scooted a barstool close to Ethan and hopped on it.

Kai stood silent.

Mrs. Tagaloa, who was no less stunned on her part, snapped out of it and greeted them, "Talofa! Nice hair, Coop." She walked from behind the bar and carried the food to a table behind them.

"Thank you, Mrs. T," Coop said.

"See, she said it looks nice, you did a good job," Coop praised Ethan, and put his arm around him.

Kai was still frozen. His mouth still hung open.

Coop waved his right hand in front of Kai's face. "Hello, Kai, helloooo, come back to me, buddy," he said, attempting to pull him from his trance.

Kai quickly shook his head and wiped his hands and arms on a towel. "Hang on," he finally said. He grabbed an empty beer glass and filled it properly. "Yo, sorry this took so long," he apologized while delivering the beer to a customer at the far end of the bar. His face was still stunned as he returned to Coop and Ethan.

"What the hell am I looking at right now, what happened to your hair? Did I hear you tell him he did a good job cutting it? Where do I even start? Is your name Coop? Are you Coop Morgan, my best friend?" Kai questioned him quickly.

Ethan laid his head on the bar and turned to face Coop, who was ignoring Kai's inane questioning. "I guess your distraction didn't work, Cooper."

"Distraction? What distraction?" Kai asked. "Oh, you mean him carrying you in here while smacking your ass? No, that didn't work. It was funny, but it didn't work."

Coop patted Ethan's head, as he sat up straight. "Who said you were my best friend?" Coop asked Kai, in a serious tone.

Kai whacked a towel at him from behind the bar.

"Ew, gross, don't hit me with your nasty bar towel!"

Kai looked at Ethan, then shifted his eyes to Coop and smiled. "Hair looks good, I just wasn't expecting it. I mean it. It's really good," Kai said genuinely.

"Thanks," Coop said as he leaned over and kissed Ethan's soft, smooth lips.

Kai shook his head slowly from side to side in disbelief at Coop's outward show of affection.

"Ugh, Kai, now my hands stink from touching that gross towel you hit me with. I gotta go wash them." He kissed the top of Ethan's head, and walked toward the restroom.

"Do you want something to drink?" Kai asked Ethan.

"No thanks. We had a drink with Cooper's dad and Levi not too long ago, I'm good."

Kai tugged at his own ears. "Did I hear that right? Did you just say that you had a drink with Coop's dad? And Levi, too?"

Ethan nodded. "Yeah. We had a beer with them. Why, what's so strange about that?"

"Okay, well, it's like this, I've known Coop since we were"—he held up his hand to indicate the size of a small child—"and in allll that time, I've never, ever, seen him do the things that he's done with you. I know for a fact that he has never had a beer with his dad and Levi together, before today. It's unbelievable. Are you a wizard or something? I mean, he seems happier than, well, ever. I haven't seen him so outwardly affectionate in my entire life. I think it's safe to say that unless you are a wizard, *which* I'm not entirely sure you aren't, my boy is definitely feeling something stronger for you than he ever did for Luke." Kai waved both hands. "Not to bring that up, because, honestly, I wasn't even supposed to know that. But, I mean, he was never like this, not even with him."

Ethan smiled sweetly at Kai. "Thank you."

Kai looked confused. "What are you thanking me for?"

"For taking such good care of him. You're a really good friend. I mean, I'm not going to lie, the hair thing set us back a bit, sure, but I know that you meant well. I feel happy knowing that when he went through all of the bad stuff, you were there for him."

"See, see, I knew it, you *are* a wizard! You're wrapping me up in a spell right now. You smooth talker. You got those big brown eyes, a perfect tan, and you're jacked like Coop. Definitely a wizard." He winked at Ethan. "Alright, so, seriously, though, and more importantly, what's your ship name going to be?"

"Our ship name? Don't tell me Cooper has a boat, too," Ethan said.

"Well, he does, or, well, his dad does, but no, I mean your ship name, your couple name, your relationship name. Have you not heard of that? You put your names together and"—he clapped his hands once—"boom, that's your ship name."

Ethan was perplexed as he began mashing their names up in his head while Kai said anything that came to mind aloud. "Alright, let's see, we got Coothan, Coopan." He made a disgusted face at his own suggestions.

Ethan spoke up, "What about Ether?"

Kai scoffed at him. "No, my man, your name doesn't come first," he said, while making a disagreeable face at Ethan.

As the door to Tagaloa's opened, Kai began his normal greeting, "Talo—" He stopped upon seeing the two enter the restaurant. "What's up, Luke? Kory?"

Ethan looked over toward the door. *Oh, not now. Why is he here? Stop, get ahold of yourself.* He lifted his chin in acknowledgment at Luke. "What's up? How's it going?" Ethan asked, feeling slightly nervous. Ethan's internal struggle quickly ended, when he saw Coop emerge from the bathroom.

Kory sat in the seat next to Ethan, and Luke sat on Kory's other side. Coop approached quickly, seeing two blond-haired men sitting next to Ethan. Ethan looked at him and smiled nervously.

Luke was in a state of shock at the sight of Coop's short hair. "Coop! Where is your hair?" he shouted.

"Very subtle," Kory said sarcastically. He smiled at Luke, who responded by kissing him on the cheek.

"Two bottled beers, please," Kory said to Kai.

Coop smiled, unaffected by Luke and Kory's presence. "Hey, Luke, how's it going?" he asked. He reached his hand around Ethan's back toward Kory for a handshake. "Nice to meet you, I'm Coop."

Kory returned the handshake. "Hey, it's good to finally meet you, I'm Kory."

Coop, who remained standing, pulled Ethan's stool further to the right, away from Kory. "Well, Kory, this guy is mine, and you are just a liiiitle too close." He pulled Ethan another foot to the right and sat close beside him.

Kory found the sight quite entertaining. *I thought Luke said Coop isn't outwardly affectionate, look at him dragging his guy away, claiming him out loud. I'd hardly call that unaffectionate. Like I would be interested in him. Keep pulling, pal. He's all yours.*

Ethan turned to his left and extended his hand to Kory. "Hi, I'm Ethan Prescott; nice to meet you."

"You too," Kory said, shaking his hand.

"Hellooooo, Coop, helloooo," Luke waved wildly from the left. "Where is your hair?"

"Ethan cut it for me," Coop said, while putting his left arm around Ethan and pulling him in even closer. Ethan leaned into Coop's chest and nuzzled against him.

Luke leaned in front of Kory to see better. "You did a good job, Ethan. It looks great!"

"Thanks," Ethan replied, shooting Luke a smile.

Kai grabbed two bottles and slid them to Luke and Kory. "Alright, where did we land, Ethan? Did you pick one?" Kai asked.

"Pick one of what?" Coop asked, tilting his head at Ethan.

"Ship names, we were talking about ship names," Kai said.

"Cethan," Coop answered quickly.

"How do you get that from your names? You're saying 'Key-than' how would you spell that?" Kai asked.

Coop shrugged and spelled it for Kai. "C-e-t-h-a-n, how else would you spell it?"

Kai furrowed his brow. "Yeah, it sounds cool, but I don't know if that's how that would be pronounced."

"Who would decide how it was pronounced if not Ethan and me? You?"

Kai winked. "Alright, alright. It's a good one, better than what we came up with."

Luke's eyes were wide with shock, he couldn't believe he was hearing Coop talking about ship names. He thought Coop hated those types of things.

"Wait, Cooper, I like the name. I really do. But why can't my name be first?" Ethan asked in a sweet voice.

Luke spit his beer out. "Pfttt." *He called him Cooper?! How does he really not know why his name can't be first?* Luke wondered. Then he noticed how gentle Coop was being with Ethan and couldn't help but stare. He watched him kiss Ethan quickly on the mouth, then kiss his hand softly. *This is so different than what I've ever seen from him. Look how comfortable he is with Ethan touching him. Not only that but he's holding him so close out in public and kissing him. He seems like a different person. He even let him call him Cooper…* Luke was brought out of his trance hearing Kory's voice.

"Do you really not know why?" Kory asked Ethan.

"No, I don't. What is it? Bad luck or something?" Ethan asked, while looking at Coop. He tilted his head as he waited for an answer.

"You look like a little puppy right now," Coop said as he rubbed his nose against Ethan's. He continued, "It's nothing, it's stupid and it doesn't even make sense." He then whispered something into Ethan's ear, prompting Ethan to cover his mouth in embarrassment.

"Cethan it is!" Ethan announced proudly. Luke and Kory raised their beers in salute.

Ethan looked over at Luke and Kory. "So, what's your ship name?"

Luke and Kory exchanged glances. Luke replied, "We don't have one. We've been busy with this huge case, and honestly, we never even thought about it."

Ethan looked at Coop with eyes that indicated he was ready to go. Coop nodded in understanding, and the two stood up.

"What, are you guys leaving already?" Kai asked.

"Yeah, we just came for his car, I told you we were just stopping in," Coop replied. The two said their goodbyes and quickly left the restaurant holding hands.

Luke laid his head on Kory's shoulder and giggled. "What's funny?" Kory asked, as he looked down at him.

"I've known him for my whole life. He has never let *anyone* call him Cooper. He would walk around all the time yelling at people, old and young, it didn't matter. 'My name is Coop, call me Coop,' he would say."

"Sounds like a brat," Kory joked as he took a long sip from his bottle.

Luke gazed adoringly at Kory and replied, "That was a new Coop Morgan. I'm happy for them."

Kory finished his beer and kissed Luke softly. "I'm so happy being with you," he said, as he kept his mouth near Luke's.

"I'm happiest with you," Luke said, moving in for a kiss.

Kai smacked his hand on the bar and raised his hands in frustration. "Is everyone going to make out in front of me today? What the hell? Respect that some people are single. Everyone is flaunting their damn love in my face. Blech."

Coop and Ethan walked hand in hand toward their cars. "Let's head back to my place, and hit the pool," Coop said.

Ethan leaned against his door and put his hands on Coop's waist. He looked into his eyes, while gripping his hard sides firmly, allowing his pinky fingers to tease just under the hem of Coop's shirt.

Coop raised his eyebrows at him. "Or maybe not a swim?" he asked. He tilted his head and approached Ethan's mouth with his tongue half out and quickly drove it inside. Ethan's head pushed against the window, and he slid his hands all the way up Coop's back, lightly scratching it.

The two continued the kiss for a few moments until Ethan pulled back. "Let me just go to my dad's and grab some stuff first."

Coop stared at him for just a moment, seeming to struggle with letting him go.

Ethan looked at him and said, "It'll be real quick. You follow behind me, little puppy."

Coop gave him a quick smooch. "I'm not the puppy. You're the puppy, Ethan."

Ethan hopped into his Jeep, he whimpered like a puppy at Coop, while he closed his door for him.

Chapter 20
Living The Dream

After leaving Tagaloa's, Luke and Kory headed to the store.

Kory looked over at Luke. "Coop doesn't seem so bad. He's not as arrogant as I imagined." He kissed Luke's hand, then held it.

"I'm glad. I don't think we'll see him much unless we're around my dad for the holidays."

"Do you really think things will work out with your dads?" Kory asked.

"Without a doubt," Luke said. "Neither will ever let the other one go. I can tell."

Their first trip grocery shopping was a lot of fun. Luke felt like a kid grabbing snacks and putting different things into the cart. "I've never gone full grocery shopping with anyone else," he said, smiling at Kory.

"Me neither, it's much more fun with you. When I go alone it's such a chore."

Luke continued piling things in, while Kory pushed the cart along. When they reached the register, they were greeted by an employee who seemed to be in the worst mood ever.

Kory watched as Luke greeted him.

"Hello, how are you today?" Luke asked the employee who ignored him, and quickly began scanning their items.

Grabbing the box of condoms, he stopped and looked at Luke and Kory. "Living the dream…" he finally replied.

"Well, that's great," Luke said with a smile. "We're living the dream, too. Was a bit of a journey for us to get here, but now we're here, and we just went grocery shopping together for the first time. How fun is that?"

Kory bit his lip watching their awkward interaction. He found it adorable that Luke was really trying to converse with the employee, who truly seemed to want nothing more than for Luke to stop talking, but Luke, being the incessant chatterbox, didn't let up.

"I can't remember ever having so much fun in a grocery store," Luke said, with a smile.

The employee rolled his eyes and continued scanning. "Good for you…I don't know what you want me to say," the employee mumbled, while scanning the last few items.

The employee probably thinks he's bragging but he's just so happy that he can't contain it. He's absolutely perfect. Kory grinned, watching Luke take the receipt and thank the associate.

The two finally left the store and headed back home. Kory looked at Luke as he stopped at a red light. "So, the professor really said it was fine to just do extra work online, even on a Saturday? My professors would only allow me to do extra work online during actual class days, not on off-days."

Luke nodded. "Yep. He said it was fine. I can do the extra work whenever I want. He even said I really don't have to come back into class. I told you this on Thursday, remember?"

"You did and I do remember, but the extra work part I didn't hear on Thursday. Well, you should probably use the home office today. I don't know if I'll be able to keep my hands to myself for two hours. It's already been too long today; the office is your safest bet." Kory laughed.

When they arrived home, Kory playfully shoved Luke into the office, before he put the groceries away. "Go, hurry up, you said you needed two hours to finish the assignment. I'll be working in the bedroom until you're done."

Luke sat inside the office and tried to focus on the project that he was working on. He felt more than happy, thinking of not only his relationship with Kory, but also how happy Coop and Ethan seemed. He then thought of his father and Mr. Morgan.

He questioned if he would be willing to sacrifice years of his life for Kory's happiness, the way his father did for Mr. Morgan. The short time they'd been a couple couldn't begin to compare to the eighteen years that his dad and Mr. Morgan spent together while growing up, nor the eighteen years that they spent apart. For the first time, he truly understood why his father made the decision he did. Luke already knew that he would do anything to protect Kory, his happiness already mattered more to him than his own.

He quickly finished up his extra credit project, and just a few minutes later, walked into the bedroom where Kory was.

Kory lifted his gaze from his tablet when Luke entered. "What is happening? You have reading glasses? How haven't I seen these before? You look like a sexy professor. Get over here, right now." He patted the bed.

Luke sat down and laughed. "Why am I always something? What about you? Here, you take the glasses, you be the professor."

Luke put his glasses on Kory's face. Kory pumped his eyebrows at him. "You ready for class?" he asked, pinning Luke to the bed.

After a few "lessons" and a shower, they packed an insulated beach bag with a bottle of wine, cheese, crackers, and fruit. Kory grabbed a large blanket from the linen closet and held the bag.

They reached the beach only a few minutes later. The two found a perfect spot and set their picnic up. There were very few people walking by, which was nice and added to the romantic ambience.

Kory poured the wine, and Luke graciously accepted it, while snacking on grapes. Kory watched him through lovestruck eyes. *I never want to be away from him,* he thought.

Luke popped another grape in his mouth, smiling at Kory. Kory held him close as both faced the water, sitting on their blanket. They stared at the water in silence, listening to the waves.

After a few minutes, Kory kissed the top of Luke's head. Luke sat up straight, he turned and looked deep into Kory's eyes.

Kory tilted his head, trying to read Luke's expression.

"I never want to be away from you," Luke said.

Kory held his face. "You never will be." He sat thinking about what he wanted to say next as he softly kissed Luke. He felt nervous but really wanted to say it.

Luke pulled back gently. "Kory, I—"

"Luke, I love you," Kory interrupted.

"I love you, too," Luke said, pulling Kory's face in.

The two kissed and held one another listening to the waves crash. After they cleaned up their picnic, they walked back home, and headed straight for their bedroom. Kory sat on the bed, while Luke stood near the dresser.

Kory looked at him softly. "Come here," he said to Luke.

Luke stood in front of him, holding his hands. He tilted his head and looked at Kory.

Kory kissed the top of Luke's hands and looked up at him. "Will you marry me?" he asked.

Without pause, Luke shouted, "Yes!" and bent down to kiss him.

"One condition," Luke said.

"Anything you want."

"I want to get married right away, at City Hall. I don't want to wait."

Kory kissed him. "We'll do it Monday, on our lunch break."

Chapter 21
Tina & Gina

Coop and Ethan pulled their cars in front of Coach's house.

Ethan jumped down from his lifted ride and walked over to Coop, who was already headed toward him.

"Hey, that's the car that was here last night," Coop said while pointing.

Ethan nodded and took Coop's hand as he walked with him up the driveway. "Yeah, that's my mom's car. It's weird seeing it here. I don't understand what's happening, but"—he shrugged his shoulders—"let's just get in and out before they get back. My dad's car isn't here, so I'm guessing they went somewhere together."

Ethan unlocked the door, and they both entered the living room. The smell of fabric softener filled the quiet home. The room I'm staying in is this way," he said, placing his keys on the counter.

Coop had picked up on the fact that Ethan never called any place home or his room. He remembered Ethan saying he never felt at home, growing up in between two houses. He felt a bit sad thinking about a little version of Ethan feeling that way. Looking at him now, he wanted to be his comfort, his place of solace. He wanted to make Ethan feel at home wherever he was.

"Do you need a drink or—" Ethan suddenly froze.

The faint sound of a shower could be heard from the direction of the master bedroom. Coop made an uncomfortable face. "Your mom?" he asked.

Ethan's eyes bulged in horror, while he pulled Coop down the hall. "No questions, yes, it's most likely my mom. My dad is a creature of habit, and he wouldn't be taking a shower at this time. Plus, his car isn't here."

Ethan rushed into the bedroom and began pulling clothes out of his drawers. Coop looked around the room as he watched Ethan having the most adorable freak out, he'd ever witnessed. He glanced at the trash bin, scanning it intently, trying to see if he could get a peek at the picture that Ethan drew of the ice bath incident. A large drawing pad stood in the corner of the room. The sheet that was showing was blank, Coop approached it and asked Ethan if he could take a look at what he'd drawn.

"Yes, yes, of course, go ahead," Ethan said, not really paying any attention to what Coop was doing. Ethan was a man on a mission and would not be distracted.

Coop flipped the most recent picture over and stared silently. The large white paper showed a very toned, good-looking man, lying flat on his back atop a locker room bench, one leg on each side of the bench. His face was solemn, and faced a row of lockers, his gaze focused on one that displayed "Morgan 1." There was a single tear drawn leaving the man's eye. At the top right corner of the portrait, a closed office was shown with two men, one standing with his hand on the shoulder of a seated man whose hair was in a topknot and face was in his hands.

"Ethan," Coop said softly, unable to take his eyes off the picture.

"Yeah?" Ethan responded, not looking up from his dresser. After not receiving a reply, Ethan turned his head to see Coop staring at the picture he'd drawn. He stood up from his squatting position and approached Coop. "Yeah, that was a rough one to draw."

Coop's eyes were tearful as he stared at the picture while talking to

Ethan. "This is you lying here? And me crying in your dad's office?" he asked, in the gentlest tone ever, voice cracking. Coop rubbed his finger on the Ethan in the picture. He wiped the cheek with the tear drawn on it. "I'm sorry, Ethan," he said.

"What for? You didn't do anything. I was supposed to meet up with my dad that day, but when I got to his office, I saw you in there. I could see how upset you were. I just wanted to go in and make whatever it was better, but how could I, when I hadn't really even spoken to you? I felt like I could fix it, and I wanted to, but I found myself unable to do anything. So, I walked away, went into the locker room, and laid on the bench next to your locker. It's over; don't think about it anymore," he said, as he flipped a clean sheet of paper over it.

Coop pulled him into a soft, warm embrace and held him close, each feeling the other's rapidly beating heart. Coop wanted to cry as he held him. *How was he feeling these things for me? How did I not notice? I'm such an idiot. It's okay, I have him now, and I won't let him cry ever again.*

A knock sounded, and a woman's voice with a very thick northern accent said, "Ethan, sweetie, open up. I want to talk to you. I haven't seen you in so looong…I want to hear about the ice bath and Coop Morgan," she joked through laughter. "No, seriously, open up let's talk." She wiggled the doorknob.

Ethan's face was still tucked in Coop's neck, as he looked up at him and shook his head slowly from side to side, breathing in Coop's intoxicating scent.

She knocked again. "What is that smell, did you change to a new cologne? I like that, what brand is it?" she called through the door.

Ethan exhaled and looked at the ceiling. "Mom, no, I didn't change cologne. Can you please go away? We're just grabbing some stuff really fast, then leaving." Ethan realized his error as soon as he said the word *we're*.

Footsteps could be heard as his mother walked back down the hall, the sound of blinds rattling as she presumably looked out the front window. Ethan pulled away from Coop's embrace and began rifling through his small closet.

She returned and knocked again. "Is Coop Morgan in there with you? Open up, I want to meet him."

"No, Mom. I'm not opening it."

"We both know I'm not going away. So just open up already."

Coop walked across the room to Ethan and whispered, "Is your mom from New York?"

"Yes, and she's Italian. Cooper, go out the window, she is not going to leave, and I really can't deal with her right now. She already brought the ice bath up. I'm so embarrassed."

Coop gave him a quick smooch on the lips.

"Ethan, I can hear you," she said. She changed tactics and started again. "Hi, Coop, I'm Ethan's mom, Gina. I'm not leaving this doorway until I see my baby's face, so tell him to open the door, please. I want to meet you."

Coop nodded at Ethan and pointed at the door.

Ethan sighed and walked over to it, looking at the floor. He took a deep breath in and exhaled while opening the door.

Ethan's mother, who must have had her ear on the door, nearly fell in. She came in wearing a navy-blue men's bathrobe, with her hair wrapped in a towel.

"Mom! You're not even dressed. Get out!"

She made a face at him in annoyance, and cupped his face in her hands. "Mimmo," she said, as she pinched then kissed both of his cheeks. Ethan refused to say anything to her, his face burning in embarrassment.

She lightly patted his cheeks, then let go and walked over to Coop.

In what seemed like one breath she addressed him, "Oh my, you are good-looking and tall, and built, but, wait, I thought you had long hair? I'm Gina, it's nice to meet you. My husband talks about you *all* the time." She extended her hand toward him.

Coop tried to hold in a laugh, as Ethan quickly placed his body in between the two.

"Mom, back up. You're in a bathrobe. You do not shake people's hands in a bathrobe. What is wrong with you?!"

She swatted Ethan aside like he was a fly and reached toward Coop. "Adorable, isn't he?" she asked, as she shook Coop's hand.

"It's a pleasure to meet you, and, yes, I agree, he is adorable," Coop said, grinning.

"Your hands are strooong," she said, as they finished the handshake.

"Oh my God, okay, Mom, we're leaving, we just came to grab some stuff." He grabbed Coop's hand and pulled him toward his closet. He pulled out a black backpack and stuffed a few things that he'd pulled out earlier into it, and quickly zipped it up.

Ethan's mom stood behind them. "What are you doing? Packing a bag? You're not staying for dinner?"

"No, we're not staying for anything." He shook his head at her, while he yanked Coop out of the bedroom.

He continued pulling Coop along toward the front door as his mother followed. "Are you coming back tonight? Or shouldn't I ask that? I'm sorry, I'm just too excited to see you and to meet Coop."

Ethan opened the door and shoved Coop outside, as Coop shouted back, "It was nice to meet you, I'm keeping him for the night, by the way."

"Nice to meet—" The door slammed in between them, leaving Coop standing outside alone and Ethan inside with his mother.

"Oh my gosh, Mom!" he screamed. Then started again, this time softer and very calm. "Mom."

"Yes, Mimmo?"

"Mom, words cannot express the absolute embarrassment that I feel right now…I truly want to crawl into a hole and hide there for the rest of my life…but there is a very, very perfect man waiting outside for me. So, I must go…now."

"Sweetie, I'm sorry. I didn't mean to embarrass you. But listen, really, now that I've met him," she tilted her chin down and her eyes grew to the size of meatballs, "you really need to be careful because I mean, I shook his hand and the picture—"

Ethan walked out and shut the door on her.

"Love you! Be safe!" she shouted through the door.

Ethan looked up to see a giggling Coop leaning next to his car. "Come here," he said, beckoning him. He held his arms wide and hugged Ethan tightly.

"I want to die," Ethan said.

Coop rubbed his back and quickly kissed him on the side of the neck. "No, you don't want to die. You want to be with me. Your mom is nice. That was fine," Coop said, as he continued rubbing his back. "Do you want to leave your car here? You can just ride with me; you won't need it."

Ethan nodded looking at him. "Yeah, I'll just ride with you."

Coop began to separate from the hug, and something caught his attention. He turned Ethan around to face the house. Ethan's mother stood inside, looking through the window, while waving and blowing kisses. Coop waved goodbye and smiled, while Ethan ignored her and got into the passenger side of the car. Coop jogged around to the driver's side, got in, and drove away.

Coop thought Ethan's mom was hilarious, but after meeting her, he now understood why Ethan never moved in with his dad before this year. He was quite certain that she wouldn't have let him.

A ringtone sounded from Ethan's pocket. Coop knew it was his mother before Ethan even looked at it. "The embarrassment continues, if I answer this," he said to Coop.

"Answer it, it's fine," Coop encouraged him.

"Yes, mother," he answered.

She was so loud Coop could hear her, even though the phone wasn't on speaker. "Oh my gosh! You guys are so cute. That was so sweet. He was rubbing your back and I just melted, honey, I melted!" Ethan looked over at Coop, with an *I told you so* face. "Listen, I want you both to come over for dinner tomorrow," she said. "I'm making gravy, your father hasn't shut up about it since I got here. You looked thin, so I'll make extra. I'm not worried about Coop, though, as he seemed healthy enough. Oh, honey, I hope I didn't really embarrass you. He was just so handsome, but of course you are, too." She finally took a breath and paused. "Ethan, well, what do you say, you'll do it, right?"

"Hang on, Mom." Ethan covered the phone and looked at Coop. "Do you want to go there for dinner tomorrow?"

"Sure, if you want to. We don't have practice until Monday, and I don't have plans."

"Yeah, Mom, that's fine. We can, but, seriously, don't bring *that* up again. Or else I'll leave, and you'll never see me again."

"Okay, yes, of course, honey. I'm terrible. Worst mother ever. I know. But, gosh, he really is so tall and…never mind. I'll see you tomorrow. Love you."

"Love you, too," Ethan said, as he ended the call. He smacked his head backward onto the headrest.

"Hey, I thought your parents were divorced, but your mom called Coach her husband."

"Yeah, well they separated when I was ten, but never legally divorced. Didn't really see each other, but they still spoke. I have no idea what's going on, to be honest."

"You seem close with both of them, that's nice."

Ethan looked out the window as he replied, "Yeah, I'm close with both. Maybe a little closer with my mom, but, yeah, they're both great and awful… Oh noooo," he sighed, holding his phone against his forehead.

"What's wrong?" Coop asked.

"She's gonna call my Aunt Tina."

"Tina and Gina that's funny," Coop said.

Coach walked inside the front door to see Gina sitting on the couch wearing his bathrobe, talking on the phone. He smiled at her and headed down the hall. "Ethan?" he called out. He looked inside the open bedroom. "His Jeep is here, where is he?" he asked Gina in the living room.

"Mimmo's not here, you just missed him, he left in Coop's car." She returned to her conversation, pausing only in between her sister's replies. "Oh my God, Tina, and it was a BMW, black and slick. I mean, yes…but you know I just worry…"

Coach walked into the kitchen to grab a snack as her conversation continued.

"But his hands were so strong! Huge!" She cackled. "I know! But it was like a weapon! A weapon, Tina! I'm worried for my baby! He had just gotten out of the ice bath, so how big co—"

Coach interrupted her. "Hey, I'm standing right here," he said, as he bit into a potato chip.

She looked at him quickly. "Tina says hi." Then she resumed her conversation. "Where were we, Tina?"

Coach put his hand up in frustration. "No, no, there's no where were we. That kid is like a son to me, and the other one is our actual son! What's wrong with you two?"

She looked at him and rolled her eyes. "Oh, wait, Tina, remember when Ethan was ten, and he lost that big game, yeah, the juniors, right. Tell Paul what I told you that day."

She turned the phone to face Coach. No speaker was needed, Tina was loud enough without it. "You said that Ethan hearing Coop's name seemed to do something to him."

Gina held her hand up. "Ha! See, I told you! I'm never wrong!"

Coach shook his head and walked away.

Chapter 22
Give Me Goosebumps

Coop pulled through the Estate gate. Luckily, there was no one around, so he parked without incident. He and Ethan hopped out quickly and walked toward the front of the car.

Ethan held a hand on his head and one finger up. "I just need a minute." Ethan had experienced a plethora of emotions very quickly, and not only was the heat outside getting to him, but the heat he was feeling for Coop was burning white hot from deep within. *Gotta block my mom's warning out of my head. We may go upstairs and actually do this. But now I'm feeling a little nervous. I want him, though; I can't be afraid.*

Coop rubbed Ethan's shoulders and took his backpack from him. "You okay?" he asked.

Ethan tugged at the collar of his own shirt. "Of course, of course, I'm fine, just trying to calm myself. I feel a little hot."

The fire Ethan saw in Coop's eyes told him that he wanted him just as badly. Suddenly he felt like a piece of meat under the gaze of a hungry wolf.

Coop let out a large breath and led Ethan by the hand up to his bedroom. Neither said a word, as Coop threw Ethan's backpack on the floor and pinned him on the bed. Coop looked him over, like a starving beast. They both wanted the same thing. They wanted the goosebumps, the goosebumps that came only when the unceasing passion erupted from within them.

Ethan, with his mouth slightly open, in eager anticipation, pulled Coop's shirt up and slid his hand down the front of his pants. Coop dove into Ethan's mouth, he moved quickly to Ethan's neck and aggressively bit and sucked the side until both were a panting mess.

Ethan's hand reached further down the inside of Coop's pants.

Coop looked down and gently pulled Ethan's hand out, bringing an annoyed, "Ugh, Cooper!" from a dismayed Ethan.

Coop squeezed his eyes shut. "No, no, we're not doing this right now."

"What? Why not? Look at me, why are your eyes closed? Why did you stop?" Ethan tried to paw back down Coop's pants.

Coop grabbed both of his hands and kissed them lightly. "Listen, I can't open my eyes because you look so hot right now, and if I open them, I won't be able to stop again," he said, in a pained voice.

"So, don't stop then, do it. Why are you stopping?" Ethan asked, as he looked at Coop, who still had his eyes closed.

"Ethan, listen. I'm going to be straight with you here. I like you so much and I really want you, but right now, I want you in a dangerous way. I don't want to hurt you. If I take you like this…well, I mean it's going to hurt either way, honestly, but I want to be gentle with you for our first time." He opened his emerald eyes, which pleaded with Ethan, silently begging for understanding. Taking Ethan's hands and kissing them again, he said, "Let's just take a breath, and go cool off in the pool."

Ethan closed his eyes and silently nodded.

When they got up, Ethan grabbed the backpack that was on the floor and pulled out his navy and white swim shorts.

"You don't want the ones in the bag? From the store?" Coop asked.

"Well, you bought them for me, so I don't want to be rude. But you only bought them so I wouldn't have to grab mine from home, which I ended up doing. So, you should just keep them."

Coop blinked his eyes hard and shook his head. He brought Ethan with him into his closet. Using his foot, he pulled open a drawer full of swim shorts, in all colors. "I bought them for you because I wanted to. I don't need them. You said you liked them, so just keep them." He ruffled Ethan's hair, then bent down and grabbed a seafoam pair of shorts, with a black waistband and outline. The two put their swim shorts on, grabbed towels, and headed to the pool.

It was an exceptionally clear, warm day, so the crystal blue water was especially welcoming as the sun reflected off it. This time of the year in Florida was the best time to be in the state. It was either mildly cool, or just warm enough that you wouldn't sweat when you walked outside, unlike summer which felt like a constant burning furnace.

Ethan, wearing his new black swim trunks, walked around for a bit, skimming his foot around the edge of the pool, and decided to sit near the waterfall.

Coop dove in and drenched Ethan with a huge splash. When he surfaced, he found Ethan wiping the water off his face, his tan skin shimmered as the beads of water dripped down his washboard abs.

Coop swam over and looked up at him mischievously as he grabbed both of Ethan's feet that were underwater. "Aren't you coming in with me?" he asked. His eyes carried a light threat of pulling Ethan in, regardless of his answer.

"I'm coming in, just looking around at this place. It's crazy. I've never been in a pool like this." He gestured toward the grotto and waterfall areas. "It's absolutely beautiful."

Coop smiled and released Ethan's feet. He went underwater, and quickly resurfaced, while rubbing his head, with a confused look on his face.

"What? What's wrong with your face?" Ethan asked, half joking.

"Nothing, my head felt light, and I forgot for a minute that my hair was gone. This is the first time I've ever swam in the pool without it weighing me down. It feels great."

Ethan smiled. "I'm so glad I didn't mess it up," he said, as he slid down into the pool and swam into Coop's arms. Coop quickly scooped him up, and Ethan wrapped around him like a slippery eel.

He held Ethan's bottom in his hands firmly, pressing Ethan's body against himself. Ethan was weightless in the water, not that it mattered to Coop, whose arms were considerably larger. Ethan rubbed his body against him, and took Coop's earlobe into his mouth, lightly sucked it and panted heavily in his ear.

"You really are naughty," Coop said, as he gripped Ethan's ass harder.

Ethan nodded his head and brought his face directly in front of Coop's, with desperate eyes, and a thirsty voice he begged, "Please, Cooper. I really want it."

Coop shook his head at him softly. "What am I gonna do with you? I want to make you dinner, and romance you first, don't you want that?" he asked him.

Ethan, eyes half closed, replied by tracing his tongue on Coop's mouth and sucking on his bottom lip, leaving his tongue out as he pulled back. Coop squeezed Ethan's face and licked his exposed tongue.

Ethan moaned in want, as Coop suddenly looked concernedly around the pool, while still holding his face in his right hand. "Do you hear that?" he asked Ethan.

Ethan, deep in the throes of lust, shook his head no, and forced his tongue inside Coop's mouth. Coop stood unmoving, his brows furrowed, as Ethan pulled back and looked at him, legs still wrapped around Coop tightly. "What is it?" he asked.

"I hear yelling," Coop replied. He walked through the pool with Ethan clinging to him like a koala. He carried him in this position out of the pool toward the noise, walking around the estate.

Chapter 23
Mimmo's Gonna Sock Him

The main gate was open, as Coop's dad, Levi, Coach, Ethan's mom, and someone Coop didn't immediately recognize stood locked in argument.

Coop quickened his pace, trying to hear what was happening and attempting to process the bizarre scene. Coach and Gina stood side by side, Gina's arms folded, and to the right of them stood Levi and Coop's dad, and in the center, standing near a white Mercedes, was the unknown man, who sounded drunk.

Gina spotted Coop carrying Ethan, both dripping wet, in their swimsuits. "Oh…my sweet mother…" she said. Then she gestured to Coop's dad to look in their direction.

"Coop, do not come over here right now, take Ethan and go inside!" his dad yelled. He then did a double take at seeing Coop's hair and added, "What happened to your—"

Levi quickly finished his dad's thought, "Your hair!"

Coop continued walking toward the group, as Ethan turned to get a better look. Coop gently put him down and held his hand.

"What is happening? Why are my parents here, who is that guy?" Ethan asked frantically.

Coop finally realized who the drunk man was, it was none other than Collin Pyle, standing drunk yelling at his dad. He stopped his approach as he realized who it was. "That's the scout," he told Ethan.

Ethan's mouth dropped open. "The one that—"

Coop nodded.

Ethan pushed Coop behind him and sped up, moving closer toward the group. Coop quickly grabbed his arm, held his hand, and walked beside him.

"Oh, there he is!" Collin Pyle yelled, upon seeing Coop.

"Coop, I told you to take Ethan and go inside," his dad said.

Collin Pyle stood staring at Coop, his swimsuit still wet, water dripping. Ethan quickly placed his body in between the two, blocking the man's view of him.

Collin Pyle smiled, as Ethan ferociously stared him down, his brown eyes alit with fury. "Don't fucking look at him, you disgusting piece of shit," Ethan said.

"Mimmo, language!" his mother screamed from across the group.

"Mimmo? Wait, Ethan? Oh, wow, just wow, this is your boy?" Collin Pyle asked, as he looked at Coach and Gina.

Coop felt the urge to protect Ethan, wrapping his arms around his waist from behind, he gently tried to pull Ethan's body beside him. Ethan was rooted firm in his stance. *Damn his legs are strong.*

Ethan tapped Coop's hands, while keeping his gaze on the scout. "Don't try to move me. I don't want him staring at you," he whispered.

"Yes, that is our son, what of it?" Gina said, placing a hand on her hip.

Coach took a step forward. "What is it that you want, Mr. Pyle? I let you plead your case earlier after the meeting, and I listened politely because I was at school. But here, I'm just a dad. I'm not at work right now. I'm Paul and, yes, that is my son. I'd suggest getting to your point quickly because I'm not like these other two," he gestured to Coop's dad and Levi, "I have a very limited amount of patience."

"Are you threatening me? Was that a threat?" Collin Pyle asked.

Coop's dad cut in, "Mr. Pyle, I do not appreciate you coming to my home, drunk, to air your grievances. The board reviewed its findings and what's done is done. Now, I am going to ask you one more time to get the hell off my property."

Levi grabbed Coop's dad's arm and pulled him back a step. "Take a breath. You can't hit him, Tommy," he whispered.

Coop was torn between charging at Mr. Pyle and holding onto Ethan, who looked like he was going to explode if he let go for even a second. *If I move to the left and cut around, I can probably knock him out. But if I let go, Ethan may rush him first. I can't stand that this is happening.*

"I have something to say," Ethan spoke up. All eyes shifted to him as he stood there in his bathing suit, attempting to block Mr. Pyle's gaze from Coop's wet body. "What the hell gives you the right to proposition him for sex…just because of your position? You're a real piece of—"

His rant was cut off by his mother's scream. *"Sex? What?"* She rushed over and stood in front of Ethan and held her arms wide, attempting to block him from Mr. Pyle. "Don't you look at Mimmo either, you pervert." She turned to face Ethan and spoke quietly, "Sweetie, I don't really understand what's happening. Your father had a meeting at school today, I guess this guy got fired. Your dad came to talk to Tom, and now here you two are, talking about someone propositioning someone. I'm confused."

Levi, Coach, and Coop's dad also stood confused as all three looked at each other. Levi asked, "Tommy did you know that happened? I didn't know that part." Coop's dad and Coach both heard his question and shook their heads in response.

Coop's dad took a step closer to the center where the drunken Mr. Pyle stood, staring at Coop through Gina and Ethan. "Did I hear that right? Did he just say that you propositioned my son for sex?" Mr. Morgan asked, cracking his knuckles, biceps rippling…

"Yes, I did," Mr. Pyle answered. While looking around Gina's small body, he spoke to Ethan, "You know, it took me so long to get those pictures. The two of them were always so careful not to let anyone see anything. Now, here you are with a hickey on your neck, and him holding your hand like it's nothing. Not to mention him carrying you over here."

Gina quickly turned around to look at Ethan, meatball eyes almost fell out of her head as she noticed the love bite on her Mimmo's neck. She said nothing at first, then looked up at Coop, who stood biting his lip with his hands on Ethan's waist. She shot him a quick smile through gritted teeth, and she whispered through her smile to Ethan, "Mimmo you just left the house an hour or two ago, how did this—" She stopped herself as she saw Ethan's eyes still focused on Mr. Pyle, full of rage, and turned back around.

Levi now stood next to Coop's dad again, the two of them went over the situation, with Levi encouraging him to stay calm.

Mr. Pyle, ever the antagonizer, started again, this time talking to Coop. "Nice hair, I guess it's good things didn't work out with Luke, so now these two can be together." He pointed to Mr. Morgan and Levi.

Ethan's posture dropped as he started to step around his mother, Coop squeezed his hand and pulled him back against his chest.

"Do not talk to my son," Coop's dad warned in a towering voice.

Levi took command of the conversation. "Listen, you are finished, your career is over because you screwed up. There is nothing else to say. Just leave."

Mr. Pyle looked at Levi. "Oh, is this your house? Unbelievable. How dare you tell me to leave!"

Coop was finding it extremely hard to stay still. Seeing everyone get upset on his behalf made him feel guilty. *I have to stop this. Everyone is here just because of me not asking for help in the first place. What do I do? What is the smartest move here?* Coop suddenly remembered something vital. "Dad, where the hell is Tony?" he shouted

As if dropped from the sky, a large man with spiked black hair and sunglasses, dressed in a casual suit appeared. Tony. He darted in from the hole in the group and in one move pinned Mr. Pyle, arm behind his back, face against the hood of his own car.

"He's huge!" Gina squealed.

The group collectively let out a breath of relief as Tony held Mr. Pyle with one hand. "Sorry, boss. How'd he slip in here?"

Coop's dad answered, "He tagged in behind Paul."

Levi, attempting to lighten the mood, said, "Yeah, its Paul's fault, he didn't pull in quick enough. Good job, Paul."

Gina added, "Yeah, Paul! I told you to pull through quicker."

"What? You did not. You were freaking out because Ethan didn't respond to your texts, and you were going on about how big the estate is…and I don't know, a bunch of other stuff."

She waved his comments off.

Coop rubbed Ethan's shoulders and turned his strong frame around to face him. "Hey, you're good, it's fine. Tony's got him pinned down. Let's go."

Ethan felt his body being turned against his will. He looked at Coop who was trying to comfort him, and finally relaxed when Coop kissed him softly and pulled him tightly against his chest. There was something about Coop's scent that soothed him, he couldn't quite understand it. Ten seconds ago, he was ready to punch the scout and now he felt completely calm, wrapped in Coop's warm embrace.

His mom turned to face them and let out a sigh. "Oh, to be young again. Good thing Tony got here, I thought my little Mimmo was gonna sock him," she said, rubbing Ethan's back.

Ethan nestled his face in Coop's neck and closed his eyes.

Ethan's dad, Mr. Morgan, and Levi began walking to the main estate entrance. "Gina, let's go," his dad called.

Levi held the arm of Mr. Morgan, who remained silent. "Yeah, Gina, let's go. Leave them alone."

She slouched a bit and tilted her head, trying to decide if she would follow as told or stay.

"Go, Mom, I'm good," Ethan said, closing his eyes, not moving his face from Coop's neck.

Coop began slowly walking back toward his side of the estate, holding Ethan's head in place.

Tony smiled at them, while keeping the scout pinned against the hood of his car. "Banned from games, banned from the school, I'll never get a job as a scout again. Thanks," Mr. Pyle said.

Ethan picked his head up in shock and turned his foot. Coop quickly threw him over his shoulder. "My spicy little puppy, calm down. He isn't worth it." Coop patted Ethan's ass and headed for the entrance to his side of the estate.

Chapter 24
Let Coop Bang Him

Coop carried Ethan inside, placing him down before the stairs and taking him by the hand. As the two entered his room, Coop sighed and leaned against the wall.

Ethan walked over to his backpack and knelt on the floor. He pulled a pair of underwear out. "What? Where are my sweatpants? I don't have anything to sleep in. I packed my bathing suit, two pairs of underwear and two shirts. Why did I pack this stuff?" he asked himself aloud, while shuffling through the backpack.

Coop approached him from behind. "I think your mom showing up may have affected your packing skills." He squatted and winked at him.

Ethan was flustered. "Now I don't have any clothes, and I don't have my car."

Coop smiled at him and pulled him up, leading him toward his closet. "Hey," he said as he placed his hand on Ethan's chin and tilted his head up. "I'm sorry about that. That was awful," he said as he stared deeply into Ethan's big brown eyes.

Ethan shook his head while looking up at him. "What a lunatic that guy was. Really pissed me off."

Coop gave him a quick peck on the lips. "Yeah, he did. I thought my little pupper was gonna bite him," he joked.

Ethan's eyes widened. "Bite him? Wait, you…you bit me earlier and that guy said I had a hickey." He rushed toward the mirror above Coop's desk. Sure enough, there was a bright red love bite on the side of his neck. He looked at it in the mirror and ran his fingers over it.

"Sorry," Coop said, making a pouty face from inside the closet. Ethan smiled as he rubbed the mark and joined him in the closet.

"Alright, so, in here is basically everything that I don't want to stuff in a drawer. So, comfies, like track pants, sweats, gym shorts, and underwear—not the new underwear—are in the dresser out there. Just grab whatever you want. I'm going to rinse off and throw on some comfies," he winked, "then I'm going to make you dinner. The controller for the TV is on the nightstand if you want to watch something."

"Sounds good. Thank you," Ethan replied, while opening the dresser in search of bottoms. Coop kissed him quickly and headed into the shower.

As Coop stood in the shower washing his newly cut hair for the first time, he smiled and chuckled to himself. *When have I ever felt so happy? All I want to do is kiss him and make him smile. Man, I want him, really bad. I could have really hurt him earlier, if we hadn't stopped.* His lower half started to stir, as he remembered the way he held Ethan against himself in the water.

"Hey, can I rinse off too?" Ethan asked, as he entered the bathroom. He looked at Coop through the glass doors.

"No, you can't. You really are seriously naughty." He wiped the glass, so he could see Ethan's face.

"You don't want me to come in?" Ethan asked.

Coop sighed loud and long. "Ethan, listen to me. I am determined to make you dinner. If we fool around right now, which we will if you come in here, we won't do anything else today."

Ethan thought for a moment then asked, "Is making dinner that important to you?"

Coop wiped the glass again and nodded emphatically at him. "Yes, I've never cooked for anyone before. I just started cooking recently. I've been thinking of it since early this morning. I want to do something special for you. Not that I'm not turned on right now, and you coming in here has only made matters worse, so to speak."

Ethan pressed his forehead against the cleared glass that Coop wiped. His eyes were drawn downward and his mouth dropped open at the sight.

"Hey!" Coop shouted, covering himself.

Ethan gave him an innocent look.

Coop turned the water off as he finished rinsing his hair. He grabbed his black towel that hung over the glass door and wrapped it around himself. Taking Ethan's face in both hands, he gave him a slow and sensual kiss. "Ethan, I really want this, but I also want to treat you right. I want to show you how much you mean to me."

When Coop left the bathroom, Ethan stripped and stepped into the shower to rinse himself off. His thoughts were fully occupied with Coop and…well…*all* of Coop. He'd been teasing Coop all day about it, trying to seduce him into going all the way. But, in truth, it did scare him a little bit.

Will it hurt? What if I'm not good at it? He's so perfect, I'm sure it'll be amazing. He then remembered Kai and the stupid conversation about the hair rules. *If I'd ignored Kai, Coop and I would be further in our relationship. We might've even done it by now.*

Ethan turned off the shower, toweled down, and got dressed. He walked out of the bathroom wearing a pair of Coop's black track pants and a gray slim fit T-shirt. Coop was sporting gray track pants with a black Henley tee.

"Hey, those are my favorite pair of track pants!" Coop said. "They look good on you, nice choice."

Ethan smiled at him. "Thanks for letting me borrow them, they are really comfy." Ethan looked at his phone, which flashed with notifications.

17 missed texts from Mom
5 missed calls from Mom

Mom:

4:00 PM: *Hi sweetie, we are going to Tom's soon because your dad wants to tell him something.*

4:01 PM: *I think it has to do with his meeting from earlier.*

4:02 PM: *I'll let you know when we get there.*

4:05 PM: *Tell Coop I said hi.*

4:10 PM: *Have you heard of something about a guy getting kicked out of the scout program?*

4:11 PM: *Your father won't stop talking about it.*

4:18 PM: *I'll call you when we get closer so you can come see us.*

4:30 PM: *Your father said I shouldn't bother you.*

4:40 PM: *Coming around the long road to the estate.*

5:30 PM: *MIMMO WHY WAS THERE A HICKEY ON YOUR NECK?*

5:31 PM: *WE ARE HAVING DRINKS WITH TOM AND LEVI.*

5:32 PM: *LEVI IS STILL FUNNY.*

5:33 PM: *COOP LOOKS LIKE TOM.*

5:37 PM: *THIS PLACE IS HUGE!*

5:40 PM: *HOW FAR AWAY IS COOP'S ROOM?*

5:45 PM: *Sorry I didn't realize I had the texts letters wrong.*

5:46 PM: *I just meant to do the first one big letters.*

Ethan held the phone in his hand and stared in silence.

"What's up?" Coop asked. "Did you miss something important?"

Ethan shook his head and closed his eyes. "Cooper, my mother and father are having drinks with your dad and Levi. How far away is your kitchen from wherever they are?"

Coop thought for a moment. "Couldn't really say, where did she say they are?"

Ethan passed his phone over with his mother's text stream open. Coop could only guess at possible locations, as he read the texts. "Yeah, I have no idea. Not enough information. It's nice out, though, so maybe out by the pool bar where we were earlier? Or inside the main dining area. Those would be my best guesses. You could just ask her, then I could tell you."

Ethan put the phone in his pocket. "Oh yeah, let's do that, and then she can come join us for dinner, and maybe come check out your room, too," he said facetiously.

They left Coop's room holding hands. Going downstairs Ethan nearly stumbled on the bottom step, while looking around nervously to be sure his mother wasn't going to appear.

Coop smiled at him and led him into the kitchen. "I doubt she'll come, honestly. My dad and Levi would find a way to stop her."

Ethan looked at him. "You don't have experience with Italian mothers. It's not your fault that you would think two men could stop her. My sweet man, nothing can stop her when she wants to do something," he said, as he patted Coop's cheek.

Coop readied his cooking supplies on the long black countertops, while Ethan sat watching him. "So, this kitchen is not near your dad's, right? I'm just trying to get the layout in my head, so we can run if we hear her."

Coop tried to calm him. "I'm telling you, they won't let her come over here. Trust me. I just want you to relax. I'll text my dad in a minute if it makes you feel better."

"Yes, yes…please?" Ethan begged, with puppy dog eyes.

"Alright, I'll just call him really quick." Coop placed the phone on speaker and set it on the counter.

Mr. Morgan's phone rang twice before Levi answered, "Hey, Coop, it's Levi, your dad is—"

The sound of Gina's loud voice blared through the speaker. "Get him, Paul, get him, Paul."

"Don't give up, Tommy!" Levi shouted. "He still thinks he can kick your ass!" He then spoke to Coop, "Sorry, your dad and Paul are arm wrestling right now."

"Levi, tell my dad I need to talk to him."

"Tommy, Coop is on the phone, he sounds distressed."

"What?!" Gina screamed.

Coach could be heard in the background, "Yeah! Whoo! Take that, Tom!"

Ethan, only focused on his mother's reaction, froze in complete fear. He was now convinced that nothing would stop her from finding him.

Coop actually glanced up at him with nervous eyes, too, at the sound of her scream. He walked around the counter and looked outside the glass doors at the back of the kitchen.

"Coop? What's wrong?" Mr. Morgan asked.

"Dad, nothing's wrong, but I need your help with something."

Mr. Morgan was panting into the phone, seemingly out of breath from the arm wrestling.

Paul was taunting Levi in the background, "Come on, Levi, your turn, step up."

Mr. Morgan yelled, "Yeah, you finish it, Levi, I wore him down for you!"

Coach taunted Levi again, "That's right, baby doll, bring your big baby blue eyes over here. Daddy's gonna put you down for a nap."

Ethan was mortified, while Coop seemed to think what Coach said was hilarious. His phone vibrated on the counter; he didn't even bother looking at it, he knew it was his mother.

"Dad, focus," Coop said.

"So, what's up, Coop? You're not in distress?"

"No, Dad, I'm not in distress. But Ethan is. He's terrified that his mom will find her way over here."

"Hahaha," he said loudly. Then started whispering intently, "She has already asked how to get to your room at least fifteen times. Each time, Levi and I distract her with something. Levi threw me into this arm-wrestling match for that very purpose. Now, Paul is just showing off, I'm pretty sure he just called himself daddy again." He paused for a moment. "Levi, push, push!" he screamed. He started whispering again, "Okay, she's focused on her phone. Tell Ethan to text her that he's going to bed early."

Ethan sat petrified.

"Dad, no, that won't work, it's too early for him to go to bed. Come on, we really need your help."

Coop's dad resumed whispering, "Coop, the estate is huge, she couldn't find you guys if she tried. Plus, we all saw the hickey on his neck earlier, I'm sure she would be too afraid to walk in on something… Noooo, Levi!" Mr. Morgan shouted.

Coach shouted, "Yeah, take it! Ha, I'm still stronger than both of you supermodels! Ha!"

Ethan threw his hands up.

Levi came to the phone and started whispering, panting out of breath, "Coop, what is it? Your dad just gave me a look."

Ethan spoke up, "Mr. Everton, I really need my mother to stay distracted. I don't want her coming over here, or even trying to find us."

Levi whispered, "I know, I know, we're trying. Let me think…. Okay, well, if I've learned anything at all recently, it's that we should be honest." He paused, then shouted, "Gina, leave Ethan alone, so Coop can bang him, okay?"

Coop and Ethan both hung their heads.

"There, see, that worked," Levi said proudly. "She just gave me a thumbs up, and put her phone in her purse." Coop and Ethan were silent. Levi asked, "What? Are you two embarrassed? You were carrying him half naked earlier, with a hickey on his neck, do you think she's stupid?"

Mr. Morgan took the phone and spoke quickly, "That worked. We should have said it earlier. You boys be safe. Bye." The phone call ended.

Now, of course, Gina didn't exactly give a thumbs up, per se.

When Levi screamed for her to let Coop bang Ethan, Gina's eyes went meatball, and Paul quickly held his hand over her mouth, while giving Levi a thumbs up. She then dropped her phone in her purse on her own.

Gina yelled, "Levi, you are the worst, always taking things too far!" Paul chuckled from behind her. "You think this is funny, Paul? You didn't see that picture our son drew of Coop coming out of the ice bath," she said.

"What?!" Mr. Morgan and Levi shouted simultaneously.

Chapter 25
Two

Coop looked seriously at Ethan following Levi's "Let Coop bang him" comment. "You know, I was really trying to set a mood here."

Ethan was relieved. "Well, she stopped texting me, so I guess it really did work."

Coop opened a large white cabinet. He moved quickly around the kitchen pulling out the ingredients needed. "I probably should have made sure you liked what I was planning to make beforehand. I wanted to surprise you, though. Your shocked face is so cute, I can't get enough of it."

"So, what is it? I love almost all food, and since you're making it, I'm sure I'll love it."

"Not telling," Coop said. As he sliced and cut the squash and potatoes, Coop looked over at Ethan. "Tell me about this gravy that we're eating tomorrow."

"Well, see in my house, gravy is sauce, like red sauce, or Marinara, pasta sauce, whichever way you're comfortable referring to it. My mom makes her homemade sauce every Sunday. Takes her all day. I usually make it with her if I'm free. It's probably the only thing I can help with in the kitchen. Well, aside from washing dishes," Ethan said.

"That's cute. I'll just make you whatever you want, you don't need to cook. I'm excited about the gravy. I've never had it homemade before."

Once Coop finished prepping, he placed the food in the oven and set a timer on his phone. Forty minutes later, Coop's masterpiece was complete. He carefully readied Ethan a plate, with herb seasoned Chicken breast, topped with goat cheese, sundried tomatoes, and a lemon butter sauce. Sitting perfectly next to it were oven roasted potatoes, mixed with zucchini and squash. Ethan's face lit up, as Coop placed the dish in front of him.

"I can't believe you just made this for me. It looks and smells delicious. Thank you, Cooper."

Coop gave him a quick smooch on the lips and sat down with his own plate beside him, while Ethan tasted the chicken. "Oh my gosh, Cooper, this is the best chicken I have ever had. I love goat cheese so much! This is amazing! Did you really just start cooking recently?"

Coop kissed his cheek and smiled. "Yep, like I said earlier. You're the first person I've ever cooked for. I'm glad you like it. I was nervous about making it, but I really wanted to impress you."

"Mmmmm, well, you did. I couldn't be any more impressed with you. I'm sure of that."

Coop looked at him and tilted his head. He reached under the counter and slid his hand over to Ethan's thigh. In a sultry tone, he said, "Ethan, you're saying there's nothing else I can do that will impress you tonight?"

Ethan took another bite of his chicken, which was already nearly gone. He thought for a moment as he ate a few potatoes and vegetables. Coop's hand remained on his thigh, lightly massaging it. "You are the biggest tease on the planet. Let me clean up before you try and impress me any further."

Ethan looked around astonished, at some point Coop had already cleaned everything, except for their two plates and utensils. He stood and brought the plates near the dishwasher, while Coop lurked closely behind him.

"You clean as the food is cooking, that's the secret."

Ethan bent over to put the dishes on the bottom rack. Coop gripped his waist forcefully from behind. "I felt like I heard a bit of a challenge in your voice a moment ago. Did I misunderstand?"

Ethan righted his posture, turning to face him. He took both of Coop's hands and brought them to his mouth, lightly kissing his fingertips while backing up against the large, shiny granite countertop.

Coop grabbed him by the waist and lifted him up onto the counter, placing his body in between Ethan's legs. He went straight for Ethan's mouth, with his tongue leading the way. The two kissed passionately, fully immersed inside each other's warm mouths.

Ethan pulled back and brought Coop's hand slowly to his mouth, leaving his tongue slightly out, while staring into Coop's carnal green eyes. He licked Coop's pointer finger, starting with just the tip, then slowly dragged his tongue up and down both sides of his finger.

Coop finally shoved his entire finger inside Ethan's mouth. Ethan sucked and licked it enthusiastically, as if it were a melting ice cream cone on a hot summer day. Coop moved his finger around the inside of his mouth, pressing on the sides of it. "Naughty…little… puppy," Coop whispered.

He and Ethan were locked in a thirsty stare-down, with Coop's finger still being sucked on. Ethan lightly pulled the finger out, making a popping sound. He was torn between staying in this position or running up the stairs. He knew if he said what he wanted to, he may just be done right here on the counter. After a few moments of being forcefully kissed again, he decided to answer Coop's earlier question.

He grabbed a section of Coop's hair tightly, and put his mouth right next to his ear. "Cooper, you should know that every time I've imagined being with you, it's been rough. I've never imagined it being gentle. I only imagine you taking me, wholly and completely. So, to answer to your question, yes, I did challenge you." He licked Coop's earlobe, then tugged lightly on the chunk of Coop's hair he'd been holding onto. Bringing his face to meet Coop's eyes, he said, "Get the wine and bring it to your bedroom, you tease." He released his hold on Coop's hair, then hopped off the counter and darted upstairs.

Ethan ran quickly inside Coop's bedroom; he stood leaning against Coop's desk. Coop came in only a few seconds later and slammed the door. Ethan gave Coop a challenging look while he walked toward him.

"Ethan, you called me a tease again. I showed you earlier what happens when you say that."

Ethan put both his hands on Coop's chest and pushed him backward onto his bed. He sat atop Coop, rubbing his chest.

Coop grabbed Ethan's hands and looked up at him. "Did you want wine first or…?"

Ethan sat atop him thinking, while lightly moving his lower half back and forth. "Hmm…I don't know. Should I?" Coop grabbed the sides of Ethan's ass and gently moved him off his body, onto the bed. He stood up, exhaling while looking at Ethan.

Ethan looked up at him. "What's wrong? Why did you move me? I was just thinking if it's really going to hurt, maybe I should have the wine to help. I'm a little nervous."

Coop sat down on the bed next to him, lost in thought. *What am I doing? I don't want to hurt him. Not only that, but he's nervous. I'm even more nervous. I can't say that to him, though. Will I even be good at sex? Are people good at sex right away? Does it take practice? I don't even know. As much as I want him in that way, my heart wants him even more. I feel so unfocused now, this memory, this feeling, my heart is just telling me to comfort him, to hold him close.*

Ethan sat up next to him, looking quite concerned.

Coop reached over and held his hand. "I know this is silly to bring up right now, but I'm feeling really conflicted. I just… I can't concentrate. I've only ever felt my heart reach for another person like this, one other time in my entire life."

Suddenly, Ethan seemed like he wasn't sure where this conversation was going, but he looked at Coop softly.

Coop continued, "It was right after my mom passed away. I was ten years old and had just won the Junior Championship and everyone was cheering. It was really strange because I was happy for a minute, because everyone was celebrating, and it was because of my homerun. But, while everyone else was cheering and happy, I just wanted to be alone. I was thinking about my mom, she used to be the loudest one in the stands, and this time she wasn't there. All of a sudden, I noticed another boy looking over from the other field, in a white jersey. I think he was on a team that had lost. I walked over to the fence and just stared at him, as a woman pulled him away. I wanted so badly to cry with him about my mom. He looked sad, too, so I thought maybe we could cry together and make each other feel better. It was such a weird feeling, but it was like my heart was pulling me toward him. I felt like he would understand, it was like we shared something, even though we didn't talk to each other. That was the last time I felt my heart move like this. We were just kids…it must sound stupid."

Ethan stood, and silent tears fell instantly. He looked at Coop, who was still caught up in the memory, looking at the floor. While holding his number two chain in between his fingers, he asked, "Cooper, what number was he wearing?"

Coop looked up at Ethan. "Two."

Ethan nodded, showing his charm in between his fingers.

Coop instantly realized that the little boy from all those years ago was Ethan. His heart raced, and he stared at Ethan silently, trying to hold back tears. *How can this be? How could it have been him the whole time? This is why…this is why my heart warmed every time I saw him. It knew him. My heart knew he was mine before I did. My heart belongs fully and completely to him, and it always has.*

He stood and hugged him tightly while gently lifting him off the ground.

"Ethan..." Coop sniffled, as tears fell. "Ethan, it really has always been you."

Ethan nuzzled his cheek into Coop's. "Cooper...it's always been you for me, too."

The two held each other for several minutes, switching between kissing, tears, and squeezes. Ethan laid down on Coop's bed and looked up, as Coop stood next to him, rubbing his face with the back of his hand. "Ethan, I am the happiest I've ever been with you here next to me. Like deliriously, completely happy." He smiled brightly.

Ethan kissed his hand. "Me too. I have never had a day as perfect as this, I don't know how anything could ever top it."

Coop's eyes widened playfully. "Is that a challenge?" he asked.

Chapter 26
Make Me Cupcakes

The next morning Ethan opened his eyes to a sleeping Coop next to him.

Wow. Last night was amazing…I didn't know that doing that would make me feel this way. I thought it was purely physical, but it wasn't. It was beautiful and natural. The feel of his heart pressed close to mine, our heartbeats completely in sync. His soft kisses and sweet words. He was so caring and attentive. Thinking about the way I imagined it before, seems crazy now. When I imagined those things, it was like I didn't know him, and now I do. Ethan exhaled, lost in an overwhelming feeling of bliss.

He closed his eyes and placed a hand on his chest, then looked down, confused at the chain hanging from his neck. He clearly remembered taking it off before they'd gotten closer last night. Upon inspection, he realized it was Coop's number one charm. He glanced at the nightstand and didn't see his chain. *Did I put his on by mistake? I was so out of it, how did I even put it on?* He looked over at Coop's perfect chest, peeking out of the blankets and saw his own number two charm sparkling against his tanned skin. *He must have put them on us after I fell asleep,* he concluded. He pinched Coop's cheek lightly and said, "You're so cute."

Coop put his hand on top of Ethan's and kissed the inside of it.

He opened his sleepy eyes and looked at Ethan in adoration. "You're perfect," he said, as he pinched the number one charm that lay on Ethan's hard pecs.

Ethan smiled and looked at him. "When did you put this on me? I don't even remember."

Coop smiled big. "It was after we were done. I got up and kissed you after the shower. You closed your eyes and grabbed at my neck, trying to pull me back in, while you were half asleep. You kept saying, 'Mine, you're mine, Cooper,' over and over again. It was the cutest thing. So, I took my chain off and put it on you, then I grabbed yours from the nightstand and put it on myself. I knelt next to the bed and tried to show you, but you just patted my head and fell asleep."

Ethan smiled at him. "Okay, well that's adorable. Thank you. It means so much to me, that you put this on me. I'll cherish it always."

Coop smiled. "I'll do the same."

Their quiet peace was interrupted by the sound of Ethan's phone ringing. He'd left it on the desk last night, after they came back upstairs. Ethan quickly sat up without thinking as Coop placed a hand on his shoulder and shook his head no at him. "Don't try to stand up. I'll get it for you. Stay in bed. Just relax."

Coop walked over and grabbed Ethan's phone, then passed it to him.

Ethan couldn't believe the way Coop was treating him. He'd been doted on his whole life by his mother, of course, but never by another guy. "Thank you. That was sweet of you. I don't think you could be any more perfect."

Coop kissed him on the head and sat back in bed beside him. "You're the one that's perfect."

Ethan's phone continued to ring, he saw it was his mother calling and sent it to voicemail. "Sorry, my parents have no concept of the appropriate time to call people."

Coop shrugged his shoulders in response. "Nah, it's fine. We were up anyway. I shut my alarm off for the first time ever last night. I didn't want it to wake you this morning. It feels weird not running, but I'd rather just stay in bed with you."

Ethan's phone buzzed as he received a text from his mom, with several more immediately following:

Mom:
7:05 AM: *Good Morning Mimmo, what time are you coming over?*
7:06 AM: *I started prepping without you. I can wait to blanch the tomatoes if you'll be here soon.*
7:07 AM: *Are you awake?*

Ethan ran his hand down his face and passed the phone to Coop, he figured it was easier than explaining everything.

"What's up? I'm guessing it's your mom," Coop said. He read the texts and passed the phone back to Ethan.

Ethan shook his head side to side, as another two texts came in.

7:09 AM: *Call me when you get this. I can't wait too long. Your dad says Coop wakes up at 5am every day.*

7:10 AM: *Never mind, he also said I shouldn't text you. He wanted me to tell you that.*

"You should probably just call her. Your dad knows me too well after all these years," Coop said.

Ethan tilted his head. "You're too cute to argue with, it's unfair." He was about to call his mother, then realized they didn't even have a plan yet. "Wait, before I call her, what time are we going there? I don't want to help prep tomatoes. We'll be there all day if we go now."

"Well, it's up to you. How are you feeling? We can go whenever you feel up to it."

Ethan stretched his arms over his head. "I feel a little exhausted, but other than that I'm fine. I'm glad you didn't ask me to work out this morning, though." Ethan flipped his legs over the side of the bed and stood momentarily, pure exhaustion overcame him. He looked at Coop, who watched him with a concerned look on his face.

"You okay? Why don't you lie back down? We can take our time this morning. We don't have to rush."

Coop walked around the bed and tucked the covers tightly around him.

He kissed Ethan's head, ruffled his hair, then took his phone, and called his mom, who answered on the first ring. "Good morning, it's Coop. How are you this morning?"

She was so loud that Ethan, of course, heard everything. "Oh, hi, Coop, good morning. I'm fine, thank you for asking. Such a sweet man. Is Ethan asleep?"

"Ethan isn't feeling too well, we stayed up late last night and he's probably just a little tired. I know he was really looking forward to making the gravy with you, but I don't think we'll be able to make it until later this afternoon. What time is good for us to come over?"

Ethan closed his eyes and turned over in bed. *He's good, didn't pause for her to try and ask any questions. She may get him in a second, though. I think I know what's coming next.*

She replied, "Oh, between three and four would be great, but really any time before that is fine. Wait a minute, does he have a fever? Or is he really just tired? I've been worried about him, he looked so thin yesterday. Are you sure he's okay? I can come by and check on him if you want. Actually, maybe I should, no, wait… shoot, I can't trust Paul with the gravy…"

Coop bit his lip, as Ethan sighed. Coop replied quickly, "No, he's fine. No fever, he's just tired. I'll take good care of him. I'm going to bake him some cupcakes in a few, I'll bring some for you and Coach when we see you this afternoon, okay?" He winced, awaiting her reply.

"Oh, cupcakes? You know how to bake? Cupcakes are hard, you know. You mix the batter too much and you'll end up with hockey pucks. Hahaha…. Never happened to me, of course, but my sister,

Tina, you may get to meet her tonight, oh, now she has made some hockey pucks before." She cackled.

Ethan's eyes shot open, and he rolled onto his back, a look of terror covered his face, hearing his Aunt Tina may come for a visit later. Coop sat on the bed beside him.

"Well, this will be my first time baking them, but Ethan told me that he wanted some." Coop winked at Ethan.

"That's so nice, what a doll of a man. Yes, well Mimmo loves vanilla bean flavor, oh, he is such a sweet little bean. You're sure he's okay? I really gotta get this gravy ready. I can leave you on speaker, though, if you want. I can make the gravy, while you—"

Coach interrupted in the background, "Gina, hang up. Let the man make the damn cupcakes!"

"Sorry, Coop. I'll see you guys this afternoon. Add my number to your phone, too, in case you need anything while Mimmo is asleep."

"I will, thank you. Bye," he said.

Coop leaned down and smooched Ethan on the mouth. "Now, I'm gonna run downstairs and grab you some stuff to eat. You just lay here and relax." He placed Ethan's phone on the nightstand next to him while Ethan snuggled up tight in the blankets.

As Coop stepped out of the room, Ethan shouted, "Wait, come back here for a minute."

Coop walked backward next to the bed and looked down at Ethan. "Do you have a special request?" he asked.

Ethan grabbed at Coop's gym shorts. "When did I say I wanted vanilla cupcakes?"

Coop looked down at him. "Oh that, you said that when you were drunk on Friday night. You were sleep talking, or drunk talking...I don't know which one. Your eyes were closed, and I was trying to get you to wake up. You mumbled something about pushing you on a swing and wanting a vanilla cupcake."

Ethan couldn't remember that. "That's funny. I've never thought about you pushing me on a swing before."

Coop tilted his head. "Well, I swung you around pretty easily last night." He winked and leaned down, giving Ethan a big kiss on the lips.

Ethan looked at Coop as he pulled back. "Okay, but are you going to make them for me? Or did you just tell her that?"

Coop ruffled his hair. "Of course, I'm gonna make them. You asked for them, it's my job to give you what you want. But let me get some food in us first. When you have to get up to go to the bathroom, just walk slowly. Don't try to run in there and definitely don't attempt to go down the stairs. If you need something, just call me. I'll bring my phone with me, just in case." He showed Ethan his phone, placed it in his pocket and went down to the kitchen.

Ethan turned back over and closed his eyes; he really was so tired and truthfully didn't feel that great. He ached all over, and he had a bit of a headache.

Coop went downstairs and prepped two breakfast smoothies for Ethan and himself. He poured them into two airtight cups and placed them inside an insulated bag. He also grabbed some yogurt and fruit in case Ethan preferred everything by itself. Next, he tossed some plates and utensils, along with water bottles and napkins into the bag and headed back upstairs. He noticed Ethan asleep as he walked into the room. *Well, good thing everything is in an insulated bag. I'll let him rest for a while. He must be so spent.*

Coop placed the bag on his desk and walked into the bathroom, he grabbed the bottle of ibuprofen and placed it on the nightstand. He snapped his fingers, remembering something he'd read. He quickly jogged down the stairs and grabbed a heating pad and brought it upstairs with him, placing it on the nightstand beside the medicine. He rubbed Ethan's face lightly; Ethan didn't move an inch.

He decided he would make the cupcakes while Ethan was asleep, and quickly went back into the kitchen. He pulled up a recipe online and readied the ingredients. *How many should I make? His mom said that her sister may go there tonight too. Should I make extra?* he wondered. He decided on an even dozen. Luckily, he had enough supplies on hand for the recipe with the highest rating. *Wait, I don't have cupcake wrappers, but Dad usually has leftover stuff from parties, I can run over there really quick and see if he has any.*

He hurried around to the main estate, hoping that Ethan wouldn't wake up in the time that he was gone. As he walked down the foyer, he heard Levi mumbling to himself in the kitchen. Coop walked in quickly and saw Levi sitting at the kitchen bar alone, reading something on his phone.

Coop greeted him, "Good morning."

Levi looked up, straightening his satin outer robe. "Good morning, Coop. Where is Ethan? I assumed he stayed the night."

Coop quickly searched the cabinets and answered him, "Yeah, he did, but he's asleep. I'm trying to find cupcake wrappers. Dad usually keeps left over party supplies in one of these." He continued rummaging through the cabinets.

Levi gave him a big smile. "You're making cupcakes?"

Coop found the wrappers and grabbed them. "Yeah, I'm making them for Ethan. I gotta go. Don't mean to be rude, but I want to try and make them before he wakes up."

Levi smiled and nodded. "Of course, you should hurry and get back then. Let me know if you need any help. I'm great in the kitchen."

Coop seriously doubted that was true, but he thanked him anyway with a smile and dashed toward his side of the estate.

He opened the bookmark on his phone for the cupcake recipe, then mixed and poured the batter quickly into the twelve wrappers. Luckily, he remembered to preheat the oven, so he was able to place them right inside. The next step was the frosting, the recipe was quite simple with only four ingredients. He prepared it as directed and set the bowl aside. He looked at the timer he'd set for the cupcakes, realizing he still had enough time to run upstairs and check on Ethan. He peeked in through the door, Ethan was still fast asleep. Coop smiled and ran back downstairs. His stomach rumbled, reminding him that he hadn't eaten yet. He didn't want to go back upstairs for the smoothie, and accidentally wake Ethan up, not when he was so close to finishing the cupcakes.

He grabbed a banana and yogurt and quickly ate them. The timer on his phone beeped, and he pulled the cupcakes out. He checked two of them; they were cooked to perfection. He slipped them out onto a cooling rack and ran back up the stairs.

Coop was getting a little tired from all the stair running, but figured he should do it anyway, since he missed his morning run. He looked inside his room and saw Ethan sitting up, looking at the nightstand.

"Hello, sleepy puppy," Coop said as he walked over to him.

Ethan smiled at him, and gestured at the nightstand. "What is all this?" he asked.

"Well, I made us breakfast a while ago, it's in that big bag on the desk. You were asleep when I got back, so I left it. I wasn't sure what you would need, and I didn't want you to have to try and find anything yourself."

Ethan smiled. "Wow, this is just so thoughtful." He pulled Coop's arm down and embraced him. He lightly kissed the side of Coop's neck, then inhaled. "Mmmm, were you making frosting? I just tasted something sweet."

"Calm down, little puppy, we don't have time for that right now. Besides, you said you were feeling dizzy earlier." He smooched Ethan quickly on the mouth.

Coop grabbed the insulated bag from the desk and placed it on the bed. "To answer your question, I was making frosting. I'm just waiting for the cupcakes to cool, then I can frost them. Let's have our breakfast first," he said.

Ethan looked at the time, it was already 10:15 AM. "Oof, I feel bad that I slept so long, what did you make me?" Ethan excitedly rubbed his hands together as Coop pulled out the smoothie, which was still mostly frozen, along with the fruit and yogurt.

Coop unscrewed the lid of one of the smoothies and popped a straw inside. "This has all kinds of fruits and veggies in there. It's a good recovery smoothie, hopefully you like it."

Ethan took the large cup and sipped it. "Oh my gosh, it's delicious. Sooo good."

Coop grabbed his smoothie out and drank it slowly. He couldn't help his eyes being drawn to Ethan's mouth after last night. His mind cared about Ethan's well-being, but his bottom half, well, that was another story. He realized what his body was thinking and stood up quickly.

"What? What happened? Why did you jump up like that?" Ethan asked.

Coop shook his head and continued sipping from his straw, looking guiltily around the room.

Ethan looked carefully at Coop's face and body, grinning when he figured out what was on Coop's mind. "You're a menace, you know that? Who was the one that said we didn't have time for another round?" Ethan joked.

Coop chuckled. "Well, to be fair, you kissed my neck a few minutes ago and moaned, now you're happily slurping on a straw. Making me feel things, I can't help it." Coop made a pouty face at him, and Ethan smiled coyly.

The timer on Coop's phone beeped, signaling the cupcakes should be ready to be frosted. "I'll be right back, just eat whatever else you want out of the bag."

He ran back downstairs, washed his hands, and lightly touched the top of a cupcake to check the temperature. "Perfect," he said as he finished frosting the last one. He was quite proud and took a few pictures to show Ethan.

He quickly jogged back upstairs and flopped onto the bed.

Ethan was adjusting the heating pad under himself and laid on his back beside Coop. "Thank you for the smoothie and the rest of the stuff," he said.

Coop sprawled out on his back. "Ethan, I'm so tired. I've run up and down the stairs like twenty times this morning."

Ethan leaned in close to Coop, tucking himself under his arm and lying on his bare chest. Coop closed his eyes, rubbing Ethan's back lightly. "Look how good you fit, tucked in here beside me."

Feeling Ethan's warm tongue tickling his chest, Coop's eyes shot open, and he giggled. "What are you doing? Naughty. I told you we didn't have time for that."

Ethan's mouth was all over Coop's pecs. He looked up at him. "Well, this is so you don't get ants in your bed. You're covered in tiny flecks of frosting…I'm just trying to clean you up," he said.

Coop felt his body enter dangerous territory as Ethan slid down toward his navel. "Oh, I think you got some down here, mmmmm," Ethan moaned as he licked.

"Ethan, you said you weren't feeling good earlier. You shouldn't," Coop half-heartedly said, closing his eyes and running his fingers through Ethan's hair softly.

Coop's defenses crumbled and he gave into the moment with Ethan. He wanted nothing more than to make him happy, and if he wanted this right now, then Coop would give it to him. Several minutes later, Ethan rolled over and laid his head on the pillow next to Coop.

Coop leaned in to kiss him. "Thank you," Coop said.

Ethan smiled and then sat up. He grabbed a water bottle off the nightstand and took a large swig. "Oof, I feel hot, like hot, hot literally. I'm all sweaty."

Coop looked at the time. "Let's take a quick shower, then we'll see how you're feeling."

Ethan nodded. "Okay, but then I want a cupcake. That frosting…was really delicious. Mmmm, I loved the taste of it, I want more." Coop tilted his head and looked at him as Ethan pulled his head back. "What? That wasn't a euphemism for anything. I really mean it, the frosting that I licked off of you was delicious. I want more," Ethan said.

Coop smiled and led Ethan by the hand into the shower.

The two spent the rest of the morning lounging around, with Ethan enthusiastically devouring several cupcakes.

Chapter 27
Mimmo Is A Butterfly

That afternoon they headed over to see Ethan's parents. When they pulled in front of the house, Ethan noticed a familiar blue sedan parked in the driveway. "Oh, nooo," he whined.

"What's wrong?" Coop asked, as he turned the engine off and parked.

"It's my Aunt Tina. I forgot my mom slipped that in this morning. Of course, she would come. I'm sure my mom told her all about the ice bath picture and everything else." He hung his head and sighed. "This is gonna be rough."

Coop leaned over and met Ethan in the middle with a quick smooch and a bright smile. "It will be fine, don't worry about it. That's why I brought extra cupcakes. Just give her a cupcake if she starts to annoy you," Coop suggested.

Ethan lifted his chin toward Coop. "Can you see any marks on me from last night?" He pulled the visor down and checked himself in the mirror.

Coop rubbed a few small hickeys on the sides of Ethan's neck and pulled his collar up to cover them.

"No, not really, they're pretty much covered if you just leave only that top button open."

Ethan opened the car door. "Follow me into the land of crazy people," he said, stepping outside the car.

Coop carried the cupcakes in a covered dessert container with a single handle, and the two held hands as they walked up the driveway.

Ethan opened the front door, with Coop close behind him. The smell of the gravy smacked the two in the face as soon as they entered the home. "Wow, that smells great," Coop whispered.

"Yeah, I told you, it's amazing. This is the smell of my childhood," Ethan said.

Ethan's dad came out of the kitchen to greet them, "Hey, son, Coop." Coop shook Coach's proffered hand. "How are you feeling, Ethan?" he asked, with his hands on his hips, while giving the two a discerning look.

"I'm fine, feeling better. I was just a little tired. How deep into the box are they?" Ethan asked.

"The box is almost empty. They've been out on the patio for a while," his dad answered.

Ethan let out a long sigh, and walked with Coop into the kitchen. He looked outside at the patio, and saw his mom and Aunt Tina, happily sipping their wine. He quickly pulled Coop back from the patio doors to avoid being seen.

"What was that about?" Coop asked. "What does 'deep in the box' mean?"

Ethan smiled and pointed carefully outside to the table that the two women sat at, a box of red wine between them. Gina quickly flipped her head around, as Ethan pulled Coop's body backward behind the kitchen wall again.

Ethan winced. "Did she see you?"

"I'm not sure." Coop shrugged. "Maybe?"

"Cooper, if they're deep into the box it means my aunt's been here for a while. Which in turn means that my mom will not be focused on my aunt, she'll be able to focus solely on the two of us. My aunt is a special kind of strange, so just sit close to me. The same as the bar yesterday, when you pulled me in close. That's the general idea with my aunt. Just keep your distance." He heard the slider door open and smooched Coop quickly.

"Oooh, you see, Tina, you smell that, that's the cologne," his mom said loudly.

"Oh, that is nice, wow, sexy, it's stronger than your gravy, G," Tina replied. She spoke exactly the same as Gina, but perhaps a bit louder.

Ethan squeezed his fists together and closed his eyes, while Coop chuckled silently and pulled him in close.

His mom came around the corner first, she had a huge smile on her face and wrapped them both up in a hug. She smelled strongly of wine as she squeezed the two of them into a bundle. "Hi, boys! I'm so happy you're here! Mimmo, baby, are you feeling better?" she asked. She turned his face toward her, lifting it from Coop's shoulder.

Ethan looked at her annoyed. "Yes, Mom. I am feeling better. Well, I *was* until my aunt called my boyfriend's cologne sexy."

Gina rubbed his shoulder, then went around the corner to tend to her gravy.

Tina walked into the kitchen, she held a bowl of something that Coop had never seen before and was chewing loudly. Whatever it was, hung slightly out of her mouth, as she walked in and made eye contact with Coop. "Oh, my sweet mother, look at you," she said. She quickly pulled the food into her mouth and crunched it loudly. She placed the bowl down and wiped her hands on her black cotton capri pants. Her hair was frosted, and it had a large stiff wave in the front. She wore heavy eye make-up, and had a loose-fitting, low-cut, yellow T-shirt on.

She stared at Coop, then hugged Ethan. "Ethan, look at you, it's only been a few weeks since I saw you, you look so thin!"

Ethan eyed the large red bowl that she put down. "Oooh, Taralli!

Mom did you make these?" Ethan shoved one into his mouth and grabbed one for Coop.

Ethan placed a Taralli into Coop's mouth. "Here, try this, it's homemade Taralli, well, technically, this is Tarallini because of the size, but it's basically the same thing. It's like a small homemade crunchy breadstick."

Coop ate it and smiled. "Thanks, that tastes great. I've never had Tarallini before."

Tina approached Coop. "Hi, I'm Aunt Tina, but you can call me Tina," she said, leaning in for a hug.

Coop didn't normally hug other people; he tried to smile and looked to Ethan for help. Ethan quickly came in between them, as she came within a paper's-width distance. He scolded her, "You can't hug people without their permission, Aunt Tina!"

She looked at Coop, who was very uncomfortable. "Oh, oh, sorry. I didn't know. We're Italian, we're all family here, we're just very affectionate," she said, looking at Coop. She grabbed a Taralli and dipped it into her wine, then ate it quickly.

Coop smiled. "It's fine, I'm just not used to people hugging me. It's nice to meet you, I'm Coop." He extended his hand in place of the hug.

Aunt Tina smiled big, loudly chewing on another piece of Taralli. "I gotta ask you something," she said, eyeing Coop. "How do you look like that and say you don't let people hug you? You play baseball, don't baseball players always smack each other on their asses, and pick each other up?"

Ethan interjected, "What does that have to do with anything? You're a stranger. Even if he let our teammates hug him, which I haven't seen him do," he paused, "well, maybe the ass smack I've seen in the locker room, but that's beside the point. It's not the same as his boyfriend's crazy aunt pressing her body against him, without permission."

She pulled her head back and eyed Ethan. "You've seen other guys smack his ass? Didn't that make you jealous? I would be so jealous dating a guy that looked like him. Your mom told me about the ice bath picture, how can you stand other guys seeing him naked in the locker room? I'd have to put a leash on him if he were mine!" She winked at Coop and cackled loudly.

Ethan was not amused, as he stared his aunt down. Coop noticed Ethan's cheeks were quickly turning a bright shade of red. He wanted to ease the tension; he grabbed Ethan's hand and pulled him in close, then whispered something into his ear. Ethan definitely liked what he heard. His eyes went wide, and he looked at his mom. "We'll be right back. I want to show Cooper something," he said.

Ethan pulled Coop into the room where he kept his things and locked the door. He grabbed his face and kissed him deeply, while Coop lifted him onto the bed.

Coop kissed him with more force, leaning in and pressing his body against Ethan's. He kissed the side of his neck, then whispered in his ear, "Do you really want me to do it?"

Ethan wrapped his arms around Coop tightly. "Yes, do it. It will calm me down. If I don't calm down, I'm going to end up fighting with my aunt. Help me please, Cooper?"

Coop squeezed his hand between them, fumbling with Ethan's belt. Soon, Ethan had goosebumps and, more importantly, his tension had been eased.

Ethan cinched his belt tight again. "Thank you, oof, I feel so much better now." He kissed Coop gently on the mouth.

Coop looked him up and down. "You look really good wearing my clothes, you know that?"

Ethan joked, "Well, just imagine my feet every time I wear your shoes, they're about an inch too big for me."

"I wondered about that the other day, but you said they were fine.

The ones you wore today are good, though, right? Those are a little tight on me," Coop said.

"Yeah, still a little big but that's okay. I'll have to give you your clothes back tomorrow after I wash them tonight."

Coop was confused. "What are you talking about?"

Ethan tilted his head, and held Coop's chin. "What else could I be talking about? I just said I'd wash this outfit and give it back to you tomorrow. Where did I lose you?" He smooched Coop quickly.

Coop already couldn't bear the thought of sleeping without Ethan. "Well, I wasn't planning on you staying here tonight. I thought you would just come back and stay with me; don't you want to?"

"Of course, I do," Ethan said. "Do you think I'd rather stay here? I want to stay with you, but I'm new to all of this and I don't know how much space you need."

Coop pulled him in close. "None, I need zero space. I just need you. Just bring whatever you want and whenever you want to, we can always run here and grab something if you need it."

"I happily accept that offer. But I should warn you, I probably won't ever want to leave."

Coop smiled. "That's the plan." He gave Ethan a quick smooch and squeezed him.

His dad knocked on the door, just as the two separated from the hug.

Ethan opened the door cheerfully. "Yeah? What's up, Dad?"

"Your mom and Tina are going crazy over Coop's cologne again. I just wanted to warn you. Tina already asked if she could sit next to him at dinner." Coach rolled his eyes. "I did not miss Tina…what a piece of work she is."

Ethan smiled and patted his dad's shoulder. "Thanks, Dad. It's fine. I'm good. It's cool if they like the way he smells." He pulled Coop by the hand into the living room.

Coach made a confused face at Ethan's laid-back response. He watched as the two sat in the living room on the leather loveseat.

Gina and Tina quickly joined them sitting on the opposite couch. Tina pointed at them. "So, do you guys have any single friends that are into cool women in their mid-thirties?" she asked.

Gina teased, "Who's in their mid-thirties? You're thirty-eight, that's not mid-thirties!"

They both cackled loudly.

"I brought the cupcakes, we put them in the kitchen, if you hadn't seen them yet," Coop said to Gina.

"Oooh, you did? I'm so excited. How many did Mimmo eat? That will tell me how good they are."

Ethan dropped his head, while Coop smiled and raised four fingers.

"*Four?* Mimmo! That's too many cupcakes! When did you eat them? I hope you saved room for dinner. See, this is why you can't be away from me, eating cupcakes before dinner!" She laughed.

Tina said to Gina, "G, remember the hockey pucks I made for ma and pop for their anniversary that one year?" The sisters cackled together.

"Of course," Gina said. "But better than that was the crunchy frosting that you made!"

They continued laughing as Coop and Ethan leaned their heads together watching them on the couch.

"Aunt Tina, how did you make crunchy frosting? Was that on purpose?" Ethan asked.

Tina and Gina cackled loudly. Tina replied, "Of course not, Ethan. I was trying to follow a recipe and I thought more sugar would make it sweeter, but it ended up not breaking down properly. So, it was just crunchy, grainy frosting. It was awful. Terrible."

Ethan left Coop to grab some water for the both of them. Gina waited for Ethan to walk into the kitchen, and then nodded at Tina.

Tina got up quickly and sat next to Coop, she whispered, "You have to be careful with him. He seems very tough, and he is sometimes, but he's really like a delicate little butterfly." Tina fluttered her hands like a butterfly.

Gina nodded in agreement. Coop scooted to the left away from Tina, who was very close to him on the two-person loveseat.

"How is he a butterfly?" Coop asked.

Gina replied from other couch, "He is very sensitive to things."

Ethan walked back in. "Can you move please, Aunt Tina?"

Tina folded her robust arms. "Nope, move your feet, lose your seat."

Gina said, "Those are the rules, Mimmo."

The two sisters clapped their hands, cackling loudly.

Ethan raised his eyebrows toward the patio at Coop, he understood and followed him outside. The patio area was nice, with a hot tub and pool. Ethan walked over near the hot tub and sat on the edge, putting his feet inside. Coop followed him over, rolled up his navy pants to mid calves, sat down beside him, and stuck his feet in.

"So, they say you're a delicate butterfly and I need to be careful with you, Ethan."

"Pfftt. That's hilarious. The boxed wine talking."

"I'm excited for practice tomorrow, can't wait to try out my new stance," Coop said.

Ethan hung his head. "You know, I don't really like that guy, Mac, the relief pitcher. He's been rude since I joined the team."

Coop scoffed. "I don't think many people like him. He's rude to everyone. I almost punched him a couple times because of you last week."

"I thought so," Ethan said. "I was pretty sure you saw me headed toward you that one day, I thought I saw a smile, then he said something rude and cringey."

Coop rolled his eyes. "Yep, then he ran and hid next to Coach."

He put his hand on Ethan's thigh. "Don't worry about it, he's not gonna do that now that we're together. Besides, I'm gonna crack that fastball tomorrow, first one he throws, guaranteed."

Ethan made a disagreeable face, looking at Coop.

Coop pulled his head back. "What, you don't think I can do it?"

Ethan leaned back on his elbows. "Well, you've been having trouble with it… So, why don't we bet something, make it more interesting?"

"I'm always down for a good bet. What are we betting?"

Before Ethan could answer, his mother, father, and aunt came running outside with old water guns and sprayed the two of them relentlessly. Well, Aunt Tina and Coach sprayed them, Gina kept smacking hers and nothing was coming out.

"Pump it Gina, I told you to pump it first!" Coach yelled at her, while he doused Coop and Ethan.

Gina screamed, "I am pumping it, Paul, its broken!"

Ethan tried to shield Coop from Aunt Tina, who was really honed in on Coop's chest.

Coach grabbed Gina and pulled her into the pool with him. She surfaced, and screamed, "Paul, the ziti is gonna be done soon! Are you crazy?!"

Coach watched as she trudged out of the water. Since the spraying had stopped, Ethan unbuttoned his olive-green shirt and removed it, while Coop pulled his drenched white polo off. They hung their wet shirts over the backs of two chairs, while Gina stood frozen on the pool stairs just staring at the two of them.

"*Oh damnnn*, looks like little Mimmo wasn't just tired this morning. No wonder he wasn't feeling good," Aunt Tina said loudly.

Ethan quickly slid the door open and pulled Coop back into the room where he kept his things. He looked at himself in the mirror reflection. "Oof, it looks like I was attacked, no wonder my mom was frozen." He turned and saw several hickeys, a few scratches and two light bruises on both sides of his waist.

Coop looked at him softly. "From this angle it looks like I really hurt you."

Ethan turned Coop's back to the mirror. There were massive red scratches all the way down his back. Not to mention the hickeys on Coop's chest.

"There, see? Did I hurt you when I did that?" Ethan asked.

"Nope, didn't feel it and if I did, I must have liked it," Coop replied, while trying to reach the scratches.

Ethan tilted his head. "Same for me. Definitely didn't—okay, well, I definitely did feel it, especially these," he pointed to the bruises on his sides, "but I liked it, too."

Ethan walked over to the closet. "Well, now you have to wear my clothes," he said, with a smile.

Coach knocked on the door. "Hey, your mother was luckily distracted by the scratches on Coop's back, and Tina is keeping her busy talking about his nipples and his...forget it." He sighed loudly though the door. "What has my life become? Anyway, I don't think she noticed anything on you, Ethan. Hurry up and get dressed. I heard her tell Tina that the ziti will be ready in ten minutes."

"Alright," Ethan called through the door.

"I feel really embarrassed right now, I know that's probably stupid," Coop said.

Ethan kissed him quickly. "It is a little embarrassing, but it's fine. We just have to eat, then we'll leave and never come back."

Coop and Ethan both threw on gym shorts and slim-fitting T-shirts. They joined the group standing in the dining room.

Aunt Tina eyed Coop as he walked out. "Well, I guess I shouldn't have called little precious a butterfly...not with those claw marks he left on you, Coop." She let out a light growl and clawed in the air.

Gina narrowed her eyes and looked at Ethan, then stared down Coop. "You said Mimmo was sleeping earlier, did you lie to me?"

"He did sleep for most of the morning, he didn't even eat his breakfast until after ten. I made the cupcakes and everything while he slept," Coop said.

Tina re-joined the conversation, "You know, they say the deeper the scratches…"

Gina smacked her with a dish towel.

"Too much?" Tina asked, looking at her sister.

"Yes, too much, shut up," Gina said. "We're all adults here, we know how it happens. Jeez Louise…we don't need to talk about it."

Gina served the baked ziti, scooping it onto each plate. The food was delicious, and the conversation happily shifted to Gina and Paul sharing high school memories. Gina spoke animatedly as she held her fork in her hand, "Yeah and then Tom and Levi showed up, together, both barefoot! Hahaha…I think everyone figured it out then."

"Yeah, those two have always been a couple of knuckleheads, when it came to each other," Coach said. He finished off his ziti and then spoke to Coop, "Hey I've been meaning to ask how the Foundation is, you guys still planning to have the Youth Benefit Gala this year?"

Ethan looked at the both of them confused, as did Gina and Tina.

Coop smiled. "Yeah, just locking down a few other pieces concerning entertainment, but it'll come together."

"What are you two talking about?" Gina asked loudly from across the small table.

Coach, sitting next to her, wiggled his ear and squinted several times.

Coop answered, "I recently took over the charitable portion of Morgan Enterprises. We held an Inaugural Youth Benefit Gala for a local charity last year, well, we've done a lot of benefits, but this one was a little different. I'm planning to hold it again later this year."

Tina dropped her fork loudly on her plate and wiped her hands on her pants. A piece of cheese hung from her chin. She looked at Coop. "You're a damn philamannthromist, too? Oh my…I don't even know what to say. Ethan, listen to Aunt Tina, get a leash for him," she warned.

Ethan corrected her, "*Philanthropist*, is the word you're looking for, Aunt Tina."

Paul shook his head in disapproval, looking at Tina.

Ethan grinned widely and turned his attention to Coop. "I had no idea. We hadn't discussed that yet. That's so amazing."

Coop smiled modestly. "I don't do much. I'd hardly consider myself a philanthropist."

Tina shook her head resolutely. "Leash, Ethan, get a leash."

Gina grabbed her red and white linen napkin from her lap and whacked her sister lightly with it. After everyone finished eating, Ethan and Coop removed the empty plates and brought them to the kitchen.

Coop stood over the sink, prepared to wash the dishes, as Gina rounded the corner. "Drop it! You are a guest here, nope, no, thank you. Very sweet, but no thank you," she said.

Coop backed away from the sink as told. A little while later, the two started loading some of Ethan's belongings into their cars. Ethan walked past his mother, Aunt Tina, and his father, who now sat in the dining room drinking coffee. He slid the patio door open, and Coop followed behind. Coop grabbed the two shirts that were now mostly dry and shook them out.

The two walked back inside, quickly passing by the group again.

Coach followed them into the bedroom where they continued grabbing various items to bring to Coop's house. He faced Coop and Ethan. "Listen, guys, I think this is great. I just want to say that first—"

Ethan interrupted him, "But what?"

Coach put his hands on his hips. "Well, I hope you're both prepared for practice tomorrow. I can't afford for either of you to be off your game, you especially," he pointed to Coop, "I can say this now, because you're standing in my house, and our situation has shifted a bit here. I can't have you distracted, like you've been. You gotta step up. You're the team captain and I'm gonna need your best stuff going forward. I know Ethan had some tips and new tricks for you, hopefully you guys have worked them in over the weekend."

Coach stopped himself and closed his eyes, then wiped his hand down his face. "Everything sounds perverted to me now that Tina's been here all day." He shook his head. "Listen, just bring your best stuff tomorrow."

Coop smiled at him. "Understood. I already bet Ethan that I would—"

Ethan quickly covered Coop's mouth. "Shh, no," he told Coop.

Coach raised his chin. "Let go of the man's mouth, son. You bet Ethan, what?"

Coop shook his head no. "He doesn't want me to say it. I can't."

Ethan threw his hands up. "We haven't really worked on the stance, just a bit. But I think he's gonna fall back in a rhythm quickly. He bet me that he's gonna hit a homerun off Mac's first fastball tomorrow."

Coach clapped his hands. "Well, alright. That's what I want to hear. Coop, let me talk to Ethan for a minute, it'll be quick."

Coop smiled in acknowledgement, then carried Ethan's large art pad outside to his car.

Ethan had a stack of clothes on hangers bundled in his arms. "What is it, Dad?"

Coach sat on Ethan's bed. "Listen, son. I'm not used to seeing Coop this way. It's throwing me a bit. He's like a different person."

Ethan placed the bundle on the bed, standing in front of his father. "Meaning what, Dad?"

Coach looked down at the floor then up to Ethan. "I just don't want you to get hurt. It's great seeing him affectionate with you, but I'm not sure how things will be tomorrow at practice. Not to rub salt in a wound, but listen, in all the time he and Luke were together, Coop never showed him any affection outside of what a normal teammate or friend would at practices, games, get togethers…so, I'm just worried. That's all."

Ethan sighed loudly. "Thanks, Dad. It's nice that you're worried… I'm not Luke, though, and Cooper wouldn't treat me that way."

Coach smiled at him. "Well, I hope you're right. He is letting you call him Cooper, so what do I know?"

He stood up and placed one hand on Ethan's shoulder. "Also, listen, it kills me to say this to you…I can't even…okay, I have to say it. As your coach, not as your father—or maybe as your father, I don't know anymore. Listen, you are a catcher, not only that, but we need your speed." Coach exhaled. "Squatting and running are a big part of your job, so you two take it easy with the bedroom gymnastics, okay?" He patted Ethan's shoulder and walked away.

Coach walked out of the bedroom, past Coop, who walked in to see Ethan with his hands covering his mouth.

"What's wrong, did you get in trouble?" Coop asked.

Ethan shook his head and gathered the bundle of clothes off his bed. They finished packing the few things that Ethan wanted to bring, and headed out in their cars, after saying their goodbyes.

Chapter 28
The Bet

The next morning Ethan joined Coop for a morning workout. Ethan was not used to getting up at five but was happy running on the treadmill next to Coop.

Coop explained that he had two treadmills because his father used to run with him every morning until recently, when he turned eighteen and developed his own routine.

"That's really nice, it sounds like, despite a lot of things, your dad has always been supportive," Ethan said.

Coop wiped his brow. "Yeah, he has. He lets me run the Foundation and doesn't really stick his nose in at all, he's fine. He's a good dad. Just weird to think that if he had his way, I wouldn't even be here now."

Ethan looked forward but had a confused look on his face. "Why do you say that?"

"Ethan, if he had his way he would have been with Levi, and not my mom. So, yeah, I wouldn't have been born. It's just a weird feeling."

Their treadmills went into cooldown mode following their twenty-five-minute run. As Ethan walked with his hands behind his head, he turned his head to Coop. "Don't think about that. It's obvious how much he loves you."

"I'm not really thinking about that. If anything, I should thank him. After seeing what he and Levi sacrificed, I realized pretty quickly that I wanted to stop pretending and hiding my feelings. It gave me the courage I needed to scoop you up."

They hopped off their treadmills for a water break and shared a quick smooch. Coop pushed Ethan to his limit with squats, deadlifts, rope training, and other exercises that Ethan thought, truly, no human should do.

Ethan hunched over by the door on the way back to Coop's room. "Okay, your body is perfect, so hot...but at what cost? This is crazy. I thought I had a good regimen… Phew. I'm exhausted."

Coop picked Ethan's sweaty body up and tossed him over his shoulder, then took a playful bite of Ethan's bottom.

"Cooper! That tickles! Don't!" Ethan laughed. Coop carried him into the bathroom and flipped the sauna on. He pulled the door to the custom sauna open and placed Ethan inside. Ethan lay comfortably on the large wooden reclining seat, while Coop laid beside him.

Ethan looked around inside. "I turned this on accidentally the other night. I can't believe you have a sauna in your bathroom. I've never seen one inside a house before."

The two sat for fifteen minutes and then hopped into the shower for a quick clean off.

Coop pumped his eyebrows at Ethan who was washing his hair. "What are the terms of the bet for practice today?"

Ethan rinsed his hair under the shower. "Do you have any leftover frosting?" he asked.

"Yeah, I do, it's in the fridge. I think you only have one cupcake left in the kitchen, though. I can make you more before practice if you want them."

Ethan whispered into Coop's ear. Coop's eyes widened in excitement. "Wait, I get that if I hit the homerun *or* if I lose? You need to be clear here."

"Hmm, that's tricky because I want it, but I guess it is a treat for you, too," Ethan said. "Why should I have to be denied if you don't deliver?"

Coop lathered his own hair. "Well, I never said I would deny you anything. You can do that either way. I have something else that I want, *when* I win later, but conditions would have to be perfect for it to happen."

"What is it that you want, Cooper?"

Coop leaned in close to Ethan's ear and whispered.

Ethan couldn't believe his ears. "The locker room bench?!"

"Mmhmm. That's what I want," Coop said.

The two finished washing off and stepped into Coop's room.

Ethan pulled his pants on. "Okay, so if you hit the homerun, we do your thing and my thing. If you don't hit the homerun—"

Coop interrupted him, "Ethan, there is no way in the world that I won't. Don't even say anything else. I'm not gonna miss out on either of those things. Period."

Once both were dressed, Coop walked Ethan downstairs, he'd convinced him to take his BMW to class during their workout.

"Look, see? This one has the perfect plate for you, it has your number! It's announcing that you're mine."

Ethan looked at the plate—*COOP2*—and smiled.

Coop gave him a deliciously sloppy kiss, as he opened the driver's side door.

"Mmm…Cooper…" Ethan pulled back from his beast of a boyfriend. "You are making it very hard to leave," he said, sitting in the driver's seat.

"Alright, I'm sorry. Just drive safe and text me if you're bored." They shared a quick smooch, and Coop closed the door.

Shortly after, Ethan pulled into the school parking lot. Coop had a premium parking pass, so Ethan was able to pull along the front row of the building. Ethan grabbed his art pad and tossed his black backpack over his shoulders. He hit the car alarm by accident as he tried to lock Coop's car. He turned it off quickly and although the sound was brief, it was incredibly loud. Ethan noticed several other students looking at him strangely. He was certain it was because he was driving Coop's car. The class was uneventful, and Ethan found himself back in Coop's car afterward.

He called Coop, who answered after only one ring. "Hey, are you done with your first class?"

Ethan answered, "Yeah, people were looking at me weird when I got here, though people are actually still looking at me weird, right now."

"Why are they looking at you weird, where are you? Didn't you say you usually find some place quiet to draw?" Coop asked.

Ethan looked through the tinted windows, at the people walking by. "Yeah, I normally do, but I wanted to sit in your car, because…it smells like you. I miss you already. That's crazy, right?"

Coop sighed. "Not crazy. I miss my little puppy, too. What is the next class? Can you take it online?"

Ethan hadn't considered that as an option. "Honestly, I don't know if I can. I've never asked about that. It's only like my third time going. It's Advanced Art History."

"Hmmm, well, you have a few options: You're already there, so you can go today and then ask if you can take it online moving forward, you can look online and see if your schedule shows the computer icon next to it, or you can walk to the office and ask."

Ethan thought for a moment, then said, "I guess I'll just go and if he says I can take it online then I'll do that. You have a class soon anyway; there's no point in me rushing back."

Coop sounded like he was pouting. "Okay…I understand. I think that's probably the best, even though it sounds like the worst. When you get here later, just come right in, don't try to knock or something, I won't hear it because I'll be in my office."

"What are you looking at, lady?" Ethan asked aloud inside the car. "Oh, she is getting just a little too close to the car. She's putting on lipstick using the reflection. It's so cloudy, I don't think she knows I'm in here." Ethan slid the window down, and the woman jumped, making a large pink lipstick line to her nose.

"Oh my gosh, I'm so sorry." She wiped the lipstick smudge. "I didn't know anyone was in there. Wait, you're not Coop Morgan." She looked at the car, then walked back to the license plate.

"Oof, Cooper she's looking at the plate. Who even is this person?" Ethan whispered.

"I have no idea. I don't really talk to many people on campus. I'm hardly there, usually only for baseball. Ask her, if you want, or just tell her to go away."

She came back around to the driver's window. "Sorry. I'm actually a friend of his sister, Ariel."

Coop yelled through the phone, "She's lying! Arie's friends would never call her Ariel, she hates to be called that."

Ethan cocked his head to the side. "Hmm, that's interesting. Anyway, did you need something, or can this conversation end now?"

She made a nasty face and rolled her eyes. "You're cute, but that was rude. Where is Coop, anyway? He's like never here, so why are you in his car?"

Coop yelled, "Speaker! Put me on speaker now!"

"No," Ethan said calmly.

Coop shouted, "Ethan, do it or the bet is off!"

Ethan quickly placed the phone on speaker and held it near the window, turning the volume up. He wasn't about to lose out on his frosting.

Coop's voice came loudly from the speaker: "Whoever you are, can you please get away from my boyfriend and my car? You're pissing me off and you're bothering him. Also, you definitely aren't friends with my sister."

"Ugh, whatever. But did you just say he was your boyfriend? Like *boyfriend*-boyfriend?"

Ethan furrowed his brow and continued holding the phone up. "Boyfriend that I'm gonna do again in a few hours, if you must know. Ethan, if she doesn't leave in five seconds, call campus security."

The woman walked away while she quickly pulled her phone out and put her lipstick in her oversized bag.

Ethan's ears were hot with frustration. "That was really annoying. Ugh, now look at the time, I'm gonna have to jog to class. I'll be there as soon as it ends, okay?"

Cooper was equally frustrated on the other end of the phone. "Okay, just don't go into spicy puppy mode. Promise?"

Ethan smiled. "Spicy puppy mode? Oh, don't lose my temper...yes, I promise."

There were only about fifteen other students in the class when Ethan walked inside. He approached the teacher, who was standing in front of his desk looking at something on his computer. He was a younger man, very tall and thin, with long, stringy blond hair.

"Good morning, I was wondering if this class can be taken online?" Ethan asked.

The teacher didn't look up from his computer, "Yep. It can. That's why I'm over here futzing with this monitor right now. Everyone who doesn't care enough to come in can get the same experience as if they were here."

Ethan thought that was a very rude thing to say. *No spicy puppy mode.... When did Cooper even come up with that?*

Ethan thanked him and took a seat.

He heard people behind him talking rather loudly. *Oh well, whatever they're talking about, doesn't concern me. At least I don't have to come back here after today.*

A woman's high-pitched voice nearby asked, "Are you sure it was Coop? Like, really, really?"

Ethan snapped his head around. The woman who was on her cell phone looked at him. "Wait what did the guy in the car look like?" she asked whomever she was talking to.

Ethan realized what was happening, he turned back around in his seat. The woman gathered her things and sat in the empty seat next to him. Ethan sighed loudly.

She said to Ethan, "Hey, are you by chance Coop Morgan's boyfriend?"

No spicy puppy mode, damn it. I promised. Why of all days did he pick today to say such a thing to me?

Ethan looked at her calmly and smiled. "Please don't talk to me."

She lowered her eyebrows at him. "Sorry, but Coop's like super popular and I'm trying to find out if my friend who just called me is lying. So can you just answer me?"

Ethan retorted, "If she's your friend, why wouldn't you believe her?"

The professor called from the front of the class, "Good morning, please open your laptops and go to this website." He pointed to the projection screen behind him. Ethan quickly opened the website.

The girl next to him placed a folded piece of paper on his desk. Ethan looked at her annoyed and placed it back on her desk without opening it.

I'm Italian…I can't be expected to remain calm when I'm being annoyed so much. I'm gonna text Cooper. Oh, wait, he's in class right now, too. Never mind.

The professor spoke again, "Alright this website is your virtual classroom, you can access this any time we're having class. It comes in handy if you forgot something or need to partner up with someone. We have message boards, assignment boards…"

A notification chimed on Ethan's laptop.

Message from Krystal B: *Are you just gonna ignore me?*

Ethan inhaled deeply and looked up at the professor.

Message from Krystal B: *Are you his boyfriend or not?*

Ethan raised his hand. The professor acknowledged him, "Yes, guy in the front, who will never be back after today. What's up?"

Ethan asked, "Can we block someone in the classroom from messaging us?"

The professor answered, "Well, I don't know why you would need to. I'm honestly not sure."

A voice from the back called out, "You can, just right click on their name and select block."

"Thank you," Ethan called behind, he quickly blocked Krystal B. As soon as the class was over, Ethan grabbed his laptop and backpack and headed to Coop's car. As he rounded the corner, he noticed the same woman from earlier standing in front of the car, along with three others. Ethan sighed and shook his head. Krystal sped up and joined them.

He ignored them and got in the car, noticing them taking pictures of him once he was inside. He was so frustrated, that he drove straight to Coop's without even calling him.

Tony let him straight inside the gate without stopping him. Ethan walked into Coop's side of the estate and quickly went up the stairs. He looked in Coop's room, but didn't see him. He stomped his foot and called out, "Cooper, where are you? I forgot where you said the office is!"

Coop emerged quickly from a door at the end of the hall. "I said the end of the hall, remember?" He walked toward Ethan, tilting his head at him. "Ethan, what's wrong, come here." Coop held his arms open, and Ethan fell into his embrace. "What's wrong, why do you look so upset? Not because of that girl earlier, right?"

Ethan inhaled Coop's soothing scent and laid his head on his shoulder. He said softly, "I hate other people. I really mean it, Cooper."

Coop gave him a quick smooch, and Ethan righted his posture. "Come in the office and tell me what happened. Oh wait, you need lunch first. Come on." He pulled Ethan down the stairs.

Ethan sat at the kitchen counter, remembering the last time he was in the kitchen with Coop.

"What can I make you?" Coop asked, while holding the fridge open. "Come over here and tell me what sounds good. I have about fifteen minutes before I have to run back upstairs."

Ethan shook his head. "I'm really not hungry. Just water would be good."

Coop pulled his mouth to the side. "Nope. You worked out this morning and we have practice in a few hours. You want a smoothie or a salad?"

Ethan smiled at him softly. "Whichever is easier for you."

Coop pulled the freezer open and took out several different pre-portioned frozen veggies and fruits. He opened the fridge and grabbed almond milk and Greek yogurt, then tossed everything into a blender. "You can come to work with me today," he said as he passed him the finished smoothie.

Coop led Ethan upstairs to his office, and the two sat side by side at his desk. The meeting was scheduled for 1:00. Ethan sipped his delicious smoothie and leaned against Coop's shoulder. He was already feeling much better. Coop's presence truly soothed him. He began to question what he was even upset about.

Coop's meeting began. "No, I'm not coming on camera today. I don't feel like it," he said to the employees in the meeting.

The five other people in the meeting all quickly turned their cameras off. Coop called out numbers from a spreadsheet and assigned different tasks of research to the others in the meeting. "Listen, I'm good with that. If you have it under control, then I'll let you take it, but make sure that the charity is notified that the amount increased." Coop pulled up another large spreadsheet and walked through the projections for quarter one. "Yeah, I think we're good if we go all in on column B," Coop said.

Ethan had no idea what they were talking about, but he really loved watching Coop work.

The meeting ended earlier than anticipated. Coop pulled a sleepy-eyed Ethan into the bedroom with him. "You look really tired, lay down and take a nap. We still have time before practice."

Ethan didn't argue, he hopped into bed, and Coop tucked him in tightly.

Coop walked back into his office and grabbed his laptop. He came back to find Ethan already asleep. He sat in bed next to him and stared adoringly at his sleepy little puppy. *His eyelashes are so long, and his skin is so soft... How can someone so handsome, have such beautiful features? I wonder who that was earlier by the car? I still don't even know who she was. I hate that someone made him so upset.*

Chapter 29
Dropping Off Permits

Luke and Kory, dressed handsomely in gray suits, headed to City Hall. They requested a longer lunch break, which Madeline didn't question. Luke hadn't told his dad about the engagement or the ceremony.

Of course, Kory didn't mind if Luke's father joined them, but Luke was adamant that only he and Kory be there. He liked the idea of an intimate ceremony, with no one else around. He was excited beyond belief, as they reached the courthouse and parked the car.

"You're sure you're okay with your dad not being here?" Kory asked.

"More than sure," Luke replied. "This is about you and me, nobody else."

As they walked inside the building, they were greeted by two familiar faces. Andrew and Marcus from the office happened to be dropping off paperwork related to their adoption. Andrew held their small baby girl, wrapped in a mint green blanket, against his shoulder and noticed Kory.

Kory tried to avoid them, but Andrew was far too nosy to pretend he hadn't seen him. He pulled Marcus their way.

Luke was red with embarrassment as they approached. Andrew quietly introduced their baby, Lila, and asked what the two were doing at City Hall. Luke tried, unsuccessfully, to come up with something convincing.

He chided Kory, obviously not believing Luke's story. "Man, you young guys aren't doing this right. You gotta at least get Luke some flowers or something."

Luke laughed, still trying to deny what was happening. "No, I don't need flowers. We're just here to drop off paperwork."

Kory knew Marcus didn't believe that.

Marcus reached toward Kory's jacket and patted his chest. He smirked. "Pretty sure I feel a ring box in there and you two look way too nice for a regular trip to city hall."

Their daughter, Lila, let out a few soft cries, and Andrew nudged Marcus. "We gotta go."

"Alright, well, listen," Marcus said. "As much as I want to stand here and watch you two make up stories, I have to go because Andrew will have an absolute panic attack if she starts full-on crying. He just can't take it; he'll probably need to be taken away on a stretcher. But, we'll pretend we don't know anything. Congratulations, though."

Kory shrugged. "Not sure why you'd congratulate us for dropping off permits."

Andrew snapped his fingers at Marcus. "Come on, they're not going to admit it. Let's go, if she cries again, you're sleeping on the couch."

Marcus and Andrew gave them knowing glances and left quickly through the front doors.

Kory and Luke laughed, knowing they hadn't actually fooled them, but their interaction made Kory think of something. "Hey, not that I'll change my mind because I truly would do anything for you and I mean that, but do you want to have kids, Luke?"

"Oh no…never. I don't like kids. Very annoying. Loud, dirty…no. Wait, what about you?"

Kory held his chest in relief. "Me neither. Dogs, yes, kids never."

"Perfect," Luke said.

They walked quickly to the counter and were led into a small room with the Justice of the Peace.

They said their vows and stared deeply into one another's eyes as they placed gold wedding bands on each other's ring finger. Following a sweet kiss, they headed back to the office.

Luke called his father from the car and told him the news; he and Tom were ecstatic. They insisted upon giving them a honeymoon to wherever they wanted. Luke and Kory decided they would pick a destination later and get back to them.

As they walked back inside the office, Madeline was waiting for them standing near Ms. Martin's desk.

"Oh no, Andrew called her," Kory said.

Luke whispered, "She hasn't said anything yet, how do you know?"

"Just watch, you'll see how good your husband is at reading people."

Luke's face lit up. "My husband, I love the sound of that."

Madeline looked the two up and down, as she tapped her black pointed shoe while watching them approach.

Kory smiled at her. "Hi, Madeline, what can we do for you?"

She folded her arms. "Well, for starters you can explain to me why two of my favorite people in this office chose to get *married* without telling me?"

Kory smiled at Luke. "Tell me how good I am."

"Wait, Kory," Luke said. "Madeline, who told you about this?"

Kory held his hand out toward Madeline.

"Andrew," she answered.

Luke smiled and kissed Kory on the cheek. "My husband is the best. I love you."

"I love you too," Kory said.

Madeline's arms were still folded. "Alright, I don't do cute, and you guys are too cute right now. Finish your work and take the week off to celebrate. Whatever needs to be done, get Liam to do. I don't do hugs, so don't even think about it." She quickly left the office.

Kory and Luke got all their unfinished tasks together and left them for Liam, then headed out shortly after.

"Where do you want to go for our honeymoon?" Luke asked.

"I don't care, as long as I'm with you, but right now the professor feels the need to teach you something new. Let's go home and after your lesson we can figure out our honeymoon plans."

The two headed for home, looking forward to their new life together.

Chapter 30
Keep Your Pants On

Following Ethan's midday nap, the two packed up their gear and headed out for practice in Coop's Range Rover. "You didn't want to take the BMW?" Ethan asked.

"Nah, not for practice, I don't want to get clay in the carpet. Besides this one has a lot of room in the trunk if we need it for anything." He pumped his eyebrows at Ethan.

"You just focus on hitting that fastball…then after practice, we both win."

Coop licked his lips and squeezed Ethan's hand.

Dressed in their black practice uniforms, the two entered the locker room holding hands. The locker room was packed with the majority of the team already there.

Kai, whose locker was directly in the center of the room, noticed them first. "Yoooo! Coop, Ethan, what up?"

Coop held Ethan's right hand tightly.

"Holy shit, Captain, where is your hair?" Mac asked. He looked down and saw the two holding hands, then looked back at Coop who lifted his chin at him, as if daring him to say something.

Coop challenged Mac with his eyes, then said, "Ethan, my boyfriend, cut it for me."

Ethan's eyes went wide as he bit his bottom lip.

A few other teammates started to gather at the loud conversation and its current topic. Most whispered about Coop's hair, but a few were questioning if they heard him correctly.

Mac nodded his head and extended his hand in congratulatory fashion. Coop was taken aback by the gesture. "What are you playing at? You've been a dick since you were in diapers, what are you trying to shake my hand for?" The entire team laughed at Coop's comment.

Mac half-smiled at him. "Oh, I am a dick, but I'm happy that you two are together. It was obvious more than a few times that he was trying to get your attention. I think it's great that you guys are together. Seriously. I mean it." His hand remained extended; Coop reluctantly shook it. Mac extended his hand to Ethan. "Hope you can help him with my fastballs. It's no fun watching him strike out."

Ethan released Coop's hand briefly and shook Mac's hand, but he didn't smile at him or reply. Ethan was not so easily won over. He had a very mafioso mentality when it came to his relationships with other people. In Ethan's book, if he hates you, he hates you. Cross him once and you're done. He'd give you the shirt off his back, but if you crossed him, he may just strangle you with that shirt.

Coach came in at the tail end of the conversation from behind. "What are you guys huddled up in here for? Hit the field."

The rest of the team quickly jogged out to the field while Ethan and Coop remained in the locker room.

"I still feel tired, Cooper. Must have been the workout this morning. I even took a nap. I feel so worked already."

"That's not good. You're gonna need a lot more energy after practice," Coop joked.

Ethan rolled his neck and stretched his arms. He walked around to his locker on the other side and put on his chest protector and catcher's mask, which he lifted up on his head.

Coop walked around the lockers. "You all set? Your dad's gonna—"

Ethan pulled his head back. "My dad's gonna what? Are you frozen?"

Coop closed the distance between them quickly and pulled Ethan in for a quick kiss. "Your dad is gonna flip if we don't hurry. Sorry, I lost my train of thought. You're just so cute in your catcher's gear."

Ethan and Coop held hands as they walked out onto the field.

"Nice of you two to join us. Gotta love it when the captain is the last man on the field," Coach said sarcastically.

"Sorry, Coach!" Coop called out.

Coach blew his whistle, drawing the attention of the team, who were all stretching on different areas of the field. Coach yelled, "Listen up, your Captain here says he's gonna crush the first fastball that ole' Mac throws at him today! So, place your bets, lets really pile the pressure on!" Coach winked at Coop and gave Ethan a thumbs up.

Coop listened as teammates started calling things out. Mac, whose locker was to the left of Coop's shouted, "Hey, Cap, I'll trade lockers with Ethan, if you crank it out of the park, how about that?"

Coop pulled his mouth to the side in consideration, while Ethan started to get a little nervous. He had confidence based on his gut feeling, but he hadn't seen Coop at full strength on the field yet.

Coach added, "I'll throw something in, too, if you don't hit it, you and Ethan have to stay late and clean up tonight, which will make Frankie and Kai happy."

Frankie and Kai cheered from the outfield.

Coop's eyes lit up. Ethan shook his head; he knew what Coop was thinking as soon as his dad said that. He whispered in his ear, "Cooper, don't you dare miss, just so we can do your thing. I won't do it if you miss, even if my dad makes us stay late to clean."

Ethan removed his catcher's gear. The two helped stretch each other out under the watchful eyes of their teammates, who were definitely more interested in their movements than they were prior to today.

After everyone was loose, Coach blew his whistle. He yelled, "Let's go, Ethan, suit up, get behind the plate. Coop, you're up first!"

Teammates in the dugout leaned over the railing in anticipation.

Ethan leaned in, whispering to Coop while he adjusted his batting gloves. Coop nodded in understanding. Ethan squatted down behind him, while Coop took a few practice swings and adjusted everything that Ethan told him to.

Ethan spoke up from below, "Drop them just a tiny bit more for me, Cooper."

Coop dropped his hips a little more as told, and stepped into the box, eyeing Mac.

Mac lined up, staring Coop down. The pitch came in hot, straight down the middle—*crack*—the ball flew outside the field. Homerun! Coop dropped his bat, and Ethan threw his mask off and hugged him. Coop gave him a quick smooch on the mouth and gazed adoringly at Ethan. "Thank you," he whispered.

Coop turned and held his arms wide toward the rest of the team. "Alright everyone who bet against me better pay up! Mac, Ethan gets your locker. Coach, what did you bet against me?"

Coach clapped, while motioning Coop over.

Ethan stood behind the plate, as Kai came up to bat. Kai smiled at him and said, "You fixed him, bro." The two bumped fists and exchanged smiles.

"Hey, Kai, tell Frankie that Coop and I will stay and clean up tonight. Just leave me the key, but don't tell Coop, okay?"

Kai made a confused face, then shrugged his shoulders. "Alright, boss, sounds good."

Later, after practice ended, Coop bragged in the locker room, after hitting every fastball that Mac threw his way. Mac cleared out his things, as promised, and moved to the opposite side.

Ethan stood on Coop's left, facing his new locker. He whispered to Coop, "I don't want to put my stuff in yet. It's not clean."

Kai came behind Ethan and stuck the key into his hand on his way to the showers on the other side.

Coop pulled his head back and called to Kai, "Did you just put something in his hand when you walked by?"

Ethan shoved the key in the back pocket of his uniform pants. Coop looked at him curiously and whispered into Ethan's ear, "We should've asked Kai to just let us clean up. Now, I don't get to do my thing." He pouted.

Coop pulled his uniform shirt off, the scratches from Ethan had yet to fade. Ethan quickly tried to block him, standing behind him.

"What are you doing?" Coop asked.

"Your back is still all scratched up; I didn't want anyone to see anything."

Coop rubbed Ethan's head. "That's cute. Who cares what anyone thinks? I have to shower, they're gonna see them anyway."

Ethan was reminded of his Aunt Tina's warning, and her jealous feelings crept into the forefront of his mind. He looked seriously at Coop. "You're gonna shower in front of everyone?"

"Do you not want me to?" Coop asked.

Ethan sighed. "No, it's fine. That's stupid. I can't be jealous over this."

Coop leaned in and gave him a quick smooch. "They've all seen me naked. It's not a big deal."

Ethan refused to believe that Coop would not be jealous if the roles were reversed. He changed tactics and removed his jersey. His hickeys, bruises, and scratches on full display, he started to take his uniform pants off, unbuttoning them. Coop turned to face him. "Hey, hey, what are you doing? Don't take your pants—" Coop put his hand on his mouth and dropped his head, looking up innocently at Ethan.

Ethan raised his eyebrows and lifted his chin playfully. "You don't want me to take my pants off in front of anyone else?"

Coop reached over, buttoned Ethan's pants, and kissed him on the mouth. "No, I don't."

Ethan pulled the key out of his back pocket and flashed it at Coop. "Naughty. Did you get the key so we could do my thing?"

Ethan nodded.

Coop yelled, "Everyone hurry up, Ethan and I have to clean up and I don't want to be here all night!"

After everyone cleared out of the locker room, Ethan and Coop quickly sanitized the lockers, benches, and door handles. That was basically all that clean-up duty required. The college had its own janitorial staff for the rest. Coop walked over to the locker room entry and locked it, then turned the lights off. The room was only dimly lit by the moonlight from the few very high upper windows. Ethan walked into the cool-down room and grabbed a few towels.

He passed one to Coop. "This was your thing, and I'm a man of my word. But is this really what you want?"

Coop nodded with a devilish grin. "Yeah. I don't want you remembering the day you came in here and felt all helpless because I was crying. I'm gonna fix that. Shower, then the bench."

Ethan smiled. "Alright, come on. I am really proud of you, by the way. I can't believe you hit everything he threw at you tonight. I've honestly never seen anything like that before. I've seen you on film plenty of times, but tonight you were just unbelievable."

The two quickly showered, wrapped their bottom halves in towels and headed back to their lockers. Ethan laid a few towels out on the bench and sat down.

Coop sat beside him. "Now lay down for me, like you did in the picture you drew."

Ethan laid down, placing one leg on each side of the bench. Coop pulled Ethan's towel off.

Coop removed his own towel and turned his body to face Ethan's. He spoke in a soft voice, "I only want you to remember this, when you come in here. Every time you walk in here, I want you to remember who you belong to, Ethan, and what I did to you on this bench."

Several minutes later…goosebumps.

Coop gave Ethan a soft kiss. "Naughty puppy," he said.

Ethan winced as he stood up. "I'm not naughty, this was your thing. I did what I was told. I loved it, but I'm not the naughty one."

Ethan headed to the shower, it was still pretty dark in there and Ethan felt a bit uncomfortable. He screamed when he felt hands from behind.

"Whoa, Whoa, it's just me, shhh…" Coop rubbed Ethan's firm sides.

"Oof, you scared the hell out of me!" Ethan leaned into Coop.

"Sorry! Let's wrap this up and get home. It's your turn next."

They headed straight for the bedroom when they arrived at Coop's home. Ethan waited in bed for Coop, who went downstairs to grab the frosting that he requested. He came up shortly after, carrying a bowl of it.

Coop sat next to him, while Ethan pulled the clear lid off and attempted to stick his finger in it. He frowned as he poked it. "We have a problem; the frosting is hard now."

Coop poked it, with the same result. "Hmmm, maybe we could just leave it out for a bit? Or you can use the frosting off the last cupcake?"

Ethan pouted. "That is not enough frosting. This isn't fair, I did your thing."

Coop ruffled Ethan's hair. "Don't pout, little pup, I can make more. It's a very easy recipe. Five minutes." Coop grabbed the container and walked toward the door.

Ethan looked him up and down. "Five minutes is good, but I'm adding a condition since I have to wait."

Coop raised his eyebrows at him, and tilted his head. "Which is?"

"The shirt stays off while you make it."

Ethan approached him and pulled Coop's shirt off. He eyed Coop's perfect body. "Much better…now you can make my frosting."

Coop complied. "Fine, but your shirt comes off, too. I know this is supposed to be your thing. But the shirt comes off, non-negotiable."

Coop hurried around the kitchen under a shirtless Ethan's intense gaze.

"You know, Cooper, I'm just trying to figure out how he's always ready, all the time. He's a very intimidating weapon," he said, eyeing Coop's crotch.

Coop held his arms wide and looked down at his gym shorts. "He's like this because you're around. He knows what's about to go down." He licked a bit of frosting off his finger and added a bit more powdered sugar to the bowl. He gave it a few more stirs and tasted it again, while gazing at Ethan. "Mmm, I think you're gonna like it. Come try it," he said, licking his finger.

Ethan walked over and looked at the bowl, then at Coop's body. "No need. Come on." He grabbed the bowl and headed upstairs with Coop following behind him. "Should we use the guest room?" Ethan asked." I know I joked about ants yesterday, but should we actually use a different bed?"

Coop smiled and grabbed a set of sheets out of the linen closet. "We'll just change the sheets after."

Ethan carried his prized frosting in his arms and looked at Coop. "Lay down, Cooper, I've waited long enough."

Coop jumped into the middle of the bed and laid with his arms behind his head. "So, do you just want me to lay here, or can I play, too?"

Ethan dug two fingers into the frosting and scooped. He approached Coop from his feet and climbed onto the bed. He looked at Coop's chest and painted the frosting all over his body and then licked it off. After Ethan had his fill of frosting, Coop reached down and lifted Ethan's chin. "Let me give you goosebumps now."

Ethan laid next to Coop, while Coop moved the bowl onto the nightstand. Ethan's arms were covered in goosebumps at record speed.

After they showered and readied for bed, Ethan laid with his head on Coop's chest. "I forgot to tell you, during my first class the teacher mentioned there would be a display at a local gallery in two months. She said anyone from class can enter, but they'll only reserve space for the top two entries per school."

Coop rubbed his back. "That's great. You should do it. Can it be something you've already drawn?"

Ethan patted Coop's chest. "That's sweet. I'm not sure of the requirements, or how much of a chance I'd have. I've never really put my art out there before. I've been graded on things, but I don't go out of my way to show things that I draw to people."

"Well, I think your art is amazing. I told you before, I've never really felt anything when looking at art, but your drawings are really alive. There's so much emotion in them."

Ethan smiled. "Thank you. Hard to tell if you can be impartial, since you happen to be the subject of most of the pictures you saw."

Coop rubbed Ethan's cheek. "Well, I doubt I could ever be impartial when it comes to you." He gave Ethan a big smooch on the lips.

"I'll think about entering," Ethan said.

"Do you want me to wake you up at five for the morning workout? Or should I let you sleep?"

"I just ate all that frosting…so, yes, wake me up."

Coop felt bad at the thought of Ethan forcing himself to do a workout that he wasn't used to. Although Coop was accustomed to his regimen, he would much rather find an exercise that Ethan would enjoy. Even though they were getting plenty of workouts in other ways, Coop came up with an alternative. "We can do a swim in the morning, instead of the circuit. Would that be better?"

Ethan pulled an eyebrow down. "What, in the dark?"

"Yes, in the dark. Although, I have lights out there. It's hardly dark with everything lit up. Do you want to go see it lit up? I can show you. You could see it from the bathroom, but it won't be the same."

"Hmmm…yeah, let's do that. Do we need to get dressed or can we stay in our comfies?" Ethan asked.

"My puppy said comfies! Cutest thing you've ever said!" Coop planted a big smooch on Ethan's mouth.

"You taught me that word! I learned it from you! How can it be the cutest thing I've ever said?"

"It just is. Plus, I taught you something, so that alone is cute." Coop pinched Ethan's cheek.

The two, clad in their matching slim-fit black sweatpants and bare chests, headed down the stairs. Ethan regretted saying he wanted to see the pool lights. He was feeling pretty tired by the time they reached the last step.

"What's wrong?" Coop asked, looking at Ethan's slightly pouty face.

Ethan held a hand on his forehead, "Oof, I'm just tired, I think all the sex just hit me."

Coop squatted in front of him. "Hop on. I ate a ton of frosting that I need to burn off, too." He carried Ethan piggyback toward the pool area. The motion lights surrounding the pool came on immediately. Coop walked over near the bar area and flipped a few switches, still carrying Ethan. The pool water was illuminated in a bright blue light, while the waterfall and grotto areas had soft white light coming off the sides.

Ethan looked around smiling. "Oooh, this is nice. Yeah, let's do the swim in the morning." He kissed Coop on the cheek.

Coop smiled. "Alright, but now it's time for bed." He carried Ethan back into the estate.

Ethan hopped off Coop's back when they got inside. "Let me walk up the stairs myself, you're gonna hurt your back."

Coop smiled. "I carried you up that way a few nights ago. It's not that hard. Easier now, especially since you're awake."

Ethan felt uneasy, remembering his drunken state the other night. It was the greatest night ever, but also one of his most embarrassing. "I vaguely remember that," he said, as they walked upstairs.

They got back in bed and snuggled in close. Coop kissed Ethan on the cheek. He whispered, "Vaguely remember, huh?"

Ethan admitted loudly, "Okay, yes, I remember!"

The two fell asleep locked in a spooning position, with Coop holding Ethan tight.

Chapter 31
We've Been Busy

Notifications dinged rapidly from Coop's phone, waking Ethan up. He whispered, "Hey, your phone is going crazy."

Coop stretched to reach it, knocking it on the floor. He was too tired to care, he rolled back over and held Ethan, falling back asleep instantly.

Ethan heard the sound of someone coming up the stairs, they knocked on the open door of his bedroom. Ethan's eyes went wide, he shook his shoulder under Coop. "Cooper, wake up."

A woman's voice called, "Coop, are you awake?"

Ethan sat straight up, making Coop sit straight up.

Arie jumped and screamed, "Aaaah! What the eff?"

"Ugh, Arie, what the hell are you doing in my room?" Coop asked.

Ethan breathed a sigh of relief. After the incident earlier at school, he was afraid maybe a stalker had gotten inside.

Arie's eyes looked like they could fall out of her head. "Okay, so I guess what I heard was true. Hi, I'm Arie, Coop's beautiful sister. Nice to meet you, Ethan." She looked at Coop. "Nice haircut, loser."

Ethan waved to her and smiled.

Coop was still half asleep, looking at his sister. "Arie, how do you know who he is? What do you mean you heard…wait, what did you even say?"

Arie rolled her eyes and sat at the foot of Coop's bed.

Ethan scooted further back against the headboard, he gathered the sheet and tucked it under his arms, covering his bare chest.

Arie asked, "Where is your phone, Coop? I've been texting you for hours."

Coop looked at his clock. "Arie it's 12:30 AM, couldn't this have waited until the morning? Don't you have a curfew?"

Arie glanced at the nightstand. "Oh, come on, where is your phone? It will be easier if I show you."

Ethan pointed to the floor on Coop's side of the bed. Coop stood up and grabbed his phone off the floor. He got back into bed and pulled Ethan under his arm, sitting up against the headboard.

Arie's mouth dropped open, but she remained silent at the sight of Coop holding Ethan close.

Coop was confused looking at his phone. "What the hell is all this?" He passed his phone to Ethan, who scrolled through the notifications from Arie.

"I can explain," Arie said. "So, Ethan, this girl, Lila, is friends with Emma, who said she saw you in Coop's car. I'm not her friend but she knows me. She said that Coop yelled at her and called you his boyfriend, then Lila's friend Krystal, told everyone that you wouldn't deny being his boyfriend and that you straight-up blocked her in class. Someone on the baseball team added a short video to the thread with a few clips from practice today, scroll to the bottom for the video."

Ethan and Coop watched the short video together. They thought it was funny that someone had recorded them at practice. Coop raised his eyebrows and whispered in Ethan's ear. Coop gave him a kiss on the cheek, following the whisper.

Noticing that they weren't bothered, Arie asked, "You guys don't care?"

They both ignored her question and laid back down. Coop wrapped his arm around Ethan, pulled him close and closed his eyes. He sighed. "Go away, Arie, we're tired."

Arie flipped Coop's bedroom light on and looked at him. "Okay, I don't know who you are, or what you've done with my brother, but, um, what the hell? You literally have cut your hair—"

"Ethan cut my hair," Coop corrected her, eyes still closed, arm still wrapped tight around Ethan. Even as tired as he was, he still wanted her to know that Ethan was the one who cut his hair. He chose not to correct other things that Arie said, but he was quite proud of the job that Ethan did and wanted her to know that Ethan cutting it meant something deeper to him.

"Okay, Ethan cut your hair? Wow, so you're dating a guy, like, in public, you're spooning him in your bed, he drove your car to school today, *and* you told Lila that you were gonna eff him when he got home or something…then there's the video from practice where you guys are just all over each other…"

"We've been busy," Ethan said, giggling.

Coop stood up and walked toward the door. "Arie, go home. We're tired…and neither of us cares what anyone thinks. What will make you leave?"

She sat at Coop's desk, spinning in his chair. "I think that you should post something on your socials. People are gossiping because it just comes down to like a few people seeing a few things. If you go online and just say it, then people will drop it."

Coop looked seriously at Ethan. "Why should I care about this? I thought maybe the living my feelings thing would translate to everyone else too, but I honestly feel nothing about what she's saying. I really only care about you."

"I don't care about what she's saying either," Ethan said, sitting up. "I don't even use my socials, I haven't in a long time."

Arie rolled her eyes. "Okay, guys listen, here's the thing… This stuff with you two is just driving people crazy."

Ethan sighed, dropping his head. "Cooper, just—"

Arie's mouth dropped open as she looked at Ethan. "Okay, you called him Cooper?" She turned to Coop. "Are you in love with him?"

"Yes," Coop answered without hesitation.

"Me too," Ethan said.

Arie made a pouty face. "I'm sorry, I legit didn't know. This is your fault for not telling me anything."

Coop and Ethan stared at one another, while Arie looked at her phone. "Well, I know neither of you care what anyone else thinks. I can see that now. So, I would say that you should either update or delete your profiles. If you're going to keep them, change your status and just stick this video on your profiles, with a heart."

She stood up and waved goodbye to Ethan, while Coop pushed her out of his room.

Coop yelled to her, "Arie, don't come back in here in the middle of the night unless it's an emergency, okay? Like an hour or two ago, it would have been really bad for all of us if you had walked in."

She waved him off. "Yeah, I get it. Sorry. He's really cute, by the way."

Coop closed the door, and Ethan walked over to him, they stared deeply into one another's eyes. Coop tilted his head and brought his mouth directly in front of Ethan's.

"I love you, Ethan," he said searching Ethan's face.

"I love you, too, Cooper."

Coop parted Ethan's mouth slowly and gently, while holding his face with both hands. After a few soft kisses, the two laid back down, snuggled up tight and fell back asleep.

Chapter 32
My Assistant

The alarm sounded at five.

"Please don't make me get up," Ethan whined.

Coop kissed him on the cheek and got out of bed quietly. Since Ethan wasn't going to join him, he stuck to his normal morning regimen. After his workout, he took a quick shower, put on a pair of gray track pants, and got back into bed with Ethan.

Ethan scooched in close. "Good morning," he said, as he kissed Coop's chest.

Coop kissed the top of his head. "Good morning, sleepy puppy."

Ethan rolled on his back and stretched. "Sorry I didn't get up at five."

"Don't worry about it. It took me a long time to get used to it. Two solid years of my dad waking me up every day for it. Maybe we can move the time to six starting tomorrow, do you think that would work better for you? Or we can just do a nighttime work out? Whatever you want. I don't want you to force yourself."

Ethan smiled. "No, I can get up at five, you don't need to change everything around."

Coop lifted Ethan's hand to his mouth and kissed it. "Alright, so no classes for either of us today, but I was thinking…I really need an assistant. My dad gave me a big budget for one, but I didn't want to work that closely with anyone. Do you want to do it?"

Ethan sat up and looked at Coop beside him. "Be your assistant for what? The Foundation?"

Coop sat up beside him. "Yeah, then we could work together. You said you wanted to get a job. This would be perfect for you. I'll give you reign over whatever you want. Plus, I'll pay you well. I looked at the budget this morning, it's a pretty solid figure."

A smile covered Ethan's face. "How am I qualified for that?"

"Because I trust you with everything I have. Ethan, you have quickly become my entire world. I want to share everything with you. I love you."

"I love you, too. You're always saying the sweetest things. It's impossible to even say no to you."

Coop grabbed his phone from the nightstand, he pulled up a document, then paused and looked at Ethan. "So? If you can't say no, then it's a yes?"

Ethan smiled. "Yes, it's a yes. If it means I can help you and we can spend more time together, then I'm all in. I'll be your assistant."

Coop held the phone screen facing Ethan. "Your salary."

Ethan leaned in closer to see it. He smacked Coop's chest a few times in disbelief. *Assistant to Executive Director: $200,000 annually.*

Coop looked at Ethan. "What? Not enough? This number was set earlier this year when I took over. I can probably get you more if you want it."

Ethan replied sarcastically, "Oh yes, I should have more than that, with the wealth of experience I'll bring. Wait…how much do you make?"

Coop closed the document and opened his bank account summary. "It's probably easier if I just show you everything I have. You can see the pay statements for yourself." He passed Ethan the phone.

Coop stood up and stretched, reaching his toes, while Ethan's mouth fell open at the large amount he saw. He sat on the side of the bed in shock. "I don't even know what to say to this…." He continued scrolling through the account details, mouth agape.

Coop looked up as he touched his toes. "That's the checking account. The savings account has more, click the savings link if you're interested."

Ethan looked at the savings account. He jumped off the bed, with the phone in his hand. He held it facing Coop.

"What?" Coop chuckled. "Why are you showing me? I know how much is in there."

Ethan sat back down. "This is an insane amount of money. How did you…this is just crazy. I've never seen so much money in all my life. How do you have this much money?"

Coop gave Ethan a smooch on the mouth and took his phone back. He shrugged his shoulders and ruffled Ethan's hair. "It's just money. I'd give it all to you if you wanted it."

As Ethan sat back down, still appearing to be in shock, Coop's phone rang loudly. He sighed as he answered it. "Hey, Dad, What's up?"

"Morning, Levi and I are going out on the boat later today, do you and Ethan want to join us?"

Coop pulled his mouth to the side and looked at Ethan, who made an indiscernible face. "Hang on, Dad." Coop muted the phone, looking at Ethan. "Is that a no face or a maybe face? It's a yacht, not a boat by the way. He always calls it his boat."

"Of course, it's a yacht, why did I think it was a boat?" Ethan asked, shaking his head. "It's up to you. You were pretty annoyed with them the other day, though."

Coop unmuted the phone. "Not this time, but, hey, I want to run something by you about the Foundation."

"Since when? What's wrong?" his dad asked.

"Nothing is wrong. I'm going to make Ethan my assistant. You bugged me to get one when I took over anyway. Does he need to go into the office to fill out paperwork, or can Gwen email him the doc's?"

"Let me call her and find out. I have to give her a few other things for the morning. I'll give you a call in a bit."

Tom stood in Levi's bedroom, smiling, looking at his phone. For the first time in his life he finally felt like everything was truly perfect.

Levi came out of the closet, holding up two shirts on hangers. "Which one looks better, Tommy?" He held the shirts in front of himself, one at a time. Tom smiled and tapped the one on the left.

Levi kissed him quickly. "Thank you. What are you looking at your phone like that for? Are the boys going to join us?"

Tom pulled him into a hug, and Levi wrapped his arms around him, hangers and shirts dangling at Tom's back.

"No, but it's just really nice to hear him happy," Tom said. "Do you remember when we were eighteen, before we broke up, when we talked about kids and marriage? You said, in a perfect world we would be able to get married and have two sons and a daughter."

Levi looked up smiling. "Yeah...I remember."

Tom kissed his forehead. "Well, now we're together and we have the kids. Life is funny, huh?" He squeezed Levi tight, then smacked him on the tush. Levi gave him a quick kiss in return.

"Hurry up and get dressed. I have to call Gwen and give her a few things to do," Tom said. A few minutes later, he shouted in disbelief, "What?! How did that happen, Gwen? Damn it, I don't want to deal with this guy today."

Levi came into the bedroom quickly from the bathroom. "Whoa... What's going on Tommy?"

Tom stood up, frustrated. "The CEO from the Cobras, wants to meet with Coop, myself, and Luke. He wants to apologize for the incident with Collin Pyle. Shit, Coop isn't going to do that. I don't even want to do it."

Levi's mouth turned down. "There is a zero percent chance that Luke will go. Why don't you just decline?"

Tom shook his head and sighed, sitting back down on the edge of Levi's bed. "If only. As Coop's father, I could have rejected, but with my position on the board…and the school…and the relationship between the companies, I just can't."

Levi nodded. "Okay, well, I'll go in Luke's place. We can just hit the water after. It's nice and cool out today, don't worry about it. I'm sure it will be quick."

"Now I'm gonna piss this kid off," Tom said shaking his head, while he called Coop.

Coop rubbed Ethan's back as he sat across his bottom half in his track pants. "Gosh your shoulders are so tight. Loosen up for me, baby."

Ethan turned his head to the side. "Can you please not say 'loosen up for me, baby,' when you're just trying to give me a non-sexual massage?"

"Who said this wasn't sexual? We still have leftover frosting." Coop's fingers quickly made their way down to Ethan's firm ass.

Coop's phone rang, he squeezed Ethan's bottom, then stood and answered the call. "Hey, Dad, what did she say?"

His father sighed into the phone. "Listen, you guys need to go in to just sign a few papers and meet with Brody. Before you complain, I already know he's a pain in the ass, but just deal with it for a few minutes."

Coop leaned his head back and looked at the ceiling. "Okay, that's fine."

"Well, you're not going to like this next part…"

Ethan, still lying face down, peeked up at him. Coop lightly patted and rubbed his ass, drawing a smile from Ethan. "What's the next part?" Coop asked.

"I need you to meet with the CEO of the Cobras for a few minutes with me. He originally asked to meet with you, me, and Luke—"

Coop interrupted his father. "No. I'm not going to meet with him. I'm especially not going there with Luke. What the hell does Luke have to do with anything?"

Ethan quickly stood and embraced Coop from behind.

His dad replied, "I already know that. Calm down. Levi is going to go in Luke's place, and you can bring Ethan. He just wants to make things nice after everything that happened. He's probably afraid I'm going to sue his sorry ass. I won't let it drag on. You have to go there anyway to sign Ethan's paperwork. I need to get Levi set up, too."

Ethan kissed the back of Coop's neck lightly, several times, which helped to calm him. "Alright, what time do we need to be there, Dad?"

"The meeting is at eleven. We'll see you guys there."

Coop tossed his phone on the bed. He was so annoyed that he'd have to deal with more of this scout business again. Ethan's gorgeous face instantly distracted him from the frustration that he was feeling. In that moment there was only Ethan, and he needed to be closer to him, now. He turned around and parted Ethan's lips with his finger, and Ethan sucked it into his mouth, then grazed his teeth on it, biting it lightly, while Coop slid it around inside. He quickly replaced the finger with his tongue, holding the back of Ethan's head, then pushed Ethan onto the bed. Coop worked quickly giving them both the goosebumps they desperately wanted before their day got started.

Coop rubbed the sides of his neck. "Mmm, I love you, Ethan, but damn your legs are strong, my neck is all jacked up."

Ethan still lay panting. "So hot…our love is so hot. I love you, my Cooper."

Coop gave him a quick kiss and pulled him into the shower.

As the water slid down Coop's face, he looked at Ethan. "I'm sorry that we have to go do this. It's stupid."

Ethan washed Coop's body with a lathered-up body pouf. "Don't be silly, you're giving me a job. I'm lucky I don't have to interview," he said.

Coop lathered up Ethan's hair. "Well, not with me you don't but Brody is a different story. I haven't been in the office since I took over. I went once but no one was there, my dad just took me to show me around."

The two swapped places as Ethan rinsed his hair under the large rainfall showerhead. "Wait, I know Gwen is your dad's secretary, but who is Brody?"

Coop wiped some of the bubbles from Ethan's cheeks. "He's the brand manager."

Chapter 33
Don't Bite

The two looked adorable for their trip out to the executive offices of Morgan Enterprises. Coop wore a slim-fit pair of jeans, a long-sleeved gray sweater with a white button-down underneath, and white tennis shoes. Ethan sported a pair of slim-fit jeans, a navy V-neck cable sweater with a white button-down that peeked slightly out from the bottom, and camel-colored oxfords.

Coop held Ethan's hand as they approached the huge two-story building. "Ethan, you're not answering to anyone except me, I need you to understand that. My dad is the CEO, but he's not going to ever tell you what to do. That's not his style. I run the Foundation and he does his own thing."

Ethan smiled. "Got it. What about Brody? Why do we have to meet with him?"

"Like I said. I haven't dealt with him in-person for a while. I try to steer clear of him at events because he's just a lot to deal with. He doesn't really bother me. I normally just ignore him. Not sure what we need to see him about specifically."

The large glass doors slid open as the two approached. Coop nodded at the security guard that sat at a large desk in the front of the building.

"Hey, Coop! What are you doing here? Haven't seen you in a minute. How ya been?"

Coop smiled, while leading Ethan by the hand toward the elevator. "Doing good, just late for a meeting. Nice to see you."

As they entered the elevator, Coop dropped the back of his head against the wall, while Ethan leaned his head on his shoulder.

The elevator quickly arrived on the executive suite floor. The large office space was minimally decorated, with a clean, modern feel to it. The five inner offices were separated by glass partitions. Toward the farthest end of the space, in a large office, Coop's dad and Levi could be seen leaning over Tom's desk.

Coop led Ethan by the hand. "My office is the one next to my dad's, let's try to get back there before Brody sees us."

His dad and Levi looked up, as Coop pulled Ethan inside his office and closed the door.

Coop gave Ethan a soft, wet kiss, pressing him firmly against the door.

"Yow! That's how you enter an office!" Levi yelled.

Coop and Ethan's eyes widened as they separated from the kiss. Everyone in the other offices, including his dad and Levi were staring at them through the glass walls.

A small-framed man, wearing a magenta shirt, with a black tie and black dress-pants, approached Coop's office door quickly. He held a rose-gold laptop, and a large camera on a shoulder strap hung at his side. Coop shook his head no at the man who then went into his dad's office.

Ethan whispered to Coop. "Is that Brody?"

Coop nodded and led Ethan around to the back of his desk. He pulled a spare chair over, and Ethan sat next to him. Coop adjusted his own chair several times. He'd actually never sat in this chair before and was having trouble finding the right height. Ethan helped him find the right setting, as Coop leaned back and forth.

"This is a nice office, why don't you use it?" Ethan asked.

"I don't need to; I can do everything from home. I'd rather not have to deal with people all the time. Honestly, Ethan, I just don't care about half of the things that people expect me to. People waste a lot of time talking in the office."

Coop's desk phone rang; Coop raised his eyebrows at Ethan.

Ethan asked, "You want me to answer it? What do you want me to say? I haven't even signed anything yet. I don't know how to answer it properly."

The phone rang again; Coop lifted his chin at Ethan.

"I'll answer it, but—"

Coop rushed him, "They're gonna hang up, hurry, baby!"

Ethan picked the receiver up. "Cooper Morgan's office, Ethan speaking."

"That is the cutest thing I've ever heard! Tommy, look at Ethan's face!" Levi said through the speaker. Coop's dad, Levi, and Brody stared over through the glass from his dad's office.

Coop's dad spoke, "Hi, Ethan, nice job with the phone greeting. Please tell Coop that we need you guys over here in ten minutes."

"I'll tell him. Thank you, Mr. Morgan."

Coop swiveled side to side in his chair next to Ethan. Ethan looked at him. "Your dad says he needs us over there in ten minutes."

Coop pinched Ethan's chin, he really wanted to kiss him again. The way he answered the phone was too cute for Coop to bear. "What am I gonna do with you? I wish there were blinds in this office."

"Did I do it right? Is that how I'm supposed to answer the phone?" Ethan asked.

"It was perfect, and you did it right, but you won't be answering the phone. It only rang because it was my dad." Coop smiled at him. "No one else can call this line."

Ethan playfully smacked Coop's arm. "You knew it was your dad, and you made me answer it? So embarrassing." Ethan held his face in his hands.

Coop wiggled Ethan's hands off his face, tilting his head down to see him. "It was cute, I just wanted to see what you would say."

Ethan lifted his head up, and Coop gave him a smooch on the cheek, then turned his desktop computer on. The screen lit up with a generic background and screensaver. Coop pointed at the screen. "See, not even personalized. I haven't even used this computer."

Ethan looked around. "Well, when we do have to come in, will I be in here with you, or will I be somewhere else?"

Coop put his arm around Ethan and rubbed his shoulder. "You can be wherever you want. That's what's great about you being my assistant. The office right there," he pointed next door, "is the one that was meant for my assistant if I ever hired one. So, technically, that would be your office, when we come in. But we could just take the partition down and make it one big office…rearrange the desks."

Ethan stood and looked through the glass, studying the layout. "So, one big office for the both of us? Could we actually do that?"

"We can do whatever you want. Do you want us to work from here in the office, instead of the home office?"

Ethan folded his arms and pulled his mouth to the side. "Well, no, I'd rather be at home with you. But if we're here, then one big office would be nice. I don't want to ask for that, though, especially if we won't be here much."

Coop took Ethan's hand, brought it to his mouth and kissed it. "Alright, let's go meet Brody. Be a good little puppy, don't bite."

"Bite? Who would I bite?" Ethan asked.

They entered Mr. Morgan's office to the sound of Levi arguing. Levi's arms were crossed while he stood facing Brody. "I hate all of it, the whole design, the office is so plain and boring. I don't understand, with all the money Tommy has, this is the best you could come up with. Not to mention, there is no defining scent here, there are numerous ways to identify your brand with a scent. All I smell here is boredom," Levi sassed.

Brody pulled his head back as he and Levi stared one another down.

Mr. Morgan gestured for Coop and Ethan to have a seat. He whispered in close, as they sat down, "Levi really doesn't like Brody."

Brody threw his hands up at Levi. "So what? You don't like it, so I have to change it?"

Levi's mouth dropped open, and Mr. Morgan interjected, "Yes, Brody, you do have to fix it. If Levi says he doesn't like something, then I want you to fix it."

Levi smirked at Brody.

Coop spoke up, "Can we combine my office space with Ethan's? We'd rather have one big office, than two separate ones."

Brody put his hands on his hips, and looked at Mr. Morgan. "Do I have to do that, too?"

Mr. Morgan looked at Brody, who was much smaller than him. His voice started out low then turned into a shout, "Brody, Coop is your boss…of course you have to do it. Even if he doesn't ever use the damn space!"

Brody winced at the scream. "Okay, okay, okay. I get it. Yes, sir."

Brody rolled a chair over and sat in front of Ethan and Coop. "Hello, Ethan, I'm Brody, the Brand Manager for Morgan Enterprises, it's nice to meet you." He reached forward and shook Ethan's hand.

Mr. Morgan and Levi sat side by side, behind Mr. Morgan's desk. Levi was muttering about the desks, chairs, and Brody's attitude.

"Hello, Mr. Morgan, love the hair," Brody said, looking at Coop.

Ethan made a disagreeable face, which Levi quickly noticed.

"Um Brody, when you're sitting in the room with two Mr.

Morgan's what is the protocol supposed to be? Are you supposed to call them both Mr. Morgan?" Levi asked.

Brody swiveled around backward, to face Levi. He answered loudly with a fake smile, "*I don't know.* They have never been in the office next to one another like this."

Coop threw Brody a lifeline. "Brody, when we're both in here together, it's fine if you call me Coop. I don't mind."

Brody swirled around to face Coop and Ethan.

Levi shook his head in disagreement, as did Ethan.

Ethan whispered into Coop's ear.

Coop spoke again, "Actually, why don't you call one of us, Boss and the other Mr. Morgan, I don't care which one I am, but forget the Coop thing."

Brody, maintaining his wide false smile, turned backward again, to face Mr. Morgan and Levi. "Mr. Morgan, which would you prefer, Boss or Mr. Morgan?"

Mr. Morgan deferred to Levi, holding his palm open toward him. "You should be addressed as Mr. Morgan, he can address Coop as Boss," Levi said smugly.

Ethan nodded in agreement.

Brody sighed then stood up. He flipped his laptop open and removed his camera from his shoulder, placing it on Mr. Morgan's desk. "Alright, so, we have Ethan and—"

Levi interjected, "Mr. Prescott sounds far more appropriate for the Assistant to the Executive Director."

Brody smiled. "Yes, of course, forgive my unfortunate mis-phrasing, Mr. Everton." He started again, "Mr. Prescott and Mr. Everton, let's see what we have here." Brody clicked and searched, quietly clicking away without saying anything. His head moved side to side as he read through various screens. He stood up straight and sighed. "Alright, so did all four of you just decide to jump out of the closet on the same day? What the hell are you doing to me, Mr. Morgan?"

Mr. Morgan and Coop thought that was funny, while Levi and Ethan did not.

Brody turned his screen to face Mr. Morgan and Levi. "This is what I'm talking about."

On the screen, under Morgan Enterprise's social media account, several pictures and posts were shown, some with Levi and Tom, some with Coop and Ethan. Levi squinted, reading the screen, while Coop and Ethan were not interested.

Brody looked at Mr. Morgan. "What I'm saying is that, of course, I have no problem with this, zero, I'm happy with it. I support it. But as your Brand Manager, it would have been nice to be notified. Now, I have to control the narrative from the backside."

Levi was more than irritated; he rolled his eyes. "Nice phrasing," he said, with sass.

"So, what do you need us to do?" Mr. Morgan asked, leaning back in his chair.

Brody crossed his arms and looked at Mr. Morgan. "Well, it's difficult to ask, but are both you and the boss," he pointed to Coop, "serious about these two?" He gestured to Levi and Ethan.

Coop, who was previously uninterested, heard that and stood up. He approached Brody quickly, and whispered, "I can't speak for my father, but if you talk about Mr. Prescott like he's not here again, you won't be working for me anymore. That's how serious I am." He patted Brody's shoulder and sat back down next to Ethan.

Mr. Morgan shook his head and patted Levi's thigh. "Mr. Everton and Mr. Prescott are our partners. Honestly, I think you've offended everyone in this room. I know you're a good guy, Brody, but you have to realize you're treading on sensitive ground here. Just tell us what you need and let's get their paperwork started."

Coop spoke up, "Oh, Levi, are you going to be working here, too?"

Levi cocked his head to the side, eyeing Brody. "Well, yes and no, Tommy just wants to make sure that I have access and permission to do"—he smiled at Brody—"whatever I want."

"Levi will act as an advisor in an official capacity. Yes, he will have the power to do whatever he wants," Mr. Morgan confirmed.

Brody stood up from his computer. "It would be great, and I don't mean to overstep, if I could get a few pictures. I can use one of the four of you, then one of Mr. Morgan and Mr. Everton, one of The Boss and Mr. Prescott, then solo pictures of Mr. Everton and Mr. Prescott. I can use those to update the website and our social media accounts. I'd also like to have a formal press release announcing their new positions."

"Best things you've said all morning." Levi said, finally liking one of Brody's suggestions.

Mr. Morgan agreed with a nod.

Ethan and Coop were comparing hand sizes, completely disengaged from the conversation. Mr. Morgan snapped his fingers at the two of them. "Hey, guys, we need to take some pictures, then Vic is going to be here for the meeting."

Levi looked at his own hand and held it up next to Mr. Morgan's, his eyes widened at the difference in size.

Brody closed his laptop and put his shoulder strap with camera back on. "Speaking of Vic, I know sensitive information will be discussed and personal feelings involved, but I would like to remind you, as your Brand Manager, to keep your cool, Mr. Morgan, and you, too, Boss."

Coop raised his eyebrows and pointed at himself. "Not me. I don't care. I'm not interested in signing with him. Don't really care what he thinks."

Levi looked at Coop and smiled. "Such a smart man you raised, Tommy."

"Let's go," Brody said, clapping his hands. "We can use the Morgan Enterprises backdrop for the photos."

The four entered the conference room. There was a rectangular white table with a gray bottom in the center of the room, surrounded by twelve high back rolling chairs, also white and gray.

Levi looked around. "White and gray again…what a surprise. So plain," he said.

Brody didn't argue this time. "I'll change it. Just send me your preferred color palette, Mr. Everton."

Brody gestured toward the back wall; he asked the four to stand near the Morgan Enterprises logo. "Alright guys, I need you to get loose and have fun with this," he said as he readied his camera. He looked through the lens, "Oh, my stars, you four are a picture of perfection. You're straight out of a fantasy. Who dresses you guys? I don't know which one of you to look at first. Who among you is the best looking?" Each man pointed to his partner. Brody smiled. "There we go," he said, as he took a photo.

Ethan looked at Coop. "Oh, that was for a picture? I thought he was just asking."

Brody said, "Yes, Mr. Prescott, you're the most adorable, everyone knows." Brody snapped a picture.

Brody addressed Levi, "Oh Mr. Everton, you just ooze style and sophistication. I loved it when you talked down to me earlier, it was the highlight of my morning." Levi's head tilted back, he smiled with his mouth open. Brody snapped another picture. "Perfection, Mr. Everton," he said.

Mr. Morgan looked at Brody. "You got your camera in your hands and you're all better now?"

Brody said, "There it is, Mr. Morgan, coming in for the win, show me your CEO face." Mr. Morgan beamed at Levi, the two of them looked incredibly happy, like little kids again, posing for pictures. Their smiles reflected the true love they had for one another. "Wonderful," Brody said, while taking more pictures.

"Okay, now, Boss, I don't even need you to move." Brody held his camera at his side, then lifted it. "Wow, Boss and Mr. Prescott win, look at those million-dollar smiles they have for one another!" Brody took one final picture, then stepped back from the group of men. He reviewed the pictures on his camera. "Which of you would like to approve these?"

All four raised their hands.

Brody's eyes widened. "I got it, come sit."

The four sat at the long conference table while Brody displayed the pictures on the large wall-mounted screen. All four were satisfied with the result.

Coop asked, "Brody, can you please email the pics to Mr. Prescott, too, once his email is set up?"

"Mr. Prescott's email is already set up, as is Mr. Everton's," Brody said, with a smile toward Levi. "However, I do need quite a few signatures from them. Also, Mr. Morgan and Boss, I'll need two separate forms to issue their company credit cards."

Mr. Morgan and Coop both nodded in understanding.

"Thank you, Brody," Mr. Morgan said. "Please send the press release to the four of us to review, before sending it out this afternoon. We're going to be late for our meeting."

Brody winced. "One more tiny, teeny thing; Boss and Mr. Prescott, you both don't use your social media accounts and that's fine of course, no law against that, *but* at this point you have two options, you either update them, accordingly, adding your relationship status and positions within the company, or you just delete them. No third option."

Coop and Ethan looked at one another then back to Brody. Ethan spoke up, "We don't care about social media, so we'll do whatever you think is best."

Brody clapped. "Nice, very nice. Let me think about it and get back to you. Thank you, Mr. Prescott."

Ethan and Coop waved and waited near the exit for Mr. Morgan and Levi.

Levi walked over to Brody and shook his hand. "Thank you very much for taking such lovely pictures. I really do appreciate all the hard work you've put in over the years. Tommy is very lucky to have someone as insightful and creative as you, working for him."

Brody put his hand on his own heart and frowned. "That is very nice of you to say. I'm sorry that I took offense earlier, I'm very thankful to be working here. I'm even more thankful that Mr. Morgan has the other half of his heart back. It has not been easy watching him…too handsome and rich to be single! I could tell you some stories about the mood swings, though."

Levi's eyes widened in curiosity, while Mr. Morgan pulled him by the hand. "Alright, alright that's enough. Thank you, Brody."

Chapter 34
Smells Like Trache

The four walked back to Coop's dad's office. Coop and Ethan sat off to the side again, as Levi and his dad sat behind the desk.

Coop looked around the room. "Dad, I don't like this set up. I feel like I have no power over here. We look like the two kids in the corner. If Vic sits in front of you both, we're just off to the side. It feels weird."

His dad stood up. "Alright, we have a ton of meeting spaces here, I'm trying to decide which room would be best."

He pressed his in-office phone on his desk, "Yes, Mr. Morgan?" a woman's voice answered.

"Gwen, where should we go to put this guy in his place? I need a room that gives the four of us equal power, facing him straight on."

"The boardroom," she answered.

His face lit up. "Thank you." He looked at the time on his watch. "Everyone, quick, to the elevator!"

The four men hurriedly walked to the elevator and pressed the first-floor button. Upon arrival, they quickly walked past rows of employees in cubicles and small offices, until they reached the boardroom.

Tom flung the door open. The large room featured a custom, triangular-shaped, wooden table with fifteen chairs, five on each side. "Oh wow, this is gorgeous," Levi said, as he rubbed his hand across the dark, smooth wood. He frowned just a second later. "The chairs are tacky, though." He muttered to himself as he walked around the room, looking at the décor.

Tom knocked on the table to get Levi's attention. "Okay, we'll all sit on this side and stare him down."

The four sat in their chairs on one side facing the entry door. Ethan looked at the empty table, then turned to Coop. "This is my first stare-down meeting, should I scowl, or pretend to be looking at something? We don't have any papers or anything in front of us. Do I just stare at him, literally?"

Levi nudged his partner.

"Oh, you're right," Coop's dad said. He stood up and walked across the room.

Coop said to Ethan, "I don't think you're going to be very happy once he starts talking, whatever happens, just don't bite him."

Levi pulled his head back in shock. "Bite him? Ethan are you a biter?"

Coop rubbed Ethan's head. "Normally, my spicy Italian puppy only bites me. But I'm worried that his little temper may get the best of him."

"I haven't lost it all the way yet," Ethan said. He growled playfully showing Coop his bright white teeth.

"Oh, I don't know about that, Ethan, you were pretty spicy on Saturday with that scout," Levi said.

Tom walked over carrying a few files that he pulled out of the cabinet and gave one to each of them. He spoke to Ethan, "You may be tempted to lose it with Vic. Can't stand this guy."

The other three men opened their folders and saw papers they didn't understand. Mr. Morgan scoffed. "Come on, guys, don't open them, they're just for show." He turned to Levi. "Okay, well, the little puppy and the boss over there, are going to keep their tempers in check. What about you and me?"

Levi pulled his mouth to the side. "No promises."

"Fair enough." Mr. Morgan kissed him on the cheek.

Levi looked at the sky through the window from his seat. "It's too nice to be stuck inside like this, it's cool out for once. I hope he isn't late. We can rush him, right, Tommy? You said you would."

Tom agreed, as he rubbed Levi's back. "Yes, dear. I told you, this is for appearances only. I don't care if we piss him off. It'll be his word against ours anyway. Also, I doubt he's going to want to hang around for long. He doesn't want what happened getting out."

Levi looked to the right and rolled his eyes. "Oh…here he comes."

An assistant from the first floor opened the door, the room instantly flooded with awful cologne. "They're waiting for you inside, Mr. Trache," the assistant said.

"That cologne is terrible," Ethan whispered to Coop. He held a hand over his mouth, trying not to gag at the overwhelmingly horrible smell.

Mr. Vic Trache entered, wearing a blue plaid suit. He was a short, stout, balding man, with black hair.

Tom, Coop, Ethan, and Levi all stood to shake his hand. They remained standing next to their chairs, forcing Vic to approach them.

"Hello all," Vic said, as he quickly shook each hand smiling. He walked back across to the other side of the table, saying, "Nice power move, all of you bunched up over there."

Coop grabbed Ethan's hand off the table and held it on his lap. Levi crossed his arms and stared at Vic with sass.

Tom asked, "How can we help you today, Vic?"

He chuckled. "Slow down… I'm not acquainted with these two," he pointed to Ethan and Levi, "Coop I know, but who else do I have the pleasure of meeting with? I don't see Luke here, but I'm guessing there is some relation to you." He pointed to Levi and smiled inquisitively.

Levi cocked his head to the side. "Levi Everton, Luke's father."

"Nice to meet you, Mr. Everton…and you," he gestured to Ethan, "how are you involved in this meeting?"

Ethan looked at Coop, who squeezed his hand tightly under the table and spoke up, "This is my boyfriend and assistant, Ethan Prescott."

An obviously fake smile covered Vic's face. "Oh, that's great. It's a real pleasure to meet you."

Coop furrowed his brow; he didn't like that disingenuous smile. "What's great? That you're meeting him, or that he's my boyfriend?"

Tom, Levi, and Ethan stared forward, awaiting his reply.

Vic, feigning ignorance, replied, "Oh, I think it's all great. Seems like a very well put together young man."

Coop nodded his head slowly.

Tom spoke up, "Now that you're acquainted with everyone, what can we do for you?"

"What's the rush, don't you enjoy my company?" Vic asked. "The last time I came here, we had a couple of drinks and talked shop."

Levi rolled his eyes, placing his hands on the table and tapping it. Tom grabbed Levi's hand and looked at Vic. "Well, my wife here wants to get out on the water. We had plans to use the boat today, and we're stuck here with you. So, I'm not too interested in drinks or shoptalk."

Levi pulled his head back, biting his lip, as Tom quickly kissed his hand then placed it back on the table.

Ethan whispered something in Coop's ear, and Coop whispered back into Ethan's.

Vic tried to control his facial expression. "Oh, I had no idea you were married. I assumed he was just here regarding Luke."

Levi spread his fingers out flat on the table and raised his eyebrows at Tom, showing him his ringless fingers.

"Well, you assumed wrong," Tom said, taking Levi's hand and holding it.

Vic folded his hands on the table. "Listen, I want to apologize sincerely for the behavior of Mr. Pyle. He has been fired from our organization. I was especially disturbed to learn about the things that took place and was shocked to my very core upon hearing it."

Ethan spoke up, "I find that interesting..." all eyes faced him as he continued, "how can you not have been aware of the harassment that occurred? Cooper is one of the best players in the country. You sent someone to scout him, as did other teams. If he'd entered the draft last year, he would have easily been drafted at number one. Why would you have just given up on him?"

Levi backed Ethan up. "That is a very good point. Please do explain."

Vic's plump face turned red as he looked around the room, then knocked nervously on the desk. He cleared his throat. "How would I know what happens to every player that we scout? Players reject offers every day. I'm not kept in the loop on every player that refuses a deal."

Ethan looked at Coop, then back to Vic. "But he's not just *any player*, he's Cooper Morgan and you definitely wanted him. Come on. You say you came here to sincerely apologize, but you're full of it. It's written all over your face. I'd also like to know what you told the other teams that were trying to sign him, there must've been something passed along that made them back off. I haven't seen a scout around in a while."

"Oh shit," Levi whispered under his breath.

Coop rubbed Ethan's arm to calm him.

"I agree," Coop's dad said.

Vic's mouth hung open. "What did I do to deserve that? I came here to apologize, no one forced me to do that. I did it because I genuinely feel bad."

Levi leaned forward. "You're here for reputation. Just be forthright, you receive a lot of donations and support from this organization. You also don't want a lawsuit on your hands."

Vic held both his hands on the table and waved them. "No, no...

I want to apologize because it was wrong. I truly mean that. I also came here prepared to discuss a deal if you're interested." He looked at Coop.

Coop shook his head no, resolutely.

His dad stood up first. "Alright, we're done here."

Levi, Coop, and Ethan stood.

Vic sat in his chair. "If that's how you want to play this, that's fine with me."

Mr. Morgan lifted his chin toward the door, looking at Coop and Ethan. They held hands and headed for the door, understanding the gesture.

Levi asked Tom, "Can I?"

Tom nodded.

Levi faced Vic, while the other three watched. "You are a disgusting pig of a man. We all know that you were well aware of what occurred. I will be taking a very close look at my husband's contributions to your organization moving forward. We also happen to be old friends of Madeline Parson, are you familiar with her? I'm sure you are. Don't be too surprised if you're served sooner rather than later." He turned toward the door.

Mr. Morgan gave Levi's tush a light pat, and they walked out of the room.

The four men got on the elevator and relived their funniest moments of the meeting together. Levi was in stitches. "Ethan, I don't blame Coop for thinking you were gonna bite that man. You are spicy!" he said.

Ethan was nothing if not spicy when it came to defending Coop. Coop loved how protective he was over him. After spending his entire life being forced to protect someone else, the feeling that someone wanted to protect him, made him feel safer than he ever thought possible. He also thought his little Italian temper was pretty sexy.

"I told you," Coop said. "Ethan looks like a sweet little pup, but he's dangerous." Coop kissed him on the cheek.

They stepped off the elevator and were promptly greeted by Brody, who carried two separate stacks of papers. He passed one stack to Levi and one to Ethan. "How was the meeting? Everything go smoothly?" Brody asked.

The four men had guilty faces. Tom put his hand on Brody's shoulder. "We were as nice as we could be," he said.

Brody furrowed his brow. "What does that mean? Am I going to need to do damage control?"

Tom shrugged his shoulders and walked away with Levi, Coop and Ethan. They headed into his office as Brody stood in the same place, frozen.

Levi and Ethan filled out their paperwork, and Mr. Morgan and Coop signed the required forms.

Chapter 35
The Pig & The Swan

Afterward, as the group approached their cars in the private parking lot, Mr. Morgan asked, "Are you guys sure that you don't want to join us?"

"No thanks, Dad. Maybe next time,"

Coop watched as his dad and Levi sat inside Tom's silver convertible Porsche with the top down. Levi spread his fingers out on his lap and looked at Tom. "Something is missing, Tommy," he said.

Tom spread his fingers out on his steering wheel. "I know, someone called me their husband earlier, but I don't see a ring on my finger."

Levi's mouth dropped open. Mr. Morgan cupped Levi's chin and closed his mouth, then kissed him softly and said, "Let's go fix that…"

Coop chuckled and led Ethan back to their car, opening the door for him, then joined him from the driver's seat, quickly turning the car and A/C on. He leaned over and pulled Ethan in for a kiss, using his hand on the back of his neck. Their lips met fiercely, as Ethan held both sides of Coop's face, and their tongues swirled wildly around.

Coop pulled back from the kiss and whispered, "I love you, Ethan."

"I love you, my Cooper."

Coop patted Ethan's leg and backed out of the parking lot. "Let's stop somewhere and grab lunch, then we can go shopping for our home office, sound good?"

"Ooh yes! I'm starving."

Coop pulled into the drive-thru of The Pig & The Swan. It was a charming restaurant that featured both hearty filling foods, like BBQ pork sandwiches, burgers, and chicken platters, and also lighter things, like wraps, salads, and smoothies.

Beside the large picture menu, a voice spoke from a smiling, pink, standing pig, "Welcome to The Pig & The Swan, what can we make for you today?"

Ethan leaned over across Coop to get a better look at the menu. "Can we have just a moment, please?" Coop asked.

"Of course, take your time, squeal when you're ready to order," the employee said.

Coop and Ethan laughed at that. They stared at the menu for a few moments debating what they should order. Coop pointed to a chicken wrap that he wanted, while Ethan tried to decide between a burger and a salad.

"Just order them both and eat the one that tastes better," Coop said.

Ethan gave him a quick smooch and sat back in his seat.

Coop spoke to the large pig, "Hello, we're ready to order. Thank you for waiting."

"Hey, I told you to squeal when you were ready, buddy," the employee said.

Ethan raised his eyebrows and looked at Coop who shook his head no, while smiling. Coop replied, "No, I'm not gonna do that. We'll take an original chicken wrap, a chicken salad, and a cheeseburger, please."

As they approached the window to pay, a young man, leaned his body out of the window to accept Coop's payment. Making eye contact with Coop, he looked inside and saw Ethan holding Coop's hand. He smiled big and nodded. "Nice…that'll be $32.50." He held the card scanner toward Coop, who tapped his card quickly to pay.

Ethan furrowed his brow and tilted his head, he silently mouthed, "Nice?" to Coop.

The young man came back after a few moments and passed their food out of the window. "Thanks for choosing The Pig & The Swan."

Ethan couldn't help himself, he leaned over and said to the employee, "Thank you. Just wondering, though, you said nice, when you looked inside the car. What was that about?"

The young man's face lit up in excitement. "Oh, nothing, I didn't mean anything by it. I just proposed to my boyfriend last night and, well, now he's my fiancé. I'm just seeing a lot of people holding hands today. I like seeing people happy."

Ethan and Coop both congratulated him on his engagement and pulled away. They parked to quickly eat their lunch.

Ethan passed Coop his wrap. "Here you go, mmm, that smells amazing." He opened the paper container and looked at his cheeseburger, he made a disgusted face, noticing all the grease inside.

Coop was grossed out as well. "Don't eat that, baby." He closed the container and took it from Ethan, placing it back in the bag. Coop reached inside the bag and pulled Ethan's salad out. He tilted his head and asked Ethan, "Do you want my wrap?"

Ethan shook his head. "No, I'll eat the salad. It's fine." Ethan took the salad from Coop's hands and opened it.

Coop giggled and swapped with him, taking the salad for himself, and passing Ethan his wrap.

Ethan looked at him with puppy dog eyes. "Are you sure?" he asked.

Coop smooched him on the cheek. "You should just start ordering whatever I order. You always end up liking whatever I have better."

Ethan covered his mouth. "You're right. I didn't even realize that until now. I'm sorry."

Coop pinched his cheek. "Don't apologize, the salad is great. I don't mind. It's a cute thing that you do."

As they walked around the furniture store, Ethan was deep in thought.

Coop noticed his expression and was concerned. "What's up, pup? What are you thinking about?" he asked.

"It's nothing. I'm always fascinated by proposal stories. Asking someone to marry you…you're in such a vulnerable position. I wonder how he did it. I love big proposals, where one partner does something really dramatic. It's so brave. I would be so afraid to do something like that."

Coop smiled at Ethan, pulling him into a hug. "You won't have to worry about that," he said.

The two picked out all new furniture for their home office. Which turned out to be quite easy. They quickly found an entire suite that fit their preferences.

Ethan examined the order slip once they got back in the car. "Maybe we should've asked Levi to come with us. He's probably going to hate everything we picked out."

"You're probably right, but as long as we like it, who cares?"

Ethan pulled out a stack of papers from beside his seat. "Where is the paper that Brody gave us about our socials?" He thumbed through the stack. "Ah, found it, so we either update them and use them or delete them?"

Coop mocked Brody's earlier words, "No third option."

Ethan thought for a moment, leaning his head back. "I know what we should do."

Coop raised his eyebrows, still focused on the road. "What?"

"I'll show you when we get home, if you're interested," Ethan said.

"I'm interested in a turn with the frosting when we get back," Coop teased. "Let's worry about the socials later."

Ethan was definitely down for that. "Shower first, then I'm in."

As they pulled in, Ethan quickly hopped out of the car and ran up the stairs and into the shower with Coop chasing from behind. "Don't follow me in, Cooper! You said you wanted the frosting. If you come in the shower, I'll be pinned before I know it!"

Coop crossed his heart. "I won't. Promise. Let's shower, hands to ourselves this time." Coop held his pinky out toward Ethan, as they stood outside the shower. "I pinky promise. No hands until we get out," Coop said.

Ethan wrapped his pinky around Coop's. "No mouths either."

They quickly showered, keeping their parts to themselves.

Ethan instantly regretted forcing Coop to hold back. Once they dried off and headed to bed, Coop pinned him down immediately. Their breaths came quick and shallow as goosebumps came over both of them.

Later that night, Coop looked at Ethan sitting next to him in bed, appearing to be deep in thought. Ethan, too, was deep in thought beside him.

Coop held Ethan's face in his hands. "Ethan, I'm going to propose to you in the biggest way possible."

"Oh yeah? But you don't need to do that. I would marry you today, without a big proposal. I don't need that."

Coop pulled him in close. Ethan scooted in under his arm and tucked in tight.

"Well, me too," Coop said. "I would marry you right now, but I want to give you everything that you've ever wanted...and if a big dramatic proposal is something that you've dreamt about even once, I want to give it to you."

Ethan pulled his head back and put one hand on Coop's face. "Cooper, it's really not necessary... I'm already in love with you. That's never going to change. It doesn't matter how you propose."

Coop kissed Ethan's hand and held it. "I love you and hearing you say that makes me happier than you can imagine. Wait…does that mean you already plan to marry me?"

"Of course, I do. How are you even asking me this, at this point in the conversation? You're the only person that I want to be with forever."

Coop wrapped his arm back around Ethan and pulled him in tighter. "You're the only person that I want to be with forever, too, but I still want the proposal to be perfect. What if we just consider ourselves engaged and then when I propose, it will be time for the wedding. Does that make sense?"

Ethan looked up confused. "I'm not following you… You want us to get engaged now, but then you propose during something insanely big—I'm guessing, based on your face.

Coop leaned his head back against the headboard. "I don't know, I'm spitballing here. I'm just trying to figure out how to make it known that we are definitely getting married and are committed, but also give you the perfect proposal, which, yes, I've already thought of, but won't be able to do right away. I'm thinking of a specific event, but that won't take place unless circumstances work out in our favor. So, I could actually end up wasting precious time that we could have already been married by trying to just get the proposal right." He rubbed his forehead. "My head hurts just thinking about that. No, that's not gonna happen. I'll make sure of it."

Ethan was nearly moved to tears. "Cooper, I love you so much. I am yours and you are mine, rings or not. If you feel like you want to wait for the perfect moment to propose, then I won't stop you, but it really isn't necessary."

"I love you, too, Ethan. My baby is gonna have the best proposal story, guaranteed." Coop gave him a crisp smooch on the lips.

Ethan leaned his head on Coop's chest, then remembered their conversation from the car. "Oh, we gotta do that thing for Brody!" He stood and grabbed Coop's laptop off the desk and brought it back to bed. Sitting beside Coop, he flipped it open. "For the socials, this is what I was thinking." Ethan went to the social media site with his profile and hovered over the red *delete profile* button. He looked at Coop. "What do you think?"

Coop nodded. "Yep, exactly what I was thinking."

Ethan clicked the button, then several more and permanently deleted his profile. He passed the laptop to Coop who did the same.

Coop breathed a sigh of relief. "There we go, now we don't have to deal with that."

Coop opened an email from Brody. He quickly made the picture of himself and Ethan as his new wallpaper and lock screen. He smiled and kissed Ethan on the cheek. "Brody was right about one thing today; you are the most adorable."

Chapter 36
You're My Heart

Ethan stood on third base as Coop walked up to bat. The sold-out crowd of 25,000 stood on its feet in eager anticipation. It was the bottom of the ninth inning. The score was tied one to one. Coop stepped up to the plate and locked eyes with Ethan. He adjusted his batting gloves, quickly pulled out and kissed the number two charm that hung from his neck, and readied his stance. As he looked at Ethan, he was reminded of his words from their first day together: *Where is this guy's heart?* Coop smiled. *You're my heart, Ethan.*

Ethan's eyes were locked on Cooper. As Cooper kissed the charm he wore, Ethan lightly kissed the number one charm, hanging from his own neck and placed it back inside his clay-covered black and white jersey. Ethan took a big lead off the third base bag. He had already stolen twice in this inning alone.

Sweat dripped from the pitcher's face, as he tried to decide if he should focus on Ethan or Coop. The two made for a deadly combination and were both a major problem in this situation. The pitcher quickly threw the ball to third base, as Ethan got back on the bag safely. The third baseman threw the ball back to the pitcher.

Ethan watched carefully, as the pitcher shook the catcher off in disagreement several times. Coop and Ethan locked eyes. Coop could feel what Ethan was thinking. The pitcher readied a throw, and Ethan, fast as lightning, sped toward Coop at home plate. Ethan slid in, hands first, as Coop moved out of the way.

"*Safe!*" the umpire shouted and signaled.

"Milford wins! Ethan Prescott steals home to seal the Championship for Milford University!" the announcer shouted.

Coop was ecstatic and quickly reached a hand down, pulling Ethan up. Ethan jumped into Coop's arms, as the rest of the team swarmed them from the dugout.

Kai screamed as he ran toward them. His long, curly black hair flew wildly. "Whoooo! Yeaahhhh!"

Coach was overcome with emotion, as he joined the group and wrapped his arms around Ethan and Coop. "I'm so proud of you boys," he said, tears falling.

TV crews rapidly joined them on the field. Ayame Sato, a beautiful, young reporter, followed by a cameraman, approached for an on-field interview with Ethan and Coop. Her long black hair and smile shone brightly under the field lights.

"Ethan, you stole home and won the game in front of this full house. How do you feel?" she asked.

Ethan, still panting, said, "I feel great!"

Coop stood just behind Ethan, with one hand on his shoulder. He whispered into Kai's ear, and Kai quickly jogged to the dugout.

"What was going through your mind as you decided to steal at such a crucial moment?" she asked, holding the microphone closer to Ethan's mouth.

"Haah, oof, sorry, I'm just trying to catch my breath. Well, I saw Cooper there and, you know, we locked eyes and I just thought, I gotta get home. I didn't want to wait."

She turned to Coop. "Coop, what were you thinking as you

approached the plate with the score tied? We've seen you plenty of times in this situation and you seem to always be calm. How is that possible?" She held the microphone to Coop, as Ethan was pulled into another interview behind them.

Coop smiled as he looked over at Ethan. "Well, you know, with Ethan there, I knew I had to bring him home. Since he'd already stolen twice, I understood what he was thinking. It's easy to be calm when you have the right people around you."

Kai's wild hair popped over Coop's shoulder, as he shoved something into Coop's back pocket.

Ayame continued, "Your hair, which you were well known for, was cut early in the season, and your game exploded, leading to your best season yet. What led you to make such a drastic change?"

Coop smiled brightly at her, then turned to the side. "Ethan!" Coop called, while motioning for him to come over. Ethan walked over, and Coop dropped to one knee. He pulled out the small box from his back pocket and opened it, displaying a shiny black men's wedding band and held it up to him. Ayame held the microphone nearby so that everyone could hear.

"Ethan, will you marry me?" he asked.

Ethan enthusiastically screamed, "YES!"

Coop placed the ring on his finger, then picked him up, as the two shared a sweet, soft kiss, followed by lots of smooches.

"Wow!" Ayame said, while her eyeliner began to smear from tears.

Kai, who was standing close by, grabbed a tissue out of his pocket and passed it to her. She waved the cameraman off, so she could take a quick break. Kai stood beside her, enamored with her beauty. He carefully leaned in. "They're great, right?" he asked her.

She continued dabbing the corner of her eyes. "They really are great. I just love seeing people in love. It's so beautiful," she said.

Kai, still a bit starstruck, decided to take a chance.

"Ms. Sato, my parents own a restaurant nearby, would you like to go there after you finish up and get a drink with me?"

Without pause, she answered him, "Yes, Kai Tagaloa, I would love that."

Whooosh! A giant cooler of orange sports drink was poured over Ethan and Coop. Ayame moved to the side quickly as Kai stood clapping.

Chapter 37
Let's Go Home

Kory grabbed the large, wrapped gift off the kitchen counter and called to Luke. "I have the present, come on, let's get going."

Luke straightened his tie and kissed their new puppy, Toby, on the nose and closed him inside his play area. "You be good, we're going to watch your uncle Coop get married. No funny business."

The chocolate lab tilted his head at him.

Luke felt conflicted. He hated to leave him alone. Bringing him to the beach was one of his favorite things. "No, don't look at me like that, Toby. You can't come. I know you love the beach, but not this time."

Kory gave a chuckle from inside the hallway.

Luke stood turning toward Kory. "What? Why are you laughing at me? I just want him to know where we're going."

Kory shook his head. "You're so cute. I'm laughing because you insist on calling everyone his aunt, or uncle, no matter if they're part of our family or not."

Luke dropped an eyebrow at Kory squatting back down to Toby. "Don't listen to your dad. He gets grumpy when he's hungry and this wedding isn't for another two hours, he's just getting hungry." He kissed the puppy's nose again and stood up. "Will he really be okay if we leave him for this long? Maybe we should have let Madeline watch him. I'm suddenly feeling nervous leaving him like this. I don't know, Kory. Maybe we can just bring him?"

"We are not bringing him to the wedding. You were told twice, once by your father and once by Ethan's mother, not to bring him. If you think I want to deal with Ethan's mother yelling about Toby, especially after last night, you are definitely wrong."

Luke pouted. "You're right." He squatted back down. "Okay, Toby. We'll be back soon. Don't be afraid when we leave. We're not abandoning you. It might be scary, but you'll be fine."

"Luke, honey, I love you, but if you don't hurry up, you will not see the professor tonight."

Luke's mouth dropped open looking at Kory. "How dare you bring the professor into this! I'm just nervous. Look at his face. What if he gets scared? He's just a puppy!"

"I know but he'll be fine. He has his play area set up, we have cameras, you can check on him whenever you want, and we won't be gone for that long. It's just a few hours. I promise he'll be fine. Come on. Trust me," Kory said, motioning toward the front door.

Luke sighed, gave the puppy one more pat, and followed Kory out to the car.

As soon as they sat inside the car, Luke began to panic. "Did we lock the front door?"

Kory smiled. "Of course we did."

"I should probably just check the camera and make sure he's doing okay. There's nothing wrong with that, right?"

"Luke, I know you're nervous, but we've had him for a month now. You freak out like this every time we leave. You're gonna give yourself an ulcer. But, yes, if it makes you feel better then go ahead and check on him."

Pulling his phone out, Luke observed their small puppy who was laying calmly inside his play yard. A wave of relief washed over him.

Kory raised his eyebrows at him. "All good? He's probably just laying around, right?"

"Yep, all good. He's just lying down. I'm not gonna check again. I promise."

Kory continued driving while Luke leaned his head on his shoulder. "Just rest for a little while. It's almost a two-hour drive to this beach."

Luke's exhausted body gave into the warmth of his husband's shoulder. Having a new puppy was more exhausting than he'd imagined it would be.

Two hours later, he opened his eyes when Kory turned the car off. "Oh, wow. I slept for the whole drive. I'm sorry. You must have been so bored." He kissed Kory quickly on the cheek.

"It's fine. Your body needed the rest. You've been staying up so late with Toby. It's good that you got a little nap in."

Luke noticed Arie getting out of her car. "Ugh. I can't believe she brought him."

"Oh, that's her best friend, right?" Kory asked.

"Yep. Her best friend since they were really young. I don't know why she didn't bring Emma. You would really like her. She's funny. Kind of like a female version of Kai," Luke said grabbing his door handle and stepping out of the car.

Kory stepped outside of the car and grabbed the present off the back seat.

Luke walked around to him, and the two held hands down the long wooden boardwalk, leading to the beach. A familiar smell overcame Luke's senses.

"Hey, guys!" Kai said, smiling from ear to ear. "It's good to see you both. Haven't seen you since you got the new puppy. How was the rehearsal dinner? Can't believe we had to miss it."

Kory did not enjoy the rehearsal dinner. Luke squeezed his hand hoping he wouldn't go into details about the "UNO Incident." "It was fine, everyone had a great time," Luke said. "I was a little worried about Toby, but Madeline watched him for us."

Ayame stood beside Kai, extremely interested in their conversation. "We want to come over and meet him soon," she said. "When is the next time you're free? We can do a board game night, if that works."

"That sounds fun," Luke said, feeling Kory's hand tense, when Ayame said the word "game." Kory was ultra-competitive, and Luke knew the sting of defeat from last night still weighed over him, that, and since his husband was hungry, he was pretty sure his calm demeanor wouldn't last much longer.

"Yeah, we just have to check our schedules. Then we can let you know," Kory added.

"Oh, remember the resort you stayed at on your honeymoon?" Kai asked Luke.

"Yeah, of course I do. What about it?"

"Ayame has a gig lined up in Hawaii next month. She loved the pictures from the place you guys stayed at. Her agent said they'll pay for us to stay wherever she wants as long as there is availability. Can you text me the name of the resort?"

"Of course, I can. That's exciting! You guys are gonna love it there!" Luke said.

Ethan's mother waved to the group. Luke smiled watching her walk over. He got along really well with Gina, in contrast to Kory who tended to clash a bit with her during the very few times they'd dealt with one another; most recently, last night at the rehearsal dinner, when Gina and Kory were locked in an intense game of UNO. Gina won on a technicality that Kory still didn't agree with. Kory only agreed to let the game end because Madeline was watching Toby, and they needed to get home by a certain time, or risk not having a dog sitter in the future.

"Hello, everybody," she said. "I need you all to come and take your seats, okay? The boys are ready, and you are the last guests, so let's go." She clapped her hands. "I'll take that present, Kory. I can *stack* it over there for you. So nicely wrapped, too," she said, as Kory passed her the gift.

Kory's mouth dropped open. Luke hadn't missed the fact that Gina snuck the word "stack" into her brief conversation with Kory. The rule in question last night came down to stacking the UNO cards, Kory argued that the cards could be stacked in a certain way, which would have allowed him to win. Gina believed that Kory needed to draw four and his turn would be skipped. Kory continued arguing that he could stack and force her to draw two cards.

As she walked away, Luke heard her muttering about the smell, which he knew must have been related to Kai's cologne.

Luke could still feel the heat emanating from Kory. He really hated to lose. Luke kissed him on the cheek and pulled him toward their seats.

Coop and Ethan stood facing one another, both dressed in white designer suits, barefoot in the sand.

Their friends and family watched from white wooden chairs that were neatly placed in rows. Tom and Levi, wearing matching rings, looked on from the front row, seated next to Coach and Gina. Arie sat between her best friend and Gina.

In the second row were Luke and Kory, holding hands, and Kai and Ayame. Ayame leaned her head on Kai's shoulder and breathed in. "Babe, you smell so good," she said as she looked at him. Luke, overhearing the sentiment, laughed lightly as Kai gave him a big smile.

As the sun began to set, Ethan and Coop recited their vows and placed rings on one another's finger. Coop's ring was engraved with the word home, while Ethan's was engraved with the word heart.

Coop looked at Ethan. "I love you so much, you are my heart."

Ethan smiled at his new husband. "Cooper, you are my home. I love you, too."

After the ceremony, Coop and Ethan met briefly with their guests to thank them for coming. They'd decided to hold a small reception on the beach, in lieu of a large one, since they were leaving for their honeymoon in Italy tomorrow.

"Mr. Morgan," Coop said, addressing Ethan.

"Yes, Mr. Morgan?" Ethan replied with a bright smile. He loved the sound of his new last name. Hearing Coop say it filled him with such joy and pride. His giddiness couldn't be contained, he bounced a little on his toes.

"I really want to leave. How soon can we leave?" Coop whispered.

Ethan wanted to leave, too, but they still hadn't thanked everyone for coming yet, and he didn't want to be rude. "Let's just do a quick lap around and then we can go. We should at least make sure to ask Luke and Kory about the puppy."

"Oh, no. Please don't get him started on the puppy. We'll never leave," Coop said through laughter.

Ethan agreed, "Yeah if we want to get out of here, we can't bring up the puppy and we can't bring up—"

Ethan's mother's loud voice rang through the air near the food table. "You lost! You cannot stack a draw two on top of a draw four. It's against the rules!"

"I most certainly could have! The whole game is about stacking! Of course I can stack a card! I should have won!" Kory shouted.

"Yeah, let's just leave, while no one is looking," Ethan said.

"Agreed, let's go," Coop said, kissing him on the cheek.

Both their fathers, and Levi, were smiling beside Coop's car. They had decorated it in true "after wedding" fashion for them; complete with *Just Married* written on the back window, and cans tied to the bumper.

Ethan's heart was instantly warmed. He was so happy to be a part of this family. There was so much love between them that Ethan's eyes teared up at their gesture.

"Thank you for doing this for us," Ethan said to the group, while Coop walked around the car checking out their handiwork.

"Of course! You're most welcome," Levi said. "Wait, were you two about to sneak out of here without saying goodbye to us, though?"

"Definitely were," Coop said, squatting down and picking up a beer can. "Wait, these are full of beer! You're supposed to empty them first!" Coop said, looking at his father.

"No," his dad said. "That's the fun in it, they explode everywhere when you drive away. That's the whole point!"

"Those cans won't be the only thing exploding tonight," Levi said, through laughter.

Coop giggled, wrapping Ethan in a tight squeeze, kissing him on the forehead. Ethan melted into his husband's warm embrace. The two shared a sweet kiss. Ethan pulled back and said softly, "Let's go home, Cooper."

Join Cooper and Ethan on their honeymoon in *Only My Husband Calls Me Cooper*, an adult MM romantic comedy.

About Cali Kitsu

Cali Kitsu lives in a very sunny state with her amazing husband and daughters, and she enjoys making people smile. She tries to bring a little bit of her Cali sunshine and energy wherever she goes. Cali believes that love is for everyone, and she's found the perfect way to express that in her writing. Cali absolutely loves writing—she's having so much fun telling steamy boy love stories, with a bit of her Cali sense of humor!

Aside from co-hosting the *Cali & Craig Talk…* podcast with her bestie Craig, Cali is also assistant to Craig Gibb, publisher at Story Perfect Books and its family of imprints, and author of the MM YA romance books *You Can Call Me Cooper* (2024) and *Froderick, Gay Son of Dracula* (2024), and the MM adult romance books *Cookies, Candles, and Cute Butts For Christmas* (2024), *Vincent & Sivan: Book 1: Rum-Soaked Awakenings* (2025), *You Can Call Me Cooper: Author's Cut* (2025), and *Only My Husband Calls Me Cooper* (2025).

Cali's other hobbies include watching Anime, reading Manga, baking, going to the beach, and she's an avid gamer in all forms: console, tabletop, strategy card games…*Magic the Gathering* is probably her favorite strategy card game.

YA Romance Books by Cali Kitsu
You Can Call Me Cooper
Froderick, Gay Son of Dracula

Adult Romance Books by Cali Kitsu
Cookies, Candles, and Cute Butts for Christmas
Vincent & Sivan: Book 1: Rum-Soaked Awakenings
You Can Call Me Cooper: Author's Cut
Only My Husband Calls Me Cooper

Also from Deep Hearts YA

**Froderick, Gay Son of Dracula
Cali Kitsu**

My name is Froderick Dracula, but my friends call me Frode. I'm seventeen and starting my junior year of high school. My father, the famous Count Dracula, is not only the most celebrated vampire in the world, but he's also the school ruler, not to mention a huge idiot. He's completely out of touch with the world and hates anything that he doesn't understand—which is basically everything.

Being the son of the ruler of the school and the highest vampire in all of vampire society is hard enough on its own, but there's one thing I forgot to mention: I'm gay. It's pretty hard keeping such a big secret, especially with my father trying to convince me to get my first bite out of the way. I'm not interested in biting any girls, though, so that's not gonna happen.

Starting the first day of school will be just like every other year, boring, bland, full of classes that I don't care about. That's what I assumed until our opening assembly, when I saw him. Caleb Cheval. The new vampire in school. He's also a noble, and he wants to—hold my hand?

Whaaat?! What the fangs am I supposed to do?

Turn the page for a preview of *Froderick, Gay Son of Dracula*

Chapter 1
Oh My Fangs

"I vant to suck your blood," I say into my mirror before school. Ugh gross…I really don't. Being the seventeen-year-old son of the legendary Count Dracula, though, that's what people expect me to say. But if you really want to know, there's only one thing I'm interested in, and that's keeping my very secret obsession with guys a secret. "Yes, Dad, I'm gay," I say in my dreams.

In my dream, my most far away unrealistic dream, he hugs me and supports me. Hell, maybe he even takes me out to a bar afterward. But in reality, my dad would say it was Wolfie's fault for sure. Wolfie is my best friend; his dad, the Wolfman, is far more accepting than mine. If Wolfie came out today, I have no doubt that his dad would hold an honorary parade and rename a street to mark the day…shoot; he may even rename the family salon for him. His dad is all about acceptance. It's why his parents aren't together anymore. Still, Wolfie hasn't come out yet either, so me and my bestie stay locked in our metaphorical closets as we start our junior year of high school, but at least we have each other. I mean, it's not like either of us is going to come out any time soon.

It's almost time for school. What an effing chore school is. I hate it. I grab my favorite cloak from my closet. It's black, of course, so boring, but Wolfman spiced it up for me over the weekend. He sewed a sparkling red ruby in place of the black clasp that secures the cape around my neck. It looks fabulous. It gives it that nice dramatic contrast. The cape is shiny black, and the material doesn't wrinkle easily. It's plain and has no personality, but this gorgeous oval ruby that secures it makes all the difference to me. It feels like, for once, there's a little bit of me on display. I proudly button my red ruby clasp around my neck and make sure my cape isn't wrinkled. Then I tie my long black hair into a bun on top, nice and tight. My skin looks a bit tanner than normal from being at the beach over the weekend. It's funny that people always assume vampires are pale-skinned; we aren't. Well, at least I'm not; my father is Greek, and my mother is Italian, so the second I hit the sun, my golden tan pops right out. "You got this!" I tell myself in the mirror before I head downstairs. My green eyes know that I'm far from in the clear, though. I've gotta go downstairs past Dad, who is probably going to yell about something the second he sees me. But, still, you know, I am good-looking, much better looking than my father, of course, whose receding hairline is on full display.

"Good morning, Frode," my dad says while looking up from his morning paper. Yes, my father still reads the newspaper. "I'm keeping the paper business alive," he says whenever I tease him. Yeah, right, keeping the paper business alive; more like turning every beautiful woman he sees into a vampire, then reading about his exploits the next day. Ugh, such a show-off. "Did you see the article this morning?" he asks me.

He hasn't noticed the ruby yet, that's good. I debate my answer for a moment. I don't really want him to notice the ruby, especially when I'm running late, but if I seem too interested in his stupid article, he'll not only know I'm hiding something, but he'll definitely give me a lookover and notice the ruby.

"Nope, I haven't, but there's a hot new girl that just moved in; hopefully, she's gonna be in my class. I was hanging around outside her place until early this morning." That should do it. He should be happy with that. Those words disgusted me as I spoke them.

"Oh?" he says as he folds his paper and looks up at me.

Shit, I really didn't want him to look up. I grab my smoothie and spin around to face the door quickly. My cape gives a nice exaggerative flourish. Ugh, if only I were on the runway, that spin was perfect.

"Yeah, she's new this year. Her mom is half-mermaid, half-vampire," I say.

He picks his paper back up. "Absolutely not. No son of mine is going to bite a mermie, purebloods only for you."

He's such a jerk, and I want to put him in his place, but he won't listen anyway, and I'm gonna be late for my first day of school.

"Right, pureblood, got it, pops," I say on my way out before he can argue.

It's a bright sunny day, nice and warm. I'm so glad vampires aren't affected by sunlight like they are in books and movies. Flying would be almost impossible if that were true. We do hate garlic, though, not because it can hurt us, of course, but because it makes blood taste icky, and if there's one thing I hate, it's anything icky. Oooh! I just flew past a vibrant red cardinal; it was stunning. I think he sang a little tune as I went by, or maybe he noticed the red ruby and was giving it a whistle. Haha, that's funny, a bird with a personality…maybe he's a closeted bird, like me, we could be friends…what the hell am I thinking today?

"Yo, Froderick, we're gonna be late. Better pick up the pace!" my buddy Robert says to me on my left. Robert is a vampire, too, pureblood, delicious. He's flying at the same pace as me. I wish it were because he liked me, but he's just a friend. There's no way he's gay, too.

"Yo, Robbie boy, sup?" I replied. Oh my fangs, I just said sup? I hate this version of me. I must sound like an idiot.

"Nothing much. Read about your dad last night. He's next level, bro. Biting five chicks in one night, man, his fangs must be sore! Dude is legendary!" he says.

This must have been what the old sack of blood was talking about this morning. So effing embarrassing. But Robert thinks it's cool, so I'll play along. Besides, it's not like I can come out and say what I really think.

"Yeah, he is definitely something. Not really my style, though," I say. Gosh, I wish he'd pick up on my disinterest…or notice anything… or care.

We both begin our descent and land smoothly in front of the school. Robert is looking me over, as his gorgeous blue eyes pause on my ruby.

Holy fangs, he's getting closer, very close, very…his hand is touching the ruby!! I'm trying not to squeal!!

"This is gorgeous," he says. His eyes meet mine for just a moment. I can feel my cheeks warming, and I know they're redder than O-positive blood right now.

I want to bite his neck, and he's so close that I could do it. But what would happen if I did?

"I've never seen any other clasp aside from black on your capes, Frode. This ruby is a really nice touch."

OMF, he's noticed my clasps? What is happening? His smell is intoxicating, like freshly made cake or brownies, just pure hot sugar. My dad may be a dick, but he's right about purebloods; they really do give off an erotic scent. Oh no, oh no, something is happening. Shit, my pants are way too tight, and Robert is way too close. Damn it! I gotta get out of here!

"Um, hellloooo? Frody? What the hell are you doing?" Kat says.

Kat is my best girl friend; she's a pureblood, too. She's every straight male vampire's dream. Huge boobs (gross), tiny waist (blech), and a perfectly round ass (I'm kind of jealous of that). Her hair is long and brown and her skin is smooth and soft. She stands at about five-three and weighs somewhere around one-fifteen, if I had to guess. She's perfect for tossing around, or fun size. That's what she always says, anyway.

Robert is still holding onto the ruby as we both look over at her.

"Hello, Kat, Robert was just checking something out," I said.

What the? Oh my, his face is getting closer, my pants….no, no, no.

"Checking something out indeed," he whispers in my ear. He releases the ruby, smiles at me, and turns to face Kat.

Whaaat?! Did he mean to whisper that in the way I thought he did? No way. But the guy in my pants is giving me a hell of a time right now. What a personality my guy down below has. Robert whispers in my ear and shwing…near full mast at 8:00 am. I just have to stare at Kat for a bit and hold my breath. That'll get him down.

"Sup, Kat, new school year, you ready?" he says to her.

Kat thinks Robert is hot; they'll probably be banging by lunchtime. Robert is tall, six-one, about two inches taller than me. His hair is dirty blond, and his skin is lightly tanned from all the outside activities he does. He doesn't wear a cape; most vampires don't, just me. I'm meant to stand out because of my dad, the man, the myth, the legend—the insufferable bag of blood whose face is staring at us as we walk toward the school entrance.

To make being the son of Dracula even more difficult, my dad is also the ruler of the school. Basically, he's the face of the school, the reason it exists, the one everyone strives to be like. He's the perfect picture of a vampire. Normally, he isn't here, but with it being a new school year, here he is in all his proud glory, standing on the stone steps high above the rest of us, greeting the students and faculty. His cape is long and just barely misses the ground. His collar is open, and so is his top button. There are just a few offensive black hairs that can be seen peeking out from between the top buttons. He's such an effing show-off. Should a school ruler really be allowed to show off that tiny bit of chest hair? Ugh, no. Not if you ask me, but if you ask the fawning teachers, that would be a different story. Students are flocking to him as we walk up the steps. Robert to my left and Kat beside Robert. Where the hell is Wolfie? He always helps me deal with these uncomfortable situations. I look around and don't see him anywhere, but he's usually late, so it's not to be unexpected. It is the first day of school, though.

Oh wow, a breeze from the left just brushed past my face, tantalizing; it was the smell of Robert. Woah, that is going to be hard to deal with. I just got the blood from earlier to stop rushing below, and now this smell again.

"Velcome, velcome," my father is saying to a group of giggling girls. My left nostril, along with the left side of my lip, rises in agitation. Really? Velcome? He doesn't talk like that. He's such an effing cliché. He loves it, vamps falling all over him.

He breaks character for a moment and approaches the three of us. "Hello, Kat, you are looking lovely today," my dad says. Kat loves the attention, and she loves my dad. All women do; I can't understand why. They all dream of the day that he bites them. It's so stupid.

Our uniforms are highly inappropriate if you ask me. Regardless of gender, you can wear either a black and red plaid skirt with a black button-down shirt or black and red plaid pants with a black button-down. I'm pretty sure ninety percent of the skirt-wearing population have had their skirts altered, though. The skirts are so short that if a strong breeze blew by, you'd be flooded with either panties or bare asses. It's ridiculous. Then again, I'm much more interested in the pants-wearing crowd for the most part. I haven't seen any guys wearing skirts yet, but I think I might like it. Kat is wearing thigh-high black stockings along with her dress shoes, and she's giving my dad a playfully-inappropriate twirl. "Good morning, Mr. Drac," she says.

My left nostril and my lip are moving up again in disgust. "Kat, gross, that's my dad."

My dad isn't paying attention to her. "Good morning, Robert. How is your mother?" he asks.

Robert thinks my dad is the coolest. I have no idea why. The dream of most vampires is to be bitten by my dad. That goes for all vampires, regardless of gender. It's so damn weird. Sex is secondary to being bitten. I can't understand that…holy, sweet mother. If this breeze doesn't stop, I'm going to die. Never mind what I just said; at this point, with Robert next to me and his scent wafting through the air, I'm definitely feeling the need to bite, but that other urge is pretty strong, too. Man, he would taste so good. I haven't bitten anyone yet, but I'd take a piece of Robert's neck as my first.

My father's fingers snap in front of my face. "Frode, straighten up. I've adjusted your schedule; they had you in a bunch of classes with only boy vampires. Thankfully, I was there to fix it. Gotta get that first bite out of the way sooner rather than later."

Are you fucking kidding me? Did he really just say that? In front of Robert? So damn embarrassing; not only that, but he moved my schedule?

"Dad, why did you do that? What criteria did you use to decide if they were boys or girls? We've talked about this before." I hate his ignorance.

"I looked carefully at their names. I know it's a boy when I see a boy's name," he says proudly.

My mouth is wide open as I look around and really hope no one heard that. My dad's attitude toward gender is so embarrassing. I have some leeway here to mouth off a bit because he's standing in front of the school. Besides, what's he gonna do? If he laid a hand on me, my mother would destroy him. He's no match for her. "Dad, you are not very smart. I have told you, and the principal has told you at least a hundred times, not to judge vamps based on their names, their ID's, or their looks. How many times? How many times do we have to go over it?"

Ms. Tansy, the principal, cuts in and pulls my dad aside before he can answer. She didn't hear what I was saying, but it was good timing for him. I'm sure he was more grateful than I was at that moment. I don't often get the opportunity to lay into him. When one appears before me, I sink my fangs into it.

"Yoooooowwww!!!" a raucous howl from the right side came in loud and crisp. There he is, right on time; it's Wolfie. My savior, my very best…what the fuck? I can't believe what I'm seeing.

Kat just ran over to Wolfie and jumped in his arms. He's carrying her back up the stairs with his face in her chest. They're both giggling as they head my way.

Robert elbows me. "That looks like fun," he whispers while looking at Wolfie and Kat.

"What the fangs is happening?" I ask the two of them as Wolfie grips Kat's behind. The bell rings loudly before they can answer. It's time for morning assembly. On any other day, we would only have an assembly if there were an emergency or special event, but with it being a new school year, we always have one to start the first day off.

Wolfie places Kat down, and the two are holding hands, walking in front of me. They're both acting like they didn't hear my question, pretending this behavior is normal. Well, this behavior is normal, just not for them, not for my gay best friend and my other best friend. Just as I start to open my mouth to try and get some answers, Leslie pushes in between Robert and me. Leslie's skirt is even shorter than Kat's, which is saying something. "Hey, baby," she says to me as she kisses my cheek.

Fangs, I want to throw up when she kisses my cheek. I'm not going to dance around this. Leslie is my RP…my release partner. I'm not going to say girlfriend because I will never have a girlfriend. Not interested, but normal releases; yeah, I'm okay with that. Besides, the vampire I imagine, when we're doing things, is standing right next to her. With any luck, his scent will rub off on her, which will make free period easier and definitely more enjoyable.

Leslie is probably prettier than Kat, and she's definitely more popular. She has long, wavy brown hair and big brown, doe-like eyes. Her body is no better or worse than Kat's. It's all the same. She's the captain of the cheerleading squad, really smart, and pretty funny. I don't entirely hate her company. I'm just not interested in biting her, which is what she's really after. There's no way I'm marking a girl, though. It's just not happening. She knows that, but she chooses to continue this pretend game. As far as vampire families go, hers is ranked number two. The house of Marnkov is led by her mother, Darna, who was, of course, one of my father's first bites. Her mother really feels like she's special because of that, in contrast to my mother, who couldn't care less that she'd been bitten by and had a baby with my father.

"Don't call me baby," I say as I pull back from her.

She smiles and then gives me a little pout, one that I assume she thinks is sexy. It isn't.

Robert appears to be observing closely. He's probably interested in Leslie. What did he say to me earlier? He said something; I can't remember what, though. I'm too distracted by Leslie's scent. It's entirely different. It smells like watermelon, and it's far too sweet for me. Well, now free period is gonna be a problem.

The auditorium is large enough to hold the entire student population. It's decorated with pictures of famous vampire families. Of course, my father's picture, which is larger than the others, hangs proudly in the center of the room.

Kat and Wolfie head down the row to the left, and I push past Leslie and Robert to sit next to Wolfie. There's no way I'm not getting an explanation for this. We're in about the eighth row back from the stage. Leslie pushes past Robert to claim the seat beside me.

"Oh, I was hoping to sit next to Froderick." I hear Robert say.

Leslie is giving Robert a pinch on his chin. "Aww, you want to sit next to my guy? That's so cute! Like little boy besties!"

She touched Robert's chin. Oh man, I gotta get ahold of her hand. Wait, she actually moved aside for him to sit next to me? I can't believe what I'm seeing!

Robert just sat down next to me. He's smiling, and his face is getting strangely close to mine. "Oh, fangs…the smell." His mouth is right beside my face!

"Do you really like Leslie?" he whispers in my ear.

What the hell do I say? What the eff do I do? If he likes her, he can have her. Why is he whispering with his hot, sugary scent all in my ear?

Before I can answer, Wolfie is whispering in my left ear, "RP's, just for show, for both of us."

Okay, so I have pureblood delectableness on my right, the sugary-sweet scent of Robert, and my best friend on the left, who smells like a mix between mustard and, wait, he just smells like mustard.

"What the hell did you eat this morning? You smell like mustard!" I say to Wolfie.

"Dad made a breakfast casserole for the first day of school. You always say I smell like pickles and bacon, and now, today, it's mustard. You smell the weirdest shit, Frode."

I'm still a bit confused by what Wolfie said a few seconds ago, and honestly, I don't really want to explain to Robert that Leslie is just my RP. It would bother me if he knew that. RP's are pretty normal here, though; no less normal than biting someone. Sinking your fangs in is an act of marking, a territorial type of claim, and since teenagers are nothing if not territorial, it happens all the time. Not for me, though. I'm saving that bite.

Anyway, Robert already knows, thanks to my dad, that I haven't bitten anyone, which is already abnormal, especially for the son of Dracula. If he knew I really didn't like Leslie, he may start to suspect my secret. I don't want that. I'm just going to ignore his question. If he's that interested in her, he can talk to her about it. We're friends, but I'm not interested in helping him get laid or lining up a bite for him. Obviously, him biting me would be a different story, but that's not gonna happen.

"Okay, wait, you guys are actually having sex, or it's just for show? I don't understand," I say to Wolfie.

"Both," he replies.

"You had sex with Kat?" Oops, I may have screamed that a bit louder than intended. All eyes nearby have turned to face us. Damn it, now I've given away my position and, in the process, leaked a secret, or not secret, about my two besties.

"Hi, Frode!" Kressa says from the row in front of me. She turns all the way around in her seat.

Kressa is the half-mermaid, half-vampire girl we met at the beach over the weekend. She is a really nice girl. Of course, I wasn't actually around her house like I told my dad I was earlier; that was just a distraction.

"Oh fangs…" My dad is standing in front of Kressa. She doesn't even realize it.

"Excuse me, miss," my dad says to her. Students are clamoring and whispering excitedly because my dad is standing so close by. "I don't believe we've been properly introduced. I am Count Dracula, and you are?"

"Hello! Of course, I know who you are! Everyone talks about you! You're so famous! Even among mermies, you're famous! Is it true you can tell anything about someone once you bite them? Like, do you have the power to read their mind? And control them? I've always wondered. I'm only half-vampire, so I'm not sure how it works. I've never bitten anyone either or been bitten. At my school before this, it was all mermaid lessons, so now it's vampire lessons."

Now, my father loves to look cool, but he also hates unnecessary conversation, and in a conversation with a seventeen-year-old, he's definitely not going to answer her. He's going to just walk away.

"Ohhh, you're the one," he says. "Frode, is this the girl whose house you said you were outside of all night?"

Why am I alive? What is my purpose? I honestly have no idea. I can't believe he just said that. Oh shit...

Leslie is standing up from her seat. "Who the hell are you even?" she says to Kressa.

"Yeah, who the hell are you that Froderick was outside of your house?" Robert asks.

I have no idea why he cares, but it doesn't matter right now. I need to step in and save Kressa before Leslie jumps on her. "I was not outside her house; that was someone else," I say.

"Who?" Leslie and Robert ask simultaneously.

What the hell is happening? I don't even know who to respond to right now.

"That strapping young vamp behind you is my son. I'm not sure if you knew that." My dad says to Kressa.

She did not know that because I choose not to tell anyone that. When Wolfie and I met her at the beach, our band, Fangs Come First, was doing a free gig. So, no, I was definitely not introducing myself as Dracula's son.

"I had no idea! Wow! Vampire royalty!" she says.

Thankfully, Ms. Tansy, the Principal, just walked up to the stage podium. My dad left quickly to join her on stage.

Leslie sits back down, and Robert removes his hand from my armrest. Wait, when did that get there, by the way? Was his hand there the whole time?

"Good morning, and welcome to another year at Fangula High. It is wonderful to see all of your smiling faces and fangs this morning!" Ms. Tansy says. "Now, many of you know this is the first year that we've accepted transfer students, and I hope you'll all be very velcoming"—she looks at my dad—"to them!"

My dad is clapping. He thinks Ms. Tansy is hilarious. Don't even bother wondering if he's bitten her; the answer is yes, of course, he has.

Ms. Tansy just gave him a flirtatious smile. I don't even know which of them is more inappropriate.

"Ahem," Ms. Tansy clears her throat. "Now, among the many transfers, there is one in particular I'd like to introduce: Caleb Cheval. Can you come up here, please?"

There is a lot of whispering from behind me. I'm not turning around, though. I don't want to sound like a jerk, but the more vamps that know where I am, the worse this assembly will be for me. Everyone will want to talk about how great my dad is afterward and probably gossip about that stupid…HOLY SHIT!

Whistles and howls fill the room as a handsome blond-haired vampire walks on stage. He's wearing a cape, it's black, his clasp is purple… Wait? It's effing purple? I look down briefly at my own ruby and then back up. This guy is gorgeous. Who the hell is he? What did she say his name was?

Ms. Tansy is rubbing his back, and he's smiling. His mouth may be the most fangtastic mouth I've ever seen. His lips are full and almost pink, he has very light blue eyes, and his skin is just perfection. Oh wow. His shaggy blond hair is gorgeous.

"This is Caleb Cheval," Ms. Tansy says. "Caleb has transferred from another school following a family move. We are happy to have him, and I expect that all of you will show him what a fabulous place our school is. Do you have anything to say, Caleb?"

Damn, he just licked his lips. This guy is seriously fire up there. I'm getting a little heated.

"Hello, I'm Caleb," he says. Everyone is clapping, along with some whoops and hollers. Wolfie is one of the loudest whistlers in here right now, and Kat seems to find that entertaining.

My dad is walking up beside him. He smiles brightly at Caleb and takes the microphone from him.

"Frode?" my dad says while looking in my direction.

Oh my fangs, what the eff? I'm holding my forehead and trying to slink down in my seat. But I better not do that. Who knows what he'll say if I don't acknowledge him? I begrudgingly stand up and acknowledge him, in a voice full of agitation, "Yes…father?"

Caleb is tilting his head and looking at me.

"Frode, come up here. I want you to meet Caleb before anyone else does." My dad says.

Caleb is staring at me pretty hard as I walk past Wolfie, Kat, and the rest of the row. He's definitely interested in who I am.

Okay, what is happening? Caleb is walking toward me as I step onto the stage. He extends his hand and reaches for mine. Do I let him hold my hand? What? No. I wave politely and smile at him. He is devastatingly handsome, and he smells like freshly baked Italian bread with a touch of cotton candy. Oh my…I'm not gonna make it through this. He looks a bit perturbed that I didn't hold his hand; maybe I'm imagining it, though.

"Caleb, this is my son, Frode. He is the number one vamp in the school. Since you were number one in your school, you'll have a lot in common, I'm sure. I've arranged your classes to be in sync with Frode's," my dad says.

Caleb is eyeing my ruby; he's rubbing his purple jeweled clasp. I'm turning slightly so my dad doesn't see the ruby on my clasp, which is currently sparkling from the stage lights. Caleb's clasp is actually a purple crystal bat upon closer inspection. It's beautiful, very nice. This makes sense; he's vampire royalty, too. That's why he's wearing a cape. You can only be considered number one at any vampire school if you're born of a noble house. He's giving me a strangely seductive look. If we weren't on stage right now, I'd actually guard my neck. Well, on second thought, maybe I wouldn't.

As we stand beside one another, the air feels different. It's hot, very hot. I swear there is actual heat coming off this guy.

"Thank you, Mr. Dracula. I think Frode and I are going to get along more than fine," Caleb says with a wink.

What the hell was that wink? How does he know we'll get along? Ah, yes, I'm sure he's heard all about how nice I am. Eyeroll. He's probably already planning to use me for social status, too. Not that he'd need that, not with that face. He looks like he's fresh from a commercial about first bites. I could imagine that…him there with some trampy vamp pushing bite spray as a product. Some vampires believe in bite spray and the effect it has on others. I don't know if it's because I'm gay or because of my pureblood, but that shit has never worked on me. I can say that the only vampire I've considered biting is Robert, and I doubt that any spray would entice me to do that any quicker. Still, the lockers of other vamps will be lined with cans of bite spray, same as always.

"Now, Frode," Ms. Tansy says. "I want you to take some time this morning to show Caleb around. Your teachers already know that you'll be giving him a tour for most of the day. It's fine to take all the time you need. We want Caleb to feel welcome here. You two can go on ahead. The rest of the assembly doesn't pertain to either of you."

What the hell? Now I'm supposed to show him around the school? Okay, he just grabbed my hand. We're holding hands as we walk off the stage toward the exit. I'm not sure if I'm uncomfortable or turned on. This guy is something fierce. Who would hold someone's hand like this?

"Hey, you can let go of my hand," I say as we exit the auditorium into the bright sunlight.

He's squeezing my hand tighter. "Do you dislike holding my hand?" he asks as he turns his body toward mine.

What the fangs am I supposed to say? I don't know how I feel. He's hot, though. I mean, I guess I'm okay with it, but, no, I can't hold hands with a guy. Everyone will know I'm gay then. I can't do that. I have to stay safe inside my—

His face is directly in front of mine. You'd be hard-pressed to fit a piece of paper in between us. OH MY FANGS!! My back is against the wall! What is happening? I'm screaming inside. My guy below is too far gone; he's not gonna go down for the rest of my life after this.

"You're very close," I say while staring into his pale blue eyes.

"I can't help it. You smell like cotton candy and Italian bread, and I can't help but wonder if you're feeling what I'm feeling," he says.

I swallow hard. How does he think I smell exactly the same as he does? I've never asked anyone what they think I smell like, but it was just a little bit freaky to have him describe my scent that way. Can he read my mind? That's not possible. What am I supposed to do right now? How do I get out of this? Do I even want to get out of this?

With my voice full of false self-righteousness, I say, "You know who I am, and yet you are so bold as to pin me against a wall like this?" Why did I say that? What am I getting at? He's obviously into guys, but is it okay that I let him know that I am, too? If his bottom half gets any closer, I won't need to tell him anything; my guy downstairs will take care of that.

He's chuckling, and it's kind of a deviant open-mouth laugh. I like it, and it's pulling me in. His fangs are exquisite, and I can see how sparkly they are as he tilts his head back. That neck of his, it's clean and clear, delectable. He's never been bitten on it. I'm sure of that. You can tell when someone has; the scars heal, but they never go away.

"What did I say that was funny?" I ask him.

His mouth is pulled to the side, and if eyes could have sex or bite, he'd have taken me fifty times over during this brief yet strangely sensual conversation. His mouth is near my ear, and our warm cheeks are pressed together on the left side; his hand is on the right side of my waist, barely squeezing me.

Froderick, Gay Son of Dracula
is available now in hardcover, paperback, and ebook

www.ingramcontent.com/pod-product-compliance
Lightning Source LLC
Chambersburg PA
CBHW031842310726
48972CB00005B/1377